# THE SUN RUNNERS

SHADOWPAW
PRESS

# THE SUN RUNNERS

## JAMES BOW

THE SUN RUNNERS
By James Bow

Shadowpaw Press
Regina, Saskatchewan, Canada
www.shadowpawpress.com

Trade Paperback ISBN: 978-1-998273-18-8
Ebook ISBN: 978-1-998273-19-5

Cover by Bibliofic Designs
biblioficdesigns.com

Shadowpaw Press is grateful for
the financial support of Creative Saskatchewan.

*For my father and fathers-in-law. Silent heroes all.*

# CONTENTS

# PART ONE
## FRIEDA: THE WROUGHT IRON CROWN

# CHAPTER 1
# THE ROCK BEFORE
# THE DAWN

*The latitude town known as the* Messenger
*Mercury Colonies, April 30, 2201 CE*

FOR AS LONG AS SHE COULD REMEMBER, HER HIGHNESS THE
Crown Princess Frieda Koning had wanted to be an engineer.

When some of her classmates told her that it was more
likely she would have to marry an engineer, she went to her
mother, Queen Beatrix, who told her that, while she didn't have
to marry an engineer, she would have to be Stadtholder.

The young princess threw a tantrum. Beatrix stroked her
hair and tried explanations for a bit, but she was, after all, the
queen, and rather busy. She passed the kicking child to the
Dowager Queen Adelheid Koning, who simply waited Frieda
out. There was no point in arguing with Queen Adelheid.

Still, a princess needed a well-rounded education. Frieda
grew up alongside the children of trackworkers, cooks, algae
farmers, bridge crew officers, file clerks, and the walkers who
harvested the iron cornrows. She learned with her friends and
classmates about life on board the latitude town as it rolled

along its Robinson Rail across the surface of Mercury, keeping them perpetually ahead of the sunrise, safely in the dark.

Frieda never asked for special treatment, and right now, she wasn't receiving it.

"Why is this taking so long?" she muttered.

Nearby, Cara sighed and rolled her eyes. Next to her, Malika took notes for the class yearbook. "Frieda Koning was most eager to view the *Messenger's* trackworks," she muttered.

Chastened, Frieda turned away. She fidgeted. Around her, the *Messenger* rattled and hissed. This close to the Robinson Rail, the floor pulsed like the colony's heartbeat.

"I don't know why *I* need to be there." Alfons stood beside her, looking without interest at the struts and pipes around them. "I made my choice. It's the kitchens for me." He smiled dreamily. "I can still taste their caramel mousse."

Frieda smiled back. "That was really good."

"You know the rules," said Linde. She tucked her hair beneath her hard hat. "We see *all* the presentations. You never know; you might find something that changes your mind."

Malika leaned in, notebook at the ready. "Do you have anything to say about our vocation tour so far, Frieda?"

Frieda wiped any impatience carefully off her face. "No comment."

It was almost her seventeenth birthday—in Earth years; they still measured things in Earth years. She, like her classmates, was nearing the end of classroom education. It was time for all of them to pick apprenticeships in their chosen professions before completing their Master Works.

*All of us except me*, Frieda thought. *But maybe Mother will agree once I bring her the application.*

On the other side, Toshiko nudged their friend Isolde. "I bet *I* can guess what your favourite presentation was."

"Possibly flipping Meneer Koske to the mat?" Frieda guessed. Watching tiny, fierce Isolde grapple with their dignified teacher had been the highlight of *her* trip to the security office.

Isolde rolled her eyes. "You do realize they let me for the purposes of the demonstration?"

Toshiko chuckled. "I'm pretty sure Koske didn't know what hit him."

Frieda snorted.

"Students!" Koske snapped.

Frieda had gone to all the presentations, just like everyone else. She'd stared in fascination at the algae farms and pinched her nose closed at the chicken coops. She'd struggled not to fall asleep while Jian's father droned about the intricacies of his department's filing system.

*"You can see how important your math skills would be to understanding how these maps and files are classified." He looked up. "Meneer Koske?"*

*Koske snorted awake.*

And Alfons was right; the kitchens had been a tasty treat, but for her, it had been the opposite of Alfons: all of the heat but none of the importance of moving the *Messenger* forward along its Robinson Rail.

After the kitchens, they'd gone to the communications centre, where the Head of Communications had spoken animatedly about cables and cameras and how the radio towers pointed to Earth picked up the static that fed the displays of the Memorial to the Silence in the agora outside the Royal Apartment.

*"Why do we listen?" Anna blurted.*

*Head of Communications blinked at her. "I'm sorry?"*

*Anna blushed as the classroom's attention swung to her, but she pushed on. "The Earth has been silent for almost fifty years, so why do we keep listening?"*

*An uncomfortable silence fell until Koske cleared his throat. "Anyway! We're almost done here. Any other questions?"*

For Frieda, all that had been a preamble to their visit to the trackworks, but now she frowned at the glimpses she got of their young guide, obscured by the people in front of her, droning on about boring history.

"Named for the twenty-first-century philosopher Kim Stanley Robinson," their guide intoned, "the Robinson Rail was envisioned as a means to guide the majestic cities of Mercury across the planet's surface, keeping them ahead of the dawn and out of direct sunlight. Robinson theorized that the heat of the Sun would cause the rails to expand, constantly pushing the cities forward. We've gone beyond that, of course, giving us the ability to drive ourselves faster along the rail while using the rail's thermal expansion as a failsafe."

Frieda grit her teeth. *How can you make the trackworks boring? Don't treat us like tourists; we know this stuff!* "Come on, let's go!"

Cara glared at her. Alfons coughed. Frieda blinked. *Did I say that last bit out loud?*

Alfons leaned closer and whispered, "Be kind, Your—" He coughed. "—Frieda. Look at who our guide is."

Frieda's brow furrowed as she strained to look between the heads of her taller classmates at their guide. He was young but strangely familiar . . .

Her eyebrows shot up. "Josef?"

She ducked her head. She could feel Meneer Koske's frown, but she couldn't help herself. *In for a gasket, in for a cog.* "They have *you* leading us on this tour?"

Frieda's yawning classmates gasped as they looked up and saw the slim-faced young man in the blue-grey overalls of the trackworkers' guild, recognizing him as somebody they'd played floor hockey with, competed against at sums, or partnered with on presentations. He was going on eighteen and had moved into his apprenticeship last year. The chasm between schoolhood and adulthood had never seemed so narrow yet so vast. Giggles rippled through the group.

Josef blushed, but then he caught Frieda's eye, and they shared a smile. As she looked down, something out of the corner of her eye made her look up again. She caught Cara glaring at her. Frieda blinked. *What?*

Meneer Koske cleared his throat. The class came back to order.

Josef drew himself up. "Well, then, *children* . . ." He emphasized the last word so much it would have gotten things thrown at him if Koske hadn't been present. "If you study and work hard, you too can be given the task of leading those under you on school visits."

He turned to the bulkhead, pulled the lever, and yanked it open. It slid sideways on its track with a pneumatic-assisted *whoosh!*

The heartbeat pound of the *Messenger* intensified. Frieda, eager as a child on Terminal Day, pushed between her classmates and stepped through the door. The class gathered on the landing. Some sidled past Frieda and down the steps as she stood by the railing, breathing in the sting of kerosene and the thick sourness of engine oil. She smiled.

The trackworks took up the entire lowest level of the *Messenger*—all 4.5 kilometres of it. The grey-washed walls abutted directly outside. Below the network of catwalks and platforms running the length of the galley and beyond, the wheels and gears of the *Messenger* were grouped in a long line running down the centre of the room. Between these, Frieda could see a portion of the Robinson Rail sliding along as smooth as a treadmill.

Frieda grunted as someone nudged her in the back. "Ow!" She turned. "Watch it!"

Behind her, Cara rolled her eyes. "I am, Your Highness. You weren't."

Nearby, Anna and Alfons drew their breaths in.

Frieda stared at Cara. *My other classmates respect me enough not to call me by my title. Trust Cara to turn it into an insult.*

But she met Cara's sarcastic smile with one of her own. "My apologies, Ambassador." As insults went, it was at least subtler than "republican.".

That provoked a chuckle from some of Frieda's other class-mates—not too many, as Meneer Koske was in earshot—but enough that Cara's cheeks darkened.

Cara Flores wasn't an ambassador but rather the daughter of the ambassador from the *Hermes*—the premier latitude town running the *Messenger*'s equivalent distance north of Mercury's equator.

"Students," Koske chided. "No dallying! Let us continue."

"Move along, Your Highness." Cara gestured to the stairs. "You're in the people's way."

Frieda glared but hurried after the rest of the class as they descended the metal stairs to the floor of the trackworks. At the base, the students pooled at the viewing platform. Frieda pushed toward the safety rail. Settling beside a tool closet, she found herself standing next to Anna. Anna gave her a glance and a quick smile. Frieda smiled back.

As Josef began to drone on again, Frieda nudged Anna gently. "Why does Cara dislike me so?"

Anna blinked at her. "Does she?"

"She keeps calling me 'Your Highness,'" Frieda grumbled. "She's the only one in class who does."

Anna looked down at her hands, clenched on the safety rail. "Well . . . we know you. Cara's new to this class. Maybe she feels uncomfortable using anything other than the proper term of respect?"

"I don't think she means it as a term of respect."

Past Anna, Linde leaned against the railing, then pulled her hands back, yelling, "Ack! Grease!" She flicked at her blackened palms desperately.

Frieda pulled her own hand from the railing. Someone must have brushed past with a barrel of engine grease. Not the safest thing, but at least the stairs were clear. Still, Frieda smiled at the dark mark on her palms before rubbing them off on the grey leg of her school uniform.

On the outside walls, near one of the reticulations that allowed the *Messenger* to bend across the curve of the planet, students gathered at the portholes and stared out at the night-time expanse of Mercury. Beatta pointed. "Look at the iron cornrows!"

Frieda came closer. Outside, she could see the iron corn-rows shining in the floodlights of the *Messenger*, planted like their namesakes in the fields of old Earth, freshly scraped of their extremophiles, ready for their next trip around the Sun. In the distance, land speeders approached from the north, their gondolas full of material, wheels raising dust that settled softly around them.

Koske clapped his hands and shouted over the chug and rush of gears and turbines. "Students, what two ways does the Sun power the *Messenger*?" He never missed a chance to quiz his class.

It was such an easy question Frieda was surprised nobody put their hand up. She did, and Koske looked over. "Mufrau Koning?"

After Cara's use of her title, it felt better to be addressed as a standard young woman. "We rely on direct solar energy collected on the surface of our Robinson Rail on the daylight side of our planet. The second is part of the failsafe. Even if we are without power, the thermal expansion will drive this city forward, and that kinetic energy can be transformed into elec-trical power to feed the batteries and relaunch the engines."

Koske nodded. "Very good."

Cara let out an exasperated sigh, which Frieda pretended not to hear.

"We are using some of that kinetic push from the Robinson Rail right now," said Josef. "We're hanging back to within five kilometres of the Dawn Line while we do maintenance on the solar power system."

Frieda frowned. Cara blurted, "Five kilometres? That means the Sun's less than a half-hour away. Is that safe?"

"Perfectly safe," Josef replied. "The failsafe will keep us out of direct sunlight. We've done it before."

The other classmates chuckled at Cara's fretful question. Koske cut in with another test. "How long is our Robinson Rail?"

Frieda's brow furrowed. If you didn't memorize the number —and Frieda realized to her shame that she hadn't—you had to remember what latitude of Mercury the *Messenger* travelled and, from that, calculate the circumference of the circle. Toshiko straightened up, thinking hard. Malika tilted her head. Frieda gnawed her lip. They were close to the equator but not quite there. How far back? Toshiko seemed to be close to figuring it out. While it might not have been sporting, Frieda put her hand up while she was still thinking through her numbers.

Koske looked over. "Mufrau Koning?"

"Fourteen thousand, eight-hundred and ninety-seven kilometres," Cara muttered, beneath her breath, without raising her hand.

Frieda blinked. Cara was right. *I forgot to carry the one.*

The floor shuddered. Deceleration pulled at their bodies. Some students grabbed onto things. Others, like Alfons, stumbled and fell over with a cry.

The floor shook in a way that felt wrong to Frieda's feet. The *Messenger* had stopped before, but never so suddenly and never this close to the Dawn Line. More than that, the vibrations made it feel like the town still wanted to go forward. The walls, floors, railings, everything, went out of rhythm, like a cart running over corrugated metal.

Bangs ripped up the length of the Robinson Rail, growing louder and louder.

Inertia pulled them forward, sharply this time, and everyone stumbled. Cara fell over, smacking her shoulder. *"Merda!"* she gasped. Frieda would have laughed, but the forward-facing deceleration yanked at her stomach.

The lights flickered, then went out.

Classmates shouted. Some screamed. Frieda clutched the safety rail, and someone grabbed her arms, nails digging in. "Hey!"

"Sorry." Alfons's voice.

It was dark and, other than the cries of her classmates, so silent it was deafening. Frieda realized with a lurch that the wheels and generators had all stopped.

Switches clicked, then clicked again. They grew louder as red lights turned on, illuminating the trackworks, moving closer and closer before passing, flicking on farther and farther toward the forebridge.

Alfons struggled to his feet. "What happened?"

"Emergency power kicked in," Frieda muttered. The red lights illuminated only on backup power. Josef had said they'd taken the solar power system offline for maintenance. "We're running on batteries alone." The stillness beneath her feet made her heart ache. "We're parked."

Her words sent a chill through the class. All eyes turned to the portholes. "How far are we from sunrise?" Alfons whispered. "How far?"

"They said half an hour," said Cara. "That was minutes ago."

The students peered. The jagged horizon of Mercury was dark, for now.

Through the trackworks, boots pounded on the metalwork. Shouts cut through the distance. The students shifted to the walls as trackworkers came running. "Where's the obstruction?" workers shouted. "What stopped us?"

"We need to go," said Koske, but his students either ignored him or couldn't hear him. "Students!" he shouted. "We need to go, now!"

Josef stepped forward and started nudging students toward the exit stairs. "We shouldn't be here," he yelled. "Please! Let—"

A senior engineer caught Josef by the arm. "Meneer Bakker! We need you at Diagnostic Station 10!" He pulled the young engineer to a bank of dials and gauges.

There were more shouts and people running every which way. A trackworker yanked open a tool closet. He pulled a crowbar free, letting another drop to the floor with a clang. Frieda watched as he climbed over the safety rail and tightrope-walked across the gears to the Robinson Rail. He peered close, then smashed at something pressed up against it, raising a spray of dust and shards: a rock caught within the gears.

Koske began pulling individual students into a hurried line. Malika gripped her tablet and stylus and looked around, frightened but determined.

On the walls, screens flickered to life. "Tail section to trackworkers," said a woman and Frieda's heart leaped. It was her mother. Her image shuddered and ghosted. The electromagnetic wash of the Sun was rising. Soon, so, too, would the heat.

"Trackworks, report!" Queen Beatrix's voice crackled. "The Dawn Line is approaching. We have about ten minutes before the tail is in sunlight!"

People were too busy to pay attention. The trackworker balancing on the gears hopped onto a safety platform. "Ready!" he yelled. "Try the restart now!" Other shouts echoed up and down the gantries as other workers pulled up crowbars and waved.

The gears shook, making a ratcheting noise that set Frieda's teeth on edge. She touched the safety rail as if she could soothe her town's wounded heart.

Bangs ripped along the length of the trackworks. Gears jerked. Frieda saw the Robinson Rail shift, and with it, the floor shook beneath her, but it was only a few centimetres. The jumpstart had failed.

Alfons turned to the porthole. "Should we evacuate?" His voice quavered.

"And go where?" Linde snapped.

"Out!" Alfons looked at her wide-eyed. "We can walk faster than the Sun and keep ahead of the Dawn Line—"

"In spacesuits?" Linde cut in. "It will be at least an hour before the next latitude town responds with a rescue shuttle. It would be a death march."

Alfons shook. Linde bit her lip and, after a brief hesitation, hugged him. He clutched her close.

At the porthole, Anna pointed. "There's light on the mountains!"

Frieda's classmates crowded her portholes, collapsing the line Koske had organized. Someone else shouted, "Flares! I can see solar flares!"

Frieda looked away. She clenched the safety rail, staring at the gears and wheels, willing them to work.

"Again!" the trackworkers shouted. "Try it again!"

Another series of bangs drowned him out. Frieda saw the starting force jerk along the Robinson Rail. Then she saw the ghost.

Fifteen metres beyond the safety platform, where gears banged and bulged against each other, a cloud erupted behind where the trackworker was staring. It wasn't smoke or steam. It was dust.

"Hey!" She pointed, but the trackworker couldn't hear her. Frieda looked around for someone to tell. She grabbed a rushing engineer, but he ducked his head and pulled away. "Excuse me, Your Highness!"

Suddenly, klaxons rang in beats: *short-short-long, short-short-long.* A call to shelter.

"Tail section to forebridge." On the monitor screens, Beatrix's voice edged up. "I'm ordering all personnel in the back two sections forward. Prepare to receive them!"

Frieda turned this way and that, but nobody would stop for her. Koske frantically tried to gather his class again. Josef looked up from his diagnostics screen, shouting over his colleagues to be heard. Her classmates milled, looking lost and scared. Then she spotted a small hatchway below the safety rail, next to the fallen crowbar.

"Jumpstart!" someone else shouted. "Again! Now!"

The floor shuddered. The machinery jerked in a wave running up the Robinson Rail, *kachunk!kachunk!kachunk!*

Frieda's throat tightened. Her fists clenched. She could see where something was holding them—holding her town, her home, her whole life in place, while the planet's slow rotation dragged them back toward the Sun. She swore she could feel the obstruction in her heart.

She stepped to the access hatch and picked up the fallen crowbar. A smash and a few twists later and the door popped open. She held the crowbar to her chest as she crawled inside.

The workings of the *Messenger* whined around her, like dynamos straining. Frieda passed beneath a canopy of cogs, their frozen, interlaced teeth casting shadowy fingers over her. Another jumpstart attempt rattled through, making her wince in the shattering clatter. She looked up into the gears, desperately trying to find the obstruction.

There were many, but they were small. As she spotted each one, she swung up her crowbar and smashed it. Rock dust sprayed into her eyes and mouth as the gears clanged together. She spat. Still, the gears wouldn't move. She kept looking.

Finally, she came beside the Robinson Rail itself—a long beam of black metal, thick as a desk, already warm with the heat of the approaching dawn. Huge leather-edged wheels hugged it close. She searched for something that could jam these wheels and, on her third scan, found it.

It was a grey rock, almost camouflaged by the grit and the grease of the rail, about the size of her head. It was pressed hard against one of the gripping wheels, digging into the leather. She marvelled at it. *That little thing?*

She gathered her strength and swung the crowbar at the stone. Dust rained down on her, but the rock didn't budge. She swung again, grunting, and a shard broke off and smacked her in the forehead. She swatted it aside with a rush of anger. She knew it was silly; it was just a rock. But her city was in danger because of this rock. Here and now, as Crown Princess of the *Messenger*, she had to deal with it.

She struck it with the point of the crowbar. The rock crunched. Stone and wheel shifted. She struck again, raising more dust, but still, the rock would not come free. She struck a third time, and the crowbar slipped from her grip and smacked her across the face. She lay gasping a moment, sweat biting her eyes, her nose beginning to bleed, and stared back hopelessly.

What was she going to do? The rock looked like it was almost out of the rail. She felt she could reach up and wrestle it out. Maybe . . . She reached for it, then pulled her hands back. *What in Sunlight do I think I'm doing?*

The klaxons changed, going from short-short-long to steady short bursts. Frieda heard her mother, the Stadtholder, shouting over the public address system. "General emergency! We have hit the Dawn Line! Repeat, the tail section has hit the Dawn Line. We are in sunlight!"

A distant explosion shook the floor beneath her. Her mother's voice cut out. The Robinson Rail vibrated like a tuning fork.

The rock rained more dust on her. She heard screams outside. Frieda sat up, horrified. "Mom!"

The klaxons confirmed it. They were now in a steady tone. Hull breach. *We've lost the tail section!*

Frieda glared up at the rock. She picked up the crowbar again, took careful aim. "On three," she breathed. "One . . . two . . ."

She struck. The crowbar shattered the rock. The wheels smacked against the Robinson Rail and turned.

Frieda's cry of triumph turned to a scream as the wheels grabbed the crowbar and pulled. The hook caught her sleeves, and before she knew it, the crowbar was sucked into the wheels, pulling her arms with it. Her body jerked forward, then suddenly fell back.

Frieda screamed louder as she felt warm flecks spray across her face.

The heartbeat of the *Messenger* started slow, then pulsed faster. Frieda was dimly aware of shouts outside and above her.

"We're moving!"

"Engage the boosters! Get us away from the Dawn Line!"

"Somebody's in there!"

The last voice was from just outside the hatch. Cara peered in, looking frantic.

A reinforcing beam connecting the Robinson Rail to the bedrock of Mercury grazed Frieda's shoulder, with the power of the planet behind it. She took no notice, curled up into a ball, still screaming. Outside, confusion reigned.

"What in Sunlight happened?"

"The Crown Princess is in there!" Cara shouted. "Help her! Josef! Do something!"

Frieda looked up. Josef's face came into frame within the hatch. Their eyes made contact. She could see him, his mouth open in horror. She reached out with a hand that was no longer a hand.

He lunged for the opening, then froze at the sight of the whirling machinery. He went as white as a sheet. "I—I can't go in there!"

"Oh, for goodness' sake!" Cara shoved him aside.

Shadows flickered from the hatch. A shape crawled forward. Suddenly Frieda was face to face with Cara, who reached for Frieda's hand, then jerked back at what she saw.

Cara hesitated. Then she leaned in and wrapped her arms around Frieda. Hooking hands under Frieda's shoulders, she pulled Frieda away as another reinforcing pillar on the Robinson Rail swept past them. Squirming, she shifted the two of them toward the hatch. "Come on!" she grunted. "Come on!"

Frieda was dimly aware of something sticky running over her arms and Cara's school uniform smearing red. Her vision tunnelled, but she could see the gears rolling above her. That lifted her heart, even as the spinning teeth made her dizzy. For some reason, the place had become inexplicably cold.

*I saved my home*, she thought. *Mom will be proud.*

*We lost the tail section.*

Sweat dripping from her forehead, Cara slipped out of the hatch and dragged Frieda out the opening. "We need medical help!" she shouted. "Now!"

And that was all Frieda remembered.

# CHAPTER 2
# THE CLOCKWORK HAND

FRIEDA WAS FOUR WHEN SHE FIRST SAW THE *MESSENGER*'S trackworks. While her fellow kindergarteners clamped their hands over their ears, Frieda ignored her teacher's admonitions and pulled her chin over the safety rail to stare at the wheels and gears that spun on the Robinson Rail.

"Wow," she whispered.

*She frowned. Her hands hurt. They were burning. She looked down and—*

From that day onward, Frieda built rails for her toys to travel along. For school presentations, she spent hours with magnifying goggles and jewellers' screwdrivers to build a diorama model of the *Messenger* that ran on batteries. She felt rather than heard her mother step up behind her, but she smiled when her mother kissed the back of her head.

*She reached for her jeweller's screwdriver but couldn't feel it in her fingers. She couldn't feel her fingers. The screwdriver hit the floor with a ting! She looked, and her arm smacked into her diorama, smashing down a pillar and part of her train.*

Her presentation won the top prize in the science competition at the Terminal Festival. Her father hugged her while they waited at the edge of the stage. Then Frieda saw her teachers bowing low and her mother striding forward, skirts sweeping, reaching to shake Frieda's hand.

Behind her mother, her grandmother—Adelheid, the dowager—leaned heavily on her cane. She nodded at Frieda and smiled.

Frieda reached for her mother's hand . . .

*She flinched in pain, then gasped in horror . . .*

Frieda woke.

She found herself lying in a soft bed in the middle of a quiet room. She blinked up at a white ceiling, bewildered. *Where am I?*

Her vision swam the moment she lifted her head to look around. She let it fall back and closed her eyes. She drifted back to the edge of sleep.

*It's so peaceful here. I can stay like this as long as I want. It's warm and soft and quiet and still—*

*Wait. Still?*

Her eyes shot open. There was no vibration. Like an ache in the centre of her chest, the heart of the *Messenger* did not beat. Her breath caught. *Are we dead?*

Frieda spied a porthole in the wall to the right of her bed. Straining to peer through it, she saw nearby rocks shining in the lights from the *Messenger*. The rest of the landscape faded to black. She couldn't see the iron cornrows. The lights of the room were too bright to let her see stars. Nothing moved.

She struggled to sit up but swooned. Her body wasn't responding the way it should. Signals from her brain weren't reaching parts of her.

*And that would be because . . . ?*

She looked down at her sheets, tucked in tight around her, pinning her arms to her sides. Her stomach dropped. She felt an urgent need to look and a rising, deepening dread.

Behind her, someone snorted awake. "Frieda?"

The voice, so familiar, brought a flood of relief. "Dad?" Her voice cracked like she hadn't spoken in weeks.

A chair scraped. His round face, his brown eyes, his mop of peppered hair suddenly filled her vision. His smile made her feel instantly warm and loved. "Hello, Frieda! Are you with us?"

Despite everything, she found herself grinning. "Of course I am." But there was more she needed to know. "Dad, why are we parked? The Sun—"

"Don't worry," he said. "Your grandmother ordered us 1,500 kilometres ahead of the Dawn Line so we could make repairs. We have a week before sunrise."

Frieda gaped as she wrapped her head around this. The *Messenger* could travel three times the speed of Mercury's rotation. Putting 1,500 kilometres ahead of the dawn must have taken at least two days and spent most of the *Messenger*'s battery reserves. How much time did they need for repairs? And why did Grandmother give the order, not Mother—

"Dad?" She took a shuddering breath. "Where's Mom?"

Her father's gaze darkened. "Frieda? Do you remember what happened? Do you know where you are?"

Her gaze tracked away. The walls were white instead of their usual grey. She was on a metal-framed bed. The air smelled of antiseptic. "Infirmary." She glanced down at her body, a lump beneath the sheets. She wanted to sit up, but something wasn't responding the way it should. She felt the memories approach with the momentum of the dawn. "Dad?"

He sucked his teeth. "Frieda, it's all right."

And that was a lie. "Where's Mom?"

"Frieda." His voice was husky with grief. "I'm sorry. Your mother was in the tail section when it—" he waved a hand "— when it happened. She was organizing the evacuation." He sniffed, then forced a wry smile. "You know her: nobody gets left behind. She was there when the sunlight caused a faulty window seal to fail." He gulped. "The window blew out, exposing her to the vacuum." He turned, reached, then stopped. He carefully touched her arm. "I'm sorry, Frieda. She's gone."

For a moment, the words didn't register. *Gone? What does he mean, gone? Gone where?* But the memory edged closer. The sirens. Her striking at the rock holding the *Messenger* back. The alarm indicating a vacuum breach—

And why had Dad touched her so gingerly when he clearly wanted to hug—

The pull. The crash. The spray.

She sat up, but not the way she expected. Signals crossed or vanished. And this time, her father did grab her, frantic, trying to hold her back. "Frieda! Be careful!"

"I need to see," she shouted before she even knew what she needed to see. She pushed against his restraining arms. Her covers fell to her lap. She raised her arms and—

She froze when she saw her arms.

Her infirmary robes, the sheets she lay on, and the covers were all white. The pink of her right arm stood out like a gash. She couldn't see her left arm because it was wrapped in bandages. So, too, was her right hand, but her left arm demanded her attention because parts of it were missing.

Frieda moved her arm, and a dizzying wave of that alien, signal-not-received feeling washed over her. Her left arm ended just above her elbow, its tip brilliantly white in its bandage. A part of her was shocked that there wasn't any blood or pain.

She realized she was gulping in air and holding her breath, building pressure in her chest until she thought she would burst. "Oh, gods!" Her thoughts leaped all over the place. *Where are my arms? Where is my Mom? What did I do to myself? Mom's dead! The Stadtholder is dead! Long live the—*

Her mind rebelled. "No!" She shook her head wildly. "I can't do this! I can't be Stadtholder! Not like this! Not now! This can't be happening!"

"Frieda!" Her father gripped her shoulders and tried to look her in the eye. "We'll get through this, I promise. You're not the Stadtholder! The advisory council assigned a regent for a year until you come of age." He said this desperately, as if fixing this one thing could fix everything else.

It didn't. Frieda tried to cover her face with her hands and flinched when she saw what she brought near. Instead, she closed her eyes and wailed. She didn't hear the door opening. She didn't notice the person entering until a shadow fell over her.

"Are you crying, Crown Princess?" said a firm voice.

Frieda's wail cut out. She looked up and saw an old woman standing like a soldier.

*Which she was, once,* said a voice at the back of Frieda's mind. *Her Majesty Queen Adelheid Koning, mother to the Stadtholder and dowager of the* Messenger *and its client cities of Mercury. Grandmother.*

Grandmother Adelheid looked down at her. The old woman was wearing the ceremonial uniform: a blue jacket and blue pants with gold piping on the sleeves and an orange sash across her chest. The room's lights glittered off the epaulettes.

As Frieda watched, Adelheid gripped the ball handle of her cane and knelt by the bedside, her joints creaking, bringing her face level with Frieda's. Inside a face that was like taut, ridged canvas, dark eyes burned. "I said, Frieda, are you crying?"

There was no denying it. Frieda cleared her nose with a sniff.

Still gripping her cane, Adelheid pulled out a handkerchief from under her cuff and wiped Frieda's cheeks with it. "Because of your mother?"

*Of course, because of that! Because of everything,* Frieda's mind shouted, but she said nothing. New tears added their streaks to the old.

"Beatrix was my daughter." Adelheid pulled her handkerchief away and lowered her raspy voice. "And she was a great woman. She did everything Mercury expected of her and more. Just as you did down in the trackworks. I have never been prouder of both of you. But she is at rest now, and Mercury expects more from us." She touched Frieda's cheek. "There will be time for crying. Later. Do you understand?" She gave Frieda a firm look.

Frieda swallowed, but she took a deep breath and nodded.

Adelheid flashed Frieda a smile. It was so brief, Frieda wasn't sure if she'd seen it, but in that moment, her grandmother looked so much younger Frieda was reminded of a mirror.

Then the smile was gone. Adelheid put both hands on her cane and shoved herself up with a barely audible grunt. She turned to an attendant Frieda hadn't noticed, standing guard by the door. "Did you bring it?"

The attendant stepped forward, holding a box covered in black velvet. Adelheid opened the lid and removed the Stadtholder's crown.

Frieda stared at it in shock. *They must have taken it from Mom's body!* And that made her mother's death more horribly real.

Adelheid turned the crown over in her hands—a crown she'd also worn, Frieda realized, decades ago, just after the Earth's silence started. Adelheid had ordered it made: a tiara of wrought iron, with no jewels but woven with the delicacy of lace. Adelheid kissed it once, as if it were still on Queen Beatrix's head, and placed it on her own.

And it seemed to Frieda as though Adelheid grew. She walked with a cane but not with a stoop. She stretched herself straighter until she towered. Eyes blazing, Adelheid focused on the attendant. "We are ready."

The attendant opened the door. People entered. Her father hurriedly pulled the covers above Frieda's arms. Frieda saw doctors and nurses in grey-white overalls. She saw civilian uniforms as well—men and women carrying tablets and cameras. *The journalists' guild!*

Everyone filed in. They didn't shout questions as Frieda had seen them do to her mother. Instead, they formed two lines along one wall, like a regiment. Frieda lay to attention.

Adelheid stood by the bedside, the wrought-iron crown on her head. She said, "Let the people know that the Crown Princess is awake and recovering. She will be in the infirmary a few days more, before being released to assume her duties."

The reporters dutifully wrote this down. One on the end straightened up. "Your Highness—" he began, then grunted as the woman beside him elbowed him.

Adelheid laid a hand on Frieda's shoulder. It was gentle, but it made Frieda feel awkward.

Adelheid turned to the reporters. "You may mark this moment."

Cameras clicked like grasshoppers. Frieda blinked. Her eyes watered.

Adelheid lifted her hand. "And now the Crown Princess will have her privacy."

The doctors and nurses began shooing the reporters out. There was a brief confused scuffle as too many people tried to fit through one small door.

Adelheid waited until the door shut and silence fell. When it did, she let out a breath and leaned on her cane. She patted Frieda's shoulder. "You did well."

*I didn't do anything*, Frieda thought. *I just lay here and looked pretty.*

Quietly, she said, "Thank you, Grandmother."

"Your father and I have to go," said Adelheid. "You have to get well enough to leave, and I have a lot of things to organize."

Frieda watched in horror as her father went to his seat and

gathered up documents, which he put into a case. "Dad? You too?" *Don't leave me alone with this!*

Her father winced. "I have to work, honey. We have repairs to do and not much time to do them. I'll come back and stay with you whenever I can, okay?"

He looked anguished and guilty, but he didn't stop. Frieda swallowed. "Okay."

Frieda's father and grandmother walked to the infirmary door.

"Grandmother," Frieda blurted. Adelheid looked back, and Frieda shifted her injured arm and bandaged hand into view. "What are we going to do about . . ." She shuddered. "This?"

Adelheid glanced at the bandages, then looked away. "We are putting our best doctors on that, Frieda. We will give you what you need to carry out your duties."

*That answer was almost meaningless,* thought Frieda.

Adelheid turned away. At the door, however, she turned back. "There is somebody here to see you."

Frieda perked up. Friends! But was she ready to see them? "Who is it?"

"Cara Flores," Adelheid replied. "The *Hermes* ambassador's daughter." She said this with a grimace—brief, but Frieda still saw it. Adelheid continued, "She saved your life and has expressed an interest in seeing you. I've granted that courtesy . . . assuming you are willing to see her?" She gave Frieda a look that encouraged her to say "no."

Frieda's brow furrowed. *Cara? Why her and not my friends?* But Adelheid stood waiting, and to Frieda's surprise, she found herself nodding. "Yes, let her in."

Frieda's father gave her a smile, then he followed Adelheid out of the room. The door clicked shut, then reopened a moment later.

Frieda shifted on her bed and watched as Cara stepped into

the room. The young woman stood there, hands clasped in front of her. The two stared at each other for a long moment.

"Hey," said Cara at last.

"Hi," Frieda replied.

Silence stretched.

From her hospital bed, Frieda looked Cara up and down. She was wearing the overalls of a full apprentice. Her dark hair was braided in a bun on the back of her head. On her sleeve was the emblem of the medical department.

"You signed up to be a doctor?" Frieda asked.

Cara nodded quickly. "I've wanted to be one since I was four."

Silence returned. The two young women looked at each other, each trying to avoid the other's gaze. Finally, Frieda couldn't stand it any longer. "Thank you for saving me," she blurted.

Cara met Frieda's gaze. She gave her a quick but sardonic smile. "Thank you for saving the city."

The compliment made Frieda flinch. "I didn't," she stammered. "I mean, I just—"

Cara looked down again. "It's okay, I—" She took a deep breath. "You're going to say you're not a hero. You weren't brave. You just did what you had to do. I know this because that's what I've been saying to everyone as well about saving you. Anyway, I'm sorry to bother you. I just needed to see you and make sure you were all right."

Cara made to step back, and before she realized it, Frieda said, "Don't go!"

The two women blinked at each other again. Frieda nodded to the bedside chair. "Sit with me?" Then, because that sounded too much like a command, she added, "Please?"

Cara looked at the chair for a moment, then sat. This time, they were able to look each other in the eye. "Are you all right?" Cara asked.

Frieda pulled her injured arms up and set them atop her covers. "I'm alive. I don't think I'm ever going to be all right."

Cara winced. "Sorry—"

"Please don't apologize."

"Yes, Your Highness."

"Don't—" Frieda bit her tongue. "Don't call me 'Your Highness,' at least not when we're alone. Talk to me. Tell me things. How long was I out? How much have I missed?"

Cara thought for a moment. "About a week. You haven't missed much."

"But school—" Frieda began.

"Cancelled." Cara frowned at Frieda's gape. "Well, not the whole school, just our cohort. The yearbook's cancelled, much to Malika's horror." Her cheeks reddened. "Though her first-hand account of your rescue that hit all the newsletters probably made up for that. Anyway, we were quietly given our final marks and told to report to our apprenticeships."

"No graduation ceremony?"

Cara shook her head.

"Even you?"

Cara nodded.

"That's not fair!" Frieda snapped. "Why should the class be punished because of me? Why should you be punished with the rest of the class?"

"Don't blame yourself," said Cara. "And I'm glad they didn't treat me differently. Solidarity. Besides, it wasn't a punishment. It just wasn't a time to celebrate."

Frieda looked away. *Fair point.*

She turned back. "So, how did the first week of apprenticeships go? How is everybody doing?"

Cara leaned back. "Well . . . Alfons got assigned to the kitchens."

Frieda smiled. "Is he cooking yet?"

"This early? Washing dishes."

"Poor man. How about Toshiko?"

Cara shrugged. "Apprenticed with the file clerks."

"Not a surprise," said Frieda. "Who else?"

"There's Linde, who is now an intern educator at the child-care centre."

Frieda smiled as she listened to the updates. For a fleeting moment, it made her feel normal. Who else did she want to know about? "How's Josef?" she asked.

Cara's shoulders stiffened. She looked away, biting her lip.

Frieda winced. Their initial antipathy had been over Josef, and she'd walked right into it.

But, to Frieda's surprise, Cara looked sad rather than angry. "Josef . . . blames himself . . . for what happened."

Frieda's mind flashed back. *I—I can't go in there!* "What do you mean?"

Cara sighed. "Just . . . he blames himself." She looked away. "Please. I don't really want to talk about it."

"Okay." *How do I change the subject?* She noticed Cara's uniform. "So, you're taking your medical apprenticeship here on the *Messenger*? Not back home on the *Hermes*?"

Cara shrugged. "Joining an apprenticeship here seems the best way to become a doctor. Also, it lets me stay with my mother."

Frieda felt a flash of jealousy, but she fought it down. Silence returned, longer this time. Finally, Cara turned away. "I should get back to work."

Frieda jerked up. *No! Don't—I'm not ready to be left to myself!* She burst out, "I'm sorry I called you a republican!"

Cara froze, her hand reaching for the door. She turned back; her brow furrowed. "I'm . . . pretty sure you didn't."

"On the stairwell on the way to the trackworks." Frieda gave Cara a wry smile. "I said it in my head."

Cara raised an eyebrow. She nodded slowly, then gave

Frieda a sly grin. "You shouldn't be sorry. It's accurate. I'm a child of the *Hermes*. I'm no fan of monarchies."

There was a knock on the door. A nurse looked in. "Ah, Mufrau Flores. I was told you might be here. It's the Crown Princess's dinnertime." She handed Cara a tray. "Handle that, will you?"

The nurse ducked away, closing the door behind her. Cara turned, holding the tray, and she and Frieda looked at it between them.

Frieda didn't feel hungry. After all she'd faced, how could she think of food? But her mother's voice spoke up in her head. *You should eat.* She looked at the plate and saw a protein loaf cut into bite-sized cubes and a pile of bac-crackers, all pre-broken. Then she looked down at her injured arm and her bandaged hand. She looked up and saw Cara looking grimly back.

"Ah," said Frieda.

"Indeed," said Cara. She set the tray on the bedside table and pulled the chair closer. "I guess we'd better get this over with." She shifted the tray and speared a protein cube with a fork, bringing it over. "Sorry, Your Highness."

Frieda raised her bandaged hand, and Cara stopped. "If we're to do this," she said, "then you will call me Frieda. Okay, Cara?"

Cara gave her a tight-lipped smile. "Yes. Sorry, Frieda." She held out the fork.

"Don't be sorry," Frieda muttered, and she opened her mouth for food.

☿

STRANGELY, the awkwardness of having to be fed by Cara seemed to make the time after that much less awkward, and Frieda felt good about that. When Cara finally left to go about her duties, Frieda found herself looking forward to when she would be back, and that was enough to let her face this time alone.

But with Cara gone, there was nothing to do. The media screen played but with no volume. Frieda watched journalists and news pundits speaking soundlessly. The headline scroll talked about messages of sympathy from the leaders of all the other latitude towns and the polar statics, including the *Hermes*. There was a note of a cancelled protest at the Baxter-Nordley. Eventually, the headlines started to repeat, and Frieda lost interest.

Finally, at the end of the day cycle, nurses and doctors came to change Frieda's bandages.

She'd been dreading that.

She sat stoically, looking down, while layer after layer of gauze peeled away. At first, the gauze stayed white. Then she saw a small patch of brown-red. She took a deep breath. *I can handle this. I can.*

When the gauze came away, she saw the tied-off dangle of skin, and she thought, *No, I can't!*

Fortunately, Cara was ready with a bedpan for Frieda to throw up into.

Frieda wasn't surprised at how much she'd lost of her left arm—it was gone past her elbow. The bandages on her right hand revealed that three fingers and most of her palm were gone, but her thumb and forefinger remained. *Well, that's something, at least.*

*Something?* The absurdity of that thought made a laugh start in her chest. She held it down because she wasn't sure that if she started, she could stop.

*How am I not in pain?* Then she saw a nurse pull the needle away and swab her right tricep. Her vision swam. *Oh. That's why.*

The doctor—*what's his name? He introduced himself, but I've forgotten*—caught her staring at the needle and smiled sympathetically. "You're doing great, Your Highness. We're gradually weaning you, so you won't have to worry about withdrawal symptoms."

"Oh," Frieda breathed. "Thanks."

The room swooned. Cara caught her and eased her onto her pillow. Frieda closed her eyes, and when she opened them next, she was alone.

☿

FRIEDA SLEPT FITFULLY THAT NIGHT, dreaming strange dreams, before she woke up screaming.

*Lord-in-Sunlight! My arm! My arm is burning!*

She flailed against the covers. A flash of pain made her howl. Footfalls dashed down the corridor. A pair of hands grabbed her by the shoulders. "Frieda! Frieda, don't! You're not ready!"

"My arm is on fire!" Frieda tried clutching her arm to herself and wondered why she couldn't.

The person grabbed Frieda's residual arm and began squeezing and rubbing the muscles at the top of her tricep. "Frieda!" She raised her voice against the wailing. "Frieda!" More people entered the room. It was chaos, but the rubbing was making the pain go away. Frieda came back to reality gasping and found herself staring at Cara, holding her residual arm and rubbing gently but vigorously.

"Any better?" Cara asked.

Frieda blinked at her bandaged arm. "But—" It had hurt as if it was still there. She'd been sure of it! But how—she'd lost them to the Robinson Rail, so how—

*Is this what they call phantom pain?*

A doctor came closer. "Good work, Mufrau Flores." He eased Cara back, then turned to Frieda. "I'm afraid this is not unusual, Your Highness, in the weeks after such an . . ." He coughed. ". . . accident. I think we should increase your pain medication again."

Frieda blinked at him, too tired and frazzled to say anything more than, "But—"

"You should rest now," said the doctor.

Frieda didn't see the needle, but she felt its effects when her head hit her pillow.

The following day swung between painkiller wooziness and boredom. Nurses came to deliver meals that she could hardly bring herself to eat. That brought doctors to see what was wrong with her. A gloom settled on her when she could think straight. She was tired, but she hated to sleep.

The hours ticked away. The *Messenger* stayed parked. Other than Cara or her father, nobody she knew came to visit her. She watched the media screen with the sound off and saw images of her grandmother meeting people and shaking them solemnly by the hand.

Late on the second night, Frieda woke, still woozy from the latest round of painkillers, and heard somebody moving about. In the corner of the room, a silhouette moved between chair and table, folding clothes. It was a female figure, and it looked familiar, but it wasn't Cara. The wooziness overtook Frieda before she could look harder, and she drifted back to sleep.

☿

FRIEDA WOKE clear-headed on the third day—strangely clear-headed. She felt no pain in her arms, but the room looked bright and crisp, and it didn't hurt her eyes. For a while, she was glad to be out of the woozy clouds, but the focus only enhanced the boredom. The gloom became a thing that danced in her mind, going round and round.

She focused on the media screen instead. More images of

her grandmother. *They could have left me with a remote control to turn up the volume. Then, I wouldn't have to sit in silence.*

*How in Sunlight would I operate that remote?*

*I could still ask them to turn up the sound.*

She glanced at the call button beside her bed, which she could push with her bandaged hand. It was another kind of remote. But outside her room, she heard people hurrying about. The infirmary felt busy. She realized then that she couldn't have been the only patient, not after what had happened to kill her mother—

She shifted away from the call button. She stared at the silent screen.

The door opened and a young woman hurried through, wearing the uniform of the royal attendants. She carried a bundle of clothes, which she set on the table—the table the silhouette had worked in front of the night before. *So, it wasn't a dream.* The woman started sorting, her back to Frieda. When she turned enough for Frieda to see her face, Frieda blinked. "Anna?"

Anna jumped. "Your Highness! I didn't know you were awake!"

The first classmate other than Cara to see her since the accident, Anna was one of the last Frieda expected. Anna was . . . polite. She was . . . mousy. She was . . . there. And now she was here and in uniform. *Anna? A royal attendant?*

*But it fits, strangely. She always pulled away and ducked her head whenever I talked to her, just like the servants do with Grandmother and Mom.*

"Anna," said Frieda again.

Anna set down the clothes and bowed.

Frieda stared at that. Her classmates weren't supposed to bow.

Except they weren't classmates, now. They were apprentices.

"I'm sorry, Your Highness," said Anna. "I didn't know you were awake. I wouldn't have ignored you. I—"

Anna was blushing and starting to babble. Frieda squirmed. "It's okay, Anna. It's—"

A knock at the door silenced both. It opened, and the doctor—*I still don't know his name*—brightened when he saw Frieda. "Ah! You're awake, Your Highness! Good. We can begin."

He entered, as did other doctors, nurses, and interns, one of whom was Cara. She and the other intern carried in a case and set it down on the table where Anna was working.

Frieda struggled to wrap her head around everything. "What is that? What's going on?"

"We've fast-tracked work on your prosthetic, Your Highness," the doctor replied. "Measurements were taken while you were unconscious."

Frieda reddened. "But that doesn't make sense." She was an engineer. "There has to be physiotherapy. There has to be nerve mapping, prepared connections with the remnant muscles." She looked over at the case. "Is this prosthetic going to work?"

The doctor sucked his teeth, and Frieda had her answer.

But he looked at her earnestly. "There will be time to make it work, Your Highness. The important thing right now is to get the look of it right."

Frieda blinked at him. *It won't work. It will just hang off of me. Without the preliminary work, a prosthetic will just be a*— "Who ordered this?"

The doctor coughed. "The Crown, Your Highness."

—*prop.*

Cara and the other intern pulled the prosthetic from its case and set it on the bed in front of her.

It had the shape of an arm. For a half-second, Frieda wondered if somebody had donated their own. But as she looked closer, she saw that the skin was the wrong colour. Cara and the other intern hefted it as they brought it forward. Frieda brushed at the prop with her remaining wrist. It held no heat; it was as cold as—

*Iron.*

*Well, of course. We're short on plastic, but we have plenty of iron.*

She nudged the fingers on the arm, then flinched as they shifted with an audible *click!click!click!click!*

*Clockwork.* It was intended to move, at least. But right now, the fingers splayed out like a dead thing.

*And so it will stay until they get working on making it work with my arm, and I figure out how to use it. Until then, it's just going to be a dead weight on my shoulder. Why are they putting this on me now?*

Frieda looked up at the doctors, and the interns smiled at her encouragingly. Behind them, Cara frowned, her arms folded across her chest. She opened her mouth as if to object.

The door opened. "Is she ready?"

Frieda looked up and saw Adelheid looking in. "Grandmother!" she breathed.

Everyone in the room snapped to attention, except Cara, who glanced around, then straightened up also.

"Grandmother," said Frieda again. "What are you doing here? What's going on with—" She nodded at the prosthetic. "—this?"

Adelheid lifted her chin. "It's time to get ready for your mother's funeral."

Frieda saw, then, what her grandmother was wearing: a dress. It was royal blue, with a long skirt hanging loose from the hips. The jacket went with it, with epaulettes on the sleeves and, again, the orange sash across the chest.

Frieda looked at the pile of clothes Anna had been sorting on the table. She recognized the long skirt. Her dress was to be the same as her grandmother's but without a sash and white instead of blue.

She blinked again, and looked around at the room, not only

taking in its details, but how she took in those details. Her mind was clear—clearer than it had been since she'd first woken up in here. It was like she was on a stimulant, except she didn't have the jitters that regular stimulants gave her. *I guess they didn't want me fainting at my mother's funeral. I wonder what drugs they used on me.*

"We're getting ready, Your Majesty," said the doctor quickly. "We're just about to fit the prosthetic."

Adelheid nodded, then focused on Frieda. "Are *you* ready?"

Frieda looked again at the bundle of white clothes on the far table. *That and Grandmother's outfit are probably the only two dresses to be found on the* Messenger. *They make no sense at all for any worker, but Grandmother and Mom believed in pomp and ceremony when circumstances warranted.*

*And Mom's funeral . . .*

Using her remaining hand, Frieda pushed the sheets off her, moved her legs to the side of the bed, and levered herself upright. She managed to do it before the doctors and Anna rushed in to help her. She gathered herself and stood up in her hospital gown.

*Circumstances warrant.*

She took a deep breath, then let it go. "I'm ready."

# CHAPTER 3
# THE STANDING START

ADELHEID LEFT. THE DOCTOR NODDED TO CARA AND THE OTHER intern, and the two hefted up the prosthetic. Anna coughed and gestured at Frieda's hospital robe. "Your Highness?"

Frieda's cheeks reddened. She knew it was no longer possible for her to dress herself—at least, not for a while—but to be dressed in front of a whole entourage? It was surprising how little dignity there was in royalty.

She straightened up, and Anna took the hospital robe off her. Cara hurried up to help. The other intern and the doctor discreetly averted their eyes.

Over the next two hours, Frieda felt like a robot as they hung the prosthetic from her shoulder and dressed her. They removed the bandage from her hand and fitted it with a glove that covered her remaining thumb and forefinger and gave her the appearance of having the remaining fingers, except that, unlike her thumb and forefinger, they were dead things pressed against the top of her remnant palm.

Finally, Frieda emerged from her hospital room, flanked by the entourage, wearing her white dress with no sash. She stepped into a hallway flanked by doctors and nurses. Adelheid stood waiting in blue. At the front of the troupe, a royal attendant called out, "All stand to attention for the Dowager Regent, Adelheid Koning, and her granddaughter, the Crown Princess Frieda."

Each doctor, nurse, and intern bowed as Frieda and Adelheid walked past, though Frieda saw that Cara didn't bow low. Anna did, however.

With their entourage, Frieda and Adelheid swept past the reception desk and into the public corridors.

Frieda watched it all pass. There was a brightness to everything, a hyper-reality that struck her like a dream. Except for the echo of their footfalls, the corridors of the *Messenger* remained quiet. The people Frieda did see were grouped around media screens, whispering or just staring, their hands clasped solemnly in front of them.

She heard one man suck in a deep breath and saw his jaw clench. Tears streamed down his cheeks. He looked up and saw Frieda staring and looked away quickly.

Adelheid and Frieda swept with their entourage through corridors that got larger and wider with each junction. Frieda realized they were heading for the main cargo bay.

*Of course: the only space big enough for something like this since there's no room on the Messenger for churches.*

The main cargo bay was full of people, sitting in rows of chairs Frieda didn't know the *Messenger* had. She recognized a few of the attendees—a parent of a school friend in the back Meneer Koske, a council member. Others were faces she'd passed as she walked the corridors of the *Messenger* to and from school. She didn't know their names.

Everyone rose, hands clasped in front of them, as she and Adelheid entered and walked up the centre aisle. The faces got more recognizable the farther Frieda walked: members of the advisory council, the *Hermes* Ambassador, officials from other latitude towns, including their client tows, the *Rücker Eddison* and the *Baxter-Nordley Polar Static*, but also independent towns like the *Viritrilbia*, the former *Hermes* client town *Clement-Clarke*, and the *Lares Polar Static*.

In front of the audience, by the large cargo bay airlock doors leading outside, a glass coffin lay on a stand. Inside, Queen Beatrix lay in state. Four pallbearers, each wearing a vacuum suit, stood at the corners.

Adelheid and Frieda stopped before the casket. Queen Beatrix—Mom—had been dressed in royal robes of her own, white with an orange sash. Her slippers were white. She didn't have her iron crown anymore, but she held an iron staff—one of the cornrows—at an angle across her body. Her eyes were closed, and her face was pale. She showed none of the signs of death by decompression. The undertakers had performed a miracle.

*I wish I could touch her cheek one last time. I still have two fingers for it.*

The absurdity of the thought brought the start of a laugh within her chest, tinged with hysteria, but she fought it down. *Not here. Not now.*

*Still.* She glanced down at her prosthetic. *At least she won't see me like this.*

She recoiled at that thought, then closed her eyes against the tears. *Yes. I wish Mother could see me, even like this.*

She looked up at the pallbearers. Her eyes slipped past the Prime Minister, past the president of the *Leigh Brackett* (a former client city of the *Messenger*, now independent but friendly), and the chief of the trackworkers' guild.

The fourth pallbearer was, of course—

"Dad," she breathed.

"Shh," said Adelheid.

Holding his helmet under his arm, Frieda's father flashed her a quick smile. "Hey," he said softly. "Holding up okay?"

*Screw decorum!* Frieda reached for her father, who gave her a quick hug. Around them, the cargo bay whispered. The moment held.

Finally, Adelheid and Frieda took their places in a pair of seats in the front row to the right of the central aisle. After a moment's reflective silence, the *Messenger*'s chaplain stepped to the podium. Everyone rose. At the back, two singers—an alto and a soprano—began to sing the lament. For Frieda, the funeral blurred.

"We are gathered here today to say farewell to Queen Beatrix Koning," the chaplain read out. "Stadtholder of the *Messenger* and its client towns, daughter, mother, and partner, loved by all who knew her . . ."

Eulogies followed, long ones. Frieda barely heard them. Instead, she sent up a single prayer of her own. *Goodbye.*

The chaplain stepped down from the podium and faced the casket. The pallbearers put on their helmets, grabbed a handle at each corner, and lifted the casket free of its stand. The inner doors of the cargo bay airlock clanked, rattled, and slid open. The pallbearers stepped through, and the doors shut behind them. Above the doors, a screen flickered to life, showing the view of a camera looking over the shoulder of one of the pallbearers in front, waiting for the outer airlock doors to open.

The two singers started another requiem. On the screen, the outer doors parted, and the pallbearers stepped onto the surface of Mercury.

The speakers in the cargo bay chirped. "We are clear of the airlock." Static crackled in her father's voice. "We are moving toward the cairn."

Floodlights on the outside of the *Messenger* lit the way as the pallbearers walked slowly and solemnly toward a cairn of stones in the middle distance. "Fifty metres." The speaker chirped and crackled. "Thirty metres."

The cairn grew within the screen, rocks salvaged from the surface of Mercury. A dark opening within faced the *Messenger*.

The glass casket gleamed in the floodlights, then blackened as it hit shadow.

"We are placing the casket into the cairn," said her father. There was a pause, then a catch in his voice that might have been static. "It is done."

The pallbearers pulled back. The foot of the glass casket gleamed within the shadow of the rock.

The speaker crackled again—not her father's voice this time, but the Prime Minister's. "We commit the Stadtholder's body to the Sun," she said, "to the stars and to the dust of Mercury. May she watch over us through our rotation."

Throughout the *Messenger*, the audience whispered, "We say it is so." Frieda bit her lip, hard.

The singers began another mournful song, but now people began filing out. Adelheid stood and tapped Frieda's shoulder to follow. They waited as delegates filed past them, each dignitary bowing their heads in turn, saying, "Your Highness" to Frieda and "Your Majesty" to Adelheid. Some clasped Adelheid's hands as they offered their condolences. Frieda was too mired in her own thoughts, at first, to notice that nobody was reaching for her hand.

Finally, when the front rows were empty, and the crowd was filing out of the hold, Adelheid put a hand on Frieda's shoulder. They moved forward together.

"Hold it together a little while longer," said Adelheid under her breath.

Frieda looked at her. "What?"

"You're doing fine." Adelheid nodded at the way ahead. "Just a little longer before you get home. Hold it together until then."

"But—"

The doors parted, revealing a phalanx of reporters on the other side. Digital shutters chittered like locusts. Adelheid tightened her grip on Frieda's shoulder.

These reporters were far less contained than they'd been when Adelheid had let them into Frieda's room in the Infirmary. They chattered, shouting, "Regent! Regent! Your Majesty!"

"Move quickly," Adelheid muttered. "This is not the place."

Frieda blinked spots from her eyes. "The place for what?"

Adelheid said nothing. Security officers cleared a way for them until they entered the tramway platform as a tram entered. Detraining workers and off-duty residents stopped to see the crowd before them before they were swamped by security officers who gently but firmly directed them aside. The officers ushered Adelheid and Frieda into the newly private shuttle. Shutters buzzed until the doors clicked shut, cutting out the sound like a sudden vacuum.

The tram sped off. Frieda instinctively leaned against the force of acceleration, then staggered as her changed arms unbalanced her. Her hardened knuckles smacked the wall with a shockingly loud bang. Adelheid frowned at her. Frieda gave her an apologetic smile. They faced forward, waiting. Past the window flowed the views of sections of the *Messenger*: a galley courtyard, the hydroponic farms, the smelters. Frieda saw sparks from welders getting back to work. Often, the movement of the tram could lull her to sleep, but she took it all in whether she wanted to or not.

Frieda looked at her grandmother. "What did you give me?" Adelheid blinked at her, so she went on. "I should be sleeping, but I don't think I can. What did you give me, and why?"

Adelheid looked up at the clock again as they passed another factory. "You've been seen by our best doctors, Frieda. They know what they're doing."

"Why are you checking the clock?" Frieda asked. "Do you have an appointment somewhere?"

Adelheid glanced at the clock again. "Yes, we do. Don't worry. It won't take long."

The tram juddered to a halt, and the doors parted.

They were steps away from the Royal Apartment, on a fenced-off high ledge three storeys above the agora below. Attendants awaited them, but Frieda heard something else. There was a rumble in the air of many muted voices out of view that could not stay silent.

"What's going on?" she asked.

"Just a quick diversion," Adelheid replied. "Follow me."

Frieda followed Adelheid past the front doors of the Royal Apartment. Led by one of the attendants, Adelheid marched to the railing at the edge of the parapet. The Royal Agora stretched out below them.

Frieda had looked down from this parapet many times. Across from it was the memorial screen displaying the live feed from Earth, still showing static as it had for the past fifty years. On either side of the media screen were two gigantic portraits, with the late Queen Beatrix on the right and Adelheid as a young woman on the left—from before she became Stadtholder.

Frieda had never seen the agora so full of people before. She'd thought the cargo bay had been crowded, but this—!

People stood shoulder to shoulder, and as she and Adelheid stepped up to the parapet, they cheered with the force of a storm.

The attendant stepped up before them and shouted to the assembled. "All attend! Presenting Her Royal Majesty, Adelheid Koning, Dowager Stadtholder of the *Messenger*!"

The crowd roared, and he stepped back, clapping. "Come on," said Adelheid, nudging Frieda forward and stepping to the railing.

The crowd roared to see her.

Adelheid stood ramrod straight. Lights glittered off the medals on her jacket and the sequins around her orange sash. She raised a hand and gave a royal wave, then put both hands to the railing and leaned on it. At this signal, the crowd drew quiet.

Adelheid lifted her head, with the wrought-iron crown, high. "Today has been a bitter day."

Her voice projected to the masses, but Frieda thought someone must have hidden a microphone on her, somehow, because she could hear Adelheid's voice on the speakers throughout the agora. "Today, we laid to rest your beloved Queen, my daughter, Beatrix. Today, we mourn her passing."

The audience bowed their heads.

Adelheid shifted. "But today is also a day to be proud."

People in the agora looked up. There was a soft rumble of voices, curious.

Adelheid went on. "Today, we see the result of the hard work and sacrifices made by everyone on the *Messenger* to get this latitude town back on track. We mourn all who have fallen, but we honour their memory by continuing their dedication that has sustained us through the Silence!"

A roar rose from the crowd.

"Tradition and sacrifice have sustained us through isolation," Adelheid continued. "I know this personally."

Frieda frowned as Adelheid's hand slipped along the parapet railing, gently taking the curled fist of her prosthetic arm. She saw, rather than felt, her grandmother's fingers tighten over it.

Adelheid yelled, "And none knows this sacrifice more than my granddaughter, your Crown Princess!"

Adelheid lifted Frieda's prosthetic arm. Frieda's loose sleeve slipped and bunched up at her shoulder, revealing the prosthetic and the harness that attached it to her residual arm. She could only stare at her grandmother as the crowd roared its approval. The lights of the agora blinded her. What could she do? Lord-in-Sunrise, what could she do?

*My duty*, a part of her thought. *This is my duty. Say nothing for now.*

The crowd's cheers swept over her.

And the *Messenger* started forward. The sudden acceleration staggered the audience and made Frieda's muscles clench. She would have fallen if Adelheid hadn't braced her.

The audience roared louder as the heartbeat beneath their feet began anew. The *Messenger* was moving. It was speeding up.

*And it was me*, thought Frieda, feeling it like a rock in her stomach. *Grandmother timed the whole thing on me.*

☿

When Adelheid stepped back, Frieda stepped with her and followed her away from the parapet toward the Royal Apartment. The attendants held the doors open as they entered. Frieda held her tongue long enough for the doors to shut behind them. Then she said, "How dare you?"

She said it so low Adelheid frowned a moment before turning as if she hadn't heard properly, so Frieda raised her voice. "How dare you!"

Adelheid folded her arms. "What?"

"You—" Frieda's anger, powered by embarrassment and humiliation, made her words tumble together. "You could have warned me! You could have prepared me! You could have let me know what I'd be showing—" She gestured at her prosthetic hand with her gloved one. Her artificial fingers smacked against the rubber and iron. It felt like hitting a club.

"The people of Mercury needed to see that the crown princess is up and about, Frieda," said Adelheid. "I'm surprised that you're surprised. Everybody knows what you did in the engine room. You know how important civic morale is. It's not too much to ask of you after you spent all that time recuperating in the Infirmary."

Though delivered calmly, the last words were a rebuke. Frieda drew a shuddering breath. "I know my duty, Grandmother! That's why I'm shouting at you here and not on the parapet. I am *not* some prop!"

Adelheid glared at her. "What are you talking about?"

"You timed the restart for the moment we were on the parapet," Frieda snapped. "I saw you checking the time! You were afraid we were going to be late!"

"That's called stage presence," Adelheid replied. "It drives home the fact that the people of the *Messenger* are in good hands; that the *Messenger* is strong."

"They work for the *Messenger* every day, Grandmother." Frieda shook her head. "They know how strong we are."

"The other cities need to know as well," Adelheid replied. "They need to know that we won't be taken advantage of just because our Queen is dead."

Frieda blinked. *What brought this on?*

Adelheid went on. "So, yes, you were used as a prop. Get used to it because that's what we both are: props for our subjects to lean on. Now, if you're done yelling at me like a child, you might want to retire to bed. You have a long day ahead of you tomorrow: physiotherapy and your apprenticeship to be the Stadtholder."

Frieda started and stared. "But . . . already?"

*I'd hoped to talk to Mother about this. I hoped she might relent and let me be an engineer. I'd also hoped to have hands.*

Adelheid shook her head. "The days of your mother fostering your fanciful dream of becoming an engineer are over, Frieda. You no longer have the hands for it, and the Stadtholder's daughter doesn't take the jobs that fall to those who can't work the others. There's no place for you as a file clerk; you do not walk the iron cornrows. Those were never options for you. It's time for you to grow up and accept your duties as Stadtholder."

Frieda straightened up, breathing heavily but staying silent. She'd known, if she was honest with herself, that she could smudge her cheeks with engine grease, but somebody was always going to close in with a towel. Engineering was a dream and nothing more. And now her prosthetic pulled her down like an anchor. She wanted to scream, but she didn't because doing so would mean Grandmother had won.

At the other end of the room, someone cleared their throat.

Frieda and Adelheid turned. Frieda's father stood by the door opening into the hallway leading to the bedrooms. He waved a hand. "Welcome home, Frieda."

Without a word, Frieda went forward and wrapped her remaining arm around her father. He hugged her back.

Adelheid steepled her fingers and pressed them to her forehead for a moment. She sighed. "I'm sorry, Frieda." She looked up and looked suddenly older. "I know a lot has fallen on your shoulders." She winced at her own words but plowed on. "Beatrix was your mother, but understand that she was also my daughter."

Frieda glared at Adelheid, gave her father one last squeeze, and, with as much dignity as she could muster, strode from the room and to her bedroom.

Dignity deteriorates when people aren't looking. The problem with the Royal Apartment, however, was that there was always someone looking: attendants, advisers, security. People walked the corridors. Frieda would have ignored them and stomped to her bedroom anyway, but part of her reminded her that these people weren't subjects; they were people, even if she didn't know their names. She maintained her dignity for them, also.

She was finally alone when she reached her bedroom and then struggled to turn the doorknob with her thumb and forefinger. She grunted as frustration mounted. Her fingers slipped. A pain shot up from her palm. She was building up to a good swear when she managed to twist the knob enough for the door to unlatch. She kicked it open, stormed in, and realized her mistake.

Whatever stimulant her grandmother had prescribed for her still hadn't worn off. How in dawnfire was she going to sleep? She needed to pace, and her room was too small for that.

But it was still the only private place she could go.

She sat on her bed and then fell back onto her pillow. She stared at the ceiling. *I'm going to cry.* Then she could hear her grandmother's voice in her head. *Queens don't cry.*

*I don't want to be Queen.*

Grandmother again. *Your mother wouldn't want you to cry.*

*She wouldn't want me to, but she'd let me. She'd understand. She'd encourage it.*

*But she's not here. It's just me.*

The door clicked open. "Your Highness?" It was Anna, out of breath and straightening her uniform. "I hadn't expected you back so soon. Will you need to change?"

Frieda blinked and sat up. Or tried to. "What—" She grunted, got her shoulders about a foot off the bed, then slumped back. She struggled again. "What are you doing here?"

Anna hurried over and pushed Frieda upright. "I assume you want to turn in for the night. Shall I help you with your nightclothes?"

*Anna. Classmate. Here to undress me. That is so wrong!*

*But how the heck am I going to get this prosthetic off? It needed a team to get it on me.*

"Yes." With great effort, Frieda finally sat upright. She frowned as she saw Anna head for the closet and begin pulling out nightclothes. "No."

Anna turned, frowning.

"Not nightclothes, please," said Frieda. "I'm not ready to

sleep." She gestured at her prosthetic. "Just get this thing off me."

Anna looked shocked. "But Your Highness—"

"I don't want this thing on me anymore!" Frieda snapped, embarrassment and frustration coupling to anger. "Just take it off."

Anna hurried forward and began unbuttoning Frieda's top, pulling down the sleeves to access and unbuckle the harness. She pulled the prosthetic from her sleeve and set it aside. The sudden loss made Frieda gasp with relief. "Thank you," she breathed.

"You're welcome, Your Highness." Anna did up the buttons on Frieda's top. Frieda's sleeve hung limp.

That was the fourth time Anna had used that term. "Anna—"

Anna looked up from starting to take off the glove with the fake fingers. "Yes, Your Highness?"

Frieda pulled her gloved hand back. "Stop calling me 'Your Highness.'"

"Your Highness?"

"You're doing it again," Frieda snapped. "You're treating me like some artifact. We went through school together. We made a model of the Robinson Rail when we were twelve."

But as she said it, her chest tightened. They might have gone through school together, but other than Anna and Cara, she hadn't seen anybody from her class since the accident. Not Alfons, not Malika, not Josef, anybody. And those that she had were there as part of their jobs.

*And Anna hardly said a thing when I put together that model of the Robinson Rail.*

It felt like her chest had filled up like a balloon again. She let out her breath, hard. "I'm not an artifact. I'm your classmate."

"No," said Anna, quietly.

Frieda frowned at her. "What?"

"No." Anna stepped back, clasping her hands, looking defiantly at the floor. "You asked me what I am doing here, Your Highness? My job: serving the office of the Stadtholder. I have always been doing that job. At school, we were told what to do around you, what lines not to cross. That was our job, and that's the job I've chosen for my apprenticeship." She hesitated, then continued. "And, with respect to Your Highness, you have your job to do as well."

Frieda gaped at her. Anna's cheeks coloured, and she swallowed.

*I could use my job to get her fired,* she thought. *But I don't want this job.*

She turned for the door. Anna reached it a half second before her and opened it. "Where are you going, Your Highness?"

"Out," Frieda snapped.

"Shall I notify security?"

"No!" Frieda caught herself and continued more quietly. "I'm going to the balcony. I'm sure security is keeping an eye on things there." She strode into the hallway, aware of Anna's eyes on her until she turned the corner.

The Royal Apartment was quiet, lights dimming toward bedtime. Frieda saw individuals standing in shady corners, keeping watch. They'd been there throughout her life, but now she noticed them. One leaned over and opened the door to the reception room as she approached.

It was hushed here as well. The media screens were muted, showing talking heads and headline scrolls about the funeral and the restart. Frieda turned for the outer door. Another officer opened it for her, and Frieda stepped out onto the balcony area. By the corridor leading to the tram stop, she saw two security officers stiffen to attention.

*I don't dare wander. I'd attract an entourage. Unlike King Henry before Agincourt, I have the opposite of an effective disguise.*

She approached the parapet, keeping to the shadows. She looked down at the agora as she'd done many times before. The evening workers were arriving home from the trams while the night workers set out.

She leaned against the wall and brought her hand up, stopping before she jabbed her eyes with her artificial fingers. She'd forgotten to take the glove off. She sighed, then rubbed her eyes wearily with her thumb.

*What a horrible day. What a horrible week. I never thought life could get as bad as this.*

She looked down at the agora.

*And yet the* Messenger *still runs. People keep going to work. Life goes on.*

*I'd hate to think that I'd hate that.*

She watched the people move across the agora: families, couples, single workers, walking beneath the portraits of Queens Beatrix and Adelheid, through the hiss of static from the memorial display showing the lost signal of Earth.

*We're still moving, even fifty years after the Earth fell silent,* she thought. *By rights, we shouldn't be here. Maybe, just maybe, I can do the same. Maybe I can find some sort of stability after this disaster.*

She pushed away from the railing. *Let's go to bed.*

Across the Royal Agora, the display flickered. The hiss stuttered. Then, a voice issued from the speakers. "Hello?"

Frieda turned. *Did I just see that? Did I just hear that?*

In the agora, people looked around, confused. Above them, the display below the screen counted up the time since the last signal from Earth had been received: 49 years, 9 months, 4 days, 23 hours, 52 minutes, 27 seconds, 28 . . . 29 . . . 30 . . .

The live feed flickered again. "Hello, Mercury?" The voice echoed.

The static vanished from the memorial screen. The screen went blank, before filling with green text. Frieda couldn't make head nor tail of it from this distance, but she could hear the voice booming across the square, stopping everyone in their tracks.

"Hello, people of Mercury," said the voice. "This is Earth."

Frieda's jaw dropped.

"Mercury, are you receiving this? Please respond."

# CHAPTER 4
# FRIEDA AND HER MOTHER

FRIEDA RAN TO THE ROYAL APARTMENT AND STRUGGLED TO OPEN the front door. The attendants were at the parapet, staring agog at the display; this was the first time she could remember having to open this door on her own. It would have been hard enough with both her arms. But she gripped the knob tight with her thumb and forefinger, twisted hard, then leaned back, grimacing. The door swung open, and she darted inside.

It was a lot louder in the reception area. The media screens had been turned up, tuned to the Earth's message. Attendants and security officers stared in awe. As Frieda watched, the front door burst open behind her. "Is the Queen up?"

Frieda found herself staring at the Prime Minister, leading a cohort of legislative advisers. For a moment, the woman blinked at her before bowing. "Um . . . good evening, Your Highness. Where is your grandmother, the Regent?"

Before she could answer, Frieda heard a cane click against the floor. "I'm here." Adelheid strode out from the hallway, a shawl over her nightclothes. "I'm telling you now, if this is some prank that has gotten me out of bed, the people behind it will be in bright, bright trouble."

A clerk turned up the volume. "Hello, people of Mercury," came the voice from the screen. "This is planet Earth. Are you receiving this? Please respond."

The crowd of advisers and security officers parted as Adelheid stepped toward the media screen. Her cane tapped the floor once. She tilted her head. Her eyes narrowed.

Frieda frowned. *Is that an expression of anger? Or dread?*

Adelheid stabbed a finger at the green-on-black text scrolling down the screen. "What are those symbols?"

One of the advisers peered closer. Frieda recognized them from her field trip as being the head of the communications guild. Their brow furrowed. "That's data," they said. "I think that's a live stream from the Earth's Information Web."

Head of Sanitation leaned forward. "They have the Web back? How? I thought they were dead!"

"Just because they were silent didn't mean they were dead," said Head of Communications. "There have been stray signals, chatter from personal radios. Nothing worth logging."

Head of Education and the Archive gnawed his lip. "Last I'd heard, their government had fractured into hundreds of warlord-states, based on watershed lines, feuding over resources."

Head of Security pointed at another screen, showing broadcasters from the Journalists' Guild. "Our media are onto this."

"You wouldn't expect them to just ignore it," said Head of Sanitation.

"First question." Adelheid's voice cut through the throng. "Is this broadcast genuine? Are we sure this isn't somebody from the Baxter-Nordley bouncing a signal off our satellites?"

"It's genuine." Head of Communications looked up from their tablet. "All our satellites report normal. They're receiving the signal from . . ." They nodded upward. ". . . out there."

Adelheid's frown deepened.

Everyone in the room started talking over each other again.

"All the towns hear it," somebody said. "The Earth wanted to make sure everyone who could listen could hear them."

"What do we tell the people?"

"What *can't* we tell them? They already know!"

Behind the crowd, Frieda cleared her throat. "Shouldn't we reply to the message?"

Nobody answered. Frieda tried again. "Listen to me—" Then, at the top of her lungs, "Hey!"

Silence fell. Everyone looked at her. She felt her cheeks heat up, but she pushed on. "Has anyone replied to this message?"

The advisers looked at each other. One by one, they shook their heads. The prime minister turned back. "No, Your Highness."

"Don't you think somebody should?" Frieda asked.

The advisers looked at each other again, embarrassed.

Adelheid tapped her cane. Eyes narrowed, facing forward, she pushed through the crowd. "Prepare an appropriate response. Something diplomatic but welcoming. I'll review it in fifteen minutes. In the meantime, I'm going for a walk."

Frieda stared as her grandmother strode to the front door. An attendant opened it for her.

The moment Adelheid was out of the room, the advisers rounded on each other.

"You heard her: diplomatic but welcoming!"

"What do you say to someone you thought died fifty years ago?"

"Not, 'how've you been?', that's for sure."

"'The people of Mercury greet and welcome—' No, too stuffy."

Frieda turned and followed her grandmother. As she stepped onto the balcony, she heard the noise of the crowd. The agora was full again, and though she couldn't see the people from her vantage point, she felt the air quivering with excitement. Adelheid was nowhere to be seen.

Keeping to the shadows, Frieda stepped to the parapet railing and looked at the crowd below, all focused on the memorial screen between the portraits of Adelheid and Beatrix. Lines of green text continued to stream down it. The vocal message was continuing but the voices of the people drowned it out. Though they couldn't hear what it was saying, they seemed happy enough that they were here to say that they'd listened.

Starting at one corner, then spreading across the crowd, a song rose through the agora. Frieda recognized it as the international anthem of the United Nations of Earth, last sung, so far as she knew, just before the start of the Silence:

> *And did our fleets in ancient days*
> *Soar over Terra's mountains green?*
> *And was the holy Lamb of God*
> *On Terra's pleasant pastures seen?*
>
> *Bring me my bow of burning gold!*
> *Bring me my arrows of desire!*
> *Bring me my spear! O clouds, unfold!*
> *Bring me my chariot of fire!*
>
> *I will not cease from mental fight*
> *Nor shall my sword sleep in my hand.*
> *Till we have built Jerusalem*
> *On Terra's green and pleasant land!*

A new chant started up as the song ended, simple and forceful: "U-N-E! U-N-E!"

*United Nations of Earth*, thought Frieda. *It's like we're a colony again.* Despite herself, she shuddered.

*But it's good*, she thought quickly. *Mother Earth is back. We aren't alone anymore. This is a moment to celebrate, and I, as Crown Princess, have a duty.*

Frieda stepped into the light. Below her, people spotted her and nudged their neighbours. The agora turned, and a roaring cheer rose from the crowd.

She raised her good arm in a salute. *At least they are happy.* She smiled.

*The Queen should be out here for this,* she thought. Then, *Mom.* She swallowed against her grief and waved again.

She frowned. *Grandmother should be out here, at least. Where is she? Didn't she come out here?*

Frieda looked back toward the Royal Apartment. The front door was closed, but she saw a shadow move by one of the columns. She saw a light gleam off the head of the cane. Adelheid looked back.

Frieda took a step back from the railing, expecting her grandmother to come out beside her and wave to the crowd.

But Adelheid stayed in the shadows. She looked darkly at the media screen, then at Frieda. She shook her head and put a finger to her lips.

Then she turned away, keeping to the shadows, and returned to the Royal Apartment. The door shut behind her.

☿

Once, when Frieda was fifteen, she couldn't sleep. She turned over and fluffed her pillow, first with her hands, then with her fists, then finally with her head. It didn't help.

*Too many thoughts. Too many worries. And the feel of this place is wrong, wrong, wrong.*

She lay face down for a long moment.

*I hate the sleep time when we're at Terminal, with the* Messenger *parked and waiting. It makes you feel alone with your thoughts, and that makes your thoughts loud.*

*Maybe that's why the parties around Terminal Day go on for so long.*

She propped herself up on her elbows. *Well, if I'm to be awake now, then I should at least do it upright.*

She rolled out of bed and pulled a shawl over her night clothes. The floor refused to vibrate beneath her bare feet, so she put on slippers. She pattered through the Royal Apartment.

The night servants stayed discreet and in the shadows. She left the Royal Apartment and turned away from the tram, taking the stairs to the agora. If she'd listened, she would have heard the footfalls of the security officer behind her, but the sound was so normal she ignored it.

She headed for the nearest galley. Stepping inside, she found herself in a darkened room with chairs placed on top of tables.

Of course. They put this galley on reduced hours during the Terminal period. The crew were hard at work in the spaceport's galleys. "Drat."

But she spotted cupboards and the possibility of snacks within. She slipped behind the counter and found a dry goods larder. She ran a finger along the bags of cereal and flour. She spotted crackers, which appealed, but she didn't want to open an industrial-sized bag. Weren't there smaller bags, or had they all been taken into Terminal?

"Looking for these?" asked someone with their mouth full.

Frieda whirled around. Her mother sat in the corner, chewing.

"What are you doing here?" Frieda gasped.

"Same—" Her mother finished chewing, then swallowed. "Same as you, I'll wager." Then Mom, Queen Beatrix Koning, Stadtholder of the *Messenger*, held out her bag of crackers. "Can't sleep?"

Frieda shook her head.

"Worried about stuff?"

Frieda shook her head. People worried about things that could happen when there was hope that they might not. It was useless to worry about things that would happen whether you wanted them to or not.

"Frustrated about stuff?" Beatrix asked. "Angry? I know apprenticeships are coming up."

Frieda turned away. "I don't want to talk about it." *Actually, I want to scream about it, but that would just wake Grandmother, and it wouldn't help.*

Then a thought struck her, and she turned back. "Why can't you sleep? Worried about stuff?"

Her mother chuckled. "No, Frieda."

"Frustrated about stuff?"

"Frustrated about everything." Her mother tossed the bag of crackers. Frieda caught it and helped herself to one. She sat on a stepstool while her mother leaned against the wall.

Beatrix went on. "Frustrated by the complaints of all the guild leaders. Frustrated by the mayor of the *Baxter-Nordley*, frustrated by the *Baxter-Nordley*'s water workers. I understand their concerns, but if they would just take the time to listen, we could resolve things with a lot less shouting. I'm frustrated by the *Hermes* leadership sticking their nose in, and if I hear Ambassador Flores remind me one more time about the history of it all, I might cause a Diplomatic Incident." She sighed. "Most of all, I'm frustrated that this is all my problem."

Frieda watched with a raised eyebrow. Then she looked down. "Mine too, eventually."

Her mother chuckled. "See? I knew it was the same thing keeping us both up."

Frieda scowled. "Why does it have to be our problem?"

"Because—"

"I didn't ask to be Stadtholder." Frieda gestured between them. "You didn't, either. And yet, here we are."

Beatrix nodded. "And you know why we are here."

"Grandmother," Frieda muttered.

"Yes," Beatrix replied. "Mom."

Silence fell. Frieda looked around, listening, but they were alone.

"Mother," she said at last, then hesitated. "Mom. If all this is true, why did you become Queen?"

Her mother frowned at her, but Frieda faced her. "Grandmother may have been the *Messenger*'s first Stadtholder, but she was never Queen. You took that title. Why?"

Beatrix sat a moment before she said, "Did you know that, when I was your age, I wanted to be a teacher?"

Frieda nodded. That fit. "Did you tell Grandmother this?"

"Of course I did," said Beatrix. "Loudly. I was fifteen, too, once, you know." She sighed. "Didn't matter, of course. She wanted me to follow in her footsteps. She said she needed someone she could trust. I don't know why I rated higher than the civilian council representatives, but I suppose she thought she knew me better."

Frieda's brow furrowed. "But why did you decide to become Queen?"

"I felt that if I was going to be a monarch in all but name, I was going to take that title," Beatrix replied. There was a sharpness in her eyes as she said it. "Mother was running this place as she had always done, and the people were used to it. I needed to shake it up, set new boundaries. In my studies to be a teacher, I read histories. I learned about constitutional monarchies. So, I revised the power structure. I changed our civilian council into a parliament and the council leader into a prime minister, took the title of Queen, and had people call me 'Your Majesty.'"

Frieda gaped. "You enjoyed that?"

"I didn't." Beatrix chuckled. "But Mother hated it more, especially when I gave her the title of Dowager. But she'd put me in charge, so there wasn't much she could do about it."

Frieda laughed, and Beatrix laughed with her. But after that moment of laughter, Frieda's expression soured. "There wasn't much she could do except take your dreams away. How could you give up teaching?"

Beatrix shrugged. "There's a lot of teaching involved in being Stadtholder. You may find that there's a lot of engineering involved, as well."

Frieda wrinkled her nose.

"But the truth is," said Beatrix, "your grandmother and I came to . . . an understanding."

Frieda looked up.

"She had a lot on her shoulders," said Beatrix, "and I was a loving daughter. Still am. I wanted to help her. That is why, when she offered me the position of Stadtholder, I took it." She gave Frieda a rueful smile. "And I thought, once I was fully in charge and made the changes I needed to make, I could abdicate."

Frieda sat up straighter. "Abdicate? You?"

Beatrix nodded.

"But you're Stadtholder, now!" said Frieda. "You're *still* Stadtholder. If you planned to abdicate—"

"I planned to abdicate after she—" She coughed. "After she passed away. I couldn't do it while she still lived. And then you came along, and I realized that even if I wanted to abdicate earlier, I couldn't abdicate until you came of age, or else you'd be Stadtholder, and she'd be Regent, and you wouldn't have the option of abdication."

Frieda gaped at her.

Beatrix looked away. "So, I did what I needed to do. And there were things that needed doing by someone—a symbol— that stands above the *Messenger's* chain of command. Mom had her reasons for becoming Stadtholder, Frieda. They're still relevant."

"I don't see how they could be," Frieda muttered. "It's wrong that all the problems should fall on your shoulders. The people should take care of themselves."

"Maybe they'll soon be ready to," Beatrix replied. "Hopefully, the people's leaders will realize that when the time comes." She reached out. "Pass me the crackers."

Frieda didn't trust herself to throw the bag. She stood and walked the crackers over.

As she headed back to her seat, she wondered, *What could possibly have made Grandmother want to be Stadtholder?*

# PART TWO
# ADELHEID: THE LAST GOOD DAY

# CHAPTER 5
# A COLONIAL VISIT

*The* Messenger
*Mercury Colonies, August 3, 2151 CE*

THE DAY BEFORE THE END OF THE WORLD WAS LIEUTENANT Adelheid Koning's twenty-third birthday.

That day, the door to the forebridge chuffed aside as she entered. "Reporting for duty at 0700 hours."

Sub-Lieutenant Liao Fang smiled at her from his station. "Good morning!"

Sub-Lieutenant Lizabet Anderson turned, her morning cup of chicory at her lips. She grunted and cocked an eyebrow by way of salute.

The night officer, Lieutenant Gerhardt Pohl, got up from Adelheid's seat by the front window and saluted. "Lieutenant Koning."

Adelheid returned the salute. "Lieutenant Pohl," she replied. "Is it sleep for you next, or relaxation period?"

"I'm heading to the galley," he replied. "I'm hoping to take my sleep period at 1600 hours." He gave her a grin. "But right now, the *Messenger* is moving normally, and Terminal has just been sighted."

Adelheid shot a look out the front window. They'd been on the Near Curve as their Robinson Rail took them from ten degrees south of the equator to near the equator to reach the spaceport called Terminal. Ahead, in the lights of the *Messenger*, the Robinson Rail curved as they came out of their angle. Beneath her feet, the latitude town groaned as it bent into the unfamiliar turn. In the distance, the spaceport's spires gleamed. She exhaled. "That's not fair! Punish me for arriving on time instead of early, will you?"

Gerhardt gave her a grin. "Sorry, Lieutenant."

"Sure you are," she muttered. "So, is that why you're not high-tailing it out of here? Have Liao and Lizabet paid up?"

Gerhardt's grin widened. "Just waiting for you."

Adelheid felt in her pocket and slapped a coin into Gerhardt's waiting hand. "Don't spend it all in one place."

He chuckled. "Thank you."

"Tell me, at least, that we beat the *Hermes* to Terminal," Adelheid grumbled.

Behind her, Liao sucked his teeth.

"Sorry." Gerhardt shrugged. "They radioed that they arrived an hour ago."

"Flare and daybreak," Adelheid muttered. *That's one round of drinks we'll have to buy.*

Gerhardt tilted his head. "However, we do appear to be arriving ahead of the *Apollo*."

She perked up. "We beat the capital? Seriously?"

"Seriously," Gerhardt replied.

Lizabet laughed. "And we don't have to buy rounds for the *Hermes*'s officers ..."

"If the *Apollo* buys rounds for both of us," Adelheid finished. She and Gerhardt shared a fist bump as he left the bridge. The door slid closed behind him.

Adelheid slipped into the bridge commander's seat. "What's ahead of us today besides docking at Terminal?"

"That's probably plenty." Lizabet set her chicory aside and picked up a tablet. "Standing maintenance and repairs. Waking Terminal from hibernation. Meeting the Earth supply shuttle at 1200 hours." She nodded at Adelheid. "You're due to meet the Earth envoy alongside representatives from the *Hermes* and the *Apollo*. Colonel Koning is on board the shuttle."

Adelheid flipped through the documents on her tablet. "Where is the trackworkers report?"

Liao flipped through his own tablet. "Not here."

Adelheid glanced at the clock and then punched a set of keys by the intercom. "Trackworkers, please confirm status," she said. "Your report is fifteen minutes overdue."

The intercom crackled. "Sorry, ma'am. We're still checking things here. You did ask us to be thorough."

Adelheid scowled and reached for the intercom, but Liao caught her eye. "They're not like us; they're civilians," he said. "What's five more minutes going to do?"

She frowned. "Just because the Colonel's away doesn't mean discipline takes a holiday."

Liao shrugged. Adelheid sighed. She flipped on the intercom. "Confirmed, Trackworks. Let us know in advance next time?"

"Confirmed, Forebridge. And thanks."

Adelheid leaned back. The bridge apprentice, Arend Schol, set a cup of chicory beside her. Adelheid picked it up. "Thank you, Adjutant." She sniffed the aroma deeply, took a sip, and savoured the bitterness. When she set the cup down, she noticed something beside it. The corners of her mouth quirked up. "Who brought the cupcake?"

It had white frosting and a single electric candle flickering on top.

She looked up. Her fellow officers grinned at her.

"Happy birthday, Adelheid," said Liao. "Twenty-three Earth years."

Lizabet chuckled. "You don't look much older than ninety-five Mercurian ones."

Adelheid laughed and reached into her pocket for something to cut the cupcake with. "I'll see if I can divide this for everyone. Then we must look alive. You never know when Tail Command will call."

The intercom chirped. Lizabet's eyes widened. "It's Captain Ramkin in the tail section, ma'am!"

Adelheid looked around. "Do you think he has this place bugged?"

Liao gave a short laugh. "What would your father have to say about that?"

"A lot," Adelheid grumbled. She flipped a switch. "Lieutenant Koning here. Good morning, Captain."

"Where is the trackworkers report?" Ramkin's voice rang clear through the static. "Why is it overdue?"

Adelheid did a quick mental calculation. "Ten more minutes, Colonel. You asked that it be thorough."

"Fair enough," Ramkin grumbled. "But not a moment longer."

"Yes, Captain." Adelheid turned off the intercom. She glanced over and saw Lizabet and Liao staring.

Lizabet grinned at her. "I'm sure he's like that with everybody."

Despite herself, Adelheid smiled back. "Without fear or favour." She looked ahead as the Robinson Rail straightened out, the spires of Terminal pulling closer. "At least he does it by the book." She turned back to her cupcake. "Now, who wants a piece?"

☿

TERMINAL FILLED HALF the front window as the *Messenger* approached alongside, a complex of towers rising the height of the latitude town and launch spires rising even higher. Beacon lights flashed under the stars. As the *Messenger* pulled up to the loading bay, lights along the side of the structure flickered on. The airlock gaskets ballooned as they filled with air.

"Cut power," Adelheid called. "Let us coast into place."

Lizabet pulled a lever on her console that sent the signal down to the trackworkers. Seconds later, the *Messenger* slowed.

"Nine hundred metres to the stop point," Liao reported. The metal struts of Terminal crawled past.

"Begin applying brakes." Adelheid straightened in her seat.

Lizabet sent the signal. The brakes were applied to quarter power, and a low squeal rose alongside the vibration of motion. The bridge crew leaned back against the deceleration. It took several seconds to overcome the *Messenger*'s momentum, but gradually, the vibrations eased, and the latitude town stopped with a final jerk.

Adelheid looked at a monitor showing the *Messenger*'s starboard side. Rubber airlocks pushed out from Terminal and met the *Messenger* along all the airlock doors. A row of LEDs flickered from red to green.

"Gaskets sealed," said Lizabet. "All airlocks report normal. We are parked."

Adelheid tapped the console. "Right. Shut us down to skeleton staff. Start the countdown to Sunrise, announce to the public we are parked, and open the airlock doors. We have arrived at Terminal."

The forebridge crewmembers clapped. Screens shut off. Above the front window screen, a display flickered to life with the words, "SUNRISE IN:" followed by the measurements in kilometres, as well as days, hours, and minutes, all slowly counting down. The dawn was eleven days behind them.

Adelheid stood as Sergeant Jenkins came forward to take

her seat. She walked over to Liao, who smiled at her. "You ready?"

"Just finishing up," he replied.

Lizabet stood and stretched. "I'll see you at the galley after your duty is done."

Liao frowned at her. "You've got a break?"

"Yup!" Lizabet beamed as she trooped off.

Liao glared at her retreating back. "She didn't have to rub it in."

Adelheid chuckled. "Yes, she did. We'll get a chance to do it to her in future. It all balances out."

She and Liao left the forebridge for the nearest airlock, which already had a crowd of people lining up. Claxons buzzed, red indicators turned to green, and the doors parted, slicing smoothly along their tracks. The crowd filed through into Terminal's loading platform. Lights flickered to life along it, shining on other *Messenger* passengers emerging from other doors. Adelheid stared down the platform that ran the whole five-kilometre length of the *Messenger*. Engineers went to terminals, tapped at keyboards, and called out readings. The kitchen staff shouted and cursed as they brought out crates and headed for the freight elevator.

Adelheid stretched and saw Liao watching her. She grinned. "It feels good to stretch your legs."

He raised an eyebrow. "There's less space on this platform than there is on the *Messenger*'s airlocks leading to it."

"I know," she said. "But it's still new territory—or, rather, territory we only get to walk on every Terminal Day. On a floor that doesn't vibrate. It's different. Change is good."

Liao glanced at the floor, then shrugged. "If you say so."

Along the walls, screens flickered to life. "Attention, everyone!" The picture showed Captain Ramkin, a tall, narrow-faced man in his mid-fifties. "Attention, please. Terminal is ready for us. The *Hermes* is already in, but it looks like we beat the *Apollo* by almost an hour."

People cheered. Adelheid smiled and clapped. She nudged Liao, who grinned at her.

"I'm sorry to report that the Earth shuttle has been delayed," Ramkin continued. "Their new ETA is 1500 hours."

People groaned. "Just like the Earth to leave all the opening chores for us," a young corporal grumbled nearby.

Liao shook his head. "Again? Even after we adjusted *our* schedules? If they keep this up, they're going to be landing in daylight. What will they do then?"

Adelheid said nothing. *The Earth shuttles have been getting later and later. Why? What's wrong with their ships?*

Out loud, she said, "Still, that's plenty of time for doing what needs to be done. Come on. We're the *Messenger*'s liaison officers; let's get a-liaising."

They walked through the corridors of Terminal, passing galleys where the *Hermes* and *Messenger* crews argued about the placement of supplies. They followed shining white corridors where maintenance crews were doing clean-up. A woman swept past holding a French horn, followed by a young man with a snare drum.

Adelheid and Liao followed the gathering crowd of musicians and technicians until they reached the spaceport waiting room. People were already gathered along the northern wall, activating consoles and peering at displays. A growing group carried their own musical instruments: the *Hermes* Welcoming Committee.

The room was as wide as the *Messenger,* which left the southern half of the room mostly empty as the *Messenger*'s crew entered. People among the *Hermes* crew looked up as the *Messenger*'s people spread out. Some waved, others nodded. Most within the two groups, however, stayed in their half of the waiting room, standing like awkward partygoers.

A prominent set of doors dominated the eastern wall of the room, announcing the way to the Earth shuttle's landing pad. On the western wall, a large viewport spanned the width of the room, looking out onto Mercury.

Liao and Adelheid drifted closer to the plexiglass. They looked out on the Milky Way above the horizon. They could see the extra-wide trench of the *Apollo*'s Robinson Rail, widening from the vanishing point before vanishing beneath them. In the distance, the lights of the *Apollo* approached.

Adelheid drew a deep breath. "It's beautiful, isn't it?"

Liao shrugged. "I suppose. The stars are outside my porthole, too."

"Well, here you can really see them," said Adelheid. "They don't get this view on Earth, apparently. All their dark places have gone."

"But the Earth has a blue sky," said Liao. "That's worth seeing, I think."

The floor beneath their feet rumbled as the *Apollo*, the ten-kilometre-long equator city, approached and passed beneath them. Adelheid and Liao watched as the city's roof and reticulations slid past.

"Hi," said a voice behind them. "It's Lieutenant Koning, right?"

Adelheid turned, then straightened up.

A dark-haired young man stood there. He was tall and lanky, so much so that his military uniform seemed to hang off him. His stripes identified him as a lieutenant from the *Hermes*. Adelheid's glance slid over his brown skin and settled on his dark eyes. He smiled and extended his hand. "Hello! Somebody should be the first to break the ice, here, so . . . I'm Lieutenant Cristavao D'Cunha, liaison officer for the *Hermes*."

Adelheid realized she was staring, so she ramped back her stare into a professional smile and shook his hand. "I'm Lieutenant Adelheid Koning, and this is Sub-Lieutenant Liao Fang. We're both of the *Messenger*."

Cristavao nodded. "I've seen you two around."

"But I haven't seen you." Adelheid tilted her head. "New to the job?"

"Just promoted," he replied, grinning.

"What happened to Lieutenant Almeida?" Adelheid asked.

"She's a captain now," Cristavao replied. "She's serving a command in our tail section."

"Lucky her!"

"So, this is my first assignment," said Cristavao. "Greeting you, the *Apollo*, and the Earth shuttle."

Adelheid found herself smiling when he said 'you.' "Well, same for us. I'm particularly looking forward to having the *Apollo* buy us the first round of drinks since they're the last ones here."

Cristavao laughed. "Yeah. I'm also looking forward to the *Messenger* buying the second round of drinks."

Adelheid rolled her eyes. *He would bring that up.* But she laughed and patted his arm. "Fine. I'll buy you a drink."

Liao coughed, but Adelheid quite liked how Cristavao's eyebrows shot up. She smirked. "So, what do you think? Has the ice been sufficiently broken?"

He laughed.

They looked out at the room. Where before, people from the *Hermes* and the *Messenger* had left a gap between them, that gap was now filled. People came forward, reaching out, shaking hands. Groups of *Hermes* and *Messenger* officers stood together, chatting. The noise level rose steadily.

"Mission accomplished, Lieutenant." Cristavao snapped a salute.

Before Adelheid could salute back, a flash from outside brought her attention around. She stared as a section of the *Hermes* Robinson Rail crumbled into a hole.

"What—" she gasped.

"Give it a minute," said Cristavao.

As the dust settled and people gathered by the window to watch, Adelheid saw the *Hermes* Robinson Rail start to ripple with shadows in the rear lights of the latitude town. They moved to the broken end of the rail. Adelheid could see the face of the shorn rail growing, pushing forward to the other side of the gap.

Liao whistled. "You still have construction bots? I thought they'd gone extinct."

Cristavao looked a little smug. "We've a few cases still. Enough for one more rotation."

"How can you use them like that?" Adelheid asked. "With the prices the Earth has been charging, we've been thinking about setting up a blacksmiths' guild."

Cristavao stepped away from the window, leading Adelheid and Liao away from the gathering crowd of onlookers. "We're already setting up a blacksmiths' guild. And a concrete-setters' guild. These will be the last construction bots we can reliably get from Earth, and so we're using them on the urgent big projects, getting what we can done so we can focus on routine maintenance afterward."

Adelheid raised an eyebrow. "You're well ahead of us."

"The writing's on the wall," said Cristavao. "If the Earth keeps raising prices and making excuses for delays, well . . . the new guilds may be slower, but they'll get the job done. We may not be able to cut ourselves loose from Mother Earth's apron strings, but we might loosen them a bit."

Adelheid glanced at Liao, who glanced around the room, looking nervous. She smirked at him. "It's okay. It's not like the Earth can have this place bugged, what with Terminal's sweep through eighty-eight days of full sunlight."

"Still . . ." Liao kept his voice low. "There's the *Apollo*."

"Well, they're not here yet," Cristavao replied. "And we've

checked for listening devices, too." He leaned closer. "As fellow people interested in loosening Mother Earth's apron strings, let me say that the people I work for are looking forward to seeing your father's report, Lieutenant."

Liao drew a sharp breath, but Adelheid patted his arm. "Even if the *Apollo* leadership overheard that comment, there are many in their government who'd support our mission."

"You're right, though, Sub-Lieutenant," said Cristavao. "I shouldn't speak so recklessly. And we probably shouldn't get our hopes too high until things are . . . fully in our possession. So . . . *have* you heard from your father, Lieutenant?"

She looked at Cristavao again, focusing on his lean figure, his dark eyes, his warm smile. She found herself smiling back. "Not yet," she replied. "But soon. And you can call me Adelheid."

She liked the way his smile widened.

They were interrupted by a new voice, boisterous and full. "Ah, there you all are!"

A tall, white-haired man strode toward them. He looked like Captain Ramkin but with a heavier build. The old NASA-X logo was prominent on his sleeve as he shook Adelheid and Cristavao's hands vigorously. "Captain Alistair Banks, liaison officer for the *Apollo*. My first time here, but I've seen you two around. Sorry we're late. I suppose you secondary-towners are looking forward to your free rounds?" He chortled.

Adelheid, Liao, and Cristavao shared a look.

"We hadn't really talked about that," said Adelheid.

"It'll be awfully nice of you, I'm sure," Cristavao added.

"Well, business first, pleasure later, right?" Alistair beamed. "It's always an exciting time, these colonial visits. Good to let our hair down once in a while."

Back around the shuttle arrival doors, a new group of people had joined the crowd. All consoles were manned now, and there were three groups of musicians jostling and gesturing about where everyone should stand.

"There are negotiations to be done," said Adelheid.

"Oh, yes, there is that," said Alistair. "But most of that's mere formality. We've always benefited from the Earth's benevolence. No reason why that should change."

The floor shook like they were on the *Messenger* again. Claxons warbled across Terminal. Over the intercom, a woman's voice intoned, "Attention! Earth shuttle arriving! Earth shuttle arriving!" Throughout the waiting room, people rushed to organize themselves into lines. The musicians pulled together. The space around the shuttle arrival doors widened.

"Well, fellow officers?" Alistair raised an arm. "Shall we go meet our guests?"

He turned away. As soon as he was out of earshot, Cristavao grinned and leaned closer to Adelheid. "I'm surprised he didn't say 'our colonial masters.'"

Adelheid stifled a laugh. She, Liao, and Cristavao followed Banks to the shuttle arrival doors.

# CHAPTER 6
## LIAISON

THE SPACEPORT DOORS PARTED, REVEALING AN HONOUR GUARD OF UNE marines wearing their dark green uniforms with their traditional blue berets. An officer at the back carried the UNE flag with its image of the Earth over white olive branches.

The marines flanked about two dozen men and women, all in their forties or older, wearing civilian leadership uniforms— dark blue blazers, white turtlenecks, no ties.

*How short they look*, thought Adelheid. *Built like tanks, too. I think the tallest is about five centimetres shorter than I am.*

The Earthlings also walked differently, holding their arms out slightly to keep balance, as if uncertain of their footing.

As the party stopped in front of the Mercurians, three bands with three conductors drew breath to play. People stood with hands clasped as the bands and the audience launched into the international anthem.

> *And did those fleets, in ancient days,*
> *Soar over Terra's mountains green?*
> *And was the holy Lamb of God*
> *On Terra's pleasant pastures seen?*

*And did the Countenance Divine*
*Shine forth upon those clouded hills?*
*And was Jerusalem builded there*
*Among those dark Satanic mills?*

Adelheid stood proud, Liao on her left, Cristavao on her right, as everyone sang. As the last bars faded, the welcome party clapped and cheered before coming forward to shake the hands of the new arrivals. Alistair Banks stepped up to a white-haired, bronze-skinned man in the middle of the group—the Earth envoy, Adelheid realized—and shook the man's hand vigorously. The envoy, Adelheid noticed, handled Alistair's hand gingerly.

"Envoy Govendor," Alistair burbled. "As the representative of the equator-city *Apollo* and joined by representatives of the premiere latitude towns of the parallels north and south of us, the *Messenger* and the *Hermes*, it gives me great pleasure to welcome you to Mercury!"

Govendor gave Alistair a brief bow. "Thank you, Mr. Banks. As always, it's an honour to meet the Sun Runners of Mercury. Your resilience and tenacity are an inspiration to everyone on Earth."

Adelheid stepped to a tall, thin man standing to the left of the group, near the back. She saluted. "Welcome home, Colonel!" Behind her, Liao matched her salute.

Colonel Koning saluted back. "Thank you, Lieutenant. Thank you, Sub-Lieutenant. It's good to be back." He smiled at Adelheid. "At ease, Adelheid." He opened his arms.

Adelheid stepped forward and hugged him. "Welcome home, Dad."

Behind them, Cristavao cleared his throat. Adelheid stepped back as he extended his hand to her father. "Successful trip, sir?"

The colonel shook Cristavao's hand but lowered his voice. "I'll have more to talk about with your superiors later, Lieutenant." He glanced between him and Adelheid. "I'm sure Lieutenant Koning can keep you apprised."

To Adelheid's surprise, Cristavao started to blush. "I look forward to it, sir."

Colonel Koning turned his smile to Liao. "Sub-Lieutenant. Is all in order?"

Liao straightened up. "Yes, sir. Preparations are going well."

"Good," said the colonel. "Sub-Lieutenant, can you oversee things on behalf of the *Messenger* for a little while? I'd like to talk to my daughter."

Liao's chest swelled. "Yes, sir!"

"Excellent!" Colonel Koning offered his arm to Adelheid. "Lieutenant? Walk with me."

Adelheid clasped her father's elbow. The Earth envoy and Captain Banks were still talking together while Cristavao stood to one side, unable to get a word in edgewise. Adelheid caught his eye, and he nodded to her as she and her father walked away.

"How was Earth?" Adelheid asked.

As soon as the doors to the shuttle arrival area closed, Colonel Koning slowed. He took a deep breath, then let it out slowly. "It feels good to walk in Mercury's gravity again."

She frowned. "Are you all right?"

He shuddered. "I hated Earth."

She gaped at him. "But the blue sky! Clouds! Not having to wear a spacesuit outside! Wasn't that a miracle?"

He shrugged. "Not having to wear a spacesuit outside is a blessing, but I had to wear an exoskeleton instead. It helped me walk and lift things. I could almost believe things weren't three times heavier than they should be, but it didn't help my lungs." He put his hand to his chest. "Or my heart. Whenever I lay down, it was like a great weight settled on me. I couldn't sleep worth a damn."

Adelheid touched her father's shoulder. "Well, you're home now. How did the negotiations go?" She glanced around for listening ears, then lowered her voice. "Did you get the supplies?"

Colonel Koning kept walking. "Three crates," he replied. "There's a sample package as well. Let's go to your quarters. I'll give it to you there."

Adelheid grimaced. "Just three crates? We'll need more than that if we want to be self-sufficient. With three crates, it would take years to make the caverns big enough."

"It's what I could get," her father replied. "The Earth government guards these things like biohazards. Nanobots can be dangerous if not controlled properly."

"We know what we're doing," Adelheid grumbled. "The restrictions are more to keep us under Earth's wing."

"Maybe," said Colonel Koning. "I'll keep trying to arrange further deliveries. We'll see if I can get more."

She frowned at him. "What do you mean, 'if'?" She straightened up. "Do they know what we're doing?"

Her father shook her head. "I don't think so. It's something else. Let's get to your quarters to talk about this. This should be in private. And I can do with a sit-down."

Adelheid nodded. They hurried on.

☿

Adelheid opened the door to her quarters, and she and her father entered. As soon as the door closed behind her, Colonel Koning handed her a cylinder from his pocket. Adelheid held it up and looked at it in awe.

It was made of Perspex, about fifteen centimetres long and

five in diameter. It had heft. A thin line was the only evidence that the top could be screwed off. Inside was what looked like silver sand, except it didn't move like sand. As Adelheid turned it over, the granules shifted, rising into the middle of the container like dust in still air.

"It's beautiful," she breathed.

Her father moved to a chair and sat with a grateful sigh.

Adelheid smiled at him. "Tea?"

"Thank you."

She set the canister on the table next to an arrangement of test tubes and Petri dishes, an electric Bunsen burner, and an incubator oven. As she reached for the kettle, her father nodded at the scientific apparatus. "How have your experiments been going?"

Adelheid filled the kettle with water and set it to stand above the Bunsen burner. "I've had some success with the latest batch of thermophiles."

He perked up. "Really?"

She nodded. "They're showing excellent nutritional properties. Unfortunately, the growth factor is too small. I could grow enough for a serving of finger foods at the Terminal Festival . . . assuming I had a few weeks' notice, that is."

He chuckled. "And assuming you had people willing to eat genetically modified bacteria. Do you spend all your spare time with your chemicals and Petri dishes?"

She shrugged. "If we can speed up the growth factor and add to the nutritional value, we'll have another source of food. Between it and the nanobots, we could declare independence from Earth within a couple of years."

Her father laughed. "Let's not get ahead of ourselves." He sighed. "I wonder if the military was the best choice for your apprenticeship. You're much more at home in a science lab."

She shrugged. "I think I made the right choice, Dad."

"If you think so, then I agree with you," he said. "And there's no reason you can't do both."

Something in her father's voice made Adelheid frown at him. "Dad, is something wrong? What happened on Earth? What did you mean when you said, 'We'll see'?"

He looked away. "A bomb went off in New York during the trade meeting."

Adelheid gaped. Beside her, the kettle began to boil and whistle. "Lord-in-Sunlight! Were you hurt?"

He shook his head. "It was several blocks away. We weren't the target. I did, however, see the rising fireball and hear the sirens."

The whistling was loud now. Adelheid turned off the Bunsen burner and poured out the tea. She handed a mug to her father. Then her brow furrowed. "Wait—*during* the trade meeting? That was over two weeks ago! Why am I only learning about this now?"

"The UN representatives told me not to talk about it," her father replied. "In fact, they made me sign a document *promising* I wouldn't. They were working on a cover story about a gas line rupture."

"Why would you sign such a thing?"

He shrugged. "I negotiated additional space in our diplomatic cargo. Enough to surreptitiously add a third crate of nanobots."

Adelheid whistled. "Quick thinking. But why would they want to block that news?"

Her father clasped his mug. "I turned on the news when I got back to the hotel, and this time, I paid attention. I switched between channels to make sure. The news is full of grim stories. There's strife in Edinburgh and Melbourne. The Middle East is fighting again. The Laotian regional government is struggling with an outbreak of blight, and China is arguing with India and Pakistan about the Himalayan glaciers. The

Mississippi Delta states are fighting drought and arguing loudly with the Appalachian states about water rights. The cameras are all showing UN personnel hard at work at these hotspots, working heroically. The newscasters use the word 'heroic' a lot."

He leaned back. "But there's no news about New York. There's no news about Geneva, Johannesburg, or Buenos Aires. For most people logging into the news services, the bad news is happening far from the power centres. Even in China, the news never talks about disruptions in Beijing. The UN officials told me the explosion was nothing to worry about—just a small IED, or 'improvised explosive device'—but blocks from the UN headquarters? Less than a mile from the Manhattan Sea Wall?" He shuddered. "I think the UN believes that the people of Earth can handle news about catastrophes at the edges of their world as long as the capitols remain strong and safe. If news got out that, even at the heart of the world government, things were barely holding together, I think the UN thinks that people would start panicking, making the task of holding things together much, much harder."

"What are you saying?" asked Adelheid.

Colonel Koning turned and stared out the porthole at the Mercurian landscape. After a long moment, he said, "We need to put these nanobots to work, even if we might not get any more. The sooner we loosen ourselves from Mother Earth's apron strings, the better I'm going to feel."

Silence descended. Adelheid didn't know what to say, so she drank her tea.

After a long moment, Colonel Koning patted the pockets of his jacket. "I have a gift for you."

Adelheid raised an eyebrow. "In addition to these beautiful nanobots?"

Her father chuckled. "That present is for Mercury. This

one's for you." He pulled out a small box wrapped in colourful paper and handed it over. "I'm glad I didn't miss your birthday."

"Dad! You didn't have to!" But she smiled as she took the box and ripped off the wrapping. She frowned as she pulled out its contents. "A . . . key?"

It was not a key that could open any lock in the *Messenger*. It was black and heavy on her palm. It was a single rod with a ring at the end and a simple design cut into the square at the other end. There were no jewels, but it had age and heft. She raised her eyebrows at her father. "How old is this?"

"Early nineteenth century."

Her mouth dropped open. *Three hundred years?* "Where did you find this?"

"At an antiques booth in the Times Square marketplace."

She clasped it close. "Thank you!"

Her tablet chirped. Adelheid picked it up and then blinked at the message. "Huh."

"What?" her father asked.

"Somebody's invited me to dinner," Adelheid replied without thinking as she read Cristavao's short, quick message: *Say, do you want to have dinner at Terminal? Around 1800 hours?*

"Is it a date?"

She looked up sharply. "Why would you say that?"

He raised an eyebrow. "You were grinning."

She looked away, touching her cheek. *I need to work on my poker face. Why did I just blurt out what I said like that?* She looked again at the message.

"Anyone I know?" her father asked.

She glanced at him. "Cristavao D'Cunha, the new liaison officer for the *Hermes*."

"Maybe he wants to liaise?"

She glared at him.

He stood, raising his hands. "Backing off. I know there are

few things creepier than a father enquiring after his adult daughter's social life, even if he does hope that she's happy."

Adelheid rolled her eyes. "Yes, Dad. I'm happy. Thank you."

He drank the last of his tea and set the mug aside. "So, I'll leave you to your duties and to planning your date."

"Don't make me hit a superior officer, sir."

He laughed and came over, and they hugged before he turned away. The door clicked shut behind him.

Adelheid glanced at her tablet, where Cristavao's request sat open. *It's been a while since I've made this sort of time for myself. Yes, there are potential complications, but . . . it might be fun to see where this goes.*

She tapped her answer on the tablet.

☿

ADELHEID RETURNED TO WORK. Briefings, preparations for the Terminal Day Festival, and dozens of other duties kept her busy through the morning. When she allowed herself to think about her coming off-duty activities, she found herself smiling.

On her lunch break, as she sat with a sandwich in the *Messenger's* galley, she saw Liao approach her table, tray in hand.

*Ah,* she thought. *Potential complications.* "Hi!"

"Hi." Liao smiled as he took the seat across from her. They ate in silence, casting occasional glances at each other. Finally, Liao frowned. "Something on your mind?"

Adelheid swallowed. "So . . ." She found herself twiddling her fork in her fingers and set it aside. "Cristavao D'Cunha invited me to dinner."

Liao looked up. "Oh?"

"Yes." Adelheid rubbed the back of her neck. "Him and me. In the mess hall at Terminal. At 1800 hours."

"Ah." Liao nodded. "About inter-ship business, I suppose?"

"I suppose," Adelheid replied.

Liao frowned at her awkward silence. "And . . .?"

She nodded. "And."

Liao leaned back. "Oh." Silence stretched, and Adelheid waited him out. Finally, he said, "And why are you telling me this?"

"Well..." Adelheid shifted in her chair. "I didn't want things to get awkward later."

"So, you decided to move that awkwardness up to right now."

"Liao—"

"You don't need my permission to see other people," said Liao firmly. "Gods, what century is this? Do you really think we have any hold over each other just because of what we shared? We agreed to go back to being just friends. Mutually. I agreed as much as you did."

Silence descended. The two stared at each other, hurt and chastened.

"We *mutually* agreed," Liao repeated.

"Yes, we did," said Adelheid quietly.

Silence resumed, and this time, neither could meet each other's gaze. Finally, Liao took a deep breath. "So, you and Lieutenant D'Cunha and dinner." He gave her an awkward smile with an edge of slyness. "Looking to enjoy yourself?"

Adelheid chuckled softly at that look. She thought a moment about Cristavao, and her smile widened. "Maybe. Why not? It's Terminal Season, after all. A time to enjoy ourselves, as well as fostering inter-city relations."

Liao rolled his eyes. "Is that what they're calling it these days?"

Adelheid slugged his shoulder.

☿

ADELHEID'S DUTIES took her to 1500 hours. When she booked off, she returned to her quarters and set to work on her test tubes and Petri dishes.

But as she swabbed and set, she found herself looking up from her microscope at the clock on her bedside table. 1600 hours. 1630. 1645.

She closed the mini-incubator door with a huff, picked up her father's key, and turned it over in her hands. *Why am I having so much trouble concentrating? It's just a date. We could have fun and move on.*

*What if I don't want to move on?*

*I could still have fun . . .*

She pushed away from her desk and went to her washroom to prepare herself.

At 1730 hours, wearing her best off-duty clothes—white trousers, a white blouse, and a red blazer to go with them—she left her quarters and boarded the tram to the airlock. She was alone until the first stop, when the doors parted and Lizabet entered. The woman raised an appreciative eyebrow at Adelheid's blazer before facing forward while the tram pulled away with the hum of dynamos.

"So," said Lizabet after a moment. "Hot date tonight?"

Adelheid sighed. "A date. I didn't gauge the temperature."

Lizabet grinned. "Well, enjoy yourself. I'm rooting for you."

Adelheid cast her eyes heavenward. Then she gave Lizabet a smile. "Thanks."

The doors parted. Adelheid stepped out.

The Terminal Day celebrations were starting early. She walked through gleaming corridors, dodging crews of the *Messenger*, the *Hermes*, and the *Apollo*, preparing for the festivities. People in off-duty clothes walked past or chatted by the picture windows. Adelheid caught a glimpse of a flask but ignored it.

The Terminal galley was in full swing when she arrived,

tables laid out and occupied by people taking the first supper. She paused at the door and looked out at the crowd of faces for Cristavao. She couldn't see him. She was about to ask a galley assistant for help when someone tapped her shoulder. She turned to see Cristavao behind her.

"Hey," he said, and his smile made her heart lift.

"Hi," she replied.

He was wearing a blue shirt and black trousers—less formal than her red blazer—but he was there and smiling, and the two would have stood staring at each other if it hadn't occurred to Adelheid how silly they were being, blocking the door. "So . . ." she said. "Shall we eat?"

"Yes!" Cristavao snapped out of his trance. "That's our table, there." He pointed to the long window framing the Milky Way on the horizon.

Adelheid nodded as they walked over. "Did you pull rank to get it?"

He ducked his head. "Um . . . yeah?"

"Good work! Lead on!"

They sat, ordered dinner from a galley attendant, and looked out at the stars. Silence asserted itself as they glanced from the window to each other. This close, Adelheid could see the depth of Cristavao's dark eyes, the curve of his cheek, the nervous twitch of his smile. Butterflies fluttered in her stomach. She could feel the blush rising in her cheeks.

*This is what we get for going to dinner together on a whim,* she thought. *We have to talk about something. What? Work? No, not work!*

"How's work?" *Flare and Dawnfire!*

He took a deep breath. "Busy, as you'd expect. I had to mediate a scheduling dispute between the sanitation engineers and the electricians about when to replace the effluent pipes. The electricians weren't willing to give way until they realized what the pipes carried."

Adelheid chuckled. "Nobody appreciates coordinators until people start treading on each other's toes. And even then, not really."

"Well, I've heard good things about you," Cristavao said.

She blinked. "Really? What?"

"That you're firm but fair-minded," he replied. "You're demanding, but you defend those under you to the hilt." He shrugged. "Gossip travels."

Adelheid remembered her birthday cupcake. She smiled.

Their galley attendant set plates before them. They offered the standard rations of protein loaf, potato wedges, and algae crisps, but also an extra treat . . .

"Apple slices!" Adelheid held one up in awe. "Direct from Earth."

Cristavao smiled and took a bite. "Happy Terminal Day."

"Happy Terminal Day," she replied and took her own bite. The brilliant taste made her close her eyes to savour it—sweet and tart together!

They tucked into their meal. Adelheid found herself looking up occasionally to see Cristavao looking down. Then, at one point, their eyes met. He smiled, and she smiled back, but then their eyes returned to their food.

*This is getting silly. Say something else.*

"Did you hear about the bomb blast in New York?" She kept her voice low.

He looked around for listening ears, then leaned closer. "We haven't heard about it officially, but news gets around."

"Isn't it alarming that the UN would cover up something like this?"

He frowned. "Well, maybe. They've always been more secretive than I'd like, but I suppose they want to keep people from panicking."

"I'm worried it might be more than that."

He blinked. "How so?"

"Well, the Earth's ice caps are half gone," she replied. "Whole cities are on stilts. So many regions are under drought, I'm actually surprised we can get some of the supplies at the prices we've negotiated. Given the troubles we've had negotiating with the United Nations, and with news like what happened in New York being covered up . . ." She bit her lip, then continued, "What if the UNE isn't as stable as we think it is?"

"I know they're having problems," he replied. "But for all that they've faced, they're still here." He nodded over his shoulder at the level above them, where the shuttle arrival bay was. "They can still hold themselves together enough to launch a supply shuttle and send it to Mercury. That should say something, shouldn't it?"

She sucked her teeth. "Maybe . . ."

"People were sure the apocalypse was going to arrive two centuries ago," he said. "That's one reason the UN launched the colonies in the first place. And yet, there are still ten billion people on Earth. Yes, they have problems to deal with, but they've managed it so far."

She narrowed her eyes on him. "Do you always look on the bright side of things?"

He shrugged. "I'd like to think that I'm a realist, but much of the world is affected by how you look at it. I guess I'd rather look at the world with hope than fear."

"Hmm." She took a bite of protein loaf.

"Are you a realist who prefers to look on the darker side of things?" he asked.

Adelheid stared at him, opened her mouth to say something sharp, then caught herself. He was smiling, teasing her a little. He seemed happy, and happiness was a valuable commodity. "Well, of course not. But you know what they say: prepare for the worst—"

"—hope for the best?"

"I was going to say, 'and you're never disappointed.'"

"That sounds kind of morose," he said.

She sipped her drink and looked at him over the rim of her glass. "It is until you realize that sometimes you can be pleasantly surprised."

He tilted his head. "Are you often pleasantly surprised?"

She matched his smile. "More often than you'd expect."

"How about your colleague?" Cristavao asked. "Sub-Lieutenant Fang. Does he share this worldview?"

She blinked and frowned. "Why do you ask?"

"Just curious," he said quickly. "I see you two working together a lot, so I wondered. I haven't been assigned a coworker."

"Well, he's fine," she said. Then she frowned. Liao deserved better than that assessment. "He's a good man," she added. "A good fellow officer. A good friend."

"Friend?"

"We've been friends since vocational school," Adelheid replied. "We've been working together on things for about as long—homework, projects, even our apprenticeships. We work well together, and he's a great help. He's a good friend."

Cristavao nodded. "It's good to have a friend who works hard for you. We're all working hard. But what makes it all possible are the good moments. Good days. Good friends. As long as we have these moments when we can ease back and enjoy the fruit of our work together, even knowing there's work to be done tomorrow . . . well, that's why we can go to sleep wanting to get up the next day." His brown eyes held hers. "It's good to have these days. It's even better to have these days to share."

Adelheid stared at him, focusing on his eyes. *He's about my height, no more than an inch taller. And his face is so close. It's a simple matter to just lean forward and . . .*

Cristavao let out a grunt of surprise as she half got out of her chair, leaned forward, and kissed him. The table shook as his foot knocked against its leg, but he didn't pull back. He pressed closer. The moment lengthened and softened until Adelheid pulled away.

"When are you back on duty?" Her voice was husky. "I clock in at 0700 hours."

"Um . . . 0400 hours." He cleared his throat, then looked around, nervous and sheepish and delighted. "Um . . . what was that for?"

Adelheid stood. "Because it's been a good day, and a good day gets better when you have someone to share it with." Her mouth quirked up. "Maybe we can have a good night?"

He looked panicked and hopeful at the same time. He took a deep breath, then gave her a serious look while Adelheid's heart raced. "Where . . . do you want this to go?"

She thought for a moment, then took his hand. "This is not a promise. This is a shot in the dark, just to see where things go. Do you want to see?"

He stood, holding her hand. "Will you lead?"

She squeezed his hand. "If you'll follow."

They left the galley, heading for the *Messenger*.

☿

A SING-SONG CHIRP yanked Adelheid from pleasant dreams. Her arm patted the empty space beside her. Why was her doorbell ringing at this hour? What, in fact, *was* the hour?

She peered into the gloom until she found the clock display: 04:39.

*That's over two hours before I report to duty!*

The doorbell chirped again.

She slapped the communications button on her bedside table. "Whoever is using the emergency protocols to unlock my do-not-disturb setting, if you don't outrank me, you are in bright trouble."

"Adelheid!"

The tone of the voice made her sit up. "Liao?" He sounded terrified, but not of her. "Liao, what are you doing calling me so early?"

"Adelheid, answer the door! The United Nations is underwater!"

# CHAPTER 7
## THE FALL OF EARTH

ADELHEID LEAPED OUT OF BED BEFORE SHE EVEN THOUGHT ABOUT it, then was caught up by the strangeness of it. Why wasn't the floor vibrating beneath her feet? Why wasn't their city moving?

*Oh, yes. We're parked at Terminal. We're here for a week.*

The pause made her realize she wasn't dressed. In the darkness, she groped for her robe and wrapped it around herself as she stumbled to the door and leaned on the opening mechanism. She squinted into the lights of the corridor outside.

Liao stood in front of her, breathing heavily. *Did he run all the way here?* She blinked at him, her heart rate picking up. "Liao, what is it?"

He looked at her, his eyes haunted. "Someone's attacked the Manhattan Sea Wall."

"What? Who? Why?"

"No one knows yet."

"How much damage?"

"I told you: the United Nations is underwater."

She stumbled into the corridor, her bare feet smacking the metal floor as she pushed past Liao. There was a media screen in the barracks' common room. Her fellow officers stood around it, staring, their shoulders slack. Nobody was sitting down. Adelheid shouldered her way through.

"These images were caught earlier this hour," said an off-camera female voice. "These are scenes of mayhem throughout Lower Manhattan as people struggle to get free of the waters."

Adelheid gasped. On the screen, people clawed and scrambled over submerged debris. A boat rushed forward from a pack that was holding back, an officer reaching out to help. Dozens of people clambered on, fighting the officers and others to stay on board. The boat vanished beneath the muck and the murk.

Adelheid's breath caught. New York had been six metres below sea level for the past century. If the sea wall had been breached...

She took a deep breath. "Has the Secretary-General made any announcements?"

A junior officer shook his head. "There's been no government response. None." He nodded at the screen. "The media have only had scenes like this to show."

*No UN*, she thought, then rebelled at that thought. *No way! It couldn't happen that fast! There'd be contingencies, a chain of command—*

*Why haven't we heard from the Earth Space Command about this?*

But what had Dad said? The bad news had been multiplying for weeks. The UN government had coped by trying to keep a lid on the media to stem any rising panic. And if there were no government officials responding to this...

*No. There have to be people. Somebody has to be in charge.*

*Then why hasn't Earth Space Command contacted us?*

For no reason she could name, Adelheid remembered one of her teachers' earliest science experiments. He'd brought a jar of water, set it on his desk, and told everyone to look at it. While everyone wondered why they were staring at a jar of water, he talked about supersaturated solutions, and then he dropped in a single grain of sugar.

Suddenly, white and grey lines reached out all through the water: crystals crashing into each other, crashing into the side of the jar, until what had previously been liquid was now a solid mass of crystalline matter.

*Sometimes, things reach a point where one small disturbance changes everything.*

She grabbed Liao's wrist. "We need to get to the bridge."

Liao cleared his throat, then glanced at her meaningfully. She looked down at her robe and her bare feet.

"I need to get dressed," she amended. "Then we need to get to the bridge."

"Right."

She ran to her quarters.

☿

ADELHEID AND LIAO rushed through the corridors of the *Messenger*. Usually, they'd have to slip through the morning crush of people heading to their posts. Now, however, people stood around every available media screen. These knots of people were even harder to walk through.

"Let us pass, please." Adelheid slipped along toward the tram bay, arriving as a tram pulled up. "Everybody out," she called as the doors parted. "Bridge business."

Two startled maintenance workers stumbled out, and Adelheid and Liao stepped in. Adelheid tapped the controls to take them directly to the forebridge. The doors slid shut, and the tram sped along.

On the tram media screen, the Mercury reporters were talking about the Earth.

"Why are they reporting from Quito?" one commentator asked. "What's happening at the other bureaus? Where's Johannesburg? Where's Tehran? Why hasn't anybody from the United Nations addressed the press?"

Another pundit cut in. "This sort of power vacuum doesn't happen overnight. Clearly, things have happened that we haven't been told about."

*And so, the crystal grows*, thought Adelheid.

The view from the tram window flipped and changed between scenes, from factories where workers weren't working to public atriums where crowds of people focused on screens. Adelheid realized she was holding her breath. She let it out slowly. She glanced at Liao and saw him looking at her. She didn't have anything to say, so she focused in front of her. A moment later, Liao looked ahead as well.

As they left the tram and headed for the forebridge, Adelheid broke into a run. Liao rushed to keep up. They both got to the forebridge out of breath. The other officers didn't look surprised. Gerhardt, the night officer, stepped from his seat as Adelheid came to sit down.

"Report," said Adelheid to the bridge.

"People are rioting," Sub-Lieutenant Lizabet replied.

"Where?" asked Adelheid.

Lizabet gave her a dark look. "Everywhere. On Earth, I mean, not here. The old nations have started to declare their independence."

Adelheid pulled up her monitors. They were a babble. Disasters were multiplying. The media couldn't keep up. They talked frantically over scenes of chaos, but certain phrases kept coming up again and again: breakdown, loss of control, power vacuum.

Every second, more people who were in charge suddenly weren't in charge anymore, and nobody stepped forward to replace them.

Adelheid scrolled through her communications reports.

"Lizabet, have there been any messages from Earth Space Command?"

"No," Lizabet replied. "And, yes, I tried calling them."

For a moment, Adelheid couldn't look at her screens. She leaned back in her seat, staring at the *Messenger*'s front display screen, showing the surface of Mercury. On the right, she saw the edge of the Terminal spaceport. Ahead, the trench and guide of the Robinson Rail stretched into the darkness.

*We are hundreds of millions of kilometres away from Earth*, Adelheid thought. *How is it that the news makes us feel like we're right there, yet powerless to do anything?*

*Can it get any worse?*

On the media screen, a newscaster looked up from her tablet. "Earlier this hour, the states of China, Pakistan, and India all announced their independence from the United Nations, citing the world government's loss of control. Fighting between these regional governments has already broken out along the Himalayan border."

On another screen, another newscaster. "Mississippi Delta forces launched air strikes on Louisville in an attempt to destroy the dam holding back the Ohio River—"

"Dammit!" Adelheid muttered. She pinched the bridge of her nose. Then she put in earphones and tapped a button on the intercom. "Colonel, sir," she said. Then, lowering her voice, she added. "Dad. Are you seeing this?"

He coughed. "Yes."

"What are your orders, sir?"

"Keep monitoring the situation," he replied. "That's all we can do for now. Things are quiet here, but who knows how long this will last."

"Yes, sir." She turned off the intercom.

She looked up and saw Liao staring back. As per protocol, he had earphones in. He pulled them out and came closer, keeping his voice low. "What does he mean, 'how long this will last'?"

Adelheid looked away. "He's waiting for the other shoe to drop."

"What other shoe?" asked Liao.

Suddenly, they realized that all eyes on the forebridge were on them. Lizabet turned in her seat, as did the adjutants.

Adelheid took a deep breath. "This has been coming for a while. The Earth has been fighting against its environment for centuries now. Sea levels rise, they build sea walls. Temperatures rise? They build climate control domes and plant genetically modified crops. Droughts increase, and they seed the clouds to make it rain. But in the end, there's only so much they can do."

Behind the ensigns, an Earth newscaster had stood up from his desk, ignoring his colleagues' pleas to calm down. "There's a lot we haven't been able to tell you," he shouted. "Now that government control has broken down, we can tell you about increasing anger over food shortages. Unfortunately, without government control, people are in the streets looting."

"Food shortages?" Lizabet exclaimed.

Liao sucked his teeth. "Suddenly, those supply price increases make a lot of sense."

Adelheid nodded. "I think the UN was covering up a lot of things until they just couldn't anymore."

"But why?" Lizabet snapped.

Adelheid turned to a media screen, which showed a mob of people stampeding the camera operator. "To try to prevent this panic."

A light on Lizabet's console flashed red. She checked the display and stiffened. "Lieutenant, it's a message from Earth Space Command. Priority red."

Adelheid straightened up and pushed in her earphones. "Patch it through."

The logo of Earth Space Command appeared on Adelheid's screen, but it stayed there. She frowned, reached for the volume control, and then jerked her hand back when a burst of static blared in her ears. Then . . .

Her brow furrowed. Even with earpieces in, she tilted her head, trying to make out individual voices, but all she could hear were shouts and crashes in between bursts of static.

Then, suddenly, a man's voice cut in. "To all outposts and colonial commands: this is the Earth. I—" More static. More shouts. Something shattered.

The man drew a shaky breath. "We . . .."

In the distance, a woman screamed. More confusion.

Then the man: "Please forgive us."

Then, the feed to Earth Space Command cut out completely.

Adelheid leaned back, blinking. She looked at her colleagues and saw them bringing their hands down from their earpieces. The silence stretched.

Finally, Liao breathed. "Did we . . . did we just lose the Earth?"

"No," Lizabet snapped. "No, they can't go. We'll starve." Her voice rose. "They know we'll starve, don't they?"

There was the sound of gunfire from one of the media screens. Everyone on the forebridge turned to see the news-caster leaping back and people scattering into view. The camera shook, and then the signal cut out, first to screensaver colours, then to bare static.

Lizabet flipped switches, trying different channels. The screen flickered and jumped between blue screens and static.

"What are we going to do?" Liao whispered.

Adelheid swallowed.

"Adelheid." Liao's voice rose. "What are we going to do?"

Adelheid stared at the blank screen.

At her console, Lizabet gasped and brought her hand to her mouth. "Gods! Somebody just dropped a nuke on Kathmandu."

Throughout the bridge, officers whispered fearfully.

*This is it.*

*The Earth is done for.*

*We're on our own.*

*There's not enough food. What are we going to eat?*

*We're going to starve.*

*We're going to die.*

Adelheid jumped when Liao touched her shoulder. He stared at her wide-eyed. She looked around the bridge. Lizabet stared at the monitors, both hands over her mouth. Gerhardt stared at the blank media screens, mouth agape. The adjutants stood where they were, looking lost.

*We're stunned*, Adelheid thought. *We have no idea what to do next.*

*So, what does happen next?*

*It's the Earth that's tearing itself apart, not Mercury —at least, not right now. Once we come to our senses, the first question we're going to ask is where our food is going to come from. So, where is that food now?*

*Apple slices.*

She cleared her throat. "Have we unloaded the Earth shuttle?"

The bridge crew looked at her in confusion. She brought her hand down hard on a console, making everyone jump.

"Sub-lieutenant Fang!" Her voice was firm, not sharp—a steel floor to stand on rather than a blade to cut. "I asked a question: have we unloaded the Earth shuttle?"

Liao turned to his console. "Not really. The bulk of the work yesterday was refuelling and repairs."

Adelheid stood, fixing Liao with a look. "I've got to get to Terminal right now."

His brow furrowed.

*He doesn't fully understand yet. Good. If he's an average person, maybe I can get there before the riots start.*

"Stay here," she said. "Prepare the *Messenger* for early departure. We may have to move quickly."

Liao saluted. "Yes, sir!"

"Lieutenant Pohl, you're in charge here." Adelheid strode for the door. "Coordinate with the Colonel when he calls."

Gerhardt saluted, even though they shared the same rank. But he didn't question her order.

Adelheid ran from the bridge.

☿

ADELHEID LEFT the tram and ran through the *Messenger* airlocks into Terminal. As on the *Messenger*, she dodged stunned people staring at the media screens. Now, however, people whispered. A din rose in the corridors, edged with panic.

There were guards standing by the doors to the shuttle arrival bay. Someone else was thinking things through. They recognized her rank and let her enter.

The sound hit her. It wasn't a roar, and it wasn't chaos, but there were a lot of people at the consoles shouting about readouts. All were officers of the *Apollo*—she was the first officer of the *Messenger* to arrive and the highest-ranking. Where was the *Hermes* crew?

The door on the *Hermes* side of the arrivals bay parted, and Cristavao entered. She ran to him. "What have you heard?"

He shuddered. "Cairo's been hit with a nuke. More are coming. It's going to be hell on Earth."

"I know. But what about here?"

He pointed. "The shuttle arrival doors are closed."

An *Apollo* officer looked up from a nearby console. "The Earth envoy pulled his team back to the shuttle fifteen minutes ago. We arrived as the doors closed. They've locked them and aren't answering our hails."

"I don't understand," said Cristavao. "Why would they do that? What do they want?"

"Not to be looted, probably," Adelheid replied. She tapped the *Apollo* officer on the shoulder. He glared at her, but she didn't step back. "What is the state of the *Apollo*?" she asked. "How are people reacting?"

For a moment, he looked like he wasn't going to answer, but he steeled himself. "It's tense. People know what's at stake. Now, excuse me, Lieutenant, but I have work to do." He turned back to the console.

"What do we do?" Cristavao asked.

"We have to talk to the shuttle crew," said Adelheid.

"How? He just said they weren't answering our hails."

"They can still hear us. If we can convince the shuttle crew that *we're* not panicking, maybe *they'll* have less reason to panic."

She marched to the communications console, where an officer of the *Apollo* shouted into the microphone. "Earth shuttle, respond now!" he yelled. "We demand—hey!"

Adelheid shouldered him aside and grabbed the microphone.

"I was trying to raise them!" he snapped.

She glared at him. "Really? I wonder why they wouldn't talk to you."

The officer stepped toward her, but Cristavao blocked his way. Nodding, Adelheid flipped a switch on the microphone, took a deep breath and, keeping her voice steady, said, "Earth shuttle ship, this is Lieutenant Adelheid Koning of the *Messenger*. Please stand down your departure preparations. We only wish to talk."

She turned up the volume on the answering speaker, but it only played static.

"Earth shuttle," she tried again. The chatter in the room eased as people looked up from their work and watched her. "Earth shuttle, I give you my personal guarantee of your safety. Please talk to us."

She flipped the switch. Still nothing but static. The *Apollo* officers looked at each other and grumbled.

Cristavao sighed. "You did your best," he said quietly.

The speaker crackled. "This is Earth shuttle. Captain Emmanuel Botha speaking. With respect, Lieutenant, I don't think you speak for all your people."

Adelheid leaned into the microphone. "I have the authority of my father, Colonel Abraham Koning of the *Messenger*." *Technically, I'm jumping the gun, but I know he'll back me up.* "So, when I say you have my personal guarantee, it means something, Captain Botha. We will keep order here. You have nothing to fear from us. Just open the doors and let us talk."

"I think we can do our talking just fine where we are," said Botha. "We're deciding what our next steps are, and we'll tell you as soon as we've reached a decision."

Cristavao leaned past Adelheid and shouted into the microphone. "We are offering you asylum!"

Adelheid gently shoved Cristavao aside and brought the microphone closer. "You can stay with us. You can share our food. All we ask is that you deliver the supplies you promised."

"And how long will those supplies last?" Botha shot back. "Don't you think we know how much you need what we have in our holds? This is a doomed planet. If we stay here, we'll starve to death with the rest of you!"

"And Earth is going to be any better?" Cristavao snapped.

"At least there, we'll stand in normal gravity and breathe its air," said Botha. "At least there, we'll have a chance."

"Wait," shouted Adelheid. "There are three crates in your hold. Give those to us. Those could—"

"Our patience has run out," said a voice behind her. Alistair

Banks shoved Adelheid aside and snatched the microphone from her hands. She stumbled. Cristavao caught her.

"What's he doing?" Cristavao gasped.

Adelheid steadied herself and glared. "He's panicking."

"Flare and sunlight," Cristavao breathed.

Alistair spoke into the microphone. "Earth shuttle: you have a contractual obligation to release your goods to us within three days of landing on Mercury. We've seen little of your supplies. Open the doors and give us access to your holds this instant."

The speaker crackled. "What are you going to do?" said Botha. "Call our superiors? They're busy—"

Suddenly, Botha grunted. "What are you doing? Stand down! We agreed on this—"

In the background of the speaker, Adelheid heard someone shout. "Hoarding? For what? It makes no sense!"

Adelheid leaned back to Cristavao. "Why haven't we heard from Envoy Govendor? Why is the shuttle captain speaking to us? The crew aren't of one mind on this."

"That's good," Cristavao replied. "If we can just sway a few over—"

Suddenly, Adelheid's radio buzzed in her ear. She tapped it. Her father spoke. "Adelheid, report! What's going on?"

She turned aside. "The Earth shuttle crew have barricaded themselves in their shuttle. Captain Banks is telling them to open up or else."

The Colonel swore. "Is he trying to get us all killed?"

Behind her, Alistair shouted into the microphone. "We have blowtorches. If you don't open this door, we're cutting our way in."

"And I have my fingers on the fuel dump button and ignition key," Botha shouted. "If you try to cut your way in here to loot us, we'll blow everything up. We may be dead already, so don't see if we'll take you with us."

Adelheid tapped her earpiece. "Colonel? This is escalating.

The Earth crew are threatening to self-destruct if the officers try to cut their way in. We can't be here if that happens."

She listened for a response but got none. She tapped her earpiece. There was nothing wrong with the connection. *Why would my father hesitate? Why?*

On the radio, the Colonel coughed. "Adelheid . . ."

Her stomach dropped. *If he ordered the* Messenger *to move forward now, he could be ordering me to stay behind and face my death.* "Dad," she said. "Don't. We can't wait. If we have to, all remaining *Messenger* personnel will evacuate Terminal on land speeders. I'll go with them, but the safety of the *Messenger* comes first. You know this. Move us forward."

He sighed. "I know." He took another deep breath. "Lieutenant, order all non-essential personnel to board the *Messenger* immediately. Tell Banks I demand that the *Apollo* stops what it's doing. Then, organize the evacuation of anybody left behind by our departure. Got it?"

"Yes, sir," she replied.

"Stay safe."

"Yes, Dad."

She turned back and grabbed Alistair's arm. "Colonel Koning demands that you stand down before this situation spirals out of control."

"The *Hermes* Council agrees," Cristavao added, tapping his own earpiece. Other *Hermes* officers were entering the room and walking purposefully toward the *Apollo* personnel. "You're risking three cities with your recklessness."

Alistair shook himself free of Adelheid's grip. "That food is vital to our survival! There is no way I'm letting them leave here without unloading it!"

Then Terminal vibrated beneath their feet. Adelheid swung around to look out the large window. She saw the roofline of the *Messenger* slipping past, slowly picking up speed. It would be clear of Terminal in just minutes. She breathed a sigh of relief.

Then Terminal vibrated harder, with a roar that buffeted their ears. People staggered. Some ran. Adelheid turned to the shuttle doors and saw monitors showing a wall of flame inside. "What the Hell?"

"They're trying to launch," shouted Cristavao.

"No!"

They rushed to a console, but a technician shook his head. "They've started ignition. Their fuel is burning. We can't stop it."

The shaking intensified. The screens, however, showed the nose cone of the Earth shuttle staying where it was.

Adelheid goggled. "Why isn't it moving?"

The technician tapped frantically at the console as gauges tipped to red. "I—I don't know!"

The shaking got even worse. The Perspex windows wobbled in their frames. Adelheid imagined them cracking, sucking them into the vacuum.

Then, at the consoles, she spotted a cluster of technicians around Captain Banks. The *Apollo* liaison officer looked determined as he held down a button. Above it, a panel flashed red, reading DOCKING LOCK.

She stumbled across and lunged at Alistair. "What in Sunlight are you doing? You'll kill us all!" She shoved him away from the console so hard he fell over backwards. She slammed her hand on the button marked RELEASE.

The shaking ebbed, and a new roar echoed through Terminal. On the screen, the Earth shuttle rose toward space.

"What have you done?" Alistair waved his officers forward. "Security! Arrest this woman!"

Cristavao stepped in front of them. "I don't think so." Around him, *Hermes* security officers placed their hands on their guns, looking grim.

"The Earth shuttle is clear of Terminal," a technician reported. "The first-stage rockets have jettisoned. Second-stage ignition commencing."

"Do you know how many calories you've let escape?" Alistair yelled at Adelheid. "That food! That equipment! It could have kept us going for months!"

"The rocket would have destroyed this base and our three cities if it blew up on the pad," Adelheid shot back.

"Second-stage rockets jettisoned," the technician continued. "Beginning third stage." Then he frowned. "Wait. Something's wrong."

The surface of Mercury flashed, as Adelheid imagined lightning would do on Earth. The light flooded through the windows, making everyone flinch.

"What happened?" Cristavao shouted.

The technician straightened up and stared wide-eyed at the screen, which had shown a rising shuttle but now showed a dying fireball. He shook his head. "There . . . there was a fault."

Klaxons rang.

"We have impact warnings!" another technician shouted. "The shuttle's coming down in pieces. Ninety seconds to impact."

"Where?" Alistair yelled.

"Calculating," the technician replied.

Adelheid held her breath.

"The largest site of impact will be . . ." The technician tapped on a keyboard and then looked at the screen. "Eight hundred metres forward," he said at last. "About one hundred metres starboard. It will miss Terminal."

People sighed with relief.

The technician stiffened. "The impact site is across the *Messenger*'s Robinson Rail."

Everyone turned and stared out the starboard windows, where the *Messenger* had just departed. Adelheid rushed forward to the glass. She could just see the rear of the *Messenger*, leaving Terminal's platform.

"Eighty seconds to impact," said the technician.

Adelheid turned away from the window. She tapped her earpiece. "Colonel Koning! Come in!"

Her radio crackled. "Lieutenant. We're getting the same impact warnings you are."

"Where?" she gasped. She meant, *which part?*

"Seventy seconds," the technician shouted.

"I'm ordering the *Messenger* to speed up," the Colonel replied. "At current trajectory, the shuttle will crash a kilometre ahead of the tail section. By speeding up, we can save all but the last five hundred metres."

"But—" Adelheid stuttered. *That will kill the tail section. Where command is. Where Dad is.*

"Sixty seconds!" The words stabbed the background noise.

"Contact the forebridge," the Colonel said. "They'll soon have to manage the clean-up."

*Why?* Adelheid thought. The answer came like a punch in the stomach. *He's not evacuating. There's no time.*

She choked. "Dad—"

"Fifty seconds!"

"Be brave," her father whispered. "Do not waver. Tell the forebridge to keep their speed up. Save as much of the *Messenger* as they can. Those are my orders."

Adelheid drew a shuddering breath. "Yes, Dad."

"Goodbye, Adelheid."

The connection clicked off. She tapped her earpiece. "Forebridge!"

"Adelheid." It was Liao's voice, whispering, though it was silly to. "We shouldn't speed up. If the shuttle falls less than five hundred metres from the aft, the tail section won't be protected by pressure doors."

"Forty seconds!"

"Liao, what—" She got a hold of herself. "No! You heard the Colonel! Keep to the ordered speed!"

"But—"

"We are not sacrificing residents for command," she snapped. "The people of the *Messenger* come first! Go!"

"Adelheid—"

"That is an order, Sub-Lieutenant! Go!"

She clicked the radio receiver off and ran back to the window. Cristavao came up beside her. She pressed her face to the glass and stared at the *Messenger* as it picked up speed.

"Twenty seconds to impact!" the technician shouted.

Small gouts of dust rose from the surface of Mercury as the first shards of the shuttle hit. Adelheid could see the *Messenger* accelerating, even as it faded into the dark. Her heart pounded. Maybe they would be fast enough. Maybe—

The metal hulk of the shuttle swept into view, descending like a guillotine. It smashed into the roof of the *Messenger* in total silence and with a blinding flash.

The *Messenger*'s Robinson Rail shuddered, the vibrations shaking Terminal like a tuning fork. People yelled. Adelheid staggered back, legs shaking. Cristavao caught her. They sank to their knees, clutching each other close.

Adelheid buried her face in Cristavao's shoulder and wept.

# CHAPTER 8
# THE START OF THE SILENCE

GRADUALLY, ADELHEID BECAME AWARE OF RADIO CHATTER IN HER ears. She pulled back from Cristavao, pushed herself away, and staggered to her feet.

"Is there anybody in charge?" shouted people. "Who's alive? Who's the highest-ranking officer still alive? Any civilian council members still alive? Who's in charge?"

She tapped her earpiece. "This is Lieutenant Koning. Report. Somebody, report."

Her voice was like a drop in the ocean.

She twisted the dial again. "Fore-bridge crew, report! Liao! Are you there? Report!"

The radio warbled. Lizabet's voice came on. "We still have air," she called. "The pressure doors have held. All sections report green, except for—" She choked. "The last five hundred metres. The—"

Lizabet couldn't say it. It hurt for Adelheid to even think about it. *The tail-section of the Messenger. Command.*

Liao's voice came on the radio. "We still have solar power from the Robinson Rail, but the rail is broken behind us. I'm sending crews out to assess the damage."

*I can see the damage from here*, thought Adelheid. "How long until sunrise?"

There was a pause. Liao's voice shook. "About ten Earth days."

Adelheid drew a shuddering breath. *We're out of construction bots. We have no nanobots. There isn't time to repair the Robinson Rail.*

*And everyone knows it.*

The radio chatter crescendoed again.

*What are we going to do?*

*Even if we can escape the burning, we'll starve!*

*Is anybody in command alive? The Colonel? Captain Ramkin? The Governor? Anyone? Who's in charge?*

The panic pressed in from the radio, cupped her heart, and squeezed hard. She closed her eyes and took a deep breath.

"Listen to me," she whispered.

The chatter continued unabated. Even around her, the *Hermes* and *Apollo* officers stood staring around, lost, or touching their earpieces. Some were talking fast, not listening, voices rising in panic.

"Listen to me!" Adelheid shouted. "This is Lieutenant Adelheid Koning! Do we want this to end here? Do we end it here?"

The radio chatter in her ears ebbed. Around her, the room fell silent. People stared at her, but she ignored them. She spoke only to the *Messenger*.

"I don't think so," she said. "We still have power. We still have most of the *Messenger* and, most important, we still have breath! As long as we have breath, we have hope, and this is what we're going to do: if we can't repair the *Messenger* and the Robinson Rail before sunrise, we move ahead. We will travel at twice the planet's rotation. In eighty-eight days, we will come upon this site from behind as it leaves daylight, and then we will have the whole Mercury night to make repairs. We will mourn, but we will rebuild. We will not give up. Do you understand?"

The radio was almost silent now. Adelheid counted to five. "Do you understand?" she yelled.

The radio crackled. "This is Deputy Clerk Daarel Hahn of the *Messenger*."

Adelheid frowned. *Where do I know him from? He's a junior civilian council member—wasn't he the head of accounting?*

Hahn coughed, then drew a shaky breath. His voice rasped. "The Governor is dead, along with most of the council. I am the most senior member of the *Messenger*'s government still alive— at least, that I know of. Therefore, effective immediately, I must assume command."

The world paused.

"And I command . . ." Hahn took another deep breath. "I command that we follow Lieutenant Koning's plan. We don't have time to repair before sunrise, so prepare the *Messenger* for departure around the world. All *Messenger* officials and personnel, depart Terminal now and return to your ship."

The radio chattered again, this time with people saying, "Aye-aye" and "Yes, sir." Adelheid let out a breath of relief and shut off the radio. She looked heavenward.

*I'm an orphan now. At twenty-three. I shouldn't feel this lost, but I do. How do we go forward from this?*

*By doing the job that's in front of you. That's all you can do, so do it well. People need it. People need you.*

She turned and saw Cristavao hovering close, looking concerned. She swallowed. "I have to go. I—"

"I understand," he said solemnly.

They hesitated, looking at each other. Then, at no signal either could identify, they embraced and held each other close. Adelheid looked up and saw Cristavao looking back. They kissed. The moment lingered.

Adelheid pulled away at last, bowing her head. She coughed. "See you on the other side?"

"I'll be waiting," he replied.

She set off for the *Messenger* at a run. A glance back showed her Cristavao standing, watching her go.

Outside, across the landscape, shrapnel continued to smack the ground, but at a slower pace and with smaller and smaller pieces. Bits of twisted metal made little craters over the pock-marked surface.

Soon, only dust fell, and burrowed itself into the surface of Mercury.

# PART THREE
# FRIEDA: BREAKING THE SILENCE

# CHAPTER 9
# VOICES FROM THE DARK

*The* Messenger
*The Mercury Colonies, May 8, 2201 CE*

MORE PEOPLE ARRIVED AS FRIEDA STEPPED AWAY FROM THE parapet. Their badges identified them as communications officers, and Head of Communications met them as they arrived. They headed into the Royal Apartment, with Frieda tagging behind, watching. Inside, they moved to a corner and began talking amongst themselves.

The reception room was almost louder than it had been in the agora, and while there was jubilation in some quarters—Frieda spotted the prime minister looking excited as she talked with Head of Procurement—there was also urgency and confusion.

At the side of the room, Adelheid watched, arms folded across her chest.

The front door opened, and a security officer raised his voice. "Your Majesty! The *Hermes* ambassador requests an audience."

Adelheid brought her cane down with a sharp *crack!*,

silencing the room. "Everybody, let's show decorum." She nodded to the security officer. "Show the ambassador in."

Frieda perked up at this. *Cara's mother*, she thought.

The door opened, and those in the room parted, providing a clear route to Adelheid as the *Hermes* ambassador *(What is her name? Flores, of course, but what about her first name? I remember reading it somewhere. Alanna? Aline?)* stepped inside.

There was no mistaking the family resemblance; the *Hermes* ambassador *(Alanza! That's it!)* looked like an older Cara, with her daughter's high cheekbones, bronze skin, and sharp gaze, but there were crows' feet around her eyes that changed Cara's air of youthful feistiness into one of seasoned cynicism.

Alanza Flores greeted Adelheid with a quick and short bow —the absolute minimum she could get away with.

*Very like Cara*, Frieda thought.

"Your Majesty," said Alanza.

"Ambassador," Adelheid replied.

Alanza straightened up. "A historic moment."

"As you say," Adelheid conceded.

"I can hear the people in the agora singing from here," said Alanza. "So, the *Hermes* president has advised me to discuss with you the nature of our response."

"We're working on that," said Adelheid shortly.

"As are we," replied the ambassador.

Adelheid's eyes narrowed. Silence stretched. Finally, Adelheid said, "What will you say?"

"We're working on that," said Alanza. "A simple message of welcome hardly seems sufficient."

"We should coordinate our message," said Adelheid, and Frieda heard urgency in her grandmother's voice.

Ambassador Flores leaned back. "I doubt that multiple messages of welcome and joy over the Earth's release from the Silence would somehow be an embarrassment. This *is* what you intend to say on behalf of yourself and the *Messenger*, isn't it?"

Frieda, along with everybody else in the room, looked from Adelheid to Alanza like spectators in a badminton match. *The ambassador is right*, she thought. *Why would we object if the Hermes wanted to send its own message? They're not our colony.* But another part of her—possibly the patriotic part—rankled. *Why make such a big issue of it, then?*

Adelheid folded her arms across her chest. "It's unprofessional and makes us sound like desperate children rushing back into their parents' embrace." She tilted her head. "We should have more dignity."

Alanza shrugged. "I'm sure it will be extremely dignified. However, I am here as a courtesy. You will hear our president's message to the Earth shortly, and we look forward to hearing your own. Thank you, Your Majesty."

She nodded, then turned away with a slight smirk on her face. That smirk vanished when she came face to face with Frieda, who was standing between her and the door. She smiled again, and this time, the smile was warmer, if tinged with fluster. "Your Highness—" She started to extend her hand before she caught herself and changed the movement to a bow —a deeper bow—instead. "May I extend the thoughts and prayers of the people of the *Hermes*? We were . . . horrified to learn of your accident and the death of your mother, but we are heartened to see you recovering."

Frieda stood with her remaining hand halfway raised. She tucked it behind her back. "Thank you," she said quietly.

"And, personally . . ." Here, Alanza's voice changed, becoming less formal, and her expression less stiff. "I wanted to thank you for taking the time to see my daughter Cara. It's not easy growing up away from home, but you made her feel welcome."

"Thank you," said Frieda again, less stiffly. Out of the corner of her eye, she saw Adelheid frown.

The ambassador nodded to the room and left. The door clicked shut behind her.

From their corner, Head of Communications led their team toward Adelheid. "Your Majesty, on the subject of a reply, I've taken the liberty of bringing in my team to craft a response. We already have some ideas—"

Adelheid waved them away. "I don't need anyone to write me a speech, Greer. This is a greeting, not trade negotiations. I know what needs to be said."

"But a response, after fifty years of silence . . ." Greer cut in.

Frieda raised an eyebrow. How long had Greer been Head of Communications? Not long, clearly. They hadn't even noticed that everybody else had sidled a step away and were now engaged in quiet conversation with somebody—anybody —else.

Adelheid glared. "I know what needs to be said."

"But—" Greer pressed on. "Your Majesty, who gives the response? You? Or the Crown Princess?"

The room fell silent, and Frieda realized that everybody was now staring at her. She fought off the urge to fold her arms around herself and just stood there, staring back. However, her mind reeled. *The Head of Communications has just asked who is Stadtholder.*

The silence stretched.

*Well, who is?*

She looked around. *I don't want it. I fight my nerves presenting before my class at the best of times. Given a speech I haven't written, talking to another planet with an amputated arm? I don't want this duty!*

She opened her mouth to object.

"I'm doing it," Adelheid growled, bringing everyone's attention around.

Frieda stiffened. She looked at her grandmother and saw her grandmother looking back. She opened her mouth again, but Adelheid shook her head subtly.

Frieda closed her mouth. She stepped back.

The officers in the reception area shifted toward Adelheid. "We can give you text within thirty minutes—" Greer began.

Adelheid waved them away. "I told you, I know what needs to be said. Just set up the cameras. I intend to go live in fifteen minutes, ahead of the *Hermes* President."

Officers bustled away, some dodging around Frieda as she stood staring. The babble in the room picked up. The front door opened, and more people came in, bearing video equipment. Frieda felt herself increasingly in the way, so she left for her bedroom.

*That hurt*, she thought as she walked. *Why did that hurt?*

☿

As Frieda returned to her bedroom, she felt the stimulant she'd been given ebb away. Fortunately, an attendant opened the door for her as she approached. Once inside, she flopped on her bed and stared blearily at the media screen on her wall. It showed her grandmother behind a podium.

"As Stadholder of the *Messenger* and its client latitude towns," said Adelheid, "I convey Mercury's delight at Earth's perseverance as it reaches out for the first time since it fell silent fifty years ago. On behalf of the people of Mercury, I bid the Earth welcome and look forward to further communications."

She turned from the podium, then, and walked away, taking no questions.

As Frieda struggled to blink the bleariness from her eyes, she frowned at the media screen. *That's . . . diplomatic. And perfunctory. A planet we left for dead has come back to life. The people of the* Messenger *are singing colonial anthems. Why isn't Grandmother celebrating?*

Suddenly dizzy, she fell back on her pillow.

*And what in Sunlight did they give me to make me so alert before now?*

She had just enough time to thank the fates that she'd already taken her prosthetic off before she fell asleep.

☿

IT WAS NOT A RESTFUL SLEEP.

Frieda's dreams were a jumble of pain and grief, and she woke with her phantom limb blazing.

This time, she stifled the scream, letting her breath out in short, sharp gasps. *"Dawnfire!"* she gasped. *"Daybreak!"* She pushed what remained of her right hand against what remained of her left tricep and rubbed the muscle, hard. Eventually, the pain eased. She slumped back on her pillow, exhausted. She needed a bigger swear word, and she picked it: *"Fuck!"*

Someone gasped, "Your Highness!"

Frieda looked over. Anna stood halfway through the door, mouth agape.

Frieda stared back, then raised an eyebrow. *I can see how un-queen-like I'd been but . . . but right now, I don't particularly care. You* try being queen-like with this amount of pain.

She struggled to sit up. "Well, don't just stand there, help me!"

Anna hurried forward and helped Frieda get to her feet. Frieda stood, taking deep breaths. Her residual arm throbbed, but at least it was just her residual arm and not pain from some part of her that wasn't there anymore. *How in Sunlight does that work?*

Anna frowned at Frieda as Frieda wobbled on her feet. "Your Highness, would you like your pain medication?"

Frieda blinked at Anna a moment, then remembered that the painkillers were delivered by syringe and came with crushing wooziness—except for the one that Grandmother had somehow slipped her yesterday, which cleared her mind but made it feel taut and fragile as glass.

*Pain, or wooziness, or some other state I can hardly describe? Are those my only choices? Or is there a fourth one?*

She glanced at her residual arm, then looked away, shuddering. "Not right now."

Anna frowned. "Are you sure? You're in pain, Your Highness—"

Frieda gritted her teeth against her title. "Not now!" she snapped. More quietly, she added, "I want the clarity."

Anna hesitated, then nodded. "As you wish, Your Highness." She gave Frieda a quick bow. "I'll fetch breakfast."

"But—" Frieda began, but Anna was already out the door. To fetch breakfast, presumably.

*Before, when Mom was alive, breakfast meant going down to the tail section's galley. Anna didn't give me that option, likely because she didn't have that option to give me.*

*The galley is off-limits to me now, isn't it? Because of who I am and probably because of my injuries. People would be staring at me, and Grandmother doesn't want that.*

*I don't want that either. But I'd still like that choice.*

To distract herself, she reached up to the media screen on the wall and tapped it on. Switching through the feeds, she came upon a man and a woman from the Journalists' Guild— Pundits' Department—talking at each other across a table. The woman looked angry. "You didn't just—"

The man put up his hands. "I'm only saying that we are blessed that Queen Adelheid was able to step out of retirement and take on the role of regent. I don't discount Princess Frieda's heroism and sacrifice in the moment, but any person her age would have a hard time overcoming their own grief to assume the day-to-day responsibilities of a stadtholder, much less dealing with her injuries."

"So, how long do you think the Dowager should maintain her regency?" the woman asked. "The Crown Princess comes of age in less than a year."

"Well, that's something we'll have to discuss when the time comes," the man replied.

Frieda narrowed her eyes at the screen. *Any person her age . . . hard time overcoming their own grief . . . he doesn't think I should be Stadtholder.*

Her frown deepened. *But I don't* want *to be Stadtholder.*

*So, why does this rankle so?*

She sighed and flipped to a different news site. She caught a newscaster in mid-sentence, saying, "Mercurians are still abuzz over the second message from Earth—"

She straightened up. *They replied? That quickly?*

There was a knock at her door. Anna poked her head in. "Your Highness, you have a medical appointment."

Frieda blinked. "I do?" *I didn't put that on my calendar. Then again, where* is *my calendar?*

Anna opened the door wider, and three people stepped in, wearing medical uniforms. Frieda recognized the doctor from the Infirmary, but still couldn't place his name. Fortunately, as he bowed, he said, "Your Highness. You may not remember me. I'm Dr. Daskivic. I am in charge of your physiotherapy and the mapping of your prosthetic."

"What?" said Frieda.

Someone coughed behind Dr. Daskivic. It was Cara. "Making it work," she said quietly.

Frieda straightened up. "Oh!" *This is good news!*

"Indeed," said Daskivic, giving Cara a disapproving frown. "You've met Intern Flores already and . . ." Here, he gestured at another young woman, who looked about two years older than Frieda. "... this is apprentice nurse Sara Vasser."

"I see." Frieda bit her lip as a stab of pain shot through her residual arm. Clearly, there was a lot of healing still to be done. She sat heavily down on the side of her bed. "So, what do we have to do today, then?"

Daskivic nodded approvingly, then motioned Sara and Cara forward to plunk more cases on the table. "First, Your Highness, we have to prepare the remnant arm to handle the prosthetic. We need to finish the healing process, then perform nerve mapping ahead of designing the control unit."

Frieda nodded. "How do we finish the healing process?"

"Well..." He clapped his hands together, looking eager. *Not something you want to see when your doctor talks about your medical procedure*, Frieda thought. "To start with, we have this."

Sara Vasser pulled a case from within her case and opened it, taking out and holding the object inside as if it were a holy relic. Frieda looked, and she leaned forward in awe, as did Cara. "A bone knitter! May I...?"

Frieda reached for it with her remaining hand. Sara hesitated long enough to glance at Daskivic and get his nod before placing it gently on Frieda's palm, keeping her hands close so it wouldn't drop.

It was a small metal device with a power cell and an emitter. *Ultrasonic*, thought Frieda. *It must be more than fifty years old! I can even see the label that says, "Made in Korea."* "I thought these had gone extinct."

Daskivic laughed softly. "Almost. That's the last working one. There are four others that we're using for spare parts. They should keep this running for another few years. Assuming we don't use it too often. Just on... important occasions."

Frieda wondered if he was referring to her medical procedure or to her directly. *If somebody else were to lose an arm, it should be just as important, surely?*

"With that in mind . . ." He smiled at his apprentices indulgently and nodded at Cara. "How would you like to have a go at working it, Mufrau Flores?"

Cara blinked at Daskivic's offer. She looked eager, then nervous, but she took up the device. Frieda fought down a surge of jealousy. Then Sara came forward to take off the bandages.

After two minutes, Frieda succumbed to temptation and looked at her injury. It was less gory than she'd imagined, but somehow, that made it worse. Without any blood, she saw how the skin was stitched together.

Her stomach churned. She covered her mouth with her bandaged hand. "Um . . ."

Sara looked up and frowned. "Your Highness?"

Frieda pulled her hand from her mouth. "Bucket!" she gasped.

Daskivic and Sara scrambled, looking for anything that could help, but it was Cara who set aside the bone knitter and grabbed up the wastebasket in time for Frieda to throw up into it, leaving the others to stand, looking sympathetic and awkward.

It was then Anna returned with a member of the kitchen staff, bringing breakfast.

"Of course," Frieda muttered.

"Uh . . ." Daskivic straightened up. "Maybe we should take this away—"

"No," Frieda cut in. She pulled away from Cara, who was dabbing at her mouth with a towel. *Anna and those workers spent all that time getting the food together; it would be a shame to send it back.* "I may be hungry later. And if nothing else, you folks deserve to eat." She hefted her residual arm. "Let's get this over with."

Cara put the wastebasket aside. Daskivic and Sara gathered

more equipment. Anna retired to the side of the room and began folding clothes.

What interest Frieda had in the pre-Silence bone knitter vanished when Cara turned it on. The emitter made the bones of her residual arm vibrate. It felt like a dentist's drill on the wrong part of her body. But she clenched her teeth and bore through the pain. *This will lead to better things*, she thought. *A working prosthetic, possibly.* She glanced over at her prosthetic. *Though how I'll be able to carry that thing . . .*

The bone-knitting work completed, the medical team moved to nerve mapping, and the dentist's drill gave way to electric shocks.

"Ow!" Frieda yelled.

"That's a good read," said Sara.

"Oh, good!" Frieda winced. "What in Sunlight does that mean?"

"It means your nerves can register the signals," Cara replied while she worked the numbers on her tablet. She gave Frieda an encouraging smile. "It makes it easier to design the interface to control the prosthetic."

"Oh." Frieda took a deep breath, held it, then let it go. "Okay, then. Carry on." Sara leaned in, and Frieda jerked. "Oh . . . dear!"

Cara flashed her a look of concern. Daskivic frowned. "Your Highness, if you wish it, there can be more painkillers—"

"No," said Frieda through gritted teeth.

"But—"

"No!" she snapped. "Just . . . give me a distraction. I heard the Earth replied last night. Anna, what did they say?"

Anna looked up from folding laundry. She blinked. "They... welcomed us. And are hoping to meet us at Terminal."

Frieda jerked up in surprise, drawing a hiss from Sara, who repositioned the needle. "They're coming here? *Now?*"

Anna's brow furrowed. "I don't remember the exact wording, but I think so."

"Apparently, they've successfully restored an ion ship," said Cara. "They're sending representatives and are looking forward to meeting us."

"Wow," said Sara, as she took another read from the needle. "It's hard to believe. Just yesterday, all was quiet. And now, in just two weeks, space flight resumes?"

"This will be good," said Daskivic. "If they still have pre-Silence shuttles, they could resume supply runs. We could start trading again. Life here could get a lot easier." He nodded at the ancient bone knitter, now back in its case. "We could replace a lot of old equipment."

"We don't know what state the Earth is in," said Cara. "We thought they were dead yesterday. They might not have much to trade."

Daskivic chuckled. "But then, why would they come here?"

Cara glanced at him, then turned back to her work in silence, even though Frieda thought, *That's a good question.*

She looked at the media screen. Though the volume was down, she could see the pundits speaking alongside images of people celebrating the Earth breaking its silence.

*They're meeting us at Terminal? In two weeks? When we just happen to be about two weeks away from Terminal? What a lucky coincidence they restored communications when they did.*

She winced. *I sound just like Grandmother.*

She straightened up. *She's going to be really busy because of this. Isn't this part of my job? Maybe there's some way that I can help?*

She paused. *Do I want to do that? Or stay in my room while my medical team pokes and prods me?*

Another jolt of electricity shot up her arm. "Ack!" *That settles it.* "Are we almost done?"

The medical team leaned back. Cara frowned. Sara looked

particularly put out. Daskivic paused for a moment, then nodded. "I think this might be a good place to break off," he said. "We'll get back to this tomorrow?"

Frieda hesitated only a moment when she realized he was actually asking permission. "Yes," she said. "I'll see you tomorrow."

The medical team packed up their equipment, with Sara being extra careful about the bone knitter, even with possible replacement supplies on the way. Finally, they headed out. Daskivic and Vasser bowed as they passed Frieda. Cara, out of sight of both of them but not Anna, gave Frieda a smile and a nod.

Anna gaped at Cara's back as the door clicked shut.

Frieda frowned at Anna, but then she shrugged. "I'm going to the meeting room," she said and walked out the door.

☿

FRIEDA HAD ONLY SAID 'the meeting room' to have a destination as an excuse. She wanted to find her grandmother. But as she headed through the Royal Apartment, she heard raised voices, including her grandmother's. They brought her to the meeting room anyway.

"They called us *in transit?*" Adelheid exclaimed. "They're not even waiting for our reply? They're already on their way?"

Frieda slipped in among the advisers, who were all staring nervously as Adelheid paced the front of the room. One adviser, who Frieda suspected had picked the short straw, cleared his throat: "Your Majesty, it's possible that, after emerging from the Silence, they want to make a grand show that they're back among the Solar System. It could be a boon. If they come with supplies, it could solve our parts issue and eliminate the possibility that we might have to . . ." He grimaced, then coughed. ". . . consolidate our mobile resources."

Another adviser cleared their throat. "And, certainly, re-establishing contact with the old colonies acts as a powerful symbol."

Adelheid waved them off. "You don't send a message like that in haste. Advertising your return is something you stretch out over months. They're rushing here for something. Why would they come here first? Why not Mars and Venus?"

"Well, we are closer," Frieda replied, louder than she'd intended. The room fell silent. Everyone stared at her with frowns or furrowed brows. She stared back at them. *Why did everybody make this mistake?* "We travel in orbits, remember? Because we're closest to the Sun and have the shortest year, we spend the least amount of time on the opposite side of our orbit in relation to the other planets."

Brows cleared. People nodded. Even Adelheid. "Still," she said. "It's worth asking what they want, to come so quickly."

Frieda shrugged. "Maybe we can ask when we meet them at Terminal?"

Again, the room focused on her. Adelheid glared. Frieda flushed to feel their gazes, but she pressed on. "They've asked to meet us there, and from what I've heard, they're already on their way. If we pepper them with questions about the purpose of their visit, it looks . . . unwelcoming." Her mind returned to the people cheering and singing the Earth's anthem in the agora. "We're not that."

The room looked back at Adelheid, who continued to frown at Frieda. "Don't you have a medical appointment, Frieda?"

Frieda raised an eyebrow. "*Had*, Grandmother. They finished the work they needed to do."

Adelheid's eyes narrowed. "I'll schedule another one, then. If you have time and energy to be up and about, you have time and energy to work on adapting to your prosthetic."

Frieda raised both eyebrows. "But—"

"Go, Frieda," Adelheid snapped. "I'll deal with this myself."

Cheeks burning, Frieda left the room. As the door shut behind her, she heard her grandmother say, "We can't wait until Terminal to ask our questions. We need to know what we're going to say to the Earth, and we need to speak with one voice. Contact the *Hermes* president."

Frieda fumed as she strode back to her bedroom. *I didn't want to be Stadtholder, and Grandmother has always held that against me. Now, when I try to help, she shoots me down? What in Sunlight does she want from me?*

*I know what she wants: she showed me off on the parapet. She wants me to be a pretty and inspiring symbol of resilience. And symbols don't get to talk.*

She swept back into her bedroom and slammed the door with her good hand. Flopping onto her bed, she saw her breakfast cart laid out beside her and, before she could think about it, shoved it back hard.

She regretted it the moment the cart left her fingers. She cringed as the cart rolled into the wall with a crash. It wobbled, and plates clattered, but nothing fell. Eventually, it came to rest. She stared at the cart, breathing heavily, as silence descended.

*You are acting like a spoiled child,* said Grandmother's voice in her head.

Then she heard her mother's voice: *You are acting like somebody in grief and pain.*

She closed her eyes against tears and thought, *I am acting like both.*

She struggled back up from her bed to turn off the lights. She moved to tap the media screen off, but her bandaged hand interfered with the gesture. She tried again, sucking her teeth in frustration, and succeeded only in turning up the volume.

"The president of the *Hermes* is issuing a statement replying to the Earth's second message," said the newscaster with professional urgency. "We are joining the *Hermes* broadcast in progress."

The picture cut to a view of the *Hermes* president standing behind a podium and before a wall showing the seal of the city — the old logo of a blue circle cut through by a yellow rocket tail, with the words *Agencia Espacial Brasileira* beneath. He was already speaking. ". . . welcome the Earth's offer and would be delighted to host the planet's envoys as we restore relations. Our representatives stand ready to meet the Earth's ion ship at Terminal in two weeks." He tapped his tablet, smiled at the cameras, and stepped back.

The newscaster flipped back into view. "At this time, there has been no message from the Office of the Stadtholder on behalf of the *Messenger*," he said. "Requests for comment have not been answered."

Frieda stared at the screen.

*Uh, oh.*

# CHAPTER 10
# NERVE MAPPING

NOT MUCH LATER, FRIEDA WAS HURRYING ALONG THE HALLWAY TO the meeting room. *So, Crown Princesses* can *be summoned.*

"Do I have to wear this?" She said to Anna, who hurried alongside her. "Seriously?"

"It was the Dowager's instruction, your highness," Anna replied. "You have to look your best for the meeting with the *Hermes* ambassador, so the full uniform is required."

*Fair enough,* thought Frieda. *If I'm to be a symbol of* Messenger *unity while Grandmother gives the* Hermes *ambassador a talking-to for the* Hermes *president's speech. I just wish my prosthetic wouldn't jounce so.*

*It's interesting that Anna called Grandmother's summons an "instruction" and not an order. Maybe one stadtholder can't order another one around . . .*

There wasn't much time to think about this before she hurried into the meeting room. They arrived to see Adelheid seated at a wide table and the *Hermes* ambassador taking her seat on the other side. Two *Hermes* officials stood behind the ambassador. Adelheid looked up as Frieda entered, then nodded at the seat beside her. Frieda came over and sat.

Adelheid dismissed Anna and turned back to the *Hermes* ambassador. "Thank you for coming," she said to everyone, but her glare was focused on the ambassador.

"You're welcome, Your Majesty," Alanza replied. "Though I don't know why you summoned me."

Adelheid's glare intensified. "What was your president thinking when he extended the invitation to Earth to come to Terminal?"

The ambassador raised an eyebrow. "Besides the fact that they're already on the way, and it seems rude to turn them back? I believe my president thinks that it might be a productive—nay, historic—meeting! A chance to reconnect with what used to be the dominant power in the solar system, which still holds the majority of the solar system's easily extractable resources and, better yet, the ships to deliver them, it seems."

Adelheid glowered. "We don't know what they want, and the *Hermes* president has no authority to speak for all of Mercury."

Alanza straightened in her seat. "The President did *not* speak for all Mercury, Your Majesty. He spoke only for the *Hermes*, which he has every authority to do. The *Hermes* has access to Terminal, just like the *Messenger*.

"Inviting the Earth delegation to Terminal affects all of Mercury," Adelheid snapped. "The Earth is coming as one agency; we need to speak with a single voice."

"You speak of them as if they're invaders," said Alanza. "I doubt invaders would herald their arrival with such messages of greeting. And even if it's true that there has to be a single voice for Mercury, I object—and I know that my president would object—to your implication that *you* are the only one who can act as that voice. You speak only for the *Messenger* and your client towns, and only for so long as those client towns choose to remain your client towns."

Frieda looked from her grandmother to the ambassador

and back. *This is escalating quickly and badly. Should I say something? What if I make things worse?*

Alanza leaned back in her chair. "Besides, Your Majesty, you don't have to meet with the Earth envoys. If you object so strongly to this meeting, feel free to sit it out."

Adelheid glared, and Frieda found she couldn't help but glare with her. *She may be right, but that's no reason to shine it over Grandmother.*

Alanza's smile widened. "Well, Your Majesty, I believe you have ably communicated your concerns regarding my president's invitation to the officials of Earth. I will pass those concerns on to him. Now that that's over with, is there anything else?"

Adelheid shot up from her seat. "We will revisit this."

Alanza stood more slowly and gave a little bow. "Until that time, then." She nodded at Frieda, who was still struggling from her chair, then strode from the room, her officials following her.

When the door clicked shut, Adelheid let out the breath she was holding. She drew in the cane she'd left leaning against the table and leaned on it.

Frieda stared at her. After a moment, Adelheid frowned at her. "What?"

Frieda slowed her breathing and willed herself down from all the tension that had been in the room. "What are you going to do?" she asked. "*Are* you going to skip the meeting?"

Adelheid laughed mirthlessly. "Of course not. The *Hermes* president has left me no choice."

Frieda drew back. "You're not going to try and stop this meeting, are you?"

Adelheid flashed her a look of disdain. "How can I? Terminal is neutral ground. Flores is right: the *Hermes* has as much right to it as we do. I can't stop them speaking for Mercury, even if they're making a mistake."

"*Are* they making a mistake?"

Adelheid flashed her another look, but Frieda stared back. Finally, Adelheid looked away. "They don't think," she snapped. "They don't *question!* Why is the Earth rushing to get here? What is so important to them that they should come so soon after they end their silence? *What do they want?*"

Frieda's brow furrowed. "Why do you think they want anything?"

Adelheid gave her a look of disdain. "Someday, you'll understand."

"I'm not a child," Frieda snapped.

"Compared to me, you most certainly are." Adelheid turned on her heel and, cane clicking, left the room, leaving Frieda staring. She hurried after her but didn't catch up until her grandmother stepped into the reception room and called over an adviser. "Alert the forebridge and the engine room: it's time to pick up speed."

The nameless adviser—*I should do something about that; they have names!*—looked up. "Your Majesty?"

"You heard me," said Adelheid. "I don't intend to let the *Hermes* beat us to Terminal. How fast can we go?"

The adviser picked up a tablet and ran her finger down the lines of figures. "Your Majesty, our energy stores are still only at fifty percent—"

"Fifty percent?" Adelheid nodded. "Good."

The adviser looked up sharply. "But, Your Majesty, that's barely enough energy to—"

"I know what this latitude town can do, Adjutant," said Adelheid firmly. "Tell the departments to get to work."

The adviser nodded and hurried off.

Frieda stepped forward. "Grandmother, what are you doing?"

Adelheid gave her a wry look. "Attending a meeting. I don't want to be late."

"But—"

"And I'm afraid that you will need to work as well." Adelheid nodded at Frieda's prosthetic and looked solemn. "We have to accelerate your medical appointments. We need you to get more used to that prosthetic."

Frieda tried to stop herself from wincing and failed. She stumbled through the first thoughts in her head, vetoing, *But it hurts.* Instead, she settled on. "What's the rush?"

"It's time for your apprenticeship to start," Adelheid replied. "If Mercury can't speak with one voice, I'm sure as sunlight going to make sure the *Messenger* does. We are going on a Grand Tour."

The door opened behind Frieda. Adelheid glanced over Frieda's shoulder. "Ah! Prime Minister Solberg. Welcome!" Frieda turned and saw more people entering. Adelheid added, "Thank you for bringing the cabinet." To Frieda, she said, "Now, if you'll excuse us, Granddaughter, I have work to do, and so do you."

She gave Frieda a pointed look. The Prime Minister and her cabinet looked from one stadtholder to the other. Frieda felt awkward.

With a sigh, she turned away and headed for her bedroom.

☿

SHE ARRIVED to find the medical team of Daskivic, Sara Vasser, and Cara waiting for her. She tried to cover her frustration and embarrassment with a wry smile. "Hello again. Did you even make it to the infirmary before the order came to come back?"

Cara matched Frieda's wry smile. Sara nodded irritably. Daskivic coughed politely. "It's of no matter," he said. "We are here to serve."

Frieda wrinkled her nose at that. She stepped to her bed and sat on it. Behind the medical team, she noticed Anna in the corner, folding sheets. The breakfast had been cleared away. She turned back to Daskivic. "Well, I'm still sorry to have to drag you back. Apparently, I have to look my best for the Grand Tour."

Anna perked up. Daskivic and Sara also looked impressed. Cara frowned at her colleagues, perplexed.

Frieda focused on Anna and her reaction. *Grand Tour. She's excited. I'd heard about a Grand Tour in the* Messenger's *past, but I must not have paid too much attention to it. I always looked forward to Terminal Day, instead.* "Anna," she called. "What do you know about the Grand Tour?"

Anna straightened up, reddening as everyone in the room stared at her. Frieda tried not to feel satisfaction at having that happen to someone other than herself. But Anna cleared her throat, gave a small bow, and said, "Your Highness. The last Grand Tour was when your mother, Queen Beatrix, came of age—though she wasn't queen then, and neither was your grandmother, only Stadtholder. Still, your grandmother walked your mother along the length of the *Messenger*. They visited every department and met all the workers. This was to intro-duce the *Messenger* to the next stadtholder, and the next stadtholder to the *Messenger*."

Frieda nodded. "Thank you, Anna." *Though how this Grand Tour is different from the pre-apprenticeship field trips I took during the last weeks of school is anybody's guess.*

Then the answer settled on her stomach like a swallowed ingot. *Because those trips were only to introduce the departments to the children. This visit is to introduce me, the child. I'm going to be on display almost constantly.* She sighed.

"So, how long do we have?" Cara asked.

The pitch of the *Messenger* picked up. The floor vibrated harder. Everyone in the room wobbled as acceleration pushed them toward the tail section.

"Not long, I think," Frieda replied. She focused on the

medical team. If she'd had both hands, she would have put them on her hips. She settled for the one, however. "So, I have to ask: how much is this going to hurt?"

☿

A LOT, as it turned out. Frieda stifled a yell as multiple jolts shook her residual arm.

Worse was when they connected electrodes to her tricep and ran the wires to the prosthetic on the table, winding up the clockwork within. Sara turned to her. "Now, Your Highness. Think about closing her left fist."

Frieda didn't want to think about that; it reminded her she didn't have one. But the reminder was enough to make her remember, and she felt a shudder in her residual arm.

The fingers flailed. The elbow bent. The prosthetic jerked so violently that it rose from the desktop, the violence increasing as Frieda gaped and cringed until Cara ducked in, flipped a switch, and cut the power.

Silence descended, save for Frieda's ragged breathing.

"Not bad," said Daskivic at last.

"What?" Frieda gaped at him.

"It's getting a good signal from your remaining nerves," he replied. "The challenge will be learning to control those impulses."

Frieda looked from Daskivic to the prosthetic and back. The thing now looked alive but occupied by a dormant intelligence that wasn't her own. She glared at the prosthetic as if she expected it to glare back and took a deep breath. "Do what you need to do, Dr. Daskivic."

The team kept going. The periods of boredom became periods of relief as the medical team shifted from nerve mapping to working on the prosthetic, and at least then, Frieda could sidle closer, glance over shoulders, and observe the mix of gears, control rods, and electronic receptors—half of which, she noticed, weren't working and were being removed. She also observed that there were no replacement electronics alongside the shiny new gears and control rods placed beside the increasing pile of rusted components and electronics.

Lunch arrived, but Frieda still didn't have the appetite to eat. Daskivic, Sara, and Cara frowned at this—Cara especially —but took a short break at Frieda's order, crunching a few bac-crackers before getting back to work and leaving Anna to take it away.

The afternoon became like the morning. At one point, Frieda stared at the media screen to distract herself. She caught news of more protests on the *Baxter-Nordley*, the *Messenger*'s terse welcome message to Earth, and her grandmother announcing the Grand Tour to start tomorrow.

Still, the medical work continued—more nerve mapping, more work on the prosthetic—with no obvious progress. Sara looked frustrated. Cara looked concerned. Daskivic tried to keep things light, but as another jolt shook her residual arm, Frieda let out a strangled scream and pulled back as far as she could. "Stop! Enough!"

The medical team flinched, with Daskivic and Sara backing away. Cara came forward to undo the buckles around Frieda's residual arm and remove the equipment. Frieda exhaled grate-fully as Cara gently rubbed Frieda's tricep, but she glared at the heavy, useless prosthetic. "Are we actually making progress with this thing?"

Daskivic and Sara looked at her in consternation and—to Frieda's shock and disgust—fear. *I don't want to make people around me fear for their jobs. Still, it* hurts!

She took a deep breath, then let it go. "Look, I know we've only been at this for two sessions. But none of you look happy. Where do things stand?"

Daskivic coughed. "It's . . . early days, Your Highness," he muttered.

"Definitely early," Sara added, unable to meet Frieda's glare.

"It *is* early," Cara said softly. "This takes a while. But . . ." She stopped, but not before Frieda heard the "but" and saw the pointed look Daskivic gave her.

Frieda looked from Cara's sympathetic gaze to Daskivic and Sara, neither of whom could face her. "What aren't you telling me? You said this prosthetic was taken from the stores; surely it was working before. Somebody made use of it. So, why is it so hard to adapt?"

Daskivic coughed again. "Your Highness. We should probably end this session here and take things up tomorrow—"

*I'll be on the Grand Tour tomorrow, lugging that thing around in its dead state. When is Daskivic going to have time to stab me with electrodes and current?*

*Unless Grandmother put something on my schedule for next evening. She probably did.*

Cara cleared her throat and turned to Daskivic. "Meneer Daskivic, it has been a long shift. If you would like, I can stay behind and clean up while you and Mufrau Vasser call it a day."

Daskivic looked as though he couldn't decide whether to be shocked, suspicious, or offended and settled on all three. "That sounds like a good idea," Frieda cut in and accepted Daskivic's look of shock as it focused on her. He dared not object, but Frieda stared back, daring him to anyway.

After a moment, he bowed. "As you wish, Your Highness." He frowned again at Cara, then hurried a startled Sara out the door. The door clicked shut.

Cara and Frieda turned to face each other. For a moment, neither could think of anything to say.

"You're not eating," said Cara suddenly.

Frieda rolled her eyes. "You noticed?"

"Yes," Cara replied. "I've also noticed that you're swaying."

Frieda blinked. The room had seemed too unsteady to risk standing up from her bed. She'd thought it was the extra speed boost of the Messenger, but as she focused on the feeling, she felt the empty whoosh of light-headedness. But her stomach was in no mood for food. Defiantly, she said, "So?"

"So? You need to eat! Especially after a medical trauma like yours."

"Well, what are you going to do about that? Force-feed me?"

Cara raised an eyebrow. "I'm pretty sure that would get me arrested and deported."

"Not if Grandmother ordered you to do it," Frieda grumbled.

Cara folded her arms across her chest. "I wouldn't do it if she did."

"Then you'd be disobeying orders," said Frieda. "That would also get you arrested and deported. You're burned either way."

"Well . . ." Cara stepped forward and sat on the bed beside Frieda. She looked at her earnestly. "Then I would choose what causes the least amount of harm. But either way, you still need to eat."

Frieda sighed. Then she tilted her head and looked directly at Cara. "What did you want to tell me? Daskivic clearly didn't want you to say it, so I doubt that it was 'you need to eat more.'"

Cara got up and started to gather the equipment together and put everything away. "You asked why we aren't making progress with this prosthetic. Daskivic and Sara are right: these are early days. Nobody expects a fully functioning prosthetic in a day; this takes weeks and months of physiotherapy."

"I know that," Frieda replied. "But you added 'but.' What was the 'but'?"

Cara paused before she closed the lid on the prosthetic's case. "What Daskivic is reluctant to tell you is that, no matter how much we work on this prosthetic, whatever we do isn't going to give you something that will be very functional. It's going to be heavy and cumbersome."

She turned to Frieda. "Daskivic is a good doctor, and Sara will be in a few years, but this team they've formed for you is entirely medical. That's not the right way to do things. We're here to make this prosthetic work for you, but that's impossible because this prosthetic is not designed for you. It's designed for someone else. To make something that works best for you requires . . . an engineer."

Frieda raised an eyebrow. *I wanted to be an engineer. I could take this project on.* She glanced at her residual arm and drooped. *No. I can't.* "So, we don't have the right people to do this."

Cara looked down. "That's right."

Frieda looked away for a moment. Then she looked back at Cara. "Thank you."

Cara frowned and tilted her head.

"For doing the best you can," Frieda went on. "Be sure to tell that to Daskivic and Vasser, will you? But also, thank *you*. For your honesty."

Cara nodded. She smiled as she turned and packed away the prosthetic and closed its case. "Well, unlike Daskivic and Sara, I've no interest in bowing before you. And I suspect you wouldn't fire me for being honest."

"Still, it's refreshing," said Frieda.

There was a knock at the door. It opened, and Anna entered, pushing a cart of trays laden with dinner. She lifted lids, set them aside, curtsied, then stepped out. Frieda glanced at the cart and groaned.

Cara gestured at the cart. "You still need to eat, though. That's my honest assessment."

Frieda's face soured. "I could fire you for being a nag, you know."

Cara gave her a wry look. "Would you rather this be at my suggestion or your grandmother's order?"

Frieda sighed and levered herself to her feet. "You're right. I should—" She stopped by the cart of trays, staring.

At her silence, Cara came forward. "What?" She followed Frieda's gaze to the plates of protein loaf and bac-crackers. The protein loaf was a slab two centimetres thick and ten centimetres to a side. Nothing had been cut into bite-sized pieces.

Cara gasped. "Dawnfire! What in Sunlight were the galley staff thinking? You should send this back; tell them—"

"Cara?" Frieda's voice was tight. The young woman stopped and stared at her. Frieda swallowed. "I don't want to make a big thing over this."

Cara looked back at the meal, then sighed. "Fair enough." She picked up the knife and fork and plated the protein loaf. "I'm on overtime already. Another hour won't hurt, will it?" She began cutting the loaf into smaller pieces.

# CHAPTER 11
# THE GRAND TOUR BEGINS

THE GRAND TOUR STARTED THE NEXT MORNING AT THE REAR OF the *Messenger*.

Frieda strode from the tram, wearing a white dress with the orange sash of the Stadtholder across her chest and shoulder, her medical team hurrying after her. She winced as her prosthetic jounced against her side and tugged at her residual arm. "I understand why I have to wear this," she grumbled to Daskivic on her right, gesturing with her head at her prosthetic. "I even understand why I have to wear *this*." She nodded at her dress with its long skirt—possibly the only dress on Mercury; even if it didn't trip her ankles, it was laughably impractical. "But I don't understand why all three of you have to follow so close."

"Your grandmother's orders, Your Highness," Daskivic replied.

"I guess it wouldn't do to have me faint while on tour," she muttered. She couldn't see Sara tagging along behind them. Cara was on her left. She gave Frieda an encouraging smile.

*Well*, thought Frieda, *at least I can appreciate the company.*

"So, what did you give me?" she asked the air. *If Daskivic won't answer, maybe Cara will.* "I feel like I did during the funeral. Everything's clear as glass and about as brittle." Her brow furrowed. "And *how* did you give it to me?" There'd been no needles. "In my sleep? Or did you slip me something at breakfast?"

"Um . . ." Daskivic coughed, and Frieda's look hardened into a glare.

"It's a stimulant," Cara replied. "It's not often prescribed because it predates the Silence, and stocks are low." She looked ahead, and her eyes narrowed. "They've been made available for . . . this occasion, though."

Frieda looked from Cara to Daskivic and back. "Grandmother's orders?"

Daskivic cleared his throat. "Yes, Your Highness."

Frieda rolled her eyes. "You need to get that looked at. You could be spreading germs to your patients."

Daskivic looked away. "Sorry, Your Highness."

They entered the agora outside the tail section's command centre and found Adelheid waiting, surrounded by people, including reporters. Frieda spotted Prime Minister Solberg and most of her cabinet. She noticed officials from the *Messenger*'s client towns and also the *Hermes* ambassador. Her grandmother stood with her back straight, well aware of her audience, showing it by not showing it.

Frieda faced forward. "I wish that people would tell me what medicines I'm taking, especially if somebody else is deciding that I should take them."

Cara perked up and flashed Daskivic a firm look. Daskivic looked uncomfortable, but he nodded. "I'll make a note of that, Your Highness."

As they approached, Adelheid turned and nodded at her. She wore the navy blue dress uniform with the orange sash that she'd worn at the funeral.

The two entourages merged and stepped through the

shutter clicks of the reporters. The doors to Command and Control opened as they approached.

Frieda wasn't surprised that the Grand Tour started at the tail section's Command and Control. She wasn't surprised by all the reporters from the Journalists' Guild. If you were going to tour something like the *Messenger*, it made sense to start at one end. And, as this Grand Tour was Grandmother's way to highlight her hold on the *Messenger* and show she deserved the respect of all of Mercury, she needed an audience. It also didn't surprise her that Command and Control was a construction zone, rebuilding after its exposure to the Sun.

What surprised her was how unprepared she was to see the scaffolding and temporary shields placed over the windows— the windows her mother and her staff had been blown out of. They drew her eyes the moment she entered, and she knew what they meant in a way that made her jaw ache.

Hammers clanged and welders hissed as the Grand Tour entourage and its orbital cloud of reporters entered. As the group spread out along the viewing platform, construction workers looked up and then set aside their tools to stand at attention. The chatter of construction faded to an expectant silence.

Frieda tore her gaze away from the blank, sealed windows to look at her grandmother. She saw Adelheid staring at those same windows, her jaw set tight. She said nothing as the silence lengthened. Then, before the pause became too uncomfortable, she looked away and faced the assembled workers.

"We remember those who stayed at their posts," she said huskily. "We remember those who sacrificed their lives for the *Messenger*. We move forward in their memory."

Reporters brought up cameras. Shutters clicked as Adelheid, wearing the wrought-iron crown, and then Frieda, wearing no crown, and then everyone else bowed their heads for a moment of silence.

*I'm starting to* hate *silences,* Frieda thought. The prosthetic pulled at her. Her remaining fingers twitched. She fidgeted in her mind, focusing on whatever minute details her lowered gaze fell upon, from the scuff mark on a construction worker's shoe to the seam of a uniform to the way a display flashed—anything that kept her mind wandering toward the memory of her mother. Then she realized how disloyal this made her feel and thought about her mom. She closed her eyes against tears.

Silence stretched.

Finally, Adelheid relaxed, and that was the signal. The attendants gathered closer. Amid the locust buzz of the cameras, Adelheid turned toward the door. Realizing eyes were now on her, Frieda followed. They and their entourages left Command and Control, the doors forcing their group into an elongated oval shape with a comet's tail of journalists behind them. Daskivic, Sara, and Cara walked with Frieda, but Frieda said nothing, lost in her thoughts about the tail section and Mom.

At the far end of the agora outside, a new crowd waited: residents living nearby, families of the command centre officers, and related support workers. Stalls had been set up, offering food. The air was filled with special cooking smells. The crowd cheered as the royal entourage approached.

Despite herself, Frieda's stomach rumbled. The staff were grilling a celebratory cull of chickens, and that smell alone was a rare treat—in the kitchens, the typical smell was of their staple diet of steamed soy-protein loaf.

More shutters clicked, bringing Frieda back to the present. Ahead of her, she saw Adelheid give the crowd a dignified smile and wave. Dutifully, Frieda followed suit, waving the glove over her remaining hand.

She gritted her teeth against the bombardment. *This is going to get old fast.* She focused on smiling and waving, so she didn't notice her first classmate until they were almost past.

She turned back, the sample on its toothpick between her thumb and remaining finger. "Alfons?"

She saw him look up from behind the grill, dressed in white, holding tongs. She looked so completely in his element she couldn't help but grin. "Alfons!" she called again.

Alfons saw her, then ducked his gaze. He looked flustered as the moment stretched. He said nothing before the entourage moved forward, leaving Frieda no choice but to follow, putting Alfons out of sight.

She moved ahead, frowning. *Why didn't he say anything to me?*

The tour moved from the rear agora to a nearby childcare centre attached to Frieda's old school. Memories of assignments and presentations in each room leaped out at Frieda like old ghosts. Her model of the *Messenger* on its Robinson Rail graced the display case at the entrance.

The staff, including new apprentices, stood to attention outside the office as Adelheid made another speech, this one about hope for the future. Frieda waited, ignoring the ache growing in her left shoulder.

The audience stayed at attention while Adelheid came forward to shake hands. Frieda followed, keeping her hands to her sides. Each apprentice bowed for each of them. Frieda, feeling awkward, hurried along the line, barely making eye contact until she came to the end of the row, where she looked up from her bow to see Linde staring back at her.

"Hey," said Frieda, beaming. "How have you been?"

Linde went scarlet and shifted her gaze down. "I'm fine, Your Highness." She shifted on her feet like she wanted to back away. "You're looking—" Her eyes widened as she thought through her next words. "It—it is good to—to see you," she finally stuttered.

Frieda stared at her old friend. "What—"

But Adelheid was already heading for the door, and security was closing in. Frieda was swept up in the entourage and hurried away. She tried to look back at Linde, but her view was blocked by trailing reporters.

They left the childcare centre and entered the old school, where the teachers and administrative staff stood waiting patiently to be greeted. When Frieda reached the first person in line, she came face to face with Meneer Koske. She smiled at him and came forward, stopping when he coughed, lowered his gaze, and bowed. "Your Highness," he said gruffly.

Frieda didn't gape, though it took a moment before she returned his bow. "Meneer Koske," she replied, then moved away as the entourage hustled her along.

*What in Sunligh?* she thought as she left her old school and walked with the entourage toward the tram. *Why do my friends —my teacher, even!—treat me like I'm some dangerous artifact? Alfons, Linde, and Meneer Koske could barely look at me. Is it the prosthetic? Or do they see me so differently now that I'm the Crown Princess and Co-Stadtholder? Why did they change? Did I change that much?*

As she settled into her seat and the tram started forward, leaving the first group of reporters behind, a grim thought settled on her.

*None of us have changed. Maybe it's always been this way. Maybe they were charged to treat the Stadtholder's daughter as a student or a friend, to give me a normal childhood education, and now that their work is done, the walls haven't so much gone up as been uncovered.*

She leaned back and closed her eyes.

*Was any of it real?*

☿

A GLOOM SETTLED ON FRIEDA. It followed her to the bacterial farms, where her grandmother spoke of hope, loyalty, and sacrifice to workers who stood by the stinking algae vats and the stacks of iron bars freshly scraped of their extremophiles. Shifting on aching legs and losing interest in the speech, Frieda glanced out a porthole and saw, framed in the floodlights of the *Messenger*, workers walking the iron cornrows.

Two groups marched along the surface of Mercury at a steady walking pace, all in helmets and vacuum suits, each flanked by wagons pulled by land speeders. In front, the first group walked between the iron rods that had been pounded into rocky ground, full of bulbous bacterial growths. Using a hooked bar, they levered each one out and passed them into the waiting hopper. The second group pulled cleaned iron rods from their hopper and passed them out to others, who hammered them into the spaces left by the first rods. When the first hopper was full, the second, now empty, pulled up to take its place, while a third hopper, full of new rods, pulled up behind.

*If I was not a stadtholder, this might be my fate if I could not be an engineer.* She pressed closer to the porthole for a better look. *Prosthetics can be designed for these simple tasks. This is the job that falls to people who can't do anything else.*

*There is honour there*, she thought. *Without their work, Mercury would starve.*

*And Grandmother made it possible*, a smaller voice added at the back of her mind.

She shook that thought away. Turning back to the entourage, she thought, *It is hard, mindless work, but would I be happier there than I am here as a prop?*

They left the bacterial farm for the iron factory. Frieda winced at the red glare and the hot blast of the forges while her grandmother spoke again. Frieda's inactive prosthetic felt heavier and heavier, such that she wondered if she was beginning to lean to one side.

She became aware of Cara standing next to her. She'd

sidled away from Daskivic and Sara and leaned closer, frowning at her. "Are you all right?" Cara asked beneath her breath.

"Tired," said Frieda softly. "I think that drug might be wearing off."

Cara winced.

"How much more?" Frieda asked.

Cara gnawed her lip. "One more agora, I think. Then we break for the night."

Frieda sighed, then drew herself up. "Well, let's do this, then." *What choice do I have?*

She looked over at Adelheid and saw her grandmother frowning back at her, but the woman looked away quickly. The entourage hurried to the next tram stop.

They arrived at another agora, this one closer to the middle of the *Messenger.* The crowd here was larger than any Frieda had seen that day. They clapped as the entourage arrived, Adelheid waving. Frieda winced at the auditory onslaught. She raised her remaining hand in its glove and tried to smile.

A stage had been set up at the far end of the agora, and the entourage moved to it. As they mounted the steps, Frieda started to move toward the left of the podium, but suddenly, her grandmother turned and gently but firmly guided Frieda toward the right.

*That would put my residual arm and prosthetic between us. Oh, no. I'm not going to let this happen a second time.*

Frieda planted her feet and, when Adelheid, stepping forward, instead stumbled and had to back up, stepped around Adelheid and planted herself to the left of Adelheid's podium. She placed the remainder of her right hand on Adelheid's palm.

Adelheid's expression clouded with irritation, but Frieda stood firm and stared ahead at the crowd, smiling—more widely now than she had all afternoon. Finally, Adelheid clasped Frieda's hand and raised it with her own. The crowd roared.

Adelheid lowered her arm and let go, stepping to the podium. The crowd noise ebbed as people leaned in to listen.

"The Crown Princess and I stand with you," she said, "as we move ahead to meet the Earth. It is right and proper, as the Earth ends its silence, that Mercury speaks with one voice."

Frieda looked sidelong at her grandmother. Beyond Adelheid, she caught Cara's eye. She was frowning and clapping half-heartedly with the rest of the entourage. *That was a pointed message to the* Hermes, she thought, *and the protesters on the* Baxter-Nordley.

But the crowd cheered and chanted, "Stadholder!" mixed with "U.N.E! U.N.E!"

Frieda winced against the headache developing behind her eyes. She took a deep, steadying breath.

☿

As THE RALLY came to an end and the crowds started to disperse, Frieda turned to leave the stage, only to have Adelheid catch her good arm. Frieda looked at her grandmother. "What—?"

"One more thing," said her grandmother and pointed. Frieda followed her gesture to a corner of the agora, where a gaggle of reporters waited. She sighed.

Adelheid glared at her. "Stand up straight. This is important. You are the face of the *Messenger* also."

Frieda straightened up and hoped the heat in her cheeks wasn't a flush of embarrassment. If it was, Adelheid didn't comment. She strode toward the waiting reporters, Frieda in tow.

The questions started almost before they arrived.

"Your Majesty! Have you spoken with the *Hermes* president? What message did you convey about Earth?"

"Your Majesty! Do you believe the *Hermes* president is deliberately slighting you by forcing himself to the front of the line?"

"Your Majesty! What will be the protocol for when the Earth envoy's ship arrives? Will you be the first to greet them?"

Frieda blinked. This was a completely different attitude from when they'd first met the reporters that day. *Grandmother must have let them off their leash.*

But these were fair questions. Frieda looked at her grandmother.

Adelheid cleared her throat. "I had a productive conversation with the *Hermes* ambassador yesterday. We will be greeting the Earth delegation with all the grace and decorum such an event demands."

*How difficult is it to speak without answering the question? Is it a skill you acquire or something you fall into?*

The babble ebbed somewhat as the reporters wrote this down. Another reporter raised her hand. "Your Majesty, do you have any comment on today's protests on the *Baxter-Nordley*?"

Adelheid's gaze narrowed. "I have every confidence that the matter can be resolved peacefully and—"

"It's that," the reporter cut in, to Frieda's shock, "this time, the protesters say they don't intend to leave their agora. They've been there all afternoon."

Whether they intended to or not, Frieda saw the reporters around the young woman edge slightly away, but the woman stood tall, waiting for an answer. Frieda blinked and looked again.

It was her old classmate, Malika.

Adelheid faced her. "We value the people's right to express themselves. The protesters have made their point and continue to do so. I am confident that, once they're sure of this, these protests will end, and the matter will be resolved peacefully."

"Will the *Messenger* respect the results of a referendum if the citizens of the *Baxter-Nordley* vote for independence from the *Messenger*?" another reporter asked.

Adelheid gave this question an irritated, dismissive wave. "I will not comment on hypotheticals."

This sparked a wave of questions from the reporters. For a moment, Frieda couldn't hear individual ones above the cries of "Your Majesty! Your Majesty!"

Then suddenly, from the tumult came, "Your Highness!"

Frieda blinked at Malika, standing again, but this time looking at her. The rest of the reporters drew quiet. Malika shifted nervously but cleared her throat. "Your Highness," she said again. "How did it feel, earlier today, to stand in the spot where your mother, Queen Beatrix, gave her life while the *Messenger* stalled on the Dawn Line?"

Frieda stared at Malika. Malika stared back—not maliciously, Frieda realized, but with professional interest and nervousness. As the silence stretched, her cheeks reddened. Frieda felt her own blush rise. Everyone else's eyes were on both.

*What in Sunlight am I supposed to say? How did I feel? It hurt to be there and know what happened. It hurts even more to hurt in front of an audience.*

The silence stretched further and became uncomfortable. Then Frieda heard Adelheid draw breath to speak, and something snapped inside her.

"It . . . was hard," she said, her voice soft but carrying across the stillness. "It was hard being there, knowing what happened. But I'm . . . proud of my mother and . . . proud of what the construction workers have done in so short a time." She hesitated before she added, "They are an example to all of us, doing the job that's in front of them."

Having pushed that thought to its end, she stopped and found herself nodding in the silence that followed. And this silence wasn't as uncomfortable. "And I thank them," she added.

The reporters nodded and wrote in their tablets. Malika smiled as she did so. Beside her, Frieda heard her grandmother mutter, "Not bad."

"Your Highness?"

Frieda turned her head and saw a young man raise his hand. "Your Highness, do you have any comment on the *Messenger*'s race to Terminal? How important is it that the *Messenger* arrives first?"

Frieda knew how Grandmother would answer that question, all bravado. But as she opened her mouth to parrot her grandmother's words, she paused. She saw Cara watching from the audience, and the answer didn't seem right. *The* Hermes *and the* Messenger *share Terminal; they have as much right to be there as we do. And the Earth didn't call just to the* Messenger; *it called to all of us. How do I answer this?*

*But I don't have to answer the question, do I? Grandmother doesn't always answer the question provided to her; she just provides an* answer.

She cleared her throat. "We're looking forward to arriving at Terminal and greeting the envoys from Earth for the first time in fifty years. This is a momentous occasion for all Mercurians. We are privileged to be a part of it."

The reporters nodded and wrote things into their tablets, but Frieda felt her grandmother tense behind her.

Frieda did not look back.

☿

ADELHEID DID NOT SAY anything to Frieda even after they re-boarded the tram back to the Royal Apartment for the end of the first day of the tour. Her medical team did not accompany her. Anna met her in the reception room and walked with her to Frieda's bedroom. She helped take the prosthetic off before departing.

Frieda sat on her bed. The stimulant hadn't fully worn off. Not wanting to lie down and stare at the ceiling, she levered herself up and tapped the media screen.

The screen flickered onto two media pundits arguing. Their titles beneath their names on screen identified them as being from the *Leigh Brackett* and the *Anson-Bova*. Frieda frowned as she watched them gesticulate. *Former client cities of the* Messenger *and the* Hermes. *It's like they're fighting our battles by proxy here.* Without meaning to, she brushed the screen, tapping up the volume.

"The strikers of the *Baxter-Nordley* have every right to demand a say over their future," said the *Anson-Bova* pundit.

"I'm not arguing against that," said the *Leigh Brackett* pundit. "But there's no reason to cast the *Messenger* as such a villain as this rhetoric does. They will listen. My city is proof of that."

The *Anson-Bova* pundit scoffed. "The *Messenger*'s not going to give up its control over half of Mercury's water supply. You're lucky you voted for independence before the parts shortages became more acute, or they might be cannibalizing you for your tech now—"

The *Leigh Brackett* pundit shot forward in his seat. "Did you *actually* use *that word*?"

Silence descended. Frieda looked up at the screen to see the *Leigh Brackett* pundit and the moderator glaring at the *Anson-Bova* representative, who stared wide-eyed, mouth agape. Frieda could have heard a pin drop. She found herself holding her breath.

The *Anson-Bova* pundit swallowed, then looked at the table. "I'm sorry. I shouldn't have said that. Of course, I mean—"

The moderator cut in, and the camera focused on her. "Let's

take a break and listen to these updates from our community events announcer."

The camera cut to a woman at her desk, blinking, halfway through her lunch.

Behind Frieda, someone knocked. She turned in time to see Anna poke her head in. "Your Highness? The medical team is here; a final checkup for the day."

Frieda closed her eyes and sighed. "Fine. Send them in."

The door opened wider and Dr. Daskivic stepped in, followed by intern Sara Vasser and . . ., no one else.

Frieda frowned. "Where's Cara?"

Daskivic's expression clouded.

Frieda's frown deepened. If it were some harmless or legitimate reason, like the end of a shift, he wouldn't react like that.

Then Frieda looked at Sara. She looked angry. "Your Highness—" she began.

Daskivic shushed her.

She glared. "She asked—"

"Know your place, Mufrau Vasser!" Daskivic snapped.

"I order you to let her speak," said Frieda.

Daskivic flinched. Sara looked flustered, but not for long. "Mufrau Flores is no longer on this medical team," she replied. The anger gave way to confusion. "By your order, Your Highness."

Frieda straightened up. "I didn't make that order."

"By your grandmother's order, then," said Sara. "Either way, it came from the Stadtholder's office."

"Why?"

Sara shook her head. "The order didn't say."

Frieda turned away. *By Grandmother's order. Why?*

*Because Cara is the* Hermes *ambassador's daughter, and Grandmother doesn't like that connection so close to me. She thinks there'll be a conflict! She hated my answer to that reporter placing the*

Messenger *on the same level as the other latitude towns. Maybe she thought Cara had put that thought in my ear.*

If she had fists, Frieda would have clenched them. *Just because she doesn't like what someone might tell me, she orders that person away? The one person from my school today who treated me like me and not some precious artifact?*

*This cannot stand.*

She turned on Daskivic. "Where is Cara now?"

☿

FRIEDA DID NOT RUN into her grandmother as she left the Royal Apartment, which was fortunate, as she might have been the only person who could have stopped Frieda from going out the door. The security attendants had little recourse when, after they asked, "Your Highness, where are you going?" she replied, "Out!"

But she noticed that two officers followed her at a polite distance and boarded the tram with her. As long as they didn't try to stop her, she was content to ignore them. She let them flank her as she departed the tram at the stop closest to the infirmary.

It was a quiet night, and it got quieter when Frieda stepped through the door and the people in the waiting room looked up and stared. Suddenly, chairs scraped back as people stood to attention.

She mustered herself, took a quiet breath, and counted to five before she said levelly to the room, "Please, sit down." She strode to the reception desk. "Where is Cara Flores?"

"Um . . ." The receptionist flipped up screens on her tablet. "She is leaving her shift. I suppose she'd be in the locker room?"

Frieda nodded. "And where's that?"

After telling the two security officers to wait, Frieda strode into the locker room and was suddenly among jocular conversations with nurses and interns laughing. The conversations ebbed as she stepped farther among the lockers. Interns, halfway changed from civilian clothes to uniforms and vice versa, stared at Frieda. She gave them a quick nod, saying, "As you were." When she stepped past them, the conversations started up again, quieter this time.

Frieda didn't call out for Cara. Instead, she walked along the main walkway, glancing discreetly into the aisles of lockers and benches, before she found Cara sitting dejected.

Frieda stepped closer. "Cara?"

Cara jerked up. She stared at Frieda with a mixture of surprise and what struck Frieda as a touch of shame, then swallowed. With a quick glance at the rest of the locker room, she said, "Your Highness?"

"Enough of that." Frieda kept her voice down. "I heard you were taken off my medical team. Is that true?"

Cara gave a little half-shrug. She set aside a piece of paper, clearly trying not to make a show of it. Frieda picked it up with her remaining thumb and finger. She shook it out to try and get it angled right to read.

Cara winced. "Please—"

There wasn't much to read. *By order of the Office of the Stadtholder . . . Issues of security . . .* The message was clear.

Frieda passed the paper back. "What are you going to do now?"

Cara shrugged again. "Clean medical equipment, probably. Mark time, I guess."

"Aren't they reassigning you?"

Cara looked up. "The Stadtholder says she doesn't want me. Who else on the *Messenger* will have me? I may have to take my chances back on the *Hermes*."

Cara looked so dejected that anger surged in Frieda. "She can't do this!"

Cara frowned up at her. "Of course, she can."

Objections rose in Frieda. *No, she can't. You did your job, and you did it well. Grandmother has no right to take that away.*

But a thought struck her. *I'm listing all my objections. I'm thinking for myself, and I'm not the only one here.*

Frieda focused on Cara. "Okay. Maybe you're right. Maybe the fact that you're the *Hermes* ambassador's daughter makes things difficult for my grandmother, the Dowager Regent. But I'm Crown Princess, and that should count for something. However, the more important question is: what do *you* want?"

Cara looked up.

"You don't have to explain why you want what you want," Frieda went on. "Just tell me what you want."

Cara looked down for a long moment. Finally, she said, "I want to be a doctor."

Frieda nodded. "Okay."

"I want to be a doctor here," Cara added.

Frieda tilted her head. "You want to immigrate?"

Cara nodded.

Frieda straightened up. "Right. Finish changing, and come with me. We'll talk to somebody."

Cara frowned as she pulled on her jacket. "Who?"

Frieda led Cara out the door.

# CHAPTER 12
# FRIEDA AND HER FATHER

WHEN FRIEDA WAS THIRTEEN AND ON BREAK FROM SCHOOL, SHE found her father at a desk in the Royal Library, taking notes as he looked through a bundle of blueprints. Something in his expression, a wistfulness, slowed her down and softened her step as she approached. She sat quietly in a chair near his papers and watched him. Their eyes met briefly, and they shared a smile before he returned to his work.

After a long moment of silence, Frieda said, "Dad . . . ?"

Her father smiled. "Yes, sweetness?"

"Do you love Mom?"

The moment didn't chill, but it did congeal into awkwardness. Her father looked up from his blueprints into the air above the desk. He frowned, calculating. "Was it something I said?"

"No," she said quickly. "Nothing like that. I just wondered. Do you?"

"Yes," he said immediately. "Very much." Then, "Why do you ask?"

"So, you chose to marry Mom, then?" Frieda tilted her head. "Grandmother didn't make you?"

Her father sat back in his seat. "Ah." He looked at her. "Have you been . . . talking to somebody?"

She kept her gaze level. "I've been overhearing my classmates."

He looked back into the middle distance. "Ah."

"In kindergarten, my classmates told me I might have to marry an engineer when I grew up," said Frieda. "I remember I threw a tantrum over that."

Her father chuckled. "Yes, you did."

"Nobody's talked about it since," she cut back in. "But you *are* an engineer, Dad. So, what happened?"

He sucked his teeth. "It's complicated."

"Did you know Mom before you married her?"

"Of course," he said quickly. "We . . . knew each other from vocational school. Liked each other. A lot. But . . . it's complicated."

Frieda's gaze hardened. "What happened?"

He gnawed his lip a moment—not trying to avoid the answer, Frieda sensed, but merely trying to figure out how best to word it. He took a deep breath. "There were power issues. Your mother and I were dating. It was getting a little serious, and who knows what might have happened if things had been allowed to run their course, but . . ." He took another deep breath, then let it go. "The trackworkers guild . . . unionized. And I was their union leader."

Frieda straightened up. "Unionized? But the trackworkers are already a guild. Isn't that the same—?"

"It's sort of the same, but it's also different," he replied. "It's about attitude, really, and the trackworkers were . . . getting angry."

Frieda settled back to listen.

"It's a hard job down in the trackworks," said her father. "It's dirty, hot, and dangerous. But we're proud to do that work because it keeps the *Messenger* moving. That covers the sentiments of most of the guilds, in fact: it's hard work, but it keeps the *Messenger* moving. But sometimes the work gets too hard, and sometimes people forget how much others are giving of themselves in doing that hard work. And they lose respect for the work that people do.

"We needed more time to rest," he went on. "There needed to be more work on safety protocols and on rebuilding and maintaining systems to keep workers safe; some of them had degraded since the start of the Silence. It's a lot to ask in a closed system like the *Messenger*, but sometimes you have to ask. And if people don't listen, well . . . sometimes you have no choice but to strike."

Frieda's eyebrows shot up. "They didn't mention this in history class."

"I'm not sure everybody agrees on the narrative," her father replied. "Even the trackworkers don't like to talk about it because things got . . . heated. And someone made a mistake and things got . . . *very* heated. And finally, your grandmother intervened.

"She opened negotiations with the union leadership. She offered more rest periods and more workers assigned to safety maintenance. She did what she could. But things had already escalated to the point that the trackworkers weren't listening to union leaders like me. Protests had been quelled, and some wanted revenge. During another protest, things got out of hand, and a mob got violent, trapping Beatrix with some security officers."

Frieda straightened up, horrified.

Her father raised a hand soothingly. "Before the security officers had to fight their way out, I ran to the scene. I talked fast. I moved fast. I protected Beatrix until help could arrive— union workers I could trust. And when they came, and when I knew we were safe, in the relief of that moment, emotions got the better of your Mom and me and we . . ." He raised his eyebrows, and he shrugged. "We kissed."

Frieda tilted her head. She was old enough that the thought of her parents kissing didn't disgust her—much. Couples in love *should* kiss, even if she didn't see the point. And, yes, she could picture her mother, in the heat of the moment, kissing Dad, but . . . *this* was the start of their marriage?

Her father leaned on the table and stared into the middle distance, remembering. "It was a fraught moment, and a journalist caught it on camera. It went on the media, and your grandmother got an idea." He clenched his jaw a moment. "There are some traditions back on Old Mother Earth in which a power arrangement is sealed by a marriage uniting two kingdoms. Your grandmother and I had negotiated a fair deal, but what the trackworkers wanted was some sense that they were being listened to—that they had a seat at the table. The marriage was one way of demonstrating that. Your grandmother turned the trackworkers guild into a kingdom and ensured peace between it and the rest of the *Messenger* by marrying the king with the *Messenger's* future queen."

"That . . . makes no sense," said Frieda at last. "And you went along with it?"

"The alternative would not have been good for the *Messenger*," her father replied. "And it seemed to work. The local media took up the narrative—union leader falls in love with the Stadtholder's daughter, bringing peace between the levels of the *Messenger*. It was a symbol for everyone to rally around. It helped."

"Did it really?"

He nodded.

Silence stretched. Frieda's father looked down at his blueprints.

Frieda frowned at her father. "But, Dad . . . do you love Mom?"

He looked her in the eye. "Yes."

☿

"WHERE ARE WE GOING?" Cara asked as Frieda strode out of the Infirmary, attracting stares. She followed Frieda across the corridor, the security officers hurrying after them both toward the doors to the government offices. Frieda was reaching for the door handles when she remembered she only had her residual arm and two remaining fingers on her other hand.

*It's amazing I could forget that, even for a moment,* she thought.

Cara hurried past and opened the door for her.

"Thanks," Frieda muttered as she strode through.

The receptionist looked up and then stood up. "Your Highness! To what—"

"Is the Prime Minister still here?" Frieda asked. "She and her cabinet haven't left, have they?"

"Actually, Prime Minister Solberg left five minutes ago," the receptionist replied. "But your father stayed behind." He pointed. "I believe he's researching in the government library."

Frieda sighed. "I guess he'll do." She turned and walked. "Come on, Cara."

They strode past desks and meeting rooms, their footsteps softened by the worn carpet. The hallway lights were dimmed for the night shift and flickered, but ahead, the library lights shone bright and steady.

Frieda entered and spotted her father at the head of a long table, a file box open beside him. He stood, sorting through the papers. Frieda frowned as she stared at him. *He looks . . . tired.*

He looked up and smiled as Frieda entered. "Hello, sweetness." His brow furrowed as he saw her expression and then Cara and the two security officers. "What's going on?"

Frieda turned back to Cara and held out her remaining hand. "The letter, please."

Bewildered, Cara handed it over. Frieda passed it to her father. "Why has Cara been removed from my medical team?"

Her father unfolded the paper and read it. He scratched the back of his neck. "Ah."

Frieda shot him a look. "You knew about this?"

"No." He handed the letter back to Cara. "However, I can see your grandmother's point." He nodded at Cara. "No offence, Mufrau Flores."

Cara waved a hand to show none was taken.

"First of all, we're not at war with the *Hermes*," Frieda snapped. "This letter makes them sound like we're enemies. This security concern is . . ." She waved her remaining hand in frustration. "Silly! And don't *I* get a say in this? Grandmother may be Regent, but it's *my* medical team."

"Well . . ." Her father frowned down at her. "*Did* you ask for a say in this?"

"How could I?" Frieda yelled. "Nobody asked me! How can you stand by and let Grandmother take over . . . everything?"

Her father raised a hand. "I only said that your grandmother had a point; I didn't say that you didn't. Have you tried talking to anyone about your staffing requirements?"

"No," said Frieda, her anger cooling. *I can do that?* "And as for talking to someone, I came here to see the Prime Minister. I found you, instead."

He looked away, eyebrows raised. "All things considered, it's probably better that you found me and didn't start a constitutional crisis. However, maybe this will help." He grabbed a tablet off the centre of the table, swiped through some files, and then placed it in front of her. "Have a look at this."

Frieda peered down at the columns of numbers. "What is this?"

"It's the budget of the *Messenger*," he replied. "A brief summary, anyway. Now, before you rebuke me, let me draw your attention to lines four and five, which are the royal budget.

Those two lines guide what you can spend. This includes office budgets, retaining servants and advisers, and hiring researchers."

Frieda peered closer but couldn't see those items. She saw numbers. She tried clasping the tablet in her remaining thumb and finger and struggled as it started to tilt out of her grip. Cara stepped forward and held up the drooping end.

Then Frieda blinked and looked again. "*Two* numbers? Why are there two numbers?" She looked at her father, realization dawning. "Because there are two Stadtholders."

He nodded. "You each control half the budget."

She gaped and looked at the numbers again. "I control a budget? What am I spending it on? The numbers are the same."

"Well, the details are on the next few pages," her father replied, "though you may need an accountant to walk you through them. However, I would wager that, in the absence of any input from you, your grandmother assigned you mostly servants and took more advisers for herself."

Frieda looked at the tablet again. "Well . . . if I understand you right, a position has become available for me to fill." She passed the folder over to Cara, stepped forward, and hugged her father. "Thank you, Dad!"

He gave her a squeeze. "You're welcome."

Frieda turned away to walk out of the library. Cara looked in confusion at the tablet and started to hand it back to Frieda's father. "Keep it," Frieda said. "We need it. Come on, Chief Medical Adviser Flores."

"What?" Cara exclaimed. She hurried after Frieda as they left the government offices. "What did you call me?"

"I can't force my grandmother to reassign you back to your old medical team, it seems," said Frieda. "So, I'm making a new team. You are my chief medical adviser."

"Ah . . ." Cara blinked and stared as they entered the tram

that the security officers had cleared for them. "That's good, I guess. But . . ."

Frieda looked at her. "But what?"

"What about the paperwork?"

She nodded at the tablet in Cara's hand. "That's your first assignment."

"Ah." Cara tapped at the screen. "Thank—" She stuttered to a stop, then looked closer at the page. Her mouth dropped open. "Um . . ." She tapped the screen dark. "Should I be seeing this? These are . . . documents. *Messenger* documents."

Frieda glanced at the tablet. It did not say "Top Secret" on it. It didn't say anything. "You're my adviser, now. This means you get to see the documents that I give you." She frowned. "But that wasn't why you stopped. What did you see?"

Cara flipped open the page again. "We have the manifest of the approaching Earth shuttle. It's being relayed to all the city governments. They're bringing a lot of supplies." She turned the tablet and pointed at a chart. "Apple slices. Animal proteins. There's even plastic . . . and 3D printers." She looked at the manifest again. "I wonder if they're industrial scale."

Frieda resisted the urge to pull the tablet back. "We haven't had 3D printers for . . . decades." *Not since shortly after the Blacksmiths' Guild was established, anyway.*

And the 3D printers from Earth before the Silence didn't just print out plastic or metal, either: they wove carbon, even cellular material. The best printers could print cells, even organs and body parts—

She took a deep breath, held it, and let it go. *I'm getting ahead of myself.*

She leaned closer. "These 3D printers. Could they do prosthetics?"

Cara looked up. "Easily."

# PART FOUR
# ADELHEID: IN THE FAR DARK

# CHAPTER 13
# DAMAGE ASSESSMENT

*The* Messenger
*Mercury Colonies, October 30, 2151 CE*
*Eighty-eight days after the fall of Earth*

ADELHEID SAT AT HER DESK IN HER QUARTERS. USING TONGS, SHE pulled a petri dish from the portable forge and set it down on a ceramic tile. She peered at it through a micro-lens. After a moment, she sighed. On the ledger beside her, she wrote: *Sample 42, Fertilizer 14: Insufficient growth.*

She traced her finger up the page. Line after line: *Insufficient growth.*

Beneath her feet, the *Messenger* purred. She took comfort in that. She flipped the ledger closed.

Her stomach gnawed.

Her intercom chirped. "Captain Koning?" An adjutant's voice. "Lieutenant Fang told me to inform you when we were ten kilometres from the Dusk Line. Terminal should be appearing within the hour. We're almost at the wreck site."

Adelheid's jaw tightened, but she nodded. "Thank you. I'll be there shortly."

The intercom clicked off. She pushed back her seat and stood up. She gripped her desk as she swayed. She took a deep, steadying breath.

Her gaze fell on the corner of her desk and her father's iron key. *His last gift.*

After a moment, she took it, slipped it into her pocket, and walked out the door.

☿

THE *MESSENGER* PLODDED through the Far Dark, slowing as the crew spotted the flares of the setting Sun's corona above the horizon. Terminal gleamed in the Sun's last rays, but as the *Messenger* approached, the gleam faded, then cut out as Terminal entered the night.

The *Messenger* stopped a half-kilometre from the spaceport. For a while, nothing moved.

Then, an airlock opened. A land speeder raised dust as it sped along the surface of Mercury.

☿

LIAO PRESSED his hand against the wall of the land speeder as it jounced. He peered through the porthole as the walls of Terminal gleamed in its searchlights. "Looks untouched."

"Hmm?" Adelheid frowned at the buzz of Liao's voice in her helmet's radio. Her eyes were on the Robinson Rail. "What was that, Lieutenant?"

"I said, Terminal looks untouched," Liao replied.

Between them, Adjutant Levi Janssen let out a chuff. "I'm surprised the *Apollo* and the *Hermes* didn't tear the place down for salvage." He chuckled morosely. "I'd be surprised if they left our wreck alone."

Liao frowned at Levi. "Why did you get this assignment? Aren't you third shift?"

Levi shrugged. "They moved me up after Herbert died."

Adelheid jerked up, then touched her comm. "What happened to Herbert?"

"Accident," said Levi. "He was repairing a junction box and crossed the wrong wires."

Liao shuddered.

Adelheid's brow furrowed. *I remember that report. I hadn't connected it to Herbert. Poor man.* Out loud, she said, "I see." *How many accidents does that make this month? Five? Six? We're getting sloppy.*

*No. We're getting tired. We're getting hungry. Tired and hungry people make mistakes. The* Messenger *is falling apart, and so are they. We need good news, and there won't be any for a while, if ever.*

Levi pointed ahead. "There's the tail section."

Adelheid and Liao leaned to peer out the front window.

The land speeder skidded and bounced alongside the Robinson Rail. Ahead, the trench and pillars of the rail ended abruptly, with a section ahead rising out of the ground at a sharp angle. Around and ahead of it, cement crumbled to boulders. Ahead of that, the combined wrecks of the *Messenger's* tail section and Earth's fallen shuttle stood out as a single mountain of twisted metal.

"So, the *Hermes* and the *Apollo* left this alone as well," said Liao.

Levi shrugged. "Well, they probably didn't have enough time to salvage—"

"No," said Adelheid, quietly but firmly, "It's a fresh grave site. They wouldn't touch it."

They drove on in silence.

They skirted around a crumpled rocket booster and parked the land speeder as close as they could to the bulk of the tail section. Levi shut off the engines. After a check of their vacuum suits, they unhooked their seatbelts and Adelheid slapped the door release. The cabin depressurized as the locks disengaged.

They stepped onto the surface, the beams of their helmet lamps playing across the stones and gleaming off hunks of mangled steel. The dust gave slightly beneath their feet, like styrofoam atop concrete. They marched in silence. Adelheid looked up at the ten-storey ruin of the tail section and saw broken portholes. The rooms and corridors beyond sucked in their light and gave nothing back.

Suddenly, Levi shouted into his radio. Adelheid flinched and swung back in time to see Liao catch Levi as the man stumbled.

"Are you all right?" Liao asked.

Levi grunted, then let out a nervous laugh. "Just put my foot wrong. The rock crumbled beneath me." He grunted again, then strained. "My foot's stuck in the hole."

Adelheid stomped back. "Do we need to call for help?"

Liao pulled at Levi's leg. "Try twisting your foot a little."

Levi grunted, then let out a cry of triumph as his foot popped out of the small crevice. He stumbled back. "No, I'm out." He looked around. There were small holes all around them. "The ground's a little treacherous here."

Adelheid glared. "Watch your step. Let's move." She stalked off.

They approached the hull. Helmet lanterns flickered across the dented, bent, and pockmarked metal. The portholes at ground level were either broken or half-buried. Adelheid peered into one that was at shoulder height and saw the inside of a cabin with furniture toppled on one side of the room. The remains of a bed—a metal skeleton—lay upended and upside-down. The drawers of a dresser gaped open.

Liao looked in beside her. "The whole thing must have been exposed to the vacuum almost instantly. Anybody who didn't make it to the shelters would have died within seconds."

*Tell me something I don't know,* Adelheid thought bitterly. She'd been there. She'd read the report. They'd rescued the people in the shelters. There hadn't been many who'd made it.

They moved along, past airlock doors that were bent and unusable, past more portholes, until they came to the rim of a crater ten metres deep, left by the rocket's guillotine impact. The tail section tipped into it. The Robinson Rail lay in ruins. On the other side, the trench and the pillars of the rail appeared in the crater wall, exposed like a cross-section.

Liao peered ahead. "We've been walking about two hundred metres, and this crater is about a hundred metres across. If we assume a similar amount of destruction on the other side, that's, what, five-hundred metres of Robinson Rail to rebuild? Maybe six?"

Levi winced. "We don't have enough construction bots to close the gap."

"We have eighty-eight days and the resources for concrete." Adelheid waved at the dust around them. "We can close the gap."

A treacherous part of her mind spoke up, asking, *And then what?*

She looked up at the ruin of the tail section. "Come on. We can enter from the front."

Levi looked confused, but Adelheid didn't wait for a reply. She slid down the side of the crater.

The front of the severed tail section was another cross-section, with the *Messenger*'s levels, rooms, and corridors exposed. Picking their way carefully over twisted and ripped metal, the three of them stepped off the dust of Mercury and into one of the open corridors. Their lantern lights danced across the interior walls, picking out detail after detail: apartment doors, a sign pointing the way to the command centre and the restrooms, a ceramic pot that had survived the sudden vacuum, and the ashes of a plant that had not.

Liao touched a darkened display. He nodded when it lit up to show static. "There's some residual battery power."

"Don't waste it." Adelheid pressed forward. "I don't want to open too many doors on manual."

Levi picked a tablet off the floor. Its screen was cracked, but it lit up at his touch. "Everything's still here. The *Hermes* and the *Apollo* didn't touch anything."

*The* Hermes *rescuers focused on finding survivors in the vacuum shelters,* thought Adelheid. That thought made her think of Cristavao, and she smiled, even if it was only one night, eighty-eight days ago.

"What's this?" Levi's voice cut through the radio. Liao and Adelheid turned to see him staring at a black lump on the corridor floor, a metre and a half long and about a metre wide, pockmarked like charcoal.

*Charcoal!* Adelheid looked around. *Where are we? Far from the vacuum shelters. A side corridor: the rescuers might not have gotten here—*

"It looks like rock . . ." Levi reached to tap it with his toe.

"Don't!" Liao stepped forward, too late.

The black rock collapsed. Dust flowed across the floor like water and settled over Levi's boots. He stared, bewildered. "What—"

"That was—" Liao began.

Adelheid cleared her throat. "The inside of this section spent eighty-eight days in vacuum and sunlight, cooking at four hundred degrees Celsius. Think of what that does to organic material."

Levi thought about it, then turned away, gagging and clutching at his helmet. Liao grabbed his arm in case he got the idea of yanking it off. He held Levi until the man calmed down.

Adelheid looked away. "Come on." She followed the signs pointing to the command centre.

They entered the rear agora, their lantern lights fading as

they looked up and around at the balconies above. The potted plants were charcoal skeletons, but the floor was clear, albeit inclined. At the far end were the large set of double doors leading to Command and Control.

The three stared at the doors and the large open space before them. Before, in the corridors, there had been plenty of handholds to pull them forward.

Levi took a deep breath. "What do you think the incline is on this?"

"Less complaining." Adelheid got on her hands and knees. "More crawling."

Crawling, puffing, and lending each other a hand, they clawed their way to the Command and Control doors. Adelheid pulled herself to her feet and, gripping a bend in the wall, tapped at the glass of a panel beside the doors. The display sputtered fitfully. The doors shuddered but stayed shut, and the display went out.

Liao sucked his teeth. "Looks like there wasn't enough residual power after all."

"That's why I brought batteries." Adelheid unshouldered her pack, then shouted as the straps slipped from her grip. Levi and Liao leaped forward, and for a moment, the three of them were holding the heavy pack against a long slide into the darkness.

The moment lengthened. Adelheid shifted her fingers forward and gripped one of the straps. "Thanks," she breathed.

"Don't mention it," said Liao.

Adelheid pulled the pack toward her. "Let's get started."

☿

THE DOORS to Command and Control parted for the first time in eighty-eight days, vibrating the deck beneath their feet but silent in the vacuum. They slid aside about a metre and then stopped dead.

Adelheid hissed in frustration. Levi chuckled. "Well, on the bright side, there's less chance for us to slip and slide out. It would be a long climb."

Adelheid pushed forward, grunting as she squeezed through the gap. Inside, their lights played across the stations. There were chairs at each console and a lump of charcoal on each one.

Liao stopped dead. Levi's breath caught. "Nobody left their post."

Adelheid climbed the lopsided stairs to the command deck. Liao and Levi walked slowly, moving carefully and reverentially. The two men focused on the stations while Adelheid stepped deeper into the back of the room.

Liao tapped at a console, which flickered to life. He nodded as codes scrolled down the screen. "We've found what we came for. We have access, the command codes, everything. A crew can have this downloaded in an hour."

Adelheid stared at a chair raised on a dais. She swallowed. "Liao?"

He looked up at her tone, then clambered up the stairs and stood beside her. Together, they stared at the chair and at the charcoal body that sat there, in command.

Adelheid swallowed. *Dad.*

Levi looked up at them, bewildered, but Liao touched her shoulder.

Adelheid breathed in a sniff. "I wasn't at the memorial."

Liao's brow furrowed. "What?"

"I wasn't at the memorial." She gulped against her grief. "I didn't have time. There was so much to do. I couldn't be there. I needed . . . I needed . . ."

He gave her shoulder a squeeze. "I understand."

She reached up and closed her hand over his. She shut her

eyes. Eventually, she got her breathing under control and pulled away.

"Okay." Liao motioned to Levi. "Radio the *Messenger*. We have work to do."

Adelheid turned to face the broken rear windows. She stared into the dark.

*I didn't have time to say goodbye.*

# CHAPTER 14
# THE NEW NORMAL

ADELHEID STARED AT HER PROTEIN BAR. THE FLAVOUR OF THE DAY was meatloaf.

*Four hundred calories.*

She took her fork and carefully cut the bar in half.

*Two hundred calories each.*

*The second of my two meals today.*

The galley was hushed. Officers sat in groups of twos and threes. Everyone stared at their food. At a table at the far end of the hall, two ensigns—a man and a woman—looked up from their meals and shared a brief smile.

A young lieutenant pushed past, a finger on her commlink. "Mark? Emma here. Where are you? Contact me as soon as you get this!"

Adelheid looked back at her food bar and made two more cuts with her fork. Then, two more. *Eight bites. Fifty calories each.*

She took a bite of her protein bar, crushing it against the roof of her mouth and letting the taste linger on her tongue. Then she took another. When she had one bite left, she looked up. Across from her, Lizabet sat, staring at her empty plate. The woman licked a finger and dabbed at the crumbs. When she glanced down again, she looked as lost as if she were on the surface and the *Messenger* had left her behind.

Adelheid glanced at her remaining bite, then pushed her plate over. Lizabet stared at the plate, then at her.

Adelheid shrugged, then smiled.

Lizabet smiled back, shy, then speared the remaining piece with her fork.

Adelheid looked away.

"That was mine!" a woman shouted. "How dare you eat it!" Chairs shoved back.

Lizabet looked around, her fork still in her mouth. Adelheid rose from her seat at the sight of the two ensigns facing off, fists balled.

"What are you talking about?" the male ensign shouted back. He grunted as the woman folded him up with a punch. He tumbled back, then scrambled to his feet. As other officers stood up, shouting warnings or encouragement, he grabbed his fallen chair and raised it like a club.

Adelheid and Lizabet dashed between the tables, scattering chairs and people. The female ensign was grabbing her own chair. Lizabet yanked it from her hands. Adelheid hauled the man back by his collar. "Don't even think about it!"

The man struggled. "I don't know what she's talking about! I didn't take anything, I swear!"

He dropped his chair and balled his fist, but Adelheid pulled him so their gazes locked. "Do you have anything further to say, *Ensign*?"

He spotted her rank. His eyes widened, and he stilled. "Sorry, Captain," he muttered. Then his voice edged up. "But I didn't steal any of her food! I really didn't!" He jabbed a finger at her plate. "Look! Right there! That's her piece just under her plate! It must have fallen off and slipped under!"

Lizabet moved the plate aside, and the morsel came into view.

Silence descended. The female ensign's cheeks reddened, but she picked up the morsel of food and put it in her mouth. "Sorry," she mumbled.

Adelheid looked at the male ensign, who could not meet her gaze. The chair he'd grabbed lay toppled on the floor.

"Walk it off," she said. She looked from one ensign to the other. "Both of you."

Both ensigns pushed away, striding out from the galley. Outside, they peeled off in different directions down the corridor.

Around the galley, officers sat. Cutlery clinked against plates. Conversations restarted, softly at first, then louder.

Adelheid let out the breath she'd been holding.

Lizabet picked up a fallen plate and looked disappointed to find it empty. She set it on the cleaning tray.

"Are you okay?" Adelheid asked.

Lizabet jerked up, and Adelheid saw a flash of shame. The woman turned away. "Come on. We have a meeting."

Adelheid watched her go. Then, picking up a fallen chair, she set it back in place and followed.

☿

LIZABET AND ADELHEID arrived at the meeting room to see Captains Wilhelm Schroeder and Gerhardt Pohl at the table, talking. Liao sat a few chairs over; he looked up from his notes and nodded. Lizabet pulled aside, grabbed two cups of water, and set one in front of Adelheid as she sat. She sat down herself, clasping her own.

"Hello, Captain," said Wilhelm.

"Captain," Adelheid replied, then, "Captains."

Gerhardt and Wilhelm chuckled. Then they looked at each other. "So, whose turn is it to chair this meeting?"

"Whoever's in charge," said Wilhelm.

"But as the highest-ranking officers here, we're all captains." Gerhardt nodded to Liao and Lizabet. "Saving you lieutenants, of course. There isn't any one of us in charge."

Adelheid frowned. *And that's because Hahn hasn't put anybody formally in charge yet. But I can't deal with this question now. We seem to be handling things well enough.* She nodded to Gerhardt. "If we go by seniority, you chair the meeting."

He flushed. "I'm only two weeks your senior, Captain."

"So, who had the task of chairing the meeting last time?" Wilhelm asked.

The three captains looked at each other. No answer came.

Adelheid sighed and stuck her fist out toward the centre of the table. Gerhardt and Wilhelm took her meaning and brought forward their own fists. They pumped, *one, two, three!*

"Rail beats Sun," said Adelheid. "Congratulations, Chairman Gerhardt."

Gerhardt scowled at the two pointed fingers arrayed against his splayed hand. He leaned back in his seat. "Fine."

The door opened, and Acting Governor Daarel Hahn entered the room. He was balding and shorter than all the officers, and his civilian clothes were plain but well-pressed. He had a wispy moustache below his nose.

The officers rose to their feet as he ambled toward the head of the table.

"Governor Hahn," said Adelheid. "I thought one of us was to report to the Civilian Advisory Council later."

"I thought I'd combine meetings and save time." Hahn gave them a thin smile. "Is it all right if I chair this meeting and get your reports?"

"Sure," said Gerhardt immediately. Adelheid and Wilhelm glanced at each other before turning back and nodding.

"Then let's get to business." Hahn and the officers sat. "First of all, congratulations to everyone on your promotions. I wish these could have been done with due ceremony during happier times, but needs must, as they say."

Around the table, everyone mumbled their thanks.

"Secondly," said Hahn, "you know about the Civilian Advisory Council meeting this afternoon. We're overdue a judicial meeting, as well, so I've proposed rolling them together. We need a judge-advocate to oversee matters. Captain Koning, could you act in such a capacity?"

Adelheid jerked to attention from her thoughts of food. "Certainly, Governor," she replied. *My experiments can wait. After all, it's not like any breakthroughs are imminent.*

"Thank you," said Hahn. "Now, to the reports. Lieutenant Anderson, what's the state of our rations?"

Adelheid winced. *Would Hahn ask Lizabet this if he saw the way she'd looked at her plate this morning?*

But Lizabet stood. "We are maintaining a steady rate of eight hundred calories per day for the average person. Our current stores should support this rate of consumption for the next six months."

Hahn nodded. "Lieutenant, what calorie level could we sustain indefinitely?"

The officers drew in their breaths. Lizabet grimaced. "Around five hundred calories per day for the average person."

"Five hundred calories?" Gerhardt shook his head. "What is that, exactly?"

Wilhelm shrugged. "Half a protein loaf," he said, "along with five saltine crackers."

Adelheid nodded to herself. *Actually, half a protein loaf sounds really good right now.*

Wilhelm leaned back. "A small plate of fried potatoes." His eyes went dreamy. "Along with half an apple."

Gerhardt licked his lips.

"People," Adelheid cut in, and the spell broke. The officers blinked at each other.

Hahn coughed. "Thank you, Lieutenant Anderson. Lieutenant Fang, give me the interplanetary communications report."

Flipping through his notes, Liao stood. "Channels remain open, and radio chatter is continuing. Mars is reporting that it has kept order, and things are stabilizing. Venus reports all its Zeppelins are present and accounted for, and supplies are safe. There's been no word from the Ganymede and Europa outposts for the past month."

"They've probably starved to death," Lizabet muttered.

Adelheid frowned at her friend, but Lizabet ignored her.

"Something is happening in the Asteroid Belt," Liao went on. "The government has closed the mines and is calling the scows to gather at Ceres and Vesta. They haven't said why, but I speculate that they're organizing convoys."

"Where would they go?" Hahn asked.

"Ceres is the largest gathering area, and right now, Mars may be within travelling distance," Liao replied. "Vesta's on the opposite side of the belt; their nearest planet is Venus."

"Lord in Sunlight, they're not coming *here*, are they?" Wilhelm exclaimed.

"Doubtful," Liao replied. "Mars is a stretch, Venus even more so. We won't know, though, until they move; all they're doing is gathering and consolidating."

Hahn looked up. "What's the situation on the Earth?"

Liao shrugged. "The nuclear detonations appear to have stopped."

"So . . ." Wilhelm counted off his fingers. "The Earth is Hell, Mars is fine, and Venus is fine. Maybe the Asteroid miners have a point; any chance we could—"

"No," Lizabet snapped.

Wilhelm blinked. "But we—"

"No," said Lizabet again. "I know what you're thinking, but the Earth had most of the spaceships. They still do; they're just stuck on the surface or in orbit with nobody to run them." Her voice rose. "It took us decades of immigration to bring us to the population we have now; it would take years to evacuate us. And even if we had the spaceships, where would we go? There's no room for us on Venus's Uber-Zeppelins, and Mars is too far away. We're on our own."

"Lizabet?" Adelheid cut in. The other officers shifted in their seats.

"No." Hahn raised a hand. "It's fine, Captain. She is, unfortunately, correct. Lieutenant Anderson, you may go."

Lizabet stood stiffly, turned on her heel, and strode from the room.

"Captain Koning," Hahn went on, as the door clicked shut, "tell us the state of communications with the other towns."

Adelheid snapped back to attention, then gathered her notes and got to her feet. "Well . . ." She cleared her throat. "There's not much to report. This far in the Far Dark, we're out of range of the other latitude towns. We've only been able to keep contact with the polar statics — the *Lares* and, sporadically, the *Baxter-Nordley*."

She glanced at her notes. "Things aren't good on the *Lares*. Their rations are down to four hundred calories per day. Their government is giving us daily reports, which is good—" *It means they still have a government.* "—but they're reporting a rash of thefts, and recently, they had to put down a hunger riot. They've imposed a curfew."

Hahn nodded. "And the *Baxter-Nordley*?"

"It's been a week since we last heard from them," she replied.

This brought a chill to the table. The *Baxter-Nordley* sat inside the Chao Meng-Fu crater in permanent darkness, where ice formed. Outside of the latitude towns' water-reclamation plants, the polar statics were the main source of Mercury's water. If the *Baxter-Nordley* wasn't responding, they'd just lost half of it.

"What are we doing to restore contact?" Hahn asked.

"Whatever we can, whenever we can spare the personnel," said Adelheid. "But . . ." She shook her head.

Wilhelm let out a morose laugh. "They're too far away for us to send a team, so I doubt there's anything we can do. We don't know if they don't want to talk to us, or if something's preventing them from talking to us, or . . ."

The point hung in the air: *or if they can't talk to us because there is no one left there to talk.*

"Actually, that's not true," Adelheid muttered, then blinked as the room went silent.

"What's not true?" Wilhelm echoed. "They're half a hemisphere away. Our land speeders can only make it to the parallels of the next two latitude towns. A single land speeder doesn't have enough oxygen, much less battery power, to go farther without re-supply, and we left the re-suppliers back close to the Dawn Line."

"That's the thing," Adelheid said. *In for a gasket, in for a cog . . .* "We can connect multiple land speeders together. One crew can run a bunch of them in a convoy, preserving the oxygen. We can use the other towns' Robinson Rails to recharge the batteries. We could get that team to the South Pole."

Wilhelm gaped. "That would take *days!*"

Adelheid nodded. "Driving non-stop. But they would still get there. And that crew could radio back to us if we placed communications boosters on each Robinson Rail we pass. That way, they could tell us what's happening at the *Baxter-Nordley*."

Liao leaned back. "It would be worth doing for half the world's water."

Gerhardt chuckled. "Are you volunteering?"

The others chuckled as well, including Adelheid, but Hahn nodded. "It's something to consider. Thank you, Captain Koning. Let's move on to the maintenance report. Captain Pohl?"

Gerhardt stood. "Repairs to the *Messenger* continue, but the pace has slowed because we've had to assign crews to start repairs on the Robinson Rail. I'm afraid we're going to have to assign extra hours to everybody's work detail dedicated to maintenance."

"Everyone?" Liao exclaimed.

"Even the file clerks?" Adelheid asked.

"Even us?" gasped Wilhelm.

Hahn rapped the table. "Relax, everyone. We all took lessons in repair work during vocational school. Those without experience will be assigned to more menial tasks to free up the experienced to handle the more challenging work. We're short-staffed and have to be mobile before sunrise, so this needs doing."

The officers settled down, keeping a mutinous silence.

"Please continue, Captain Pohl," said Hahn.

Gerhardt cleared his throat. "I have the unfortunate duty to report that six people of the *Messenger* died in the line of duty this past week. I'll now read their names into the record: Miike Milner, sanitation officer, killed by a steam pipe burst in maintenance corridor three. Eva Zhao, kitchen staff, killed by an electrical short in the main kitchen. Isaac Bauman, cargo worker, killed in a forklift accident in Storeroom 7..."

Despite herself, Adelheid tuned out. Her duty schedule stretched out ahead of her, and her stomach gnawed at her. Gerhardt continued to read out the names, all of them individuals caught up in solo accidents, many discovered only when the shift changed, each a tragedy.

Except...

"Wait." She looked up. "Something doesn't make sense."

Gerhardt stopped. The people around the table stared at her. "What do you mean, Captain Koning?" Hahn asked.

Adelheid frowned. Something had caught her attention, but she couldn't explain her misgivings. As she reached for it, it slipped away. The *Messenger*'s work areas could be dangerous places at the best of times. Add in people dizzy with hunger, and it was a surprise that there weren't *more* accidents. But the disturbing feeling remained. She looked down. "Sorry, Governor. I'm just fatigued."

Hahn nodded. "No apologies necessary. Let's move on to the last item I wanted to talk to you about." He leaned forward. "We have decided what we're doing with Terminal."

The officers looked at each other. "What do you mean, Governor?" Liao asked.

"The full report will be issued at the Civilian Advisory Council meeting this afternoon," said Hahn, "but we've determined that, while repairing the Robinson Rail and salvaging the tail section will take some time, we should still have half the night, once we're done. We should use that opportunity to salvage what we can from Terminal."

Adelheid's brow furrowed. "You're referring to the supplies? We're about to sort through the cargo bays. If there's any inventory still left over, we should have that on the *Messenger* by the end of tomorrow's last shift."

"I'm referring to Terminal itself," Hahn replied. "I don't need to remind you that there's an ongoing question of supplies and spare parts now that the Earth has gone silent. Terminal represents a tremendous resource, with all that metal and equipment."

Adelheid looked around the table. Gerhardt was nodding, as was Wilhelm. Liao looked unsure. "The *whole* spaceport?" she asked.

"As much as we can." Hahn looked down at his tablet. "The numbers don't lie; we can't let the resources of Terminal just sit there. And, I hate to be morbid, but it's not as if the Earth will be needing it any time soon."

"Governor!" Adelheid cut in. "Are we sure about this?"

Hahn blinked at her. "You propose something else, Captain?"

Adelheid stuttered, then forced out the first thought that came to her: "What about the *Hermes*, sir? What about the *Apollo*? Terminal is as much theirs as ours, and they didn't take it apart. They left it for us."

"They didn't have time," said Gerhardt. "There were only days until sunrise for them. They probably had other things on their mind."

"Still," said Adelheid, "Terminal isn't ours to take apart. We shouldn't do something without consulting with the other latitude towns first."

"But you said that we are out of range of the other latitude towns," said Hahn. "By the time they are in range, there may not be enough time to salvage Terminal properly. The *Apollo* and the *Hermes* can talk to us about getting their share when they are in communications range. The numbers don't lie. That'll be what the report says when the Civilian Advisory Council votes on it later today. Now, unless there are any further objections ... ?"

Adelheid looked around the table but found no help. Frowning, she looked at her lap. The silence lengthened.

"Good," said Hahn. "Then we start salvaging Terminal as soon as possible."

☿

ADELHEID LEFT THE MEETING, walking tall because it wouldn't do to stagger from hunger. She followed the main corridor until she found a side corridor out of the way, where she leaned against the wall. She heaved a weary sigh. *Judge advocate work? I just want to eat something and go to bed.*

Still, orders were orders. Even if they rankled.

*Dismantle Terminal? What about the* Hermes? *What about the* Apollo? *We should ask them, at least.*

Still . . . orders were orders.

She pushed herself upright and stepped back into the main corridor. As she walked toward the forebridge, she heard someone call out for her.

"Captain Koning!" Gerhardt strode up. He was smiling. "We've got good news."

Adelheid wasn't in the mood for any news, so she struggled to show enthusiasm. Fortunately, Gerhardt was too happy to notice. "What is it?"

"We've been through Terminal's storage facilities!" Gerhardt was more than smiling; he was vibrating with excitement. "We've found supplies! Food! Water! A third of what was in the stores eighty-eight days ago."

Adelheid straightened up. *The* Hermes? *The* Apollo? *They left them behind? For us?* She smiled like she hadn't done for weeks. "That's . . . amazing! Somebody should tell Hahn—"

"There's more," said Gerhardt. "That's why I came to you." He handed her a slip of paper. "I thought you should see this. It was with the supplies."

Adelheid unfolded the slip and read the handwriting.

THIS IS YOUR SHARE. *See you soon!—Cristavao*

ADELHEID'S SMILE widened into a grin. It was such an unfamiliar feeling it made her giddy and her eyes unaccountably wet. She folded the paper and put it in her breast pocket. "Thank you, Gerhardt."

He nodded and darted off. Adelheid leaned back against the wall, smiling and crying at the same time.

☿

THE JUDICIAL ASSEMBLY was held before the Civilian Advisory Council meeting in the *Messenger's* central agora. Adelheid sat in the middle of a long table in front of civilians and military officers sitting in rows of chairs in front of her. She picked up her tablet and swiped through the files.

There were five cases, all of them charges of theft.

All of the stolen items were food.

*I sense a pattern.*

She banged her gavel. "This court will come to order. Will the first defendant please stand?"

A middle-aged man got to his feet in the dock, his head bowed. Adelheid checked her notes: Daan Jolson, kitchen worker, first class.

She cleared her throat. "Daan Jolson," she called out. "You stand accused of stealing food rations. How do you plead?"

Jolson mumbled.

Adelheid frowned. "Meneer Jolson, please repeat what you said."

Jolson coughed. "I plead guilty, Captain."

There was a rumble from the audience. Adelheid looked out at the seated crowd. Jolson wilted in their glare, but as Adelheid watched, she saw some members of the audience look away in shame.

Jolson's advocate stepped forward. "Captain Koning, my client expresses regret and offers the following explanation—"

Adelheid pinched the bridge of her nose. "Let's speed this up, advocate. Your client was hungry, and he had mouths to feed, correct?"

Jolson's advocate nodded.

"The accused admits that he stole rations," said the prosecutor. "As it is his first offence, we ask that he be sentenced to four hours a day of extra labour and a ration limit of five hundred calories per day.'

Out of the corner of her eye, Adelheid saw Jolson wince. Her own stomach twinged.

She faced Jolson. "Meneer Jolson, what do you have to say for yourself?"

Jolson flushed in the gaze of everyone. He looked at the ground. "I'm sorry . . . sir. I was just . . . hungry."

Adelheid sighed. "Meneer Dan Jolson, you've pled guilty, and the prosecution has advocated for four hours per day of extra labour and a ration limit. Can I ask how this helps?"

Jolson looked up, bewildered, but Adelheid wasn't looking at him. She was frowning at the prosecutor.

He blinked at her. "Captain?"

"How does sentencing a man who stole food during a famine to a ration limit help?" she asked. "Is this the sentence I'm supposed to give to the—" She swiped through the files. "—four accused who are coming up after? What is denying food to starving people supposed to achieve?"

"Sir," said the prosecutor carefully. "In other states of emergency, the penalty for looting is death—"

"Looting only happens during a riot," Adelheid snapped. "This was a hungry man, working in the kitchens, who took a ration from storage."

The prosecutor sucked his teeth. "Captain, if we don't respect the ration system, we'll run out of food faster."

"I'm aware of that," said Adelheid. "And Meneer Jolson is, I hope, aware of the threat his act presents to the other citizens of the *Messenger*—citizens who are as hungry as he is."

Jolson looked at his feet again.

"And the fact is," Adelheid went on, "we're all as hungry as he is. It could be any of us standing in that dock. So, I ask again, how does sentencing this man to reduced rations help?"

She looked out at the crowd again. People were frowning, but more in puzzlement than anger. More were looking guilty. Some who had been glaring at Jolson were now staring more sympathetically.

*That's good*, she thought. But what are we going to do?

"Captain," said a quiet voice, and it took Adelheid a moment to realize it was Jolson who'd spoken. She focused on him, as did the audience. His cheeks flushed. "I'm sorry for what I've done. I know my hunger isn't an excuse because everybody is hungry. I'm guilty, Captain. I'll accept a sentence. I'm willing to work extra hours to repay my debt to the *Messenger*."

Adelheid glanced from Jolson's advocate to the prosecutor. They both nodded.

"And two weeks' house arrest," she added, "in between the times you're not working. Your rations stay the same." She meant it as a sentence, but there was a question at the end of it.

Jolson nodded. "Thank you, Captain."

She banged the gavel. "That will be the sentence of all offenders who plead guilty to theft here today." She nodded at the guards. "Take him to his quarters and his family. Next case, please."

The next four all pled guilty.

She banged her gavel for the last time and pushed her chair back, heading for an empty seat in the audience. It turned out to be beside Liao. He smiled at her, but something made her pause. Smiling seemed unusual enough in these days of grim reality, but he wasn't just happy. He seemed . . . proud of her.

"You did great," he said.

She didn't feel proud, but she smiled back.

A half-dozen men and women—the Citizen Advisory Council members—stood up from the first row of chairs and filed over to take Adelheid's place behind the long table. They waited as Acting Governor Hahn came from the back of the audience and took the centre seat. "I call this meeting to order," he said.

Again, Adelheid tuned out, fatigued and hungry. She half-listened as council members debated moving the start time of the vocational school. Then Hahn stood to read the reports given him by the military meeting. Lizabet's calorie report was met with grim silence. Everyone bowed their heads as Hahn read out the names of those who had died that week, and again, something about those names made her shudder, and not just because these people were dead.

*I wish I knew why.*

Finally, Hahn said, "As our last matter before we take questions from the audience, we are drawing up plans to scrap Terminal and salvage its parts for the *Messenger*."

He said it blithely before calling for questions, but the audience shifted. People frowned and muttered to each other. Adelheid's disquiet intensified. She thought about her last day there, before everything went to hell, meeting with the officers of the *Hermes* and the *Apollo*. She remembered Cristavao. And she remembered his note.

Before she realized it, she was on her feet. She barged in front of a young man stepping up to the podium and gripped the sides. She stared at the Civilian Advisory Council and felt the eyes of everyone in the room on her.

Hahn looked at her with a raised eyebrow.

"Adelheid," Liao hissed. "What are you doing?"

Adelheid took a shaky breath. "I am speaking as a private citizen."

Hahn tilted his head, curious.

"I learned about the plans to disassemble Terminal earlier today," she continued. Her stomach churned, and not because of hunger. *Everybody is staring at me as I go out on a limb.* "I believe these plans to be a mistake."

The crowd murmured. The council members looked confused. Hahn stared at Adelheid, his gavel clutched in his hand, but she pushed on. "The argument for disassembly is that we can use the resources, but Terminal doesn't belong to just us. It belongs to all of Mercury." Her voice echoed in the silence of the agora. "It's more than a way station. It's a connection to where we came from and a reminder of why we're here. We shouldn't turn our backs on that. Then there's this . . ."

She pulled Cristavao's note from her pocket. "Earlier today, our crews were able to recover a third of the food and water supplies that had been on Terminal when we left it. The *Apollo* and the *Hermes* saved it for us."

A gasp shifted through the crowd, of anticipation and hope.

"Speaking as a citizen of the *Messenger*," Adelheid went on, "I don't think we should tear down Terminal. It's bad for our spirit, and it's unfair to the towns we share it with. The Earth may be silent, but the rest of Mercury hasn't turned on us. We should not turn on them."

Hahn banged his gavel against the rising murmur of the audience. "I . . . appreciate your sentiment, Captain Koning, but it's sentiment. The plans that have been drawn up will stabilize our maintenance and spare parts inventory—"

"Point of order, Governor Hahn," said a council member at the end of the table, an older woman by the name of Ellen DeVries. "You talk about plans already having been made, but the proposal of whether or not to disassemble Terminal hasn't been put to a vote yet. Why is that? Were you going to present these plans as a *fait accompli*?"

Hahn shifted in his seat. "I wanted to have the plans settled before the matter was put to a vote in order for us to be fully informed—"

"I think we're jumping the gun if you're putting together a

plan before we decide whether or not to disassemble Terminal," said another council member, Jon Cloet, sitting at the other end of the table. "Captain Koning is right: we can't presume to snatch Terminal in the middle of the night. We presume too much if we don't reach out to the *Apollo* and the *Hermes* before we make such a move. If Councillor DeVries is making a motion to leave Terminal as we found it for now, I'll second that."

"I make that motion," said Councillor DeVries quickly.

"I second it," said a third council member, a young woman closer to the middle of the table.

Hahn spluttered. "You can't—"

"Why not?" Councillor DeVries demanded.

Silence descended.

Adelheid stood where she was, watching Hahn. The audience around her seemed to be holding its breath. She certainly was.

Hahn gave Adelheid a worried glance, then cleared his throat. "We have a motion and a seconder. All those in favour, please indicate by saying 'aye.'"

"Aye," the council chorused.

"All opposed, say 'nay.'"

Silence fell again. Governor Hahn held it for a long moment.

Finally, he took a deep breath. "The ayes have it. This meeting is adjourned for a five-minute break." He banged his gavel.

The audience broke into applause and Adelheid sat. She could feel Liao staring at her, open-mouthed, but she ignored him. Looking across the agora, she saw Hahn frowning at her before he turned and hurried away.

☿

FOR THE REST of the day, Adelheid worked on her duties. She heard nothing from Hahn.

*But I have to drop off the day's paperwork at his office. He'll be waiting for me then.*

She left the tram in the middle of the *Messenger* and entered the civilian government offices. She walked past reception and between desks and gleaming filing cabinets. She reached the door marked "Governor" and knocked.

"Enter," said Hahn from within.

She went inside and dropped her tablet on Hahn's desk. "The day's reports, Governor."

He looked up from his tablet, nodded, and then pulled Adelheid's tablet toward him. "Thank you, Captain. If you could wait a moment?"

Adelheid stood to attention while he read. Finally, he set her report down and looked up. "It all seems to be in order. No mention, I see, of your thoughts about maintaining Terminal."

"That wasn't a military matter, Governor," she replied. "I spoke only as a private citizen."

Hahn frowned up at her. Adelheid stayed to attention. Finally, Hahn said, "As acting governor, I respect the vote of the civilian council. Even though it goes against the recommendations of my experts, they decided to leave Terminal in hibernation state, and so it will stay. My position demands nothing less."

*Smiling would be a mistake.* Adelheid kept her gaze above and to the left of Hahn's forehead. "Very good, sir."

"And I appreciate your decision to speak as a private citizen," Hahn went on. "However, I feel that you underestimate the power of your voice. You are not just a private citizen."

"Sir?"

"The public looks up to you," said Hahn. "They respect you."

Adelheid's mind raced. *What in Sunlight is he talking about?*

"You're the colonel's daughter," Hahn added.

Adelheid leaned back, perplexed. *Why should that make a difference?*

"That makes you an important figure." Hahn leaned forward. "Colonel Koning was popular, so you are someone the public can rally around. That's important. I'm aware of how much the people of the *Messenger* need you. So, be there for them. Give them what they need. Just understand that what the people want often isn't the same thing as what they need. That decision is left to the civilian council, not to the civilians. Colonel Koning understood that. Do you, Captain?"

Adelheid clenched her jaw and drew her breath. "Yes, sir."

"Good," said Hahn. "You may go."

Adelheid turned on her heel and left Hahn's office.

☿

ADELHEID OPENED the door of her quarters and leaned against the frame. It was always hard to drag herself out of bed. Today, the corridor looked even longer than usual. She gathered herself and set off.

"Good morning, Captain," said a young woman who passed by too fast for Adelheid to recognize.

She nodded, mumbling, "Morning."

"Morning, Captain," said a young lieutenant coming off duty.

Adelheid nodded and kept walking, running her day's itinerary through her mind. *Morning meal. Bridge duty. Then, maintenance assignment. Damn.*

*Maybe I can have a little time for my experiments before falling into bed.*

*Bed, and then the next day.*

*And the day after that.*

She turned a corner.

"Good morning, Captain." An older gentleman from the kitchens nodded as she entered the waiting area for the tram. That made her look up and realize eyes were on her. And as she met each gaze, each person smiled and nodded, then politely looked away.

She smiled back tentatively and kept going. At the tram station, she stepped back to stand beside a potted plant near a wall. She listened to the conversations around her.

"Did you hear the speech she gave?" she heard someone say.

"I heard about it," a young man replied. "I think she's right: we can't just tear down Terminal. After we meet with the *Apollo* and the *Hermes*, maybe."

"You heard they left us a third of the rations there," someone else said. "They know we're all in this together."

Adelheid faced forward, waiting for the tram. The conversations continued.

At the edge of hearing, a maintenance worker asked, "How did he die?"

"A fault in his arc welder," his friend replied. "Honestly, it was lucky it was only him that got hit."

"Oh, gods! Somebody help me!"

The desperate shout cut through the air. Adelheid was running toward it before she fully registered it. She rushed into the nearest residential block, pushed past startled people, rounded a corner, and saw Liao running toward her. Between them, down a side corridor, the shouts continued.

Running in, they saw a young lieutenant Adelheid recognized from the galley yesterday morning. The woman clutched the edge of an open apartment door, sobbing. "He's dead! Mark's dead!" She jabbed a finger into the room.

Adelheid dashed into the apartment and stopped short. Liao followed, bumping into her.

A young man's body lay on his cot, one arm folded across

his chest. Adelheid recognized him. *Lieutenant Mark Bakker, second shift.* His bedside table was cluttered with origami models. He looked like he was sleeping, except that part of his bedsheets had been pulled back, and his other arm lay flopped, possibly from the young woman trying to pull him upright. Several of the origami models had been knocked to the floor. And he wasn't breathing. Adelheid felt for a pulse. Mark's skin was cold to the touch.

"My God," Liao breathed.

Adelheid brought her hands to her mouth. "How? Lieutenant Bakker, he's—he was—he's a year younger than us! He could do the hundred-metre dash in ten-point-five seconds!"

"Adelheid?" Liao touched her shoulder.

She shook it off. "How is this possible? *He was fine two days ago!*"

Liao stepped around her and also felt for a pulse. He stepped back, staring. Then, his voice so low, Adelheid strained to hear him, he said, "I've heard . . . stories . . . about the great wars in Earth's past. In the middle of them, people—civilians . . . in the middle of the Blitz, some would go to sleep one night and not wake up again."

She stared at him. "How? Suicide?"

Liao shook his head.

"A disease? Some kind of epidemic?"

He shook his head again. "They just didn't feel there was any point in waking up."

Adelheid gaped at him. Then the infirmary team arrived.

# CHAPTER 15
## THE LIST

LIEUTENANT BAKKER'S DEATH WEIGHED ON ADELHEID'S MIND through her duty spell on the forebridge. She was still thinking about it when she clocked off and headed for her maintenance shift.

*There's no doubt about it,* she thought as she passed people who nodded at her or slipped out of her way. *I'm angry. Why am I angry?*

*Because he left us?*

*Or is it because I'm adding his eight hundred calories to the general food pool and am happy that we have a little more to eat now that he's gone? Am I angry at myself? Or him? Or both?*

Still, she smiled to see Lizabet waiting for her at the maintenance storeroom. Then she saw the pressure suit and that Lizabet was holding a helmet. Adelheid stopped. "Do we have to work outside? In the vacuum?"

Lizabet smirked. "*You* do." She nodded to a second pressure suit folded up on a bench alongside its helmet. "I'm to monitor you at the airlock. My pressure suit is in case you get into trouble, and I have to come out to help you."

Adelheid scowled. "This isn't because I got here after you, is it?"

Lizabet shrugged. "We'll switch on the next maintenance duty."

Adelheid sighed. "I guess that's fair."

Adelheid changed into the pressure suit and stuffed her uniform in a locker. She grimaced as the suit's fabric hugged down on her body. *This may be better than the tin cans people used to wear in the early days of spaceflight, but these pressure suits still make me feel like I'm suffocating.* She pulled on her helmet and tapped its radio receiver. "Can you hear me, Lizabet?"

A brief burst of static; then, "Loud and clear. You ready?"

"As I'll ever be." She picked up a toolbox and tablet and followed Lizabet out of the storeroom and across the corridor to the airlock. She laughed when she looked at the job list: "Inspect and tighten? That's *all*? They could give *anybody* this job!"

"Well, you heard Hahn," Lizabet replied. "We take these menial tasks so the experts can focus on the big challenges."

"I'd like to see Hahn take on a menial task."

"He did," said Lizabet. "A two-hour shift this morning."

Adelheid let out a bitter laugh. "He would."

"You'd rather the system *not* be fair?" Lizabet asked. "You know what he says . . ." She gave her voice a nasal edge. "'The numbers don't lie!'"

Adelheid snorted. "Ramkin would at least have realized that an unfair system would give us something to complain about. Rest his soul."

Lizabet chuckled. "Yeah. How dare Hahn rob us of things to complain about?"

Lizabet put on her helmet and went to the airlock controls. The big door rumbled open, and Adelheid stepped inside. She put down her toolkit and made a final check of her suit.

Around her, displays lit up. She listened to Lizabet read through the checklist.

"Oxygen levels show full," Adelheid called. "Pressure containment confirmed. Everything checks out fine. I'm ready." She gathered up her toolkit again and moved closer to the outer door. "See you in two hours."

But Lizabet frowned. She peered at her display and tapped on the glass. "Wait—" Her voice crackled on the radio. "That can't be right. Adelheid, wait—"

With a burst of static, Lizabet's voice cut out.

"Lizabet?" Adelheid tapped the radio on her helmet. "Lizabet? What's wrong?" Then she realized there was total silence within her helmet. There wasn't even the hiss of oxygen.

She turned for the inner door, but it was already closing. Behind it, Lizabet ran forward, throwing herself to the floor and rolling, clearing the door just before it hit the floor with a solid *chunk!*

"There's a fault in your helmet," Lizabet shouted, though Adelheid could barely hear her through two sets of plexiglass. "You're not getting any oxygen!"

"What happened with the door?" Adelheid's voice made her own ears ring. "If there was a problem, it shouldn't have closed!"

Lizabet grabbed Adelheid's shoulder, pulled her down and stabbed a screwdriver at the helmet controls. "I don't know. I can't stop them. If the outer doors open, you're going to die!"

Alarms rang. Out of the corner of her eye, Adelheid saw a display light up, counting down the release of air. "Control!" she shouted. "Abort opening! Abort opening now!"

The klaxons kept ringing. The display continued to count down.

"Abort opening!" Adelheid yelled again.

Lizabet worked frantically. "I can't do it," she gasped. "I can't fix it!"

The displays clicked down. *Ten seconds to initiating vacuum. Nine.*

Lizabet stopped working. Adelheid straightened up. The two women stared at each other in horror.

Then, Lizabet twisted off Adelheid's helmet. She pulled it up and cast it aside.

"Lizabet!" Adelheid shouted. *Three seconds to initiating vacuum.*

Lizabet twisted her own helmet. It let out a chuff as it released. Before Adelheid could react, she pulled her helmet off and clamped it down over Adelheid's head. The locks engaged. Oxygen hissed in Adelheid's ears.

Pumps roared to life. The air pulled at Lizabet's hair and sucked the breath from her lungs.

"No!" Adelheid screamed. She reached for the catches of her helmet, but Lizabet grabbed her wrists and held tight. She shook her head.

"Abort the opening!" Adelheid shrieked. "Whoever is in control, abort! Abort!"

Lizabet choked, then let out a gurgle. She coughed, and blood trickled down her chin. Her grip slipped. She staggered, and Adelheid caught her, lowering her to the floor.

"Abort!" Adelheid sobbed. "Please! You're killing her!"

Lizabet let go of her last breath, then went limp in Adelheid's arms. The hiss of decompression stopped. The outer doors opened in silence. Adelheid stared out at the barren landscape, the Milky Way rising on the horizon.

Lizabet stared at nothing. Adelheid clutched her close and wept.

The radio stayed silent.

Adelheid blinked the tears from her eyes and looked down at Lizabet. The woman's eyes had already frozen over. Her skin was tinged blue. Gently, Adelheid let go of her and picked up Lizabet's screwdriver.

She looked around the airlock and saw the airlock's camera. It wasn't pointing at her. It had fallen or had been pulled to face straight down at its own corner. Maybe that explained why nobody was coming running. There had been no witnesses.

She looked at her tablet. The camera had been on her list of fixes, right at the end. Still, it felt too much of a coincidence to be an accident.

*Which means somebody planned this. What were they expecting to happen? Not to have Lizabet leap beneath the airlock doors and try to rescue me. They must be expecting her to radio or run for help, only for it to arrive too late for me. They must not have expected her to sacrifice herself.*

*Poor Lizabet. She'd seen enough death and wasn't willing to see anymore.*

Adelheid stood up.

*This does not feel like an accident. If it isn't, what are people expecting to find when they come and open the airlock door? What happens if they find me here alive?*

She gave Lizabet one last sad look, then turned to the open airlock door. She stepped onto the dust of Mercury.

When she was three steps away from the airlock, the doors closed behind her.

Her breath rasped over the hiss of oxygen from her air tanks. She tapped her radio but got only silence.

*So, Lizabet's radio wasn't working either. She couldn't have called for help. Was she meant to be another victim? Or was the radio fault simply to explain why nobody came in time?*

She looked up at the expanse of the *Messenger*, rising ten storeys above her and kilometres before and behind her.

*Where do I go? To the front to alert those repairing the Robinson Rail?*

*Or maybe I should let whoever was behind this "accident" think that I'm dead. That might give me time to investigate.*

*But I can't do that out here. I have to get back inside.*

She made her decision and walked toward the *Messenger*'s new tail section, staying close to the hull, ducking below portholes. *The trackworks are beside me. In this section, the floors above house the kitchens and residences.*

Ahead, she saw the large airlock doors and protruding frames that provided the gasket lock with the *Messenger*'s platform at Terminal. *Most of these connect with the main pedestrian corridor. I won't be able to stay hidden there.*

*But there are service entrances at these gaskets as well.*

She trudged the next hundred metres, the hiss of oxygen and the rasp of her breath her only company.

Finally, she stood under one of the gasket locks, grabbed a handhold, and swung up to a foothold. Slowly, carefully, she climbed the side of the *Messenger*.

Ladders were few and far between, so Adelheid's path up her latitude town meandered, shifting to where she could get a grip. She ascended one level height, then two. Then, when she got level with the gasket locks, she reached a gap. Her next handhold was a long stretch away. But if she leaned out on tiptoe, she could grab the handlebar and the next foothold would be just in reach of her toe. She grabbed the handlebar and leaned out.

Then she looked down.

The dust of Mercury stretched out in the lights of the *Messenger* until the pool of illumination ended and darkness kicked in. She was at least twenty metres up.

*If I let go now, would the fall kill me? Somebody wants me dead already, and, really, would that be a bad thing? I'd be one less mouth for the* Messenger *to feed.*

She let her grip loosen. She leaned out from the *Messenger*, clinging with the tips of her fingers.

*This could be my patriotic duty.*

Then she tightened her grip. *No.*

*There have been no suicides on the* Messenger—*at least, none that I know of. And, certainly, nobody has died from falling from a great height.*

*Damn, damn Mercurian gravity.*

*If I really wanted to end it all, all I'd have to do is pop the catch on my helmet and let the vacuum take me, like it took Lizabet.*

*Pop the hatch on Lizabet's helmet.*

*Which she gave me.*

*So I could live.*

Adelheid looked out again at the darkness. Then she pulled herself back.

She focused on the far foothold and stretched out. Hugging the side of the *Messenger*, she slipped across the gap and stood on the narrow ledge, breathing heavily.

The gasket airlocks were a set of airlock doors that ran along the side of the *Messenger*. The big main ones, which lead to the agoras, were at the centre, but near her was one of the service airlocks, leading to a set of service tunnels. *Which are more likely to be deserted.*

The maintenance hatch covering the door controls was locked, but Adelheid used Lizabet's screwdriver to remove the screws of the hinges, then snapped the lock by yanking the hinge end of the door hard toward her.

A touch screen lit up, but she hesitated.

*The moment I enter my security codes, I'll broadcast my location straight up the chain of command. Someone wanting to kill me and make it look like an accident would have to know how to bypass security and safety features. More likely than not, they were high up that chain of command. If people know I'm alive, I won't have time to find who's responsible.*

*I have to use my time wisely. I need someone I can trust.*

She tapped her radio. It was still dead. She focused on the keypad instead. The display allowed communication and private personal messages didn't require security clearance. *So, what was Liao's personal code, again?*

She tapped at the keypad. *This message should reach his console on the forebridge.* She typed, *Liao, it's Adelheid. Don't speak, just acknowledge.*

Her heart thumped in her throat. She used that to count to thirty.

No response.

She tapped again. *Don't speak. Just acknowledge.*

Her heart thumped another twenty times before text scrolled across her screen. *Adelheid? What are you doing?*

She looked at the maintenance identification plate beside the door. *Use your security code to open Gasket Airlock 7. The one leading to the service corridor. Do it.*

Ten heartbeats passed before the lights around the display turned from red to green, and, without a sound but with a vibration she felt in her feet, the airlock door opened. Adelheid let out a sigh of relief as she stepped across the threshold. The door closed behind her, and she heard the hiss of oxygen start soft and grow louder until the safety latches on her helmet clicked, and she could easily remove it.

She went to the door controls on the town side of the airlock and accessed the radio. "Liao?" she whispered.

At the other end, Liao coughed.

"Is someone watching you?"

Liao coughed again.

"Something wrong, Lieutenant?" Gerhardt's voice.

Liao cleared his throat. "No, sir. It's just ... dry in here."

"Fair enough," said Gerhardt. "Carry on."

"Liao," Adelheid whispered. She peered at an evacuation floor plan on the wall and found the arrow identifying the location. She traced the service corridor to its end. "Come up with an excuse and come to Maintenance Locker Room 5S43. And ..." She looked down at her pressure suit. "Bring an extra uniform. Will you do that?"

There was a pause, and then Liao coughed once more.

☿

ADELHEID PACED in the maintenance locker room. *If Liao doesn't come soon, I'm going out there, conspicuous or not.*

There was a knock at the door. She went over and let Liao in. "What did you tell Gerhardt?"

He looked confused and worried. "I told him I'd been called away to deal with my maintenance duty early," he whispered. "Hopefully, he doesn't find out that was a flat-out lie." He handed her a bundle of clothes. "What's going on? What are you doing here? Why do you need this uniform?"

She drew a shaky breath. "Lizabet's dead."

He jerked back. "What?"

"Shh!" She put his hand over his mouth. Taking the clothes, she set them on a bench. "It was made to look like an accident," she said, stepping out of her vacuum suit while Liao hurriedly looked away. "Somebody sabotaged my pressure suit and then opened the airlock door to expose me to the vacuum. If Lizabet hadn't . . ." She swallowed, then shrugged on her shirt. "They killed her. They were trying to kill me."

Liao turned back and stared, aghast. "Why would they do that? And who are they?"

She hopped on one foot, then the other, as she pulled on her trousers. "I don't know—not for sure, anyway. And I don't have much time to find out before they find Lizabet's body and realize I'm not dead. We have to move fast." She faced him. "Will you help me?"

The colour had gone from his cheeks. "Lizabet's dead?"

Adelheid nodded.

For a moment, neither spoke. They stared at each other, then at the floor. Then Liao reached out, and Adelheid hugged him close. The moment lengthened. Adelheid took a raspy breath, then another.

Finally, she pushed back and took Liao's hand. "Please help me."

He took a deep breath of his own. "What do you need me to do?"

♀

ADELHEID WAITED five minutes after Liao left for the airlock where Lizabet lay dead. If her plan was to work, he had to be the first to find her. Nobody had raised the alarm yet, so there was a chance he'd be the first.

She hated giving him that task, but at least Lizabet would be discovered by a friend and not somebody who'd arranged her death. At least she could count on Liao to raise enough of an alarm to keep attention off her.

She stepped from the locker room in her borrowed uniform. She followed the service corridor to where it emptied into one of the public corridors. There, checking to make sure people weren't nearby or looking, she slipped outside. She kept her head down and peered over the top of a tablet and stylus she'd taken from a service locker. She strode through the corridors toward the command deck.

The public address speakers sparked to life. "Emergency!" It was Liao's voice. It shook. "Assistance needed at Airlock 1S12. Officer down! All hands, immediately!"

Adelheid slowed, then slipped back into some shadows as people in the corridor looked up and around. A pair of maintenance workers and a command officer rushed past, fingers on their communicators, demanding more information. Everybody else's attention turned to the information screens, though it was too soon for updates. It pulled attention away from a crowded section of the corridor, however, and Adelheid hurried through.

As she walked, debating whether she should use the trams

to get to the new tail section's command deck, something about the crowds made her slow, then step behind the cover of a pillar. Peering out, she saw her face on the screens—her photograph. And people were gasping.

Whispers rose. "Did you hear? Captain Koning's dead!"

"What? Not Colonel Koning's daughter! How?"

"Some accident! She got blown into the vacuum!"

Hands went to cover mouths. "No! No, not her!"

From the shadows, Adelheid stared out at the knots of people who were gathering together, whispering in shock. Some . . . many! Many were . . . weeping!

"Lord in Sunlight, not her!"

She stared in astonishment. Then, after a moment, she slipped farther into the shadows and walked carefully away. The first chance she got, she ducked into a service corridor away from the grieving people.

☿

ADELHEID STEPPED from the service tunnel closest to the relocated command deck of the new tail section. There were crew quarters here and a large agora. There were people around, wandering, looking lost. To her chagrin, she saw more people weeping.

She followed the edge of the agora toward the crew quarters, wondering what to do next.

Then, in front of her, Captain Wilhelm ran up and knocked frantically at a door. Adelheid froze, then sidled behind a pillar.

The door opened, and Hahn looked out. "What is it, Captain Schroeder?"

Wilhelm saluted. "Governor! They've found Captain Koning's body!"

Hahn looked grim. He glanced around the corridor at the people, and his frown deepened. "The news is already out?"

Wilhelm nodded. "Lieutenant Fang used a public channel to broadcast his alert."

Hahn shook his head. "That's unfortunate. I'd best go address the public. This will be hard news to take, but we can rally them to her memory."

He stalked off, Wilhelm following.

Adelheid sidled to keep the pillar between her and Hahn and Wilhelm as they hurried past. She glanced at the door to Hahn's quarters, which was swinging back. She judged the distance then, trying not to make a sound, rushed over and caught the door handle just before the door swung shut. Slowly, carefully, Adelheid pulled the door toward her and then stepped inside.

Hahn's quarters were almost a mirror of her own. There was a bed and a bedside table with a small brace of books. The desk that, in her case, held her science experiments was here overwhelmed by piles of collated reports and papers.

*If there's a conspiracy to kill me, I need to start at the top. Either the evidence is here, or I'll know I can trust Hahn to help me find it.*

At the desk was a tablet that Hahn had not logged out of. She touched the screen before the sleep function could kick in. She called up lists of files and sorted them by date stamp. She looked through the most recent. Most stated clearly what they were—crew timetables, calorie reports, and maintenance schedules—but one stood out, labelled only *List*.

Curious, Adelheid selected the file and opened it.

She read it.

She stared at it.

She felt behind her for a chair and sat heavily. She stared at the tablet some more.

The public address speakers crackled to life, broadcasting Hahn's voice. "Attention all. It is with great sorrow that I'm forced to read into the record the death of Captain Adelheid Koning in an airlock accident. As you know, Captain Koning was a loyal officer of the *Messenger*. Her father, and now she, gave their lives in the service of their fellow citizens so we could live. We stand in honour of her memory."

Adelheid said nothing. She stared in the middle distance as funereal music played over the speakers. She waited.

And waited.

On the public address system, a call went out for Lieutenant Anderson to report to the bridge. Adelheid continued to sit. *I hope Liao can keep the deception going a little longer.*

She waited some more.

Finally, she heard the door creak open, and Hahn step in.

"You jumped the gun," she said without turning around. "You announced my death before you positively identified my body. Yes, Liao probably said it was me, but you should still have checked. It suggests you were anticipating things."

Hahn stopped dead. She felt him standing by the door, staring at her.

"That was careless," she went on. "Which is surprising from someone who plans so far ahead."

She turned in her seat and held up the tablet. She began to read off the names. "'Miike Milner, sanitation worker.' He was killed by a steam pipe burst in a maintenance corridor. 'Eva Gladner, kitchen staff.' She was killed by an electrical short in the main galley. 'Isaac Bowman, cargo worker.' He was killed in a forklift accident. There are checkmarks after their names. My name is on this list, but there's no checkmark yet."

She looked up at him. "But the really frightening thing is that there are many more names on this list, all without checkmarks, but space for one. None of them are dead . . . yet."

Hahn stared at her. He let the door go. He said nothing as it clicked shut behind him.

Adelheid waved the tablet. "This list is a cull. One-quarter of all the males between the ages of thirty and fifty-five are on this list. Every person over the age of sixty is on this list." She lowered her voice to a growl. "And you picked out half of the forebridge crew—*my* crew!—people who might challenge your leadership. Lizabet's name is on the list." She drew a shaky breath. "If she hadn't sacrificed herself for me in the airlock, she would have had a different 'accident' awaiting her!"

Still, Hahn said nothing.

"What gets me the most, though," said Adelheid, "is that you chose to write all of this down. I didn't have to look hard for this. What in Sunlight made you produce an actual list?"

Hahn looked down for a moment, but he answered her. "Of course, there has to be a list." He walked forward. Adelheid turned, watching him warily, as he stepped around her and stood at the other wall by his desk. "When you have to reduce the surplus population of the *Messenger* without depleting key departments, you have to be careful about who you choose to die."

Adelheid nodded. "That's what alarmed me when Gerhardt read the names of the people who died into the record. Those accidents were spread across all departments as if they were designed to ensure there were others to take up the slack."

"We had to do all that," Hahn added, "without people realizing what was happening and starting a panic."

Adelheid's jaw tightened. "So, you decided who lived and who died."

Hahn leaned back. "I didn't. The algorithm did."

Adelheid let out a terse laugh. "Oh, yes! I'm sure you left this all to an algorithm. I'm sure you didn't play any favourites—"

"Look at the last name on the list, Captain."

Adelheid stared at Hahn, then brought her gaze down. She picked up the tablet and scanned the list of names.

At the bottom was "Daarel Hahn."

She gaped at him. Then, she set the tablet on her lap. "So, what happens now, Governor?"

Hahn looked down. "One of two things, Captain Koning. Either you tell the people what you've learned and start a panic . . . or we find a way to stop you."

Adelheid heard the door click. She swung around, but Gerhardt was already striding through, bringing up his gun. She saw the muzzle rising toward her head.

And she saw Liao step in behind him and strike him down with a pipe. The air rang with a tuning-fork hum until Liao put his hand on the pipe to stop it. Gerhardt crashed to the ground, groaning. Liao picked up Gerhardt's gun and held it ready.

Adelheid faced Hahn, who stared in horror at Gerhardt's prone form. "I didn't just sit here, looking at your list, while you read my eulogy," she snapped. "I called someone I could trust, and he brought a camera and a microphone."

She pulled the microphone from her collar. Hahn stared at Adelheid, then followed her gaze as she looked at his desk and the camera she'd placed on it.

They stood in silence, and, in that silence, they heard a growing noise—a rising rumble of low voices outside Hahn's door.

Adelheid looked at Liao, who shrugged. She stepped past him, opened the apartment door carefully, and peered outside.

A crowd had gathered—*was* gathering. She could see more people stepping off the trams and coming over. They stood in a wide arc around the door in near silence, but enough of them were muttering to each other to make the rumble they'd heard inside the room.

They looked angry. They waited.

Adelheid stepped into the open. The people's expressions didn't change when they saw her. They waited with a sense of purpose that made her shiver. "What do you want?" she said.

"Bring us Hahn," somebody muttered, then somebody else. The low chant filled the agora: "Bring us Hahn. Bring us the murderer!"

Adelheid backed up, felt behind her for Hahn's door handle, and stepped back inside the apartment.

"What's happening?" Liao asked.

Adelheid gripped Liao's hand and pointed the gun back at Hahn. "Stay focused." She turned to Hahn. "The people know. They've come for you."

Hahn clenched his jaw, then forced himself to relax. "You've created a mob."

"Not a mob." She looked back at the apartment door. "I'm not sure what it is. But they've come for you. They know you've gone too far."

"They don't understand." Hahn's voice rose. "They'd never understand! The numbers don't lie! We do *not* have the food to sustain us!"

Adelheid glanced at her microphone. *Should I have stopped recording?*

But Hahn carried on. "A quarter of the people of the *Messenger* have to die! And they have to do it quickly if we're to have any hope of surviving!" His voice rose higher in panic and madness. "The numbers don't lie! You can't argue with the numbers!"

"Yes, you can," Liao whispered.

Something in his tone made Adelheid look at him. He stood still, but she could tell he was forcing himself to do so against a flood of emotion that would otherwise have left him shaking.

"Yes, you can!" he repeated. He stepped forward, the gun in his right hand pointed at Hahn's head, his left hand balled into a fist. "You must! How dare you not? How *dare* you leave us survivors with this?"

"Liao—" Adelheid touched his arm. He shook it off.

"There is a story my grandfather told me," he said. "From one of the Earth's great wars in the twentieth century. They had ships carrying supplies across the oceans and ships beneath those oceans shooting at them. One of the supply ships sank, and the survivors found themselves in frigid water, with one lifeboat among them. Thirty sailors, many of them injured, all of them freezing. The lifeboat could only hold ten."

Hahn grimaced. Gerhardt looked woozily up from the floor, but Liao pressed on. "So, what did the sailors do? They took turns using the lifeboat. The weakest went in and stayed there while the rest held onto the edge and swam for as long as they could. If there wasn't room at the edge, people held onto the people holding onto the edge. When somebody got too tired, they switched out. Somebody inside the lifeboat got into the frigid water and helped somebody else back in. This went on for two days before they were rescued. Everybody was almost dead when they were found, but not one person was lost."

Liao lowered the gun, his glare at Hahn shifting into disgust. "The biggest problem they had to face was convincing people not to tough things out too long in the water." He turned away, then suddenly swung back, bringing the gun up again. "You cannot ask the strong to leave the weak behind to die! You cannot—" His voice cracked. He drew a shaky breath. "It's the worst thing you could ever ask them to do. It's the worst burden they could ever carry!"

He stopped, then. He kept the gun aimed at Hahn. Silence descended. Finally, Adelheid drew herself up. "Acting Governor Hahn, I am relieving you of command and placing you under arrest."

"You have no authority—" Hahn began.

"I have no choice!" Adelheid shouted. "I will follow the law as far as I'm able, but if the law prevents me from making sure you see justice, then I will go around it. I have to because the alternative is out that door—" She jabbed a finger at the crowd beyond in the corridor. "—and we don't want to go there. But I will not let you get away with mass murder!"

She stopped, took a deep breath, then continued more quietly. "You will receive a fair trial—a jury of your peers. You will get a chance to defend your actions, and then you will be judged." She took another deep breath and spoke up so the microphone and the people outside could hear. "I will do this. I'm not leaving you to the mob. I know what I'm doing, and I will accept the consequences."

Hahn turned away, chuckling softly. "A fair trial? Tell me, Captain: what do you think the verdict will be?"

Adelheid scoffed. "You've admitted you arranged the deaths of dozens of people. What do you think?"

"Yes," he said. "And still, the calorie problem would remain." He pulled his hand from his pocket. "But I can help with that, at least."

Adelheid saw the gun. She yelled and ran forward as Hahn tucked the muzzle under his chin and pulled the trigger.

The bang and spray stopped Adelheid in her tracks. Hahn's body crumpled to the floor.

☿

LIAO MOVED FIRST. With his gun now trained on Gerhardt, he backed to the door, opened it, and shouted to the crowd outside. "We need witnesses! Two people right now. *Don't* storm this door!"

There was a brief commotion in the crowd. A moment later, two civilians—a young man and a middle-aged woman—stepped inside, eyes widening as they saw Adelheid looking down at the sprawled body on the floor. Gerhardt had pushed himself against a wall and sat holding his knees to his chest.

"We heard what happened," said the woman. "We know Hahn shot himself. We know what he did—what you had to do."

Adelheid kept staring at Hahn's body.

Liao frowned. "Adelheid?"

Adelheid stayed silent.

Liao turned to the witnesses. "Um . . . we need—"

Adelheid gathered herself and straightened. "We need people in here to take Hahn's body to the morgue." She turned and pointed to the witnesses. "You two, call the medical staff to arrange it. Then, I want the crowd out there to pick ten people they trust. They will accompany Liao and me to the forebridge. And put out the word, I want all the officers of the *Messenger*, every civilian council member, and every department head to meet us there, unarmed. They have some explaining to do. And, finally—" She swung around and jabbed a finger at Gerhardt, who flinched. "Put this man under arrest."

☿

ADELHEID AND LIAO stayed until the medics arrived to prepare Hahn's body. The room was full of civilians now. They milled around the agora, looking bewildered and grim, not fully aware of the fact they were guarding the area or what they were guarding it from. The people remained quiet and respectful. Nobody said, "He got what was coming to him." At least, not more than once.

Finally, when they were ready, Adelheid led Liao, Gerhardt —his hands cuffed in front of him—and a group of civilians out of Hahn's quarters. They boarded the tram to the forebridge. There, they met another crowd of civilians and officers. The forebridge crew stood at attention, while around them civilian council members and department heads just stood. Many looked angry. Everyone looked nervous. Their nervousness increased as they saw the civilians that flanked Adelheid and Liao. Liao placed a hand on Gerhardt's shoulder and moved him beside the officers.

Adelheid came forward and walked the line of officers. "I want to know," she said, her voice low. "Who among you knew about Hahn's list?"

The officers stiffened. Some looked at the others in fury, but nobody spoke up.

"He could not have done what he did by himself," Adelheid went on. "So, who else knew?"

Wilhelm shuddered. "Captain Koning, I swear to you, we didn't—"

"I was the only one to know," said Gerhardt.

Adelheid rounded on him. "Who helped you?"

He looked away. "No one—"

"You could not have arranged every accident!"

He took a deep breath and let it out slowly. "The people who did did not know what they'd been ordered to do. They were told to add particular pieces of equipment to particular fixtures. They were told to delay a particular act of maintenance. If nothing else, they were told to simply look away."

She stepped closer. "Who was assigned to sabotage my pressure suit?"

He flinched but faced her gaze. "Me. I'm sorry."

Silence stretched. Adelheid clenched her jaw. Finally, she said, "Thank you for your honesty."

Gerhardt bowed his head.

Adelheid turned to the other officers. "Set up the agora for a judicial meeting. We are having a trial."

The other officers stared at her. She stared back. "We are not a mob. Yes, I overthrew the chain of command, but the mob would have been worse. Except for that one allowance, we will do this by the book. We will have a trial. It will all be read into the record. And then we will have justice."

As she said this, she turned back toward Gerhardt.

"A trial?" he said quietly.

She nodded. "A fair one." Then she glared at him. "But we will see to it that justice is served."

☿

HOURS LATER, a hatchway opened on the side of the *Messenger*. A single land speeder nosed out. It hesitated, then rolled forward, raising dust as it headed for the horizon.

At one of the portals, Adelheid watched it go.

Behind her, Liao cleared his throat.

"Mark Bakker's name wasn't on the list," Adelheid muttered.

"What?"

"He wasn't on the list." She kept her gaze on the departing land speeder. "Gerhardt and Hahn didn't arrange his death; he died in his sleep. The others, though—the accidents . . . that was all them."

Liao stood silent. He shifted on his feet.

Adelheid didn't look around. "Gerhardt got a fair trial. He pled guilty. All the captains agreed on the sentence. The civilian council backed us up."

"But . . . banishment?" said Liao. "Those land speeders have a limited range for oxygen. Gerhardt could make it to the *Apollo* or the *Hermes* if they were this far forward, but they aren't. The closest town is the *Baxter-Nordley*, and there's no way his oxygen will last that long."

"I know," said Adelheid.

There was a long silence between them as the lights of the land speeder vanished in the distance.

Adelheid pushed away from the portal. "It's more of a chance than Lizabet got."

She stalked off.

# CHAPTER 16
# HAPPY NEW YEAR

RECONSTRUCTION CONTINUED FOR THE NEXT SIXTY DAYS. THERE was a lot to do, and not enough people to do it. Adelheid and the other captains focused heavily on organization, with Liao and the other lieutenants helping. Soldiers and civilians alike worked hard.

*The better to not think about what comes next,* thought Adelheid.

But there were no more accidents. Nobody else died in their sleep.

*They have new hope,* she thought. *They don't realize that the choice Hahn faced hasn't gone away. We're just ignoring it.*

*And, Lord-in-Sunlight, I can't bring myself to tell them otherwise.*

The debris of the crash was cleared away and recycled. The Concrete Workers Guild laid their first mix on the dust of Mercury. The supports for the new Robinson Rail rose.

There were meetings to attend and crews to organize. Except for a couple of hours each night when Adelheid pursued her experiments, she did nothing but work, eat, and sleep. The end of the sixtieth day found her at her workbench in her quarters, staring at her protein loaf. The water rations had increased, but the food rations had stayed the same.

*There may be fewer mouths to feed, but there still aren't enough calories. That's our choice: eat now and starve sooner, or stay hungry now and starve later.*

She turned away from her plate and, using tongs, pulled the Petri dish from its portable forge. She peered at it through her microscope, then sighed. She wrote in her journal, *Sample 87, Fertilizer Candidate 23: Insufficient growth.*

She put her face in her hands. *No, no, no.*

There was a soft knock at the door she'd forgotten to close. "Adelheid?"

Liao stood waiting. Adelheid sat up and smiled at him. "Yes, Liao?"

He stepped into her room and closed the door behind him. "Are you okay?"

She rolled her eyes. "I'm as well as can be expected."

His frown deepened.

She looked at him. "What is it, Liao?"

"I've, uh . . ." He looked lost. "I've been asked to invite you to the main agora. The celebrations are starting. Maybe you heard?"

"Celebrations?" She peered past him at her closed door and listened. It took her a moment, but at last, she heard it: people shouting and laughing, music starting up in the distance. Her brow furrowed. "What's so special about today?"

"It's New Year's Eve." At her frown, he added, "December 31, 2151." He looked at his watch. "Twenty-three forty-two Greenwich Mean Time, apparently. It was suggested you should be present."

She stared at her workbench. "They won't be saying 'Happy New Year' on Earth, you know. Assuming there's anybody left there to say it at all."

Liao shifted on his feet but stayed silent.

"Do you think we'll keep the Earth calendar?" She laughed morosely. "Do you think we'll still measure things in Earth years, when there's nobody back there to keep time?"

Liao sucked in his breath. "Look, there's something you should know. The reason I've been asked to bring you is because the captains—the other captains—and the remainder of the civilian council have made a decision and would like you there."

She turned to him. "What are you talking about?" Then she noticed his sleeve. "And when were you made a captain?"

His cheeks reddened. He ducked his head. "We've all been promoted. Including you. We wanted to present you with your stripes."

"But why? Who authorized this?" She shook her head. "With Hahn dead—"

Liao shrugged. "It came to a vote. The other captains had a meeting, and the civilian council concurred. You've been holding this town together the past five weeks, and after Gerhardt, you were the most senior captain. Wilhelm and the others think you're the obvious choice to assume the senior rank, so . . ." He stepped back and saluted. "Congratulations, Colonel Koning."

The title made bile rise in her throat. *No.* "Liao, don't—"

His brow furrowed. "What's wrong?"

*I'm not my father! I'm not ready!*

His frown deepened. "Adelheid?"

"You can't do this!" Her voice rose. "We have no official governor! We have no official commander! We can't just—"

"Assume that we're now the ones in charge?" Liao cut in. "What do you think we've been doing these past few weeks? You've more than filled the role. People have rallied around you, Colonel Abraham Koning's daughter. The repairs are finished now because of that. It should be you."

"Why?" she snapped. "Do they think leadership is in my DNA?"

He shrugged. "Maybe they just know it when they see it?"

"But you can't—" She stuttered. "You shouldn't—I can't—I don't want to have to make this choice!"

"What choice?"

"Hahn's choice!"

Silence descended. Liao stared at her, perplexed but also sympathetic. *A rock.* Adelheid took a deep breath and held it until she felt her heartbeat slow. "Hahn's plan was evil, but he was right. We can't sustain a ration limit of eight hundred calories per person per day. We will lose most of the *Messenger* that way. People are going to start dying in the next few weeks and months. We need to increase our calorie intake, and the only way to do that is to reduce the number of mouths to feed. Put me in charge, and I'm going to have to make that choice."

"Well, *we* will," said Liao, firmly.

"You're not making that choice," Adelheid replied. "We've all been delaying. But it has to be made. And it has to be made soon."

"Well, what would you do if you had to make that choice?" Liao asked.

Adelheid shook her head. "Maybe . . . maybe a call for volunteers. Possibly, if that didn't solve the issue, a lottery." She glared at him. "Should we propose that during the New Year's Eve festivities?"

Liao sucked his breath. "Maybe not during the party."

Adelheid let out a short, terse laugh. She leaned back her head. "Still . . . that might be the best solution—something the public understands and agrees to. Not something done in secret."

Liao nodded. "That . . . sounds like a reasonable decision from someone capable of making that decision." He stepped closer. "And that's a decision people will back you up on. You don't have to make the decision alone, but by making it, it will be easier for everyone else."

She shook her head. "Why should it be me? There has to be others who could be in control."

"Well, that's the thing. The civilian council decided Hahn was in charge, and you saw what happened with him. They're reluctant to make a second choice, and I can understand why. But there's one thing worse than nobody knowing who's in charge."

She looked at him. "What's that?"

"More than one person thinking *they* should be in charge."

Adelheid drew back, thoughtful. *What would happen if I said no? People are pulling together now, but they're pulling on me to do that. If I'm not there to be pulled on, who will they turn to? Liao's right: what if it's more than one person? What if we get factions? What if we get power-hungry people? What if they get it wrong?*

*But what if I get it wrong?*

"You know," said Liao, "it's not like they're asking it to be forever."

She looked up at him.

He shrugged. "Things change. We adjust."

She looked away. "And sometimes we get so comfortable with temporary solutions they become permanent." She sighed. "But, you're right. As long as this is temporary. I'm not the new governor. The people deserve more than to be ruled by a military government. I'm a placeholder, a *stadtholder*, nothing more."

Her brow furrowed as the word echoed in her mind. *Stadtholder. Dad used that term once, teaching me the history of my ancestors' homeland. Not a king, at least not originally. A steward. Someone who was in charge until the right person or people came along.*

"Fair enough." Liao pulled something from his jacket. As Adelheid watched, he placed two cups on her workbench, took out a small flask, and poured a clear liquid into both. She frowned up at him.

"Alcohol ration," he explained. "For today."

She picked up her cup and turned it in her hand, watching the light play across the sharp-smelling liquid. "I asked, and you didn't answer: do you think we'll keep the Earth calendar and measure dates in Earth time?"

Liao shrugged. "Maybe?" He tilted his head. "I don't like the idea of measuring things in Mercury years. Too many New Year's festivals, and I'm not really in the mood to celebrate that much."

"Neither am I," Adelheid replied.

"But we *do* have to celebrate," he said. "At least once every Earth year."

"Why?"

He stepped back and opened the door. The sounds of celebration echoing through the corridors intensified. "Because, despite yesterday, we're here today. We've stabilized our rations. We've repaired the *Messenger*. We got through today. But we need something to get us to tomorrow."

She gave him a wry look. "An inspiring speech. How long did you work on it?"

"It's true, though." He took a deep breath, then stepped closer again, looking her in the eye. "We're here today, and we're going to be here tomorrow. So, let's celebrate that. Celebrate . . . and remember." He gestured to the door. He raised his glass again. "Happy New Year?"

Adelheid hesitated, then tapped her glass to Liao's. She slugged it back, then set it down on her workbench before standing up.

This brought her close to Liao, and she hesitated. They stared at each other, and the silence lengthened. In it, Adelheid thought, *Liao. Always been there, looking at the bright side of things. Making me hope rather than fear. My best friend since we were in pre-vocational school. For a time, more, until we backed down. He's my best friend. I'm so glad to have him here.*

She frowned. *My best. Friend.*

Liao looked away and cleared his throat. "We should get going. As Colonel, you should address the people."

"Yeah," said Adelheid quietly.

Liao opened the door and stepped aside, letting Adelheid lead the way toward the sounds of celebration.

There was laughter and babbles of conversation. People passed them in twos and threes, arms over each other's shoulders, cups in hand. Adelheid frowned at that, and Liao noticed. He shrugged. Then, from under his uniform jacket, he pulled another small flask of alcohol. He tilted his head, and, in his glance, she could see the question, *Would you like to share?*

"Maybe later," she whispered. They walked on.

Then she stopped because the babble of celebration had suddenly stopped. They were at the entrance of one of the *Messenger's* agoras. It was full of people who had been celebrating. They were now all staring at her.

The silence stretched. Adelheid sensed Liao moving closer to her. *He's going to put a comforting hand on my shoulder. That would be nice, but here and now, I can't have that.*

She stepped forward. The crowd drew back, then parted, forming a channel that shaped itself as she headed to the stairs leading to the balcony overlooking the agora. As she walked, Liao following, she heard people start clapping, one or two individuals at first, then more, faster until, by the time she climbed the stairs and stood behind the railing overlooking the agora, the air echoed with it and the stamping of feet. People waved. People cheered. People saluted. Adelheid frowned. *Civilians shouldn't salute the military.*

*Maybe I'll fix that later.*

She clasped the railing and took a breath to speak.

Footsteps hurried up behind her. "Colonel Koning!"

She turned. An officer saluted, then handed over a tablet. "We've received an urgent message from the *Hermes*! It's from Lieutenant Cristavao D'Cunha."

Liao gaped. "How? We still haven't heard from any of the other towns."

Adelheid snatched the tablet and read the message.

*Emergency! Oxygen failing! Let us in! We have to talk!*

Liao peered over Adelheid's shoulder. "What does he mean, let us in?"

She looked at the message header. "These aren't the *Hermes*'s coordinates. They're on our latitude." Suddenly, it made sense: *oxygen failing*. "They're in a land speeder."

Liao blanched. "Then they must be way out of range of their town. Whatever it is they want to tell us, it must be really important."

She handed the tablet back to the officer. "We have to help them."

"I'll order crews to their location," said Liao. "If they're low on oxygen, they may need medical attention; the sooner the better."

"How far out are they?" she asked the officer.

He winced. "At least two days."

She sucked her teeth, then let out her breath. "Then we'd better shorten that time."

Liao frowned as he put this together, but he nodded.

"I'll tell the people," Adelheid added.

She turned back to the railing and looked out at the crowd that had gone quiet while she, Liao, and the other officer huddled. They looked back at her, expectant. It was like a weight. *But it's a weight I have to bear.*

*What do I tell them? What do I feel in my heart?*

After a moment, she cleared her throat. "We have sacrificed

so much for this day." She swallowed, then continued louder. "We have worked hard, with little thanks, for this moment. So, let us have this moment."

People nodded. Applause rose.

"I am honoured to tell you what many of you already know," she went on. "That repairs to the Robinson Rail and the *Messenger* are complete. You already know this because you have all been part of those repairs. You may be looking forward to us moving forward after more than sixty days stationary. And I'm here to tell you that we will move."

The audience clapped heartily.

"But we are not moving forward," she said.

People stopped clapping. They looked around in confusion.

"I have received a message from behind us." Adelheid's voice echoed through the agora. "The first in nearly a hundred and fifty days. The *Hermes* has called for our help. Remember that they gave us a third of the supplies in Terminal. They've helped us, and now we must help them. Whatever is happening near the Dawn Line, we have a duty to our fellow Mercurians to see it through."

Through the crowd, she saw people straightening up, looking determined. She nodded and raised her voice. "Reverse the *Messenger*! We're going back!"

The audience cheered. Behind her, a babble went up among the officers. Orders were relayed through the agora. Looking to the back, Adelheid saw Liao tap a comms unit on the wall and speak into it. Beneath their feet, the purr of the *Messenger* amped up. Then came a jerk of acceleration, pushing everyone toward the front rather than the back. People in the agora stumbled and caught each other as the *Messenger* slowly began reversing along the Robinson Rail.

Adelheid pushed away from the railing. She glanced at Liao and found him staring back. His look matched hers.

She looked in the direction the *Messenger* was heading, even though all she saw was the corridor to the tail section. She frowned, determined but nervous.

*What are we going to find back there?*

# PART FIVE
# FRIEDA: THE SHADOW CABINET

# CHAPTER 17
# GATHERING HER TEAM

*The* Messenger
*The Mercury Colonies, May 14, 2201 CE*

WHATEVER THE TIME WAS, THE KNOCK AT FRIEDA'S BEDROOM door came far too early. She tried to struggle upright before she remembered and slumped back with a groan. "Come in!"

Anna entered, hurried over, and helped Frieda sit up. Finally, Frieda sat at the edge of the bed, feeling both embarrassed and grateful. "Thanks," she grumbled.

Anna did a quick curtsy. "Your Highness, Secretary Tova Caarson is here to see you."

Frieda straightened up. *Who? Anna said "secretary," so one of Grandmother's advisers, likely. Which one? I need to be better at names.* "Send them in."

Anna drew back. "Your Highness? Now? You're not dressed!"

Frieda looked down at herself. She was wearing nightclothes that were not revealing at all. She glared at Anna, pulled the edge of her coverlet over one shoulder, and gave her a meaningful look. *Let's get this over with!*

Anna took the hint and draped the bedcover over Frieda's shoulders like a shawl. "Send them in," said Frieda again.

Anna hurried off, and Frieda struggled to her feet as she returned with a tall, blond individual who looked deceptively young. Frieda recognized them as one of the advisers that often helped Mom.

Tova bowed. "Your Highness. We received notice of your appointment of Cara Flores as your medical adviser."

Frieda kept her face neutral, even though she thought, *Am I in trouble?* "Oh? There's not a problem, is there?"

For a moment, Tova looked nervous, but they shook their head. "No, Your Highness. Your decision was perfectly legal. So, given your decision, I thought it best to hand over the documents confirming it and relating to it. Ms. Flores's personnel file, for instance." They set a tablet on her bedside table.

Frieda stared at it. "We have a file on her?"

"We have files on lots of people," Tova replied. "Everyone who works for the Stadtholder has a file as a matter of course. There are files on visiting diplomats. As Mufrau Flores is the *Hermes* Ambassador's daughter, she has her own file."

Frieda looked at the tablet again. "Ah."

Silence stretched. Tova looked at her expectantly. Finally, Frieda said, "All right, then. Thank you, Secretary Tova . . .you may go."

Tova nodded and left.

Frieda picked up the tablet and took it to her desk, setting it beside another tablet. She tapped the media screen above her desk and then tapped the tablet's screen. When the tablet flickered to life, she flipped through to the new set of files she'd gathered. She tapped open folders marked "Personnel," "Correspondence," and "Potential Candidates." Then she looked at Tova's file on Cara.

*I'm Stadtholder now. I need to be organized like a stadtholder.*

*Grandmother has advisers. She has files. She reads them. I'll need files, too, if I'm to add to my team of advisers.*

*But it doesn't feel right to read Cara's personnel file, even if I am Stadtholder. And if it doesn't feel right, maybe it isn't right?*

She hesitated a long moment, then tapped the file open.

Cara's face stared back at her, alongside lines of text listing Cara's height, weight, and eye colour. *We keep tabs on this information?* A list of grades followed (top marks, of course).

Frieda frowned when she saw Cara's address on the *Messenger.* It wasn't in the diplomatic quarter. She'd asked for and been assigned a simple accommodation a few levels above the main agora, close to the infirmary, and a few tram stops away from the Royal Apartment. *She's not living with her mother after all.*

Behind her, Anna entered, bearing a bundle of clean clothes. She started to put them away. On the wall, the media screen played on.

"This morning again saw protesters filling the main agora of the *Baxter-Nordley,* joining the crowd that was already there," said the newscaster. "People chanted for a referendum on self-determination before dispersing back to their jobs, leaving the core group behind.

"The mayor of the *Baxter-Nordley* dismissed the protest," the newscaster went on, "saying that the protesters represented a minority opinion. Protest organizers maintained they will continue to speak out and warned their government to expect further disruptions until their demands are met."

The screen flipped back to the newscaster. "Asked to comment on the *Baxter-Nordley* protests, the president of the *Leigh Brackett* said that she was hopeful that an equitable solution could be found through negotiation."

Frieda looked up at the screen and its image of a crowd of people waving their fists. *The president of the* Leigh Brackett *was asked to comment? Why are they asking for comments from the other towns?*

Behind her, Frieda heard Anna suck her teeth. She gave Anna an appraising look. "Do you have an opinion about this, Anna?"

Anna jerked upright from folding laundry, cheeks reddening. "No more than anybody else, Your Highness."

Frieda tilted her head. "Then what is the opinion of anybody else?"

Anna blinked at her.

Frieda sighed. "Anna, please tell me what you think. Honestly, I want to know."

Anna lowered her gaze but, after a moment, said, "I see no reason for the protesters' complaints, Your Highness. The *Messenger* has been nothing but good to them. They're *from* the *Messenger*. We sent them there after . . . after what happened at the start of the Silence."

Frieda did a quick calculation. "Their *grandparents* are from the *Messenger*. People can change their minds over generations, surely?"

Anna sniffed. "If they have a reason for it, I haven't heard it." Then, she added, "Your Highness." She set to work putting the rest of the clothes away.

Frieda stared at her. *That sounds like something Grandmother would say. Less forcefully, but still.*

She turned back to her tablet. On another file in Cara's folder, Frieda found the woman's apprenticeship application. Cara's three listed choices were the infirmary, the emergency forces, and the library. *I suspect she put down "library" only because she had to write a third choice.*

Another file, however, was more detailed and personal, and Frieda realized that this was Cara's security profile. On it, someone had written, *As a citizen of the* Hermes, *Cara Flores's access to the Crown Princess should be monitored and limited. We recommend moving her to the cohort after the princess.*

Beneath that note was another: *We are at peace with the* Hermes. *It is good for my daughter to meet a wide range of children, both from within the* Messenger *and without. Overruled. —BK.*

*Mom's initials.* Frieda closed the folder. "Huh."

There was a knock at the door, and Anna answered it. "Your Highness," she called. "It's time to get dressed. Her Majesty requests your presence for the second leg of the Grand Tour."

Frieda closed the file and set the tablet aside. "Thank you, Anna. Let's get started."

Anna hauled the prosthetic case onto the desk. Frieda sighed to see it. A part of her had hoped that somebody would forget about it—just this once—freeing her from its dead weight.

But as she let Anna dress her and set up the harness, she remembered the gifts the Earth was bringing.

*Maybe I can do something about that. Maybe that something starts today.*

☿

WITH ANNA FOLLOWING, Frieda stepped out of the Royal Apartment to the balcony above the agora, where the Grand Tour entourage was being staged. Again, the babbling crowds parted as she pushed through, dressed in the white dress of the Crown Princess.

She spotted Daskivic and Sara Vasser off to one side, waiting, and approached. "Back again? Where's Cara?"

Daskivic frowned. "She was reassigned, if you recall, Your Highness."

"I reassigned her reassignment," Frieda replied. She looked out at the crowd. "It's not like her to be late."

Cara hurried up to them, looking harried. "I'm sorry," she

breathed. "Security seemed confused about my new badge." She held it up. The title was clear across the front: *Medical Adviser to the Crown Princess.*

Behind Cara, Daskivic frowned.

Frieda glared. "I told people—"

"No, it's all right." Cara took a deep breath. "Somebody came along and explained it. I'm here. When do we start?"

"Soon, I guess," said Frieda. "I'm not sure. Anna, hand the tablet over to Cara, please?"

Frowning, Anna passed the tablet she had under her arm to Cara. Cara took it and stared at it and then at Frieda.

"Thank you, Anna." Frieda didn't look back. "I assume you have other duties?"

Anna glanced at Frieda, nodded curtly, and departed. Cara watched her go.

Adelheid stepped out of the Royal Apartment, and the entourages turned toward the trams. Frieda, Cara, and the others fell into step.

"I'm sorry about all this . . . drama," said Frieda as they approached the trams.

"It's all right." Cara glanced over at Dr. Daskivic, then quickly looked away. "I'm not quite sure why I'm here."

"Right now? Be my arms." Frieda gestured with her remaining hand. "I'd like you to keep an eye on the schedule. This looks like it's going to be another long day."

"Why didn't you let Anna do this?" Cara asked. "I see her all the time."

Frieda shook her head. "I feel she's Grandmother's servant. I can't let her run my life, so I'm taking control."

Cara frowned, but she nodded.

"I can see that's a lot of work, though," said Frieda, *now that I think of it.* "So, I'll be getting more advisers. In the meantime, though, there's just you and me, so that's why I'd like your help. Be my arms, watch my schedule, that sort of thing."

"Okay." Cara wrinkled her nose. "It doesn't exactly fit the definition of 'medical adviser' . . ."

"I'm sorry. I'll get more." Frieda smiled at her. "So, what's your medical advice, then?"

"Well . . ." Cara looked serious. "I have to ask: are you sure you should be doing this? You're still recovering. If you wanted to rest, maybe you should."

*I could imagine what Grandmother would think of that. That alone makes it tempting, but . . .* "No," she said. "I can do this. I want to show Grandmother that I can do this." *Also, I need to see the trackworks again.*

The first stop of the day was the sanitation department, which Frieda thought was a mistake so soon after breakfast. However, she bore up and, noticing how proud all the workers were of their work, stood with respect.

She also bore up in the heat of the foundry, nodding appreciatively at the intricate lacework of the blacksmiths, their stalwart structures, and the corded piles of iron cornrows fresh off the line.

But she felt a shudder ripple through her as they approached the door to the trackworks, and it wasn't anticipation. She stared at the door as the attendant—not Josef—bowed to Adelheid. *I will not let this get to me,* she thought. *I will not.*

The attendant also bowed to Frieda before he opened the door to the trackworks. The air swelled to the heartbeat of the *Messenger.* Even up here, Frieda could tell that it was beating faster. Straining gears screamed amid the pounding clatter. The sound made her wince. *The* Messenger's *going double-speed. Still trying to overtake the* Hermes *to Terminal. How much of the battery reserves will we have left when this is over?*

She stepped out onto the long gallery overlooking the trackworks and looked across at the machinery and turning gears.

Her gaze turned as if pulled to the inspection hatch from that horrible day. The lock had been repaired.

She barely heard Adelheid shout to an attendant, "It's too loud to make a speech here. Just a few personal greetings, and then we'll go."

*Then I'd better move fast.*

Standing along the gallery, ranks of trackworkers stood to attention, watching expectantly as Adelheid led the entourage to them. Frieda looked at each face in turn. She recognized many, but she couldn't find the one she wanted.

*But this gallery isn't big enough to hold all the trackworkers,* Frieda thought. There were others farther back, standing on catwalks and platforms, halting production and watching as Adelheid went up to the first worker in line and shook their hand.

*Where is he?*

Frieda nudged Cara and nodded to the far end of the plat-form, which led to a catwalk over the spinning gears alongside the Robinson Rail.

Cara blinked at her. "Um ... what are we doing?"

"Taking a side trip," Frieda replied. She glanced at the rest of the entourage. *How do I step away?*

*Maybe just step away.*

*But Security is not going to like this ...*

After a brief hesitation, she stepped to the nearest security officer and said, "I'm going this way. Please follow discreetly."

The officer blinked, then nudged his partner. They both looked at Frieda as she and Cara kept walking, without haste, along the platform. The two glanced at each other, then followed.

Frieda kept her pace steady, eying the watching ranks and nodding to each worker she made eye contact with. They all returned the nod and blushed with pride.

When she reached the end of the platform and looked

down the catwalk at other waiting trackworkers, she still hadn't found who she was looking for. She tsked in frustration. *I could search for hours. I'm going to have to ask . . .*

She backtracked to where she'd last seen a manager and saw one frozen in bewilderment as he saw her walking back toward him. "Ah, Meneer . . ." She checked his name tag. ". . . Zeller. Hello."

Zeller swallowed and looked around as though unsure whether Frieda was referring to him or another Zeller—possibly someone more worthy of attracting the attention of the Crown Princess. He coughed. "Your Highness?"

"I wanted to—" She hesitated. If what Cara said was true, the moment she said Josef's name, Zeller, like anyone in the trackworks, would register it as "the person who hesitated when trying to rescue the Crown Princess from the gears." Did Josef want that sort of attention? But how else could she ask for him?

*Best to dive in.* "Is Josef here? I need to see him."

She sensed Cara stiffen beside her. In front of her, Zeller nodded. "No, Your Highness. I'm sorry . . ." He looked around, then leaned closer. "He no longer works in the trackworks."

Cara drew in her breath. Frieda looked aghast. "You didn't expel him, did you?"

Zeller looked flustered. "No! We wouldn't have done that! It's just . . . he asked for a transfer, and . . . we gave it to him."

Frieda looked at Cara, who looked shocked. Finally, Frieda turned back. "Where did he go?"

☿

A YEAR BEFORE HER GRADUATION, the teachers at Frieda's school assigned a science project and told them to pick partners. She planned to build a model of the *Messenger*'s trackworks, of course, and chose Josef to work with her.

She peered at the gears. "I think we have the wrong ratio." Around her, the library hushed to the work of students.

Josef leaned in. "It should work. Our calculations—"

"We must have slipped a digit somewhere. It's not turning properly."

Josef sighed. "Well, back to the drafting program."

"No." Keeping her eyes on the model, she made grabbing motions with her hand. "Pass me the one-to-six. If we substitute the main gear with that one, maybe the link will work." Her eyebrows shot up. "Huh. It might actually work better than what's already down there."

Josef chuckled as he searched for the proper gear. "You'll have to tell the trackworkers that."

Frieda laughed. "Like they'd listen to me."

"You could make it a royal proclamation."

"Shut up, you," she said, but she smiled as she said it.

"Ah, here it is." Josef passed the gear over, and, for a moment, their hands brushed.

The touch, not quite an electric shock, made Frieda pause. She took the gear and, keeping an eye on the model, slotted it into place. But while she worked at it, part of her mind went elsewhere.

*I like Josef. He likes the same things I do, and he's nice to be around. We think the same thing about lots of things.*

She looked up and saw her classmates grouped around the library, gatherings of friends but also, increasingly, couples. Alfons and Linde. Toshiko and Malika. *I see these things are happening, so why aren't they happening to me?*

She looked at Josef. He smiled at her.

*Am I supposed to do something? Am I supposed to feel something? I feel . . . friendship when I look at Josef. Maybe I have to build on that?*

Josef kept smiling at her, though his brow furrowed as Frieda kept staring at him. "Did it work?" he asked.

*So, how do I lay that first gear?* "Yeah," she said, leaning back. "Have a look."

Josef came forward, peering into the model, and Frieda leaned into him. He looked up in surprise, and suddenly, their faces were close enough that she could feel his breath on her. It wasn't a bad feeling.

*In for a gasket*, she thought. And she leaned forward and kissed him.

Josef let out a surprised grunt. Their teeth knocked together, which made Frieda squeak. But she held the kiss, as did Josef. Frieda gave it to the count of five before she pulled back.

Josef blinked at her. Frieda blinked at herself. *Should I have felt something there? Beyond a toothache?*

She looked up then into Josef's eyes and frowned at his shocked expression. He looked almost horrified.

Nearby, somebody dropped a book.

They looked up and saw Cara staring. Her face went red. She closed her mouth and stormed away through the stacks, her pace quickening until it was almost a run.

"Cara!" Josef gasped. He ran after her.

Frieda watched him go, feeling an ache inside her.

*What have I done?*

☿

NOBODY CONFRONTED Frieda over her side jaunt in the trackworks, so she felt more confident as they arrived at the Civilian Government Office and Archive. As they filed through the double doors to the reception area, Frieda nudged Cara and tapped the two security officers who'd followed them in the trackworks. *I must remember to get their names.* She turned to the right, marching so fast that Cara and the rest of the mini-entourage had to follow.

Despite its size—half the width of the *Messenger* and with considerable length—the CGO was as hushed as a library compared to the trackworks. As Frieda walked between rows of desks before turning aside into an aisle between tall shelves, she heard Adelheid near the entrance begin her speech. "On behalf of myself and my granddaughter—" There was a moment's pause, then, "On behalf of myself..."

*I'll be hearing about this later. Oh, well. In for a gasket, in for a cog.*

She walked, glancing in aisle after aisle and coming up empty. It struck her, then, that she'd been foolish. Nobody would be at their desks or working, not with the Stadtholder come to visit. She clenched a fist. *All this for nothing.*

But then she turned a corner and saw, to her shock, someone she recognized. "Toshiko?"

Her classmate looked up from the stacks and almost dropped the bundle of tablets in her arm. She looked around, frantic, as though out of place and wondering where that place was.

Frieda hurried over. "Toshiko! I heard Josef transferred to your department from the trackworks. Is that true?"

Toshiko still looked bewildered, but she said, "Yes, Your Highness. A couple of weeks ago. Um . . . am I supposed to be here?"

Frieda dropped her voice further, from princess to student. "Toshiko?"

Some distance behind Frieda, Cara, and the two security officers, she heard someone call, "Your Highness? Your Majesty is asking after you. Come back to the entourage, please ..."

Frieda winced.

Toshiko looked at her, and, for a second, the barriers dropped. They stared at each other as though over homework.

"How is Josef?" Frieda asked.

Toshiko grimaced. It was all she needed to say.

"I need to see him," said Frieda.

Toshiko nodded. "This way."

☿

Toshiko led Frieda, Cara, and the two security officers through the shelves and past rows of servers as the careful calls of other security officers faded behind them. They emerged into an area with smaller desks and narrower aisles between them. Frieda suspected that this was where the apprentices worked.

There were topological maps of Mercury on the walls and spread across some of the desks, showing Robinson Rails cutting through the pits and peaks of the planet's surface. Josef sat at a desk before a keyboard, an island in the sea of monitors. All was silent save for the hiss of the server fans and his fingers tapping on the keyboard. He looked up and blinked to see Toshiko, Frieda, Cara, and the two security officers spread out around him. His eyes settled on Cara, who reddened and looked down.

Frieda pulled a chair over using her remaining hand and sat beside Josef's desk. He started at this, then shifted back as Frieda scooted closer. He swallowed. "Your Highness." He didn't bow, but only because that was almost impossible to do while sitting down. "Aren't you supposed to be with the Grand Tour?"

"Aren't you?" she replied. *Come to that, shouldn't Toshiko be out there, too?*

He looked away from her gaze. "Under the circumstances, it didn't seem appropriate."

Frieda nodded. Then she looked at Toshiko, asking the same question. Toshiko shrugged. "I'm not a monarchist, and attendance wasn't mandatory. Besides . . ." She nodded at Josef. "He needs looking after."

"I see." Frieda turned back to Josef. "Josef . . . I remember the accident."

He stared at her, holding his breath.

She shuddered but went on. "I remember that you froze when you tried to come in and get me. But I chose to go inside that hatch. I chose to hit that rock. *I* was the one who got my arm caught by the crowbar and—" She shuddered again. "You didn't do any of that. So, why are you here?"

Josef looked away from Frieda, only to have his eyes fall on Cara, who stared back at him. He looked at his lap. "I still froze," he said. "You may not know this, Your Highness, but . . . I was diagnosed with claustrophobia at a young age."

*I did know that. I read your employment profile before I came here. It meshes with how you used to play at school. You were always so easy to find—you never hid under things.*

Out loud, she said, "But you chose to apprentice with the trackworks."

"I wanted to be an engineer," he replied. "So, I worked at it. I did breathing exercises. I gradually forced myself into smaller and smaller spaces. But the one moment I most needed to control my phobia, it beat me. I couldn't stay where I was."

"I understand why you might want to go elsewhere, Josef," said Frieda. "But, still: the file clerks?"

"I'm standing right here," said Toshiko.

Josef looked at his lap again. "I also like maps. Maps are a sub-department here. It was the only other skillset I had. Well, that and sanitation workers often have to crawl into small spaces themselves."

"Josef." Frieda leaned closer. "Look at me."

He looked at her.

"I won't tell you not to be ashamed," she said. "Only you can decide that. But, personally, I can say—" She hesitated then. *Do I really mean this? Or am I only saying it to make him feel better?*

She looked into his eyes and winced at the guilt she saw in them. At that moment, she knew. "I forgive you."

He let out his breath as though he were punched.

"That's me, speaking for me," she added. "Speaking as the Crown Princess, I'd like you to make another transfer. I need you to be an engineer." She pulled a small tablet sheet from her pocket and slid it along the desk toward him. "Come to the Royal Apartment at 0800 hours tomorrow and show this at the door. The attendants will bring you right in."

Josef picked up the tablet, tapped it, and read it. His eyebrows shot up. "Uh . . . why?" He looked at her. "What's the assignment?"

Frieda hefted her residual arm and set her prosthetic on the desk between them. "I need you to look at this and help me design its replacement."

☿

ADELHEID DID NOT SAY anything to Frieda about her side trip in the archive, and Frieda gave her grandmother as few chances to speak about it as possible. Instead, Frieda hurried to her bedroom and, after Anna had helped her undress and remove her prosthetic before going on her way, sat at her desk and pulled over a tablet. She tapped open one of the programs and picked up her stylus, twisting her good arm back and forth before pressing her stylus to her cheek so it would sit in the crook between her thumb and forefinger.

She stared at the carefully gripped stylus. "This isn't going to be fun," she muttered.

But she got to work. After a few practice swipes, a few soft clunks of a dropped stylus, and some swearing, she started to draw.

# CHAPTER 18
# A NEW HAND AT THE WHEEL

AT 0730 THE NEXT MORNING, FRIEDA WOKE TO A KNOCK AT THE door. She struggled up from the bed as Anna entered, bringing breakfast. "Good morning, Your Highness," said Anna. "I trust you slept well."

Frieda yawned. "Eventually," she muttered. More loudly, she said, "What's the schedule today?"

Anna tapped on the media screen. "At 1000 hours, you and the Dowager Regent will depart for the final leg of the Grand Tour, ending at 1800 hours, when we are expected to arrive at Terminal."

*Ending the tour at arrival. Well timed, Grandmother.*

Anna went on, "Your medical team is due here at 0800 hours." Her brow wrinkled. "Something else has been double-booked for the same time: a personal meeting. Shall I cancel?"

"No!" said Frieda, more sharply than she'd intended. "It's fine. It's somebody else meeting with the medical team."

Anna frowned at her but nodded and gathered Frieda's clothes for the morning. When Frieda, dressed, finally sat before the breakfast tray and lifted the lid, she noticed that the food had been cut into bite-sized pieces this time. She nodded, ate a bac-cracker, then speared a piece of protein loaf with her fork. Her gaze trailed up to the media screen as she ate.

She wasn't surprised to see herself on it, trailing after Adelheid as they walked through the agora above the trackworks. The woman on the voice-over was saying, "The Stadtholders walked the second leg of their Grand Tour yesterday, with the Dowager Regent showing off more departments along the length and breadth of the *Messenger* to the Crown Princess. Reporters from all the latitude towns were on hand to observe—"

*Oh, really*, thought Frieda. *I wonder what they had to say . . .*

She opened a search query and, finger-by-finger, called up "Grand Tour" among the media feeds from the other latitude towns. Other newscasts popped up.

From the *BepiColumbo*, she heard, "The *Messenger*'s stadtholder and her granddaughter continued their tour of their latitude town today . . ."

Frieda raised an eyebrow. *The Stadtholder and her* granddaughter? *Okay.*

She swiped her hand. The feed switched to the *Leigh Brackett* in mid-stream. "—traditionally seen as a way to introduce a new leader to their people, and introduce the people to their new leader . . ."

*Twice is a tradition, I guess.* She swiped her hand.

The *Hermes* feed had a shot of Frieda stifling a yawn. "The Crown Princess looks bored," said the pundit. "Frankly, I don't blame her. How many speeches has her grandmother given?"

Frieda grimaced. *Oops.* She moved on.

From the *Viritrilbia*: "A show of unity by the leaders of the *Messenger*, with pointed comments at their critics, particularly aimed at the strikers at the *Baxter-Nordley* . . ."

*Hmm . . .*

There was a knock at the door, and Anna poked her head

in. "Your Highness, Cara Flores is here to see you." She ticked disapprovingly. "Early."

Frieda glanced at the clock. 0745 hours. Not very early. "Send her in, please."

The door opened wider before it closed. Frieda kept her eye on the media screen. "Cara, what do you think of this Grand Tour business? What exactly am I doing out there?"

Cara didn't answer. After a moment, Frieda looked back and found Cara staring at her with a complicated expression—a frown that was kept under careful control.

"What's the matter?" Frieda asked.

Cara took a deep breath. "Why are you bringing Josef here?"

Frieda's brow furrowed. "Because I need him. You said it yourself: I need an engineer on my medical team. Josef is available, and I know what he's capable of, so I need him."

"You're sure it's not more than that?" Cara snapped. Then she faltered—and not like some servant who'd spoken out of turn. Her gaze shifted to the floor and Frieda was shocked to see her look nervous and uncertain. Eyes on the floor, Cara continued. "I know about the *Messenger* tradition: to preserve the peace among the levels of the *Messenger*, the Stadtholder marries someone from the trackworks—"

Frieda exhaled. *Lord in Sunlight!* "Cara, first of all, that happened only once! It's bad enough calling it a tradition if it happens twice, but *once*? Second, I'm not ready to think about marriage. At all. If Grandmother were to try to force me into marrying someone, there'd be a constitutional crisis."

Cara looked up, eyes skeptical. "Are you sure?"

"I'll make sure."

"The thing is . . ." Cara fidgeted. "I know that you and Josef—"

Frieda sighed. "That was a crush, and it didn't last long. And, to be honest, I think I worked myself into that crush because I felt that I should have one. Others were having crushes at the time, and I thought, here's Josef, a year older than me, who likes engineering as much as I do. I thought maybe that would be enough to build something on. You saw the one time I kissed him. That was a disaster. I haven't tried to kiss him since." She looked away, frowning. *I haven't really tried to speak to him since. I ruined that friendship, and for what? To try and feel something that might not be there?*

Cara tilted her head. "So, you *don't* have feelings for Josef?"

*But you do, clearly.* "No more than I have feelings for you," she replied. "Honestly, I haven't had any real feelings of that sort . . ." She gestured at herself. ". . . for anybody. Yet. So, don't worry. I haven't brought Josef here for any reason other than the fact that I need his skills. That's the same reason I brought you here."

Cara raised an eyebrow, but she nodded slowly.

Frieda shrugged. "Besides, you said it yourself: he needs to stop blaming himself for what happened. He needs to stop hiding in the archive. I hope that, as my adviser, he comes to see this is true."

Cara's eyes narrowed. "So, you've decided to be his therapist instead? You're not a medical officer. Are you sure it's wise to pull him out of the archive so soon?"

Frieda spluttered. "But . . . you were worried about him. And it's Josef. He's no file clerk!"

"But what if he's not ready—"

"If he really wasn't ready, he didn't have to come."

Cara scowled. "Like he'd refuse an order from the Stadtholder!"

Frieda gaped. "I didn't make it an order!"

"You didn't *not* make it an order!"

The two women glared at each other. After a moment, however, Frieda lowered her gaze. "I'm sorry. I assumed . . .

maybe it's accurate to say that I needed to forgive Josef as much as he needed to be forgiven."

Cara nodded slowly. "I want Josef to be happy too," she said more quietly, "but . . . just understand that you can't fix everything. I know it's tempting to try, but . . . be careful, okay?"

Frieda nodded. Cara smiled, and the moment cooled to something more comfortable, albeit still awkward.

"There's something else," Cara added. "By bringing Josef aboard, I think you're going to have to deal with Daskivic. He's not going to be happy."

"What do you mean?"

The door knocked again. Anna opened it. "Your Highness, your medical team is here. And Meneer Bakker."

Daskivic and Sara entered, with Josef following behind, looking uncomfortable. Frieda saw Josef look up, his eyes falling on Cara. The two stared at each other a moment before looking hurriedly away.

Frieda stood. "Dr. Daskivic. Mufrau Vasser. Josef. Thank you for coming." Daskivic, she noticed, was fidgeting, so she said, "Dr. Daskivic, you seem troubled. How can I help you?"

Daskivic coughed. "Your Highness . . . I think I need . . . " He coughed again. "I feel I should offer my resignation."

Frieda straightened up. "Whyever for?"

For a moment, Daskivic didn't say anything; didn't look her in the eye. Sara, looking grim, nudged him in the back. He glanced at her and she raised her eyebrows at him.

Frieda focused on Sara. She didn't look uncomfortable, but she did look stiff and angry. She kept her gaze on Daskivic, pointedly avoiding Frieda's gaze. *She's angry*, thought Frieda. *Angry at him? No. Angry for him.*

She looked back at Daskivic and realized he looked humiliated.

Daskivic coughed again. "Your Highness, I feel I've done the best job I can on your prosthetic. If you had any concerns about your treatment, you should have told me, and I would have done my best to resolve them, but—"

Frieda winced. *I did this. I did this by trying to be like Grandmother and see how that hurt? But now I have to do something about it because it's my responsibility. My actions, my responsibility.*

She raised her remaining hand. "Dr. Daskivic." *How do I soothe him? It's true we weren't making progress with my treatment, but that wasn't his fault.*

*Maybe that's where I start.*

She gathered her breath. "Dr. Daskivic, I don't want you to resign. I know you've served with distinction for decades. Clearly, Grandmother assigned me the best doctor available. I appreciate that." She nodded as Daskivic looked slightly mollified. "But there have to be changes to my treatment. Yes, I should have talked to you about them before acting, and I apologize for that. So, let's do that talking now."

Daskivic blinked at her, confused, so she pushed on. "You've tried hard to make the prosthetic work, but we're not making progress. Isn't that true?"

"Well, Your Highness." Daskivic looked more uncomfortable than ever. "We've had obstacles to overcome—"

Frieda tilted her head. "And those obstacles are?"

Daskivic sucked his teeth.

"The prosthetic is not designed to work the way it needs to work," said Josef quietly.

Daskivic and Sara frowned at him, but they didn't contradict him.

"Go on, Josef," said Frieda.

Josef flushed to see the eyes of everyone in the room on him, but he nodded, stepped to the table, and set down his tablet. He called up a schematic of Frieda's current prosthetic. "I've looked at the design you sent me. From what you've told me, your current device is nearly fifty years old. It's from the early days of the Silence, built to last with the materials we had at the time. And since that time, all we've had for resources beyond iron and solar is the materials we had at the start of our isolation."

Josef looked up. "The best prosthetics are made of carbon composite materials and plastics, and we lost our supplies of these materials when the Earth shuttles stopped coming. All we have remaining on Mercury is thoroughly recycled. Yes, we can grow biofuels and make bioplastics from that, but that comes directly out of our food supply."

He hefted Frieda's prosthetic. "This is a marvel of clockwork and iron, but it's not designed for Frieda. This will never give her the dexterity she needs, and with the only planetary resources we have in abundance being iron, silicon, and solar . . ." He shook his head. "Honestly, I think the only reason this prosthetic is being used is for the look of the thing."

He looked up at the silent room. His mouth moved as he went over what he'd just said, then he coughed. "I mean, Your Highness."

Frieda looked at Dr. Daskivic. "Is what Josef said accurate?"

Daskivic nodded, eyeing Josef with new respect. "Yes, Your Highness."

"Then the job Grandmother assigned you is impossible," said Frieda. "From that, I would say you have every right to resign." She came forward and touched his arm with her remaining hand. "But I propose to change that job."

She turned to her tablet and swiped at it. The media screen flickered and displayed Frieda's drawing of an arm. She'd sketched out the structure and the gears around the elbows. Another tap of the tablet brought up images of the nerve interface, the tendons that flexed the fingers, and the elastics that turned the wrist.

Josef nodded. Sara raised her eyebrows. "Huh!" Daskivic stepped forward and let out a soft whistle.

"What do you think?" Frieda asked.

"It's . . . impressive," said Daskivic. He glanced at her remaining hand. Frieda suspected he was about to say, "especially considering," but to his credit, he didn't. He did add, "But it's impossible. We couldn't forge something this fine with iron. And the plastics wouldn't be of high enough quality . . ."

Frieda smiled. "That's true for today, but not tomorrow. Cara, show Dr. Daskivic the Earth ship's manifest."

Cara picked up the tablet and tapped at it a moment before passing it to Daskivic. Daskivic looked at it, then went still. Sara looked over his shoulder, and her eyebrows shot up.

"So, you see, doctor," said Frieda. "This is not a demotion. When we get the materials we need, we'll have better options, and we'll need more than just a medical team. We need engineers, and I studied to be an engineer, as did Josef. You, Sara, and Cara are medics. Among us, and given the materials and technology that are on their way, do you think we can build something better?"

Daskivic looked at the manifest again. He smiled. "Yes, Your Highness."

Frieda's smile broadened. "Then let's get started."

☿

THE TIME WENT MORE QUICKLY than Frieda wanted. She'd barely eaten her breakfast before Anna arrived to tell her it was time to get ready for the last leg of the Grand Tour. Sighing, she dismissed Daskivic, Sara, and Josef. They left, talking about lateral balance, gear ratios, and more nerve mapping. Cara stood awkwardly to one side as Anna helped Frieda into her Crown Princess dress and hooked on the old prosthetic. Finally, Frieda and Cara set off.

The final leg of the Grand Tour started in the communications office, where Frieda noticed that far more monitors were tuned in to Earth than the last time she was here. Mindful of the media comments, Frieda stood to attention as Adelheid thanked the workers.

Then it was another agora, followed by the design engineers, then the maintenance crews. Slowly but surely, the Grand Tour advanced on the forebridge. Frieda faced the tour with her eyes wide but thinking about the design her team was working on back home. As she sat on the tram, travelling to their final destination, though, Frieda sensed a shift in the entourage around her. She looked up and saw her grandmother standing close, looking down.

"There's something different about you today," she said, her voice low.

Frieda raised an eyebrow. "Oh?"

Adelheid tilted her head. "You look less lost."

Frieda raised her eyebrow higher. The moment stretched and grew awkward as she tried to think of a response before finally settling on, "Maybe I've had time to find myself."

It was more bitter than she'd intended, but she kept a handle on the wince.

Adelheid sighed and, for a moment, looked almost contrite. "I'm sorry we haven't . . . had more time to talk, Frieda. I know this is a difficult time for you, and I should be there, but there are affairs of state I cannot ignore. You certainly don't need to be burdened with these issues. I . . . appreciate your understanding, allowing me to get on with business."

Frieda frowned as she processed what her grandmother had said. Inside her, a spark flared. *Burdened? Does she think I can't handle such a burden?* She clenched her jaw. *But this is as close to an apology as I've ever heard from her. It's a start.* "Thank you, Grandmother."

Adelheid nodded and stepped back. The tram decelerated toward the stop closest to the forebridge.

Finally, with reporters watching, Adelheid advanced on the

doors of the forebridge, Frieda a step behind her. The doors parted.

The place reminded Frieda of Command and Control in the tail section, except that it was in good repair, and the land was drawing toward them on the viewscreen. Among the officers, Frieda saw her father standing at bridge command. He straightened up as the Grand Tour entered. "Stadtholders on bridge," he called. The forebridge crew snapped to attention.

Adelheid nodded respectfully to Frieda's father. Frieda spotted Zoe Scholl, another classmate, sitting as a navigation adjunct. Zoe looked up, caught Frieda's eye, and nodded briefly before staring ahead at attention. That, at least, was a better reunion than others Frieda'd had.

Adelheid walked up to the bridge commander's chair. Frieda's father stood, bowed, and stepped back. Adelheid stood with her back to the seat, facing the bridge crew and the crowd of reporters. She cleared her throat for another speech. Shutters clicked.

Standing to one side, Frieda glanced out the window and saw the Robinson Rail rolling beneath them, curving to port. That explained the low squeal rising up through the supports of the latitude town. Despite the noise, Frieda smiled. It brought back fond memories of previous Terminal Days.

Despite her best efforts, while her grandmother spoke, Frieda found her gaze wandering to the front window while her mind ran over gear ratios and mechanical tendons. Then, a pinprick flash on the horizon caught her eye. She focused and saw lights flashing off thin spires in the distance. Her heart skipped as she pointed. "I see Terminal!" She caught herself too late. *Oops!* She blushed as the bridge crew looked at her.

But every officer turned to the viewscreen. People muttered, "She's right! I see it too!" Applause rose, and Frieda heard one of the officers say to his fellow, "Wait—do we need to buy her a drink now?"

Frieda saw her father grinning proudly. Even Adelheid smiled and gave Frieda a nod.

Then Frieda's father peered closer at the viewscreen. "Attention, everyone," he called. "The *Apollo*, coming up on the starboard side."

As one, everyone on the forebridge stood up from their consoles, faced right, clasped their hands in front of them, and bowed their heads. Frieda clasped the wrist of her prosthetic and lowered her head as well. However, before the end of the moment of silence, she looked up at the viewscreen.

The camera zoomed in as, in the distance, in spotlights placed around it, the ruined wreck of the equator city stood, grey in the dust of Mercury, its portholes open to the vacuum. Its length stretched into the distance, out of sight of the gently curving *Messenger*. Its front end sat jackknifed off the edge of a crater, its nose crumpled on the crater floor. Ahead of it, the Robinson Rail lay crumpled as though stomped on.

As Frieda stared, she realized she wasn't the only person with her head not down. Before her, Grandmother also stared at the broken city. Frieda saw her larynx bob as she swallowed hard. Slowly, she lowered her gaze and closed her eyes.

The moment passed. People looked up, but nobody had anything to say.

A red light flashed on a console. Adjutant Scholl glanced at it and then at a monitor. "Sir?"

Frieda's father looked up. "What is it?"

"Sir . . ." Scholl looked up at the viewscreen. "We're catching up to the *Hermes*, sir."

The room stirred. Adelheid straightened up, and Frieda heard her mutter to an adviser, "Excellent! Remind me to give a commendation to the trackworkers' guild."

But Frieda could see Scholl frowning, along with her father. "What's wrong?" she asked.

Scholl looked up. "I'm seeing no forward progress on the

town whatsoever." She looked down at the console to check, then looked up, eyes wide. "They're parked."

"What?" said Frieda, her father, and Adelheid in unison. Everyone turned to the viewscreen. Scholl zoomed the camera closer.

The lights of the *Hermes* coalesced into a view of the latitude town as the camera zoomed into focus. Spotlights played across its surface from land speeders dashing around it. The camera tracked along the town until it got to the forebridge. There were no signs of damage, but the lights of the land speeders were focused on the Robinson Rail in front of it.

Frieda glanced at Cara. She stared at the screen, wringing her hands. Frieda turned back to Scholl. "Is their Robinson Rail damaged?"

Adelheid looked grim. "Contact the *Hermes*. Ask if they need assistance."

Scholl pulled on headphones and looked around her console, momentarily lost. Her cheeks reddened before a lieutenant quietly nudged her and pointed to a switch. She flipped it. "*Messenger* to the *Hermes*, please respond. Do you need assistance?"

Static. No answer.

Scholl tried again. "*Messenger* to *Hermes*, please respond: do you need assistance?"

This time, the static cut out abruptly. "*Hermes* to *Messenger*, stand down. Repeat: stand down. We do *not* need assistance. Everything is under control!"

Frieda glanced at Cara. She was frowning. Then Frieda caught her grandmother's eye. Adelheid's expression matched hers. *That was curt*, she thought. *And is it my imagination that whenever someone says everything is under control, it usually isn't?*

Adelheid stepped to the console and took the microphone from Scholl. "*Hermes*, this is Stadtholder Adelheid Koning. We stand ready to offer any assistance—"

"We do not need any assistance, Your Majesty," said the voice sharply. "There are no casualties or injuries. We are simply doing repairs and will be moving shortly. Do not come here, as we are in the middle of an investigation."

Frieda and Cara shared a look.

"Stadtholder," said Frieda's father, and for a second, he was looking at her. Frieda's mouth hung open. She stood, unsure how to reply. After a moment's hesitation, her father turned to Adelheid. "What should we do?"

Adelheid looked at the viewscreen as the image pulled back from the stalled *Hermes*. "If they won't tell us directly, I wonder what the press is saying," she muttered.

Scholl perked up. "Shall I call up their feed, Your Majesty?"

Adelheid shook her head. "Later. There's nothing they want us to do right now, so there's nothing we can do." She faced forward. "Maintain speed. Take us into Terminal."

Frieda faced forward as well as the spires of Terminal drew more distinct. *So, we won the race,* she thought, *but this doesn't feel like a victory.*

*This feels wrong.*

# CHAPTER 19
## EARTH SHUTTLE ARRIVING

AND, WITH THAT, THE GRAND TOUR ENDED.

"Everyone," said one of the marshalling attendants. "We have a few hours before the Earth shuttle docks. Everybody can retire to their regular duties. The stadtholders will retire to the Royal Apartment."

Cara took a step toward the tram, but Frieda nudged her. "Let's wait for the next one."

Cara frowned at her. "I thought you'd be eager to get back—"

"I can't wait to see what Daskivic, Sara, and Josef have done while we've been out here," said Frieda. "But I'd rather not have Grandmother breathing down my neck while we plan a new prosthetic."

Cara's frown deepened. "Are we going to get into trouble for what we're doing?"

"I shouldn't think so," Frieda replied. *At least, not much.*

They walked slowly, letting people slip between them and Adelheid. By the time her grandmother boarded the tram, Frieda and Cara were far back. Then Adelheid looked around at the crowd, frowning. She caught Frieda's eye as the tram doors closed.

Frieda smiled. "And now we take the next one."

They arrived to crowds of attendants and officials heading in and out of the Royal Apartment. Adelheid was nowhere to be seen, which Frieda was glad of, but the urgency of the officials made her frown. She quickened her pace, and Cara followed.

Anna came forward as Frieda entered, looking a little put-out. "Your Highness," she said. "Mufrau Nakajima is here to see you. You arranged an appointment?"

Behind Anna, Toshiko stood, looking awkward.

Frieda nodded. "Thank you, Anna. Cara, hand Toshiko your tablet."

"Huh?" said Cara.

"I've named her my information adviser," Frieda replied. "So you don't have to handle my calendar."

"Oh, thank the gods!" Cara thrust the tablet over.

Frieda looked at Toshiko. "You are accepting the assignment, I'm assuming?"

Toshiko hesitated. Then she said, "I'm here because you were kind to Josef. And it looks like it's going to be interesting. But still . . . I have to ask . . . what in Sunlight are you thinking?"

Frieda drew back.

"I'm an intern for the Archive," Toshiko went on. "I file things. How could I end up serving the Stadtholder when I told you I'm not a monarchist?"

"Because you're a friend, and I need your help," Frieda replied. "You'd be helping—not serving—me." She nodded at the tablet. "I'm an engineer. Cara's medical. I need somebody who understands administrative things better than I do, and I know you do."

Toshiko stared at the tablet again. "All right. Perhaps we can see how it goes."

"Good. Both of you, follow me." Frieda headed for her bedroom. "Toshiko, the first thing I want to know is, what happened with the *Hermes*?"

"Their president just held a press conference," Toshiko replied. "He said the town had encountered a rough patch on their Robinson Rail." She tapped at the tablet, then looked up. "Debris got caught in the gears and dragged the town to a stop."

Cara gaped. "What in Sunlight—"

Despite herself, Frieda shivered. *Just like what happened to us.* "Any injuries?"

"Only minor," said Toshiko. "But their president did say that an investigation is taking place and asked residents not to jump to conclusions."

Outside her bedroom, Frieda stopped and turned. "Like what?"

Toshiko shrugged.

Frieda raised her eyebrows. "They're not suggesting sabotage, are they?"

Again, Toshiko shrugged. "It would explain why they refused help."

"No, that's not—" Cara blurted. She blushed when Frieda and Toshiko stared at her.

"Why do you think the *Hermes* was so snappy when we offered to help?" Frieda asked.

Cara glared. "Are you asking me because I'm from the *Hermes* and so I must know how they think?"

Frieda tilted her head. "Well, don't you, a little?"

Cara glared a moment longer before turning away, but she said, "The people of the *Hermes*—some of the people, anyway . . . many of them in the government—value their independence. They trumpet it. Sometimes, I think they find it hard living in the *Messenger*'s shadow. Given our history, I sometimes think the *Hermes* government defines itself too much as being 'other than the *Messenger*.' Accepting help, especially if it's for something they're embarrassed about, would be a blow to their pride."

"They're embarrassed," Frieda echoed.

Cara shrugged. "I suspect so. Or afraid. Or both. It depends on what stalled them."

"It wasn't us," said Toshiko, firm.

Cara frowned at her. "I'm sure the investigation will show that. But you said the investigation is still going on, and the president doesn't want residents to jump to conclusions. That means they haven't found a satisfactory answer to what stalled them yet."

Frieda nodded. "Thank you. Both of you. I'm grateful for your help."

She turned to her bedroom door. Toshiko ducked around her and opened it. They found Josef, Sara, and Daskivic within, clustered around papers piled on Frieda's desk and workbench. As Cara and Toshiko entered, Frieda could see they were running out of places to sit. *I'm going to need an office. I wonder how much more I can shift my budget before Grandmother comments?*

She stepped toward her medical team. "So? What do you have?"

Josef gave her a nod. Daskivic stood and bowed. "Your design is . . . elegant, Your Highness. And it should work. Based on the inventory you provided, you would need these items from the Earth ship." He held out a tablet. Frieda took it in her remaining hand and glanced at the list. She nodded. *I guessed well.*

She handed the tablet to Toshiko, who juggled it with the other one before clasping both. "What is this?"

"Your first major assignment," Frieda replied. "When the Earth shuttle docks at Terminal, I need you to pick up these items."

☿

AN HOUR LATER, Anna arrived. "Your Highness." She frowned as everyone in the crowded room looked at her. She held up a bundle of clothes. "It's time to prepare for the Earth envoy's arrival."

Frieda looked up from the designs spread across the table but bit back the reply *already?* She sighed. "You're right. Thank you, everyone. You've done good work."

Daskivic and Sara set about gathering the tablets.

Frieda stepped back from the table. "Josef? Cara? Would you come with me to the reception for the envoy?" *I'd like to have more friends around me.*

Cara opened her mouth to reply, but Sara cleared her throat. "Your Highness."

Frieda turned and saw the young woman looking nervous but resolute. "Your pardon, Your Highness, but Dr. Daskivic and I have reached our overtime limit. Meneer Bakker and Mufrau Flores as well. They need to be done for the day."

Frieda leaned back as disappointment flared, along with a flash of shame. *I might as well have worded my request as an order.* She nodded at Sara with respect. "Thank you, Sara. Josef? Cara? Dr. Daskivic? Thank you again."

She turned to Toshiko, who she knew was still on shift. "I'll see you in a moment." Toshiko nodded.

The room emptied out, leaving Frieda and Anna alone. Anna set out the clothes on the bed: the Crown Princess's ceremonial uniform, with trousers. Frieda's lips tightened. *Well, at least it's not a dress.*

Anna helped Frieda put on the prosthetic and then her blouse over it. "You must be excited, Your Highness!"

Frieda's brow furrowed. "Must I?"

"The first proper Terminal Day in fifty years," Anna replied, circling in front of Frieda as if she were a maypole.

Frieda considered this. "As I recall, the last 'proper' Terminal Day ended in disaster."

Anna bowled through this. "That was fifty years ago. Everybody is dressing their best to make today special. There'll be delicacies from Earth! Dancing, even!"

"Great," Frieda muttered. *I don't like dancing at the best of times. I had two left feet before —what's it going to be like with that and one less arm? Still . . .* "I'm looking forward to the food from Earth." *Though not to having somebody help feed me.*

There was a knock on the door. Toshiko poked her head in. "Your . . . Highness?" Frieda frowned but saw others standing behind Toshiko, watching. "They're asking for you. It's time to go."

Anna stepped back, gave Frieda's uniform a critical look, and then nodded. For a brief moment, Frieda both resented and admired the pride in Anna's expression. "Thank you, Anna," she said. "Enjoy the reception. I'll see you later tonight."

Anna swept off, smiling. Frieda nodded to Toshiko. "Let's go."

Again, Frieda dallied and managed to miss the first tram, with her grandmother on it. They arrived at one of the agoras outside the airlock doors that would open onto Terminal. She stood off to one side with her entourage while service workers waited with carts of supplies and engineers stood ready with toolkits prepared to awaken Terminal from its solar slumber. A cloud of advisers clustered around Adelheid, many leaning in and whispering in her ear. The air buzzed. How could she make out anything in all this chatter?

She looked out at the crowds. Even as she dreaded the long day stretching out ahead of her, the excitement was contagious. *It is the most significant event for the whole planet since the start of the Silence. It's remarkable to be a part of it.*

"Who all are here?" she asked Toshiko.

Toshiko swiped at her tablet. "We are, of course. The top

representatives of the *Hermes*. Representatives from every latitude town are arriving by land speeders. The president of the *Leigh Brackett*. The prime minister of the *Viritrilbia*. The mayor of the *Baxter-Nordley*."

Frieda raised an eyebrow. *He must be confident things are stable if he feels he can be here. I hope he's not wrong.* "What do we do? Greet the envoy, I assume. Do we have to sing the U.N.E's international anthem?"

"It's not the U.N.," said Toshiko.

"What?"

"The envoy is not with the U.N.E." Toshiko looked up from her notes. "Lots of people are making that mistake, but the diplomatic documents make it clear: he represents the Federation of Earth Nations."

"What happened to the U.N.?"

"They didn't survive the start of the Silence," Toshiko replied. "Near as we can tell, the Federation of Earth Nations dates back to about twenty years ago."

"So, what do we know about them?" Frieda asked.

"More than you'd think," said Toshiko. "We may call what happened to the Earth 'the Silence,' but that's only because they stopped talking to us. Within their own atmosphere, they were far from quiet. The first two decades after the destruction of the Manhattan Sea Wall it was chaos. Even when things stabilized marginally, it was as groups of small nations governed by warlords. Eventually, stronger ones prevailed, grew stronger still, and ..."

"And restored the world government?"

"Created one," Toshiko replied.

"Huh," said Frieda. "I wonder what that was like." And for no reason she could name, she found herself looking at Adelheid. Her grandmother stood with attendants around her, talking at her, but she stared at the airlock door to Terminal, where the Earth shuttle would arrive, with almost the same look she'd given to the *Apollo*.

Then Frieda looked at the airlock doors. People in the crowd shifted impatiently. Frieda spotted some maintenance workers frowning at a nearby access panel. Glancing around to make sure she wasn't making a scene, she stepped closer and cleared her throat. "Excuse me? What's going on?"

A maintenance worker glanced at Frieda, then quickly bowed his head. "A minor delay, Your Highness. A mechanical fault has locked the airlocks closed. We're on it. Just a few minutes."

"Thank you," Frieda replied. She turned to Toshiko and the attendants and nodded to a spot by the wall where they could wait out of the way of the crowd. They closed up in a knot beside a large, leafy artificial plant.

Then Frieda heard Cara's voice. *"Mamãe!"*

The woman was nearby, arguing with her mother. Neither of them had seen Frieda. Cara vibrated in frustrated anger.

Ambassador Flores raised a weary hand. "Now, Cara, be reasonable." Flores kept her voice low. "People are watching us."

Frieda ducked back farther behind the cover of the artificial plant.

"I'm through being reasonable, *Mamãe*," Cara snapped, though she lowered her voice as well. "You're asking me to walk away from my apprenticeship. My time here will be wasted!"

"You can resume your apprenticeship on the *Hermes*," said her mother.

"There are no medical doctorates available on the *Hermes!*" Cara's voice rose. "They've had too many applicants. The medical jobs are here or in the *Baxter-Nordley*. It'll be years before positions open up back home. I can't wait until then!"

"You could transfer vocations," her mother snapped. "There

are plenty of other ways to use your skills. Medical records clerk, maybe. And the *Hermes* always needs engineers."

"That's not what I want to be!" Cara stormed. "It's not where I want to be. Here, I can get the experience I need."

"I told you to keep your voice down!" Her mother glanced at the chattering crowds.

"Sorry." Cara took a deep breath, then let it go slowly. "I'm learning a good job here, *Mamãe*. I want to immigrate."

"You're taking a big risk," said her mother. "Your colleagues won't accept someone from the *Hermes* working in the *Messenger*'s infirmary."

"They're treating me just fine," said Cara. "Especially Frie— the Crown Princess—"

"You can't count on that." The ambassador lowered her voice; Frieda had to strain to listen. "If the political situation deteriorates, people may not be so accommodating."

Cara let out a sigh that ended with a click of irritation. "Don't judge these people, *Mamãe*."

"I'm not judging them," her mother replied. "I just know how people think. Your grandfather learned that firsthand. Now, we'll discuss this later."

"But—"

"Do as I say, please." Though polite, it wasn't a request.

Cara let out a growl of frustration.

The airlock doors parted with a *chumpf*! The assembled crowd clapped and moved forward. Frieda nudged Toshiko and waited, with her attendants, as the others in the crowd, including Ambassador Flores and Cara, stepped into Terminal.

☿

THE WELCOMING COMMITTEES of the *Hermes* and the *Messenger* stood in front of the shuttle arrival doors of Terminal. Quietly, Frieda noticed.

There were sides to Terminal, she knew. The middle of the arrivals area used to belong to the *Apollo*, but for some reason, the gap between the *Hermes* and the *Messenger* personnel seemed wider. Frieda saw Ambassador Flores standing beside a bespectacled older man—Richard Garza, the president of the *Hermes*. Adelheid stood at the head of the *Messenger* delegation, surrounded by attendants, including officials from the *Messenger's* remaining client towns. The president of the *Leigh Brackett* stood respectfully a couple of metres away. Mayor Huang of the *Baxter-Nordley* stood beside Adelheid, looking uncomfortable.

He leaned closer to Adelheid. "It's an honour to be here, Your Majesty," he whispered. Frieda had to strain to hear him.

Adelheid nodded. "Good of you to come."

Huang shifted and lowered his voice further. "There are matters I should discuss with you, Your Majesty. The referendum calls are not going away. The strikers aren't moving and are gaining supporters. I might need to—"

"We'll talk later," said Adelheid quickly. She frowned at the president of the *Hermes*, who stood watching a few metres away, and the bevy of reporters who stood in front of the musicians, shifting impatiently.

"Landing preparations are complete," said an engineer by one of the consoles. "The Earth team is proceeding to the arrival area."

Adelheid straightened up even more, and the *Messenger* and *Hermes* delegations stiffened their attention. Along the back, two sets of musicians readied their instruments.

Lights flashed. A klaxon blared. The shuttle doors parted, revealing the officials from Earth.

*Lord in Sunlight!* thought Frieda. *They're so short!*

Everyone in the Earth party was at least fifteen centimetres shorter than the pictures Frieda had seen of the Earth envoy and his delegation from fifty years ago. Not one of the Earth party could have been more than 160 centimetres tall. *I'm not tall*, Frieda thought, *but I'm at least thirty centimetres taller than the envoy.*

And they were built like tanks. Their shoulders were broad, their hands stubby. They tread carefully in Mercury's gravity, planting their feet and spreading their legs for balance.

As the Earth delegates stepped forward, the conductor raised this hand, and the musicians raised their instruments. The anthem of the Federation of Earth Nations played.

> *O Terra, our sacred state,*
> *O Terra, our beloved world*
> *Mighty of will and full of glory*
> *From South Pole to Arctic,*
> *From seas and from mountains*
> *We speak for the world, so kept by God*
>
> *Be glorified, great Terra!*
> *Glory to our peoples!*
> *Ageless union of humanity!*
> *Ancestral wisdom guide our hands!*
> *Be glorified, great Terra! Dignity for all time!*

*Not "Jerusalem,"* Frieda noted. Instead, it was something unfamiliar that was strident and military. She saw a flag-bearer standing at the back of the Earth party. This Earth's flag was green, showing their globe backed by a golden four-pointed star.

As the last strains of the anthem faded, a man at the centre of the Earth delegation stepped forward. He wore a military uniform—everybody, Frieda realized, wore military uniforms. There was nothing fancy about these uniforms either, no medals or braids. The rank stripes were subdued, and the cloth was the colour of camouflage.

Adelheid stepped forward, and Frieda followed her. The *Hermes* president stepped out on the other side. He and Adelheid walked toward the Earth envoy in tandem. Frieda, however, noticed that both strode as if it was a race. The distance between Adelheid and Frieda widened as Frieda maintained her own pace. Adelheid stuck out a hand to the envoy first, and President Garza pulled his hand back to his side, clenching it.

The man clasped Adelheid's hand and shook it. "Adelheid Koning, regent and stadholder of the *Messenger*. Your Majesty." He bowed. "I'm Colonel Alonzo Stevens. It's been too long since our planets have met face to face."

Adelheid's mouth tightened. Her eyebrows creased. Stiffly, she said, "Welcome to Mercury, Colonel Stevens."

Stevens let go of Adelheid's hand and turned to the *Hermes* president. "And you must be President Garza of the *Hermes*." He clasped the man's hand and pumped. Garza let out a squeal of pain.

Stevens jumped back, letting go. "Oh! I'm sorry!" He let out a quick, high-pitched laugh as Garza clutched his fingers. "Sorry! I forgot the difference in gravity. Don't know my own strength."

"It's okay," Garza gasped.

Frieda glanced at her grandmother and saw her quietly holding her right hand in her left, rubbing the fingers.

Stevens turned to Frieda. "And Crown Princess Frieda Koning. Nice to meet you too, Your Highness." He reached out, then hesitated, eyeing Frieda's prosthetic.

Frieda tried to stop herself sighing and failed, but hoped it wasn't too obvious. She took the man's hand with her remaining one and clasped it. "Colonel Stevens," she said as he gingerly shook. "Welcome to Mercury."

Stevens coughed, then recovered himself. "Right." He stepped back and clasped his hands in front of him—the universal sign of preparing for a speech. Frieda braced herself.

"People of Mercury," Stevens proclaimed. "Have you seen your planet from space?"

Frieda frowned. Of course, they hadn't.

"I did as we entered orbit," Stevens continued. "The rails of your cities gleam in the Sun. They mark the latitudes of Mercury like the clouds of Jupiter. It's a testament to the ingenuity and resolve of your ancestors, the space agencies and corporations that set up your towns, and the first colonists who came to live in them, just as your presence here today is a testament to Mercury's continuing resiliency after so many people said that you should never have been here in the first place."

Frieda's frown deepened, but Stevens went on. "People said it was a reckless endeavour. Even with the best technology, the plan was too expensive. But you Mercurians thrived on proving everybody wrong. You found the minerals the Earth needed most. For your first years, you were as rich as Forty-Niners, or the first mineral prospectors of Antarctica. You outpaced the colonies of Venus and Mars. What times those were."

Then Stevens clasped his hands before him solemnly. "And then the environmental catastrophe our technology had been running ahead of finally caught up and collapsed our society. We abandoned you. For that, we are truly sorry."

He grinned. "But here you are, against all odds. It's a miracle. So, let us come back together as the two miraculous survivors of the solar system. Let us be friends again and help each other. In honour of that friendship, I bring gifts."

He stepped back. At this signal, other men and women stepped out through the shuttle arrival door, pushing crates on pallets. The eyes of the Mercurians followed these. Each box was labelled, black lettering on particle board, with words like

"Protein," "Apples," "Plastic," and "Flour." Smaller metal boxes wheeled past as well, labelled "Wires," "Screws," and "LEDs."

One crate had words stencilled in white saying "3D Printer."

Frieda stared at that, then at Toshiko. Toshiko nodded and stepped discreetly away.

# CHAPTER 20
# TERMINAL DAY

From the shuttle arrival area, the gathering moved to Terminal's reception hall. The *Hermes* and *Messenger* musicians sat together, playing the classical music of Holst, Gershwin, and the Beatles. Tables lined one wall, waiting for the arrival of food. The picture window to the stars had been left clear for viewing.

The ceiling was festooned with flags, with the Earth's globe and four-pointed star hanging beside the flags of the *Messenger*, the *Hermes*, and Mercury's other cities. Frieda stared at these. *Fast work from the hospitality department*, she thought.

Kitchen attendants moved through the crowd, offering drinks. People gathered around, chatting, holding drinks and glancing at the food table. Frieda spotted Alfons there, helping prepare. She caught his eye, and he nodded quickly before redoubling his work. A young man slouched beside him, wearing the same kitchen workers' uniform but with a badge that identified him as from somewhere other than the *Messenger* or the *Hermes*. Frieda couldn't identify where from this distance. The young man looked up, caught her eye, and glared.

Frieda raised an eyebrow, then turned away. *Well, then.*

There were reporters around, too, listening to people, asking questions. Photographers moved between groups, and people posed, smiling as digital shutters clicked.

Frieda stood at a loose end. *This feels like a dance. I hated school dances. I tended to stand against the walls, feeling awkward. And here I am again, standing, feeling awkward.*

She'd just sent Toshiko away on her errand. Josef was off-duty, and Cara was . . . doing whatever it was she was doing with her mother. There was nobody around her that she really knew. *Is there?*

She looked again. Representatives of different cities stood alongside representatives of the *Messenger* or the *Hermes* and representatives from the Earth delegation.

"The big city in the northern hemisphere these days is Halifax," said a young Earthman, a whole head shorter than the crowd around him. "It does great trade, and the region it administers has most of the world's water and a fair chunk of the arable land, so . . ."

Frieda looked at a group clustered around a short young woman with red hair. "The Federation has been instrumental in pulling the Earth out of the Troubled Decades." Her blue eyes sparkled. "The Federation Council reminds the world that we're all in this together. When two nations fight over a resource, we bring things under control, sharing the resources equally. Yes, not everyone gets all that they want, but they get what we can give and with less bloodshed."

Nearby, Adelheid and the Earth envoy stood at the centre of twin entourages, speaking.

"Everyone appreciates the Earth's return after so long, Colonel," said Adelheid crisply. "Indeed, your arrival here so soon after re-establishing communications is remarkable. I have to ask: how can Mercury help the Earth?"

Stevens smiled. "I'm sure there are many ways we can help

each other, Your Majesty. We'll have plenty of time to discuss this in the coming days."

Adelheid nodded a moment. "What does that mean, exactly?"

Everyone listened to the Earth representatives with interest. But as Frieda looked from group to group, she realized she couldn't find representatives of the *Messenger* mingling in the same groups as representatives of the *Hermes*. She frowned at this. *This is a festival where the cities of Mercury are supposed to come together. Here we are, standing apart.*

*Cara's around here, somewhere. Maybe I should find her and start a mingle of my own. Lead by example.*

She stepped forward, looking for a familiar face, and the two officers subtly stepped with her. They were the ones who'd gone with her during her side trips at the trackworks and the archive. She paused. *Maybe I'm not as alone as I thought. Didn't I promise not to think of these people as nameless?* She turned on the nearest officer. "What's your name?"

The young man blinked, flustered, but he answered, "Bao Vien, Your Highness."

She turned to the other one. "And you?"

The tall, blonde young woman said, "Hilma Idunn, Your Highness."

"So, you've been ordered to follow me wherever I go, correct?"

Vien and Idunn glanced at each other. They nodded.

Frieda cocked her head. "Did you ask to be assigned to my detail?"

The two officers glanced at each other again. Idunn raised her hands. Vien shrugged. Idunn turned back. "This assignment was one of our preferences, Your Highness."

"Why did you choose me?"

Idunn coughed. In spite of a warning stare from Vien, she

said, "Well, Your Highness . . . you're rather like your mother. You're nice, and the Regent is kind of scary."

Frieda let out a laugh that she covered with a cough. "All right, you two. You're on my budget."

The two looked at each other. "We are?"

"As in, you officially work for me, not just the general Stadtholder's office," said Frieda. "Trust me, it doesn't change anything. You'll be paid the same, but this way, I'll at least know and remember your names."

The two officers glanced at each other again but then looked back.

"The same?" Idunn asked.

Frieda kept her expression neutral. "Yeah."

Idunn and Vien glanced at each other again, shrugged, and then faced Frieda at attention. "Sounds fair," said Vien.

Frieda smiled.

Doors opened, and kitchen staff emerged, bearing plates. Familiar as well as unfamiliar but promising smells filled the room. In spite of all dignity, it drew everyone near. Frieda's mouth watered.

"Let's move closer," said Frieda, and she walked toward the food tables, her security officers alongside her. Somehow, it didn't feel as awkward. They passed Adelheid at the centre of her own entourage. Mayor Huang of the *Baxter-Nordley* stood beside her, looking uncomfortable. "We really need to do something—"

"Mayor Huang," Adelheid snapped. She frowned at the Earth envoy, who was a few feet away, talking to President Garza of the *Hermes*, and lowered her voice. "Surely it can't be too hard to manage a few strikers. You just have to be firm as well as fair."

Frieda looked at the food selection. There were apple slices, cuts of preserved meats, things that looked like dumplings, but . . . different. *Makes a change from bac-crackers, at least.* She also noticed the cutlery and the plates and glanced down at her prosthetic, realizing she hadn't thought this through.

She stepped to one side so as not to hold up the line. "Okay. Meneer Vien? Mufrau Idunn? Here's a part of your new duties, if you're willing. I'd like some food, please, nothing more than bite-sized. And decide between the two of you which one holds the plate."

Idunn ended up holding the plate while Vien handed Frieda a fork. Frieda speared a dumpling and took a bite. The unfamiliarity of the taste stopped her. She blinked. *This was good!* "What—" she started to say, her mouth full. She chewed and swallowed, regretting not taking the time to savour. *There are potatoes in here. How did they make them taste so good?* "What *are* these?"

"Um . . ." Vien glanced at the sign. "Pyro—pirro—pirogies?" He raised his eyebrows. "Some dumpling with potato and cheese."

"Cheese!" breathed Frieda in awe. She took another bite.

"Your Highness," said a voice behind her.

Frieda turned, then chewed as quickly as dignity would allow. The Earth envoy stood before her.

"I wanted to speak with you personally," said Envoy Stevens. He gave her a sympathetic smile. "I offer my sympathies on the passing of your mother and the accident. I just heard."

*Why is this pirogi taking so long to swallow?* Frieda chewed desperately, not sure what to say. "Thank you," she managed, her mouth partly full.

"I'm sure we'll be seeing each other a lot over the next few days as we re-establish diplomatic links between our two planets," said Stevens. "There will be plenty of meetings, but it's good to get a chance to speak one-on-one without your grandmother watching over your shoulder."

Stevens's stare was intense like he was searching for something. *And why the comment about Grandmother?*

Frieda swallowed her pirogi. *At last!* "Thank you," she said more clearly. "Er . . . many meetings ahead, I'm sure. Though I'm not sure what we have to talk about other than to welcome you back."

Stevens laughed lightly. "You'd be surprised. We're happy to help Mercury after being away for far too long. I'm sure all of Mercury's cities will have needs we can help fulfill, and you know how it is with government business and its tendency to fill up all available space."

There was that searching look again. Frieda's jaw tightened. "I think you'll find that Grandmother keeps meetings clicking along. My mother learned from her. And you won't have too long to dally here before we have to shut down Terminal and move on. Sunrise is just a week behind us."

"Didn't your grandmother tell you?" asked Stevens. "It's our hope to stay here for one rotation—a chance for us to get to know Mercury and for Mercury to get to know us."

Frieda's frown deepened. *I'm being sized up. Because Grandmother and I are both stadtholders. He's checking to see who the weaker one is.*

*Are these my options? Prop or political pawn?*

"I look forward to getting to know the Earth, Colonel Stevens," she said firmly. "You can always count on Grandmother to do what is right for the *Messenger*, and you can count on me for the same. You are, I hope, what's right for all of Mercury."

He flinched back from her stare and covered it with a cough and a laugh. "I expect nothing less from a people that survived five decades on this planet on their own." He bowed his head. "Until next time, Crown Princess." He bustled off, heading for the *Hermes* president.

Frieda watched him go. "What was *that* all about?"

Vien and Idunn shrugged.

Frieda saw somebody approach from the corner of her eye, and she turned, expecting another official. Instead, it was Josef, looking furtive, even though, as part of her entourage, he should have had no trouble passing through security on the way there.

"Josef, what are you doing here?" she asked. "I don't think you've cleared your overtime yet."

Josef gave her a quick bow. "Your Highness." Then he lowered his voice. "Frieda. We have to talk. I've found something in the archive."

"What?" asked Frieda.

"The maps are wrong," he whispered.

Her brow furrowed. "What?"

"The mountains aren't at their right heights!"

She drew back. "What in Sunlight are you talking about?"

He fretted, clenching and unclenching his fingers. "Earlier, I measured one of the nearest tall peaks through one of the port-holes. I calculated my elevation on the *Messenger*, our position on the rail, and the angle through my sextant. Then, I looked at the maps in the archive. The nearest peak is at least five metres lower than it should be. I haven't measured the other peaks, but their heights don't look right, either."

"Why are you looking at this?" asked Frieda. "Maybe the maps are wrong?"

He gave her a haunted look. "Frieda, the incident wasn't the only reason I transferred away from the trackworks. Yes, it was a big reason, but . . . I went to the file clerks because I needed access to the *Messenger*'s maps. The *Messenger* should never have stopped. That debris shouldn't have found its way onto our Robinson Rail. There's no weather here. There've been no meteor strikes. So, where did the debris come from?"

Frieda tilted her head. "You think the debris came from the mountains?"

"I don't know." Josef fidgeted. "There's no record of any earthquakes or landslides, and that amount of stuff couldn't appear in just one rotation without something like that. I thought maybe it was a fluke, but when I heard the *Hermes* got stuck as well . . ."

Despite herself, Frieda shivered. "Have you told anybody else?"

"I tried. In the trackworks." He grimaced. "After the incident, people didn't want to hear it from me."

Frieda nodded. *So that's why Josef is here now.* "All right, then. Get me the evidence, and I'll make sure people listen." With her remaining hand, she touched his arm. *Should we go now or wait until tomorrow? Grandmother probably wants me to stay and be visible. If anything, that makes me want to leave even more.*

As she debated with herself, she caught sight of Cara by the side of the reception hall, standing near the end of the food table, smiling vaguely and swaying. She had a glass in her hand and more behind her. She took another swig.

Frieda stepped toward her. Frowning, Josef followed, along with Vien and Idunn. "Cara." Frieda kept her voice low. "Are you okay?"

"Hmm?" She smiled when she saw Frieda. "Oh, hello." Her voice slurred slightly. "Frieda. Your Highness. Oh, sorry. Frieda."

"Have you been drinking?"

Cara gave Frieda a vague smile. "Only champagne. From the actual Champagne region. The part of it that wasn't nuked, anyway. It's a gift from Earth." She raised her glass. "To Earth!" Her brow furrowed. "You know, I've heard that the carbo— the carbon—" She shook her head. "The little bubbly things. I heard the little bubbly things help the alcohol get into the body faster. I wonder how they do that?"

Frieda's eyes widened. "How much have you been drinking?"

Cara looked up, counted off her fingers, then shook her head. "Couldn't tell you."

A shutter clicked. Frieda turned sharply, but the reporter and his photographer were interviewing the president of the *Leigh Brackett*. They weren't looking in Frieda's direction, but they were nearby, and Frieda saw her grandmother eyeing the photographer and smiling to herself as she did so.

Frieda turned back and saw Cara giggle as she caught herself against the wall. Another shutter buzzed.

*This could go badly for Cara.*

"We should go somewhere else," said Frieda. She nodded at Josef, Vien, and Idunn with a look that said, *Help me, I command it!*

Josef stepped forward. "Come on, Cara." He took her gently by the elbow and eased her away from the wall. "We should be away."

"It's not your fault, you know." Cara looked up at him, her face suddenly serious. "I was there, remember? You couldn't have saved Frieda because it had already happened. A few seconds of freezing from claustrophobia didn't change anything. It didn't need to change what we had."

Frieda nudged Cara toward her left. They were on the wrong side of the reception hall. To reach the doors to the *Messenger* meant crossing the crowded space or staying to the side for a longer walk with more chances of being spotted. Another pair of reporters was close and approaching. "Let's hurry up," she said, keeping her voice level. "Wouldn't want to draw attention to ourselves."

Cara looked at her, and her gaze softened. "You're nice. You've been friendly, even after I was cold to you. You're not a princess with her nose in the air; you're just a normal person.

And you're lonely. I understand. Being from another city gets lonely, too."

Frieda nodded vaguely, focused on leading Cara away, Josef on the other side and the security officers flanked behind them. They moved slowly and quietly toward the nearest exit.

"I mean," Cara went on. "It's weird that you're a queen. I'm still trying to figure out what I am, but you: one day, you're in vocational school studying what you like and the next moment, boom, 'Hello, Your Highness!' It's not fair. How can they call you that when you're basically their prisoner?"

Frieda's jaw tightened. "Come on," she muttered. "Let's keep our voices down." They dodged to the right past a clump of dignitaries.

"I mean, what sort of system of government is leadership decided by accidents of genetics?" Cara asked. "I mean, how is it that just because you were born to a queen, you are qualified to be a queen, huh? Is there a queen gene?" She chuckled at that. "Queen gene." Then, more seriously, she continued, "Did anybody test you? Did anybody choose you? Heck, did anybody even ask you?"

"No," said Frieda quietly. "They didn't."

"I like helping people," Cara drawled. "I like making them better. I can be a good doctor; I know it. It's not my fault that *Hermes* trained too many. Why are they punishing me for it?"

Frieda glanced back at the main doors, but there were reporters there, too, talking to *Messenger* officials. "We're running out of options!"

Idunn cleared her throat. "Your Highness?" Frieda looked at her. "If you want to get out of here without being noticed, I have a suggestion."

Frieda frowned, then glanced from Cara to the reporters. They seemed to be closing in. "What do you have in mind?"

"We need a distraction," Idunn replied. "Permission to cause one?"

Frieda raised an eyebrow. She noticed that Vien cringed, and Idunn had a mischievous glint in her eye. She found herself warming to it but deeply wondered whether she should.

Then she saw Adelheid cast a glance at the approaching reporters, and a smile touched the woman's lips.

Frieda turned to Idunn. "Give it your best."

They were near the food table manned by Alfons. Pastries had been laid out in rows. Idunn came forward and leaned against it, shifting her foot against one of the table legs. Frieda felt the colour drain from her cheeks. *I can see where this is going. Poor Alfons! Maybe I should stop it.*

"Please don't speak of this," said Idunn. "Her Highness will apologize later." Alfons looked back, confused.

But before Idunn could move, Frieda caught sight of Alfons's assistant, standing beside him—the one who'd looked so hostile when Frieda had last glimpsed him. Now, she could see his insignia identifying him as from the *Leigh Brackett*. He was glaring at her again, ignoring Idunn. And he was holding a knife.

Vien tensed.

The man stepped onto a chair and then onto the table Idunn was planning to overturn. Plates went flying. "Free the *Baxter-Nordley!*" he hollered, raising the knife and jumping down. Frieda staggered back, knocking into Josef. Vien rushed forward.

Then Cara lunged in and floored the man with a punch. Vien and Idunn pounced a fraction of a second later, holding the man down and twisting his arms behind him as more officers rushed to the scene.

People shouted. Shutters clicked. Frieda stood staring, heart racing, at the fallen knife, at Vien and Idunn, and at Cara, breathing heavily and rubbing her sore knuckles. Another shutter clicked, and Frieda saw the tableau: Cara staring down at the assailant, grim and heroic.

*That's going to make the morning news,* she thought.

Frieda looked around at the crowd of confused, horrified, frightened faces and saw her grandmother looking shocked but relieved. Then, her grandmother looked at Cara and frowned. Frieda's jaw tightened.

☿

AS OFFICERS SECURED the reception hall and people calmed down, Frieda quietly ordered Josef, Vien, and Idunn to take Cara to her quarters and ensure she wasn't disturbed. The three slipped away. Frieda sidled into the safety of her grandmother's entourage while Adelheid and other officials argued over what had happened and whose security protocols had failed. The president of the *Leigh Brackett* stood mortified. She ordered her personnel to a secure area to answer questions and prepare for departure home, then she stayed to try and smooth things over.

The *Hermes* president stepped forward, offering sympathy and relief that nobody was hurt, particularly the Crown Princess. Adelheid accepted this crisply. The Earth envoy stood nearby, surrounded by his entourage, watching.

Toshiko returned, and Frieda quietly asked Adelheid if she could go. When her grandmother nodded, Frieda walked away with Toshiko and two security officers from Adelheid's entourage as escort. Frieda walked with dignity, but when they arrived at the tram, and she sat, she leaned against the wall with a sigh of relief.

"Are you okay?" asked Toshiko.

Frieda looked up. "I'm fine. He didn't hurt me. He didn't even come close."

Toshiko nodded. "Thanks to Cara. I saw that punch on the news media live. She'll be famous in the morning."

"Yes." *Better that than infamous.* "Who was that man? He

shouted about the *Baxter-Nordley*, but he wasn't from there. And the strikers haven't done anything like what he did."

Toshiko glanced at her tablet. "We'll know more when we get back to the Royal Apartment. I'm just getting some early reports from the media right now. Apparently, he had some . . . problems in the past. Reporters are interviewing medical officers on the *Leigh Brackett*. He'd apparently been obsessed about the independence movement."

"The *Baxter-Nordley*'s?"

"Well, that too, but mostly the *Leigh Brackett*'s from five years ago," Toshiko replied. "It sounds like he saw parallels."

Frieda shivered.

"You're sure you're okay?" asked Toshiko.

Frieda closed her eyes. "Not really. But there's not much you can do about that."

"But—"

"I've seen your schedule, Toshiko." Frieda looked up. "You've hit your overtime limit. When we get back to the Royal Apartment, you go home and get some rest." She gave her a tight smile. "I'll see you tomorrow."

Toshiko nodded and then bowed her head. "Thank you." She glanced around to make sure nobody was in easy earshot, then lowered her voice. "Frieda."

Toshiko stayed on the tram when they reached the Royal Apartment. The security officers escorted Frieda off and away. Other attendants opened the doors to the Royal Apartment for her, and Frieda headed for her bedroom.

She sat on the edge of her bed and rubbed at her residual arm, which was growing increasingly painful. *Well, of course. I've been wearing the prosthetic all day.*

But the pain provided a backdrop to her whirling mind. She saw the man clambering over the table, the glint of his knife. She saw Cara, and remembered the sensation that the reporters had been stalking her—and that her grandmother seemed to know and was pushing it. And Josef saying, *The mountains are not at their right heights.*

She looked at her prosthetic, and her mind ran ahead to taking it off: Anna coming in to help her undress, unclipping the prosthetic, putting it away. *I just want to be done with it now!*

She only had a thumb and forefinger, but she attacked the buttons on her blouse. It parted, and she shook off the sleeve. She grunted in frustration as the fabric caught on the prosthetic fingers of her hand. She swore and shook her arm harder, then worked on the clips of the harness holding on the prosthetic. Moments later, the prosthetic, still caught in her blouse's sleeve, sailed across the room and banged against the corner.

Frieda flopped on her side on the bed, breathing heavily.

The door clicked open. "Your Highness?" Anna darted forward, looking down, aghast. "Your Highness, what happened?"

Frieda closed her eyes. "I wanted my prosthetic off."

"Why didn't you call me?"

"I wanted my prosthetic off faster than that."

"Your Highness!"

Frieda looked up, raising an eyebrow. *Am I actually going to see Anna angry . . . at me?*

Anna turned away while Frieda levered herself upright. She stayed, facing away, running a hand through her hair while Frieda watched. Finally, Anna turned back. She looked at the floor by Frieda's feet. "I have a job to do, Your Highness," she said softly. "I ask that you let me do it." Finally, she looked up and stared at Frieda evenly.

Frieda stared back thoughtfully before turning aside. "All right. I'll try. I guess you can start by putting my prosthetic away."

Anna nodded and set about cleaning up the mess Frieda made. As she worked, she said, "I've been told to tell you that the Regent wishes to speak with you in her quarters in the morning, Your Highness."

She said it in an off-hand way, and Frieda hadn't been listening closely, so it took her a moment to process this. She straightened up. "Wait, is my grandmother summoning me? Now?"

Anna looked back. "No, Your Highness. In the morning."

"Why did she tell you to tell me now?" Frieda asked.

*And what could she want to talk to me about? If she wanted to see if I was all right, she could have come here. Summoning is something done when you want to dress someone down. Does she know what I'm doing about my prosthetic? Did she see what I did to protect Cara?*

Anna merely shrugged. "It is just what Her Majesty told me to tell you."

"Is she still awake?" Frieda asked.

Anna frowned. "She was retiring for the night when she told me."

"Then, she's still awake." Frieda struggled to her feet. "I'm going to see her now."

"But Your Highness—"

"You wanted to do your job, fine, but let me do mine." She started for the door, paused, then looked down at herself. "And help me put on a shirt."

☿

FRIEDA STOPPED in front of the door to Adelheid's bedroom suite. It was flanked by two security officers, who saluted her but did not move.

She looked at both guards and saw them eyeing her warily. She could sense the constitutional crisis going on inside their heads. *The Dowager Regent, our Stadtholder, has retired to her bedroom and does not want to be disturbed. The Crown Princess, also Stadtholder, wants entry. Either way, we're screwed.*

Then they focused on the air above Frieda's head, and Frieda sensed the decision: *But who are we to stop her?* Frieda reached out with her remaining hand and pulled the door handle down. The door wasn't locked. She stepped inside.

The lights were dim. Looking across the antechamber into the bedroom, Frieda saw her grandmother set down a small prescription canister while she swigged a glass of water. Adelheid looked up sharply as Frieda approached. "Why are you here?"

"You summoned me," Frieda replied.

"For tomorrow!"

"I couldn't sleep," said Frieda. "I thought if you wanted to talk about what happened at the Terminal festival, I should come right away."

Adelheid looked away, momentarily lost. Her eyes fell on her glass, and she set it aside. "I'm . . . glad you are all right."

Frieda nodded. "Thank you. Cara saved my life."

Her grandmother grunted.

"Is this why you called me, Grandmother?"

Adelheid looked up. "I'll keep this brief. I wanted to congratulate you on your conduct during the Terminal reception. You were very diplomatic to the Earth envoy. I'm extremely grateful for your tact there."

Frieda nodded. *She was watching even when I wasn't sure if she was.*

Adelheid looked down. "You represented the *Messenger* well. I was proud of you." She looked back up again. "However, I fear you are becoming too friendly with the *Hermes* ambassador's daughter."

Frieda tilted her head. "Are you telling me to fire Cara?"

"I can't," Adelheid growled. "Especially now that she's saved your life."

"Well, I'm sorry if her heroics complicate your life somehow!"

Adelheid frowned. "I don't think you are aware of how precarious things are between the *Messenger* and the *Hermes*, especially with the situation with the *Baxter-Nordley*. The *Hermes* leadership is agitating things, and we risk losing face and losing the B*axter-Nordley* if we don't respond properly."

"I don't see how that relates to Cara, who I'm told is looking to immigrate—"

"She faces a complicated process," Adelheid snapped. She sighed and rubbed her forehead. "But the fact is, the *Hermes* leadership is not above using any tactic to diminish our reputation. Had reporters seen Mufrau Flores's embarrassment at the reception, we might have gained more leverage—"

Frieda drew in a deep breath. "You admit that you were trying to send the reporters to humiliate Cara?"

Adelheid glared. "I didn't compel Mufrau Flores to get drunk within earshot of reporters. She put herself in a situation that could have embarrassed her government. I didn't have to do much of anything—just position myself near where the woman was drinking. It was only a matter of time before someone noticed."

Frieda gaped. "Is that all that Cara is to you? A prop? A potential tool?"

Adelheid shook her head. "Frieda." She couldn't meet Frieda's gaze, but she continued. "We're alive today because we used all the tools we had at hand. You need to be ready to do so as well." She looked up. "You think what I did was bad? There are plenty of people out there looking for us to stumble and falter. When you become full Stadtholder, you've got to anticipate that."

"I'd much rather just think like a decent human being," said Frieda.

"Then you'll lose."

"It's not a game!"

"No, it's not. But you'll still lose."

"What are you so afraid of?" Frieda yelled.

Grandmother and granddaughter stared at each other. In the dim light, the shadows darkened Adelheid's eyes. She let out her breath and leaned back on her couch.

"The *Hermes* thinks too kindly of Earth," she replied huskily. "Too many of the cities do. They're blinded by the possibilities of what the Earth could bring."

Frieda frowned. "What are you afraid the Earth will bring?"

Adelheid looked up. "The Earth didn't just rediscover how to talk to us, Frieda. It takes time to clamber out of the hole they dug. Time and ruthlessness. They chose to speak to us when they did. They had the ability to listen to us for a long time before that. Perhaps even contact us in secret. They could have talked to the strikers of the *Baxter-Nordley*. They could have talked to people in the *Hermes* government, encouraging them to encourage the *Baxter-Nordley*'s agitators."

Frieda shook her head in disbelief. "Were you always this paranoid?"

"No, Frieda, I learned to be."

Frieda let out her breath sharply.

Adelheid winced. "Frieda, we may both be Stadtholder, but I've been here longer than you. I need to find out what the Earth truly wants from us—why they would send an ion ship so suddenly. I need to defend our interests." She took a deep breath and let it out slowly. "Someday soon, this latitude town will be your responsibility, but until that day, stay out of my way."

"Grandmother—"

"Frieda, please," Adelheid closed her eyes, looking pained. "We'll talk more about this later. I've taken a sleeping pill."

Frieda stared. "You've been having trouble sleeping?"

Adelheid didn't answer. She leaned back on the couch. Her

eyes stayed closed. In the dim light, she looked gaunt and full of shadow.

Frieda watched in silence. Minutes passed, and Adelheid's breathing slowed and lengthened.

Frieda got up to leave.

"I sent her back," Adelheid whispered.

Frieda frowned. Then she leaned close. "What did you say, Grandmother?"

"I sent her back," she repeated. "Your mother. My daughter. Beatrix."

"I don't underst—"

"After we lost the tail section, I ordered the command centre rebuilt back there, and this apartment housed nearby." Her eyes opened, staring at the ceiling. She blinked, and a tear ran down the side of her nose. "It was a symbol to the people. The Stadtholder stands behind you. But I never faced the sunlight. Beatrix did."

Frieda held her breath, waiting.

"I lost my father to the tail section," Adelheid whispered. Her eyes closed again. "That wasn't my fault, that was the Earth's. But Beatrix . . . I asked her to be Stadtholder, and the tail section took her away. That one's on me."

Frieda waited for Adelheid to say something else, but she didn't. After a while, Frieda got to her feet. Using the hand of her uninjured arm, she pulled the cover higher on Adelheid's shoulders and left the room.

# PART SIX
# ADELHEID: THE HUNGER

# CHAPTER 21
# BACKTRACKING

*The* Messenger
*Mercury Colonies, January 2, 2152 CE*

AT THE NEW COMMAND AND CONTROL CENTRE AT THE REAR—
temporarily the front—of the *Messenger*, Adelheid stared at a
map of the dark side of Mercury. There were only three towns
lit up. There should have been nineteen.

Two of the lights were the polar statics—the *Baxter-Nordley*
and the *Lares*, neither of which moved. Both shone yellow.

The other light was the *Messenger*, shining green, a few
degrees south of the equator and now nearly two-thirds of the
way to the Dawn Line.

*And we're green only because we're the only ones we know are
alive.*

There was another light, flashing green, barely moving as it
headed south on the map. It had already crossed four Robinson
Rails and was now almost halfway to the *Baxter-Nordley*. This
was the convoy she'd sent soon after New Year to see what had
happened to the *Baxter-Nordley*. It had passed Gerhardt's dead

shuttle twenty-four hours after departure, stopping only to take what supplies were left before moving on.

Then, hours later, the *Lares* ceased communications as well.

*Both our water-mining cities,* she thought. *We're on nothing but recycling now. Not good. Should I send an expedition north? Maybe after the southern expedition reaches their target.*

As for the other latitude towns, even the equator city *Apollo,* their thin tracks flashed red.

*No communications. No idea where they are on their tracks.*

*Except Cristavao. He called to us. He's out there somewhere. He's alive.*

*Maybe.*

She bit down an urge to demand a report on how far they were from Cristavao's last known position. *The answer would be five minutes less travel time compared to the last time that question was asked.*

The *Messenger* rumbled beneath them. They'd been going full-speed reverse for over a day. *The land speeders can go faster, but not for long. We were always going to have to meet Cristavao's group more than halfway, but we haven't heard anything since. How long could they survive if they broke down?*

She sighed.

Liao looked up. "Are you all right, Colonel?"

She flinched at that. *I hate that title. I'm too young for that rank. Maybe "Stadtholder" would be better? Something to remind them that I'm not their leader. I'm only here until they're ready to take over.*

*What would Liao think? I should ask him.*

She glanced at Liao. *"Are you all right, Colonel" is the most Liao's said to me since I gave the order to reverse the* Messenger. Their gaze met, and Liao shifted on his feet. He looked down.

*Why is he so uncomfortable?*

She focused on her console. *Well, so what if he is? We all have things on our minds.* "I'm fine, Captain," she said. "Just lost in thought."

*And doing absolutely nothing. I'm useless here.*

She turned on her heel. "Captain, you have the comm. I'll be in my quarters."

Liao nodded and came forward. They avoided each other's gazes. This made her angry, and she left.

Outside, as Adelheid walked through the corridors of the *Messenger*, she noticed that it was quiet, even though there were lots of people about. She slowed to watch them. People saluted her as they passed, their expressions resolute. But now that she *really* looked at them, they looked . . .

*Gaunt.*

She put a hand to her stomach. It hadn't rumbled for days, even though daily food rations were still just eight hundred calories.

She looked up again at the strangely silent corridors of the *Messenger.*

*Our stomachs are used to it now. We're used to it.*

*But getting used to it isn't the same as being able to live with it. We can't live with it. Not for much longer. People are going to start passing out. They're going to start to die.*

*We're going to have to make the decision Hahn wanted us to avoid, and we're going to have to make it soon.*

She plodded the rest of the way to her quarters.

There, she paced from the door to the porthole and back. After a while, she stopped at her desk. She hadn't touched her Petri dishes or the portable forge for days. She picked up the logbook, flipped it open, and ran her finger down the list of results. *Fail. Fail. Fail.*

She looked at the Petri dishes and the forge again. *Maybe it's time to wrap this up. Move on.*

Her eyes fell on the antique key, the gift from her father.

She set the logbook aside and picked it up, turning it over in her hands.

*Lord in Sunlight, I miss him. He'd know what to do.*

She stopped turning the key.

*No, he wouldn't. He couldn't know. Because it's an impossible decision. He'd just keep going forward.*

*That's all anyone can ever do.*

She set the key down beside the Petri dishes.

The intercom chirped. It chirped a second time before she realized it. She pressed the button beside the speaker. "Yes?"

"Colonel." Liao's voice. "We've found the *Hermes* land speeder. We have them aboard."

She straightened up. "Stop the *Messenger*."

☿

ADELHEID MARCHED into the infirmary and made for the crowd of doctors surrounding the gurneys. "How are they?"

At the back of the group, Liao turned, looking haunted. "They'll live. Most of them."

Adelheid felt her stomach drop. "Most of them?"

"One of them . . ." He shuddered. "One of them sacrificed his oxygen so the others could live. They said they couldn't stop him."

"Who—" Then a gap in the doctors opened, and Adelheid saw Cristavao on the gurney, his eyes closed, his skin pale, his lips tinged blue. She lunged forward, then struggled as Liao held her back. "Is he—"

Liao tightened his grip and planted her on her feet, putting himself between her and the gurney. "He's unconscious," he said firmly.

His words got through to her, and she swooned with relief. Then she remembered the man who'd sacrificed his oxygen, and she looked down, guilty. Liao put an arm around her.

Adelheid stiffened, then reached over and clasped his hand in hers.

Suddenly, Cristavao gasped and cried out. He flailed blindly on the gurney and smacked one of the medical officers trying to hold him down. He yanked aside his oxygen mask. "No—! Antonio! Don't—" He shoved a doctor aside and twisted toward the edge of the gurney and a fall.

Adelheid caught Cristavao's shoulders and pushed him down. "Cristavao! It's okay! You're safe, now!" She grabbed his oxygen mask and pushed it over his nose and mouth.

Cristavao's eyes cleared, but they remained wide and desperate. He grabbed at his mask.

Adelheid held it fast. "Stay still! You have to rest!"

"I'm ... fine!" he wheezed.

"No, you're not," she snapped. "You were unconscious a minute ago. Your lips are still blue!"

"We ... can't ... wait!" He struggled. "They're attacking the other towns! They're—"

Out of the corner of her eye, Adelheid saw a doctor fill a syringe with a sedative. She caught his eye. His look was a question.

She looked back at Cristavao, who still struggled. "Cristavao, please! You need to calm down! We're still days away before we can talk to the *Hermes*. You need to recover from your hypoxia."

He gasped for air. *Hyperventilating.* She nodded at the doctor, and he leaned in with the syringe.

Cristavao shouted. "No!" Then, the fight was out of him. He slumped on the gurney, his eyelids fluttering. Adelheid stroked back his hair as he drifted off to sleep. She looked up. "Who attacked them?"

In a bed at the far end of the room, a young woman struggled to turn on her side. She lifted her oxygen mask. "The *Apollo*," she rasped before she slumped back, unconscious.

☿

ADELHEID AND LIAO rode the express tram alone to Command and Control in the tail section. After a moment, Adelheid said, "You're awfully quiet."

Liao glanced at her, then looked away. "Sorry."

"Don't be sorry," she said. "Just tell me what's on your mind."

Liao said nothing, so Adelheid stared at him. She saw him look down, pensive, choosing his next words with care. Finally, he said, "I'm worried. I'm worried about what we're going to find as we approach the Dawn Line. I saw the *Hermes*'s land speeder. They took enemy fire."

Adelheid faced forward. *I'm pretty sure that's not the only thing on your mind, but fine. We do have more important things to talk about.* "People shot at them?"

"Yes. Cristavao and his crew tried what we did with the *Baxter-Nordley* expedition, hooking a convoy of speeders together to provide extra oxygen. The other cars were destroyed."

*Flare!* "I'm leading us back into hell, aren't I?"

Liao said nothing for a moment, so Adelheid looked at him. She saw him smiling sadly. "I think it was a good move, stopping the *Messenger* here," he said. "There really are only three things you can do when you lead this latitude town: go forward, go back, or stand and wait." He looked at her. "Really, though: all three choices are just another way forward."

The look on his face made her feel strange. It was sad but also composed. It was acceptance, and it made her heart ache.

She gave him a soft smile. "Forward, then." Her heart lifted when he smiled back.

Their tram drew to a stop. The doors parted.

Liao and Adelheid walked into Command and Control.

"Colonel on the bridge," Liao called. The other officers turned and whipped off quick salutes.

She acknowledged their salutes quickly and headed for the communications station, her mind on what the *Hermes* officer had said before falling unconscious again. *The* Apollo *had attacked them, she said. Why?* She'd been speaking to Alistair Banks just five Earth months ago. *They sent condolences and best wishes as we moved ahead to the Dusk Line to recover and repair. They'd been sane enough to depart Terminal and leave a third of the supplies behind. What could happen in less than half an Earth year?*

*A cull, for one thing. That happened here. And the* Apollo *has more mouths to feed.*

*But why attack Cristavao's convoy?*

*Does it have anything to do with why the* Baxter-Nordley *won't respond?*

She stepped up behind the communications chair—her old chair—and frowned at the junior officer, a corporal, who now occupied it.

*He's just out of vocational school or possibly still in it. We're running out of personnel.*

She cleared her throat, and he turned to face her. His eyes widened, and he banged his forehead in salute.

"Calm down, Corporal . . ." She glanced at his name badge. "Copley." She gestured at the screen. "Any update on communications?"

Copley grimaced. "Nothing to report, I'm afraid. I'm hearing some signals from some of the towns, but they're too weak to identify. We're too far out."

Adelheid frowned. "No communications at all?"

He shrugged. "Other than our expedition to the *Baxter-Nordley*."

"We're twenty-five days from the Dawn Line," she muttered. "We should be hearing more."

Copley shrugged again.

Adelheid straightened up. "Open a channel to our expedition."

"Yes, Colonel." Copley leaned over his controls. "*Messenger* Command to expedition force, *Messenger* Command to expedition force, please respond."

The speaker crackled, then, "Expedition force responding. Captain Schroeder here. How can we help you?"

Adelheid gestured for Copley to hand over his headset. She put it on and took Copley's seat. "Wilhelm. How's it going out there?"

"Colonel." There was a scuffle at the other end of the line, possibly as Wilhelm rearranged himself to attention. "It's going well. Oxygen remains at optimum levels, and we've been able to replenish our batteries from the other Robinson Rails. We're approaching the *BepiColumbo*'s latitude now. Another thousand clicks, and we'll be at the *Baxter-Nordley*."

"How are you holding up?" she asked.

"Well . . ." She could picture him grinning ruefully. "Six of us in a confined land speeder leading a convoy across the surface of Mercury for days? Colonel, I would appreciate an honest answer: did you assign me this mission because you thought I was too close to Hahn?"

There was a teasing edge to his voice that, despite herself, made Adelheid smile. "And are you asking me now because you're over three thousand klicks away?"

"Yes."

She laughed. "No," she lied. "You're there because you're the most qualified officer I could spare." That last part, at least, was true. She grew serious. "Captain, you've been installing signal boosters at each of the Robinson Rails you've crossed. Have you had a chance to listen to each town's communications as well?"

"I didn't realize that was part of my orders, Colonel," said Wilhelm warily.

"I'm just asking if you did."

"Aye," he replied. "We didn't hear much; just enough to tell if they were still active, and . . ." He took a deep breath. "And I'm sorry to say that the *Brook Johnson* and the *Rücker Eddison* were not."

"At all?"

"All we got was solar power," said Wilhelm. "They're as silent as the Earth."

Adelheid winced. "But you *did* hear signals from the other rails?"

"Correct," Wilhelm replied. "Regular background chatter."

She nodded. "Thank you, Captain. You've been a big help."

"Thank you, Colonel. Over and out."

She gnawed her lip. *Two towns silent. Does that mean dead? Did the* Apollo *attack them, too? Why would the* Apollo *do that? And how?*

*And what about the towns that are still alive? Why could Wilhelm hear them but we can't?*

She handed the headset back to Copley. "Corporal, do you know anything about signal jamming?"

He blinked. "Just what I've read in textbooks, Colonel."

"Get those textbooks, Corporal, and figure this out."

He snapped to attention. "Yes, Colonel!" He hurried off.

She turned to face Command and Control's front display. *Signal jamming would explain why we can't hear the latitude towns yet. Perhaps the* Apollo *is blocking communications.*

*But why would they do that?*

*What is happening back there?*

# CHAPTER 22
# RECOVERY

A FEW HOURS LATER, ADELHEID ENTERED THE INFIRMARY BUT held herself back from shouting for answers. Instead, she nodded to the doctor who approached her. "You said someone regained consciousness?"

He nodded. "Yes, and he's asking for you."

She brightened when she saw Cristavao standing beside his infirmary bed, shrugging on his uniform jacket. She came forward, arms outstretched, before she remembered herself. She squeezed his wrists instead. "Are you all right?"

He breathed deeply. "I've been better, but I've been worse. They keep insisting I should stay in bed, but I can't just lie down anymore." He nodded over his shoulder. The other members of his expedition lay in their beds, asleep or unconscious. The young woman who'd told her about the *Apollo* attack before falling unconscious sat up but looked wearily at her bowl of thin soup before taking a sip. He looked to Adelheid. "I need to help."

Adelheid glanced at the waiting doctor. "How is he really?"

"I would like him to rest some more, Colonel," the doctor

replied. He glanced at Cristavao. "But he seems unwilling to. He's been wearing a trench into the floor."

"Fair enough." She turned back to Cristavao. "I know you need to be by your people, but can you come with me for a little while? We need to talk."

For a moment, Cristavao looked at his officers, torn.

"Commander D'Cunha," said the doctor. "Your fellow officers are in stable condition, I assure you. We're giving them the best treatment we can. We will contact you if anything changes."

Cristavao looked at Adelheid and, after a brief hesitation, nodded.

"Good." She took his hand. "Follow me."

☿

THEY ARRIVED at the tram bay as the doors parted. An officer and two civilians approached, but Adelheid called out to them. "Could you not board, please? We need this to be a private car."

They glanced back, looking annoyed until they saw it was Adelheid. Then, they backed up immediately. Adelheid swept Cristavao in. The doors shut behind them.

Adelheid set the tram to express, then turned back to see Cristavao staring at her, perplexed. She couldn't think why.

"What's happened with the *Apollo*?" she asked.

He faced forward, looking lost. "I'm not sure. They were . . . under control when we left them at Terminal. It was a hard thing to convince them to leave behind your third of the supplies, but they did it, and we moved forward as the dawn approached. And, for the first month or so, they kept control. They shared some of their supplies. They offered to mediate disputes. And then . . . something happened."

"What?" said Adelheid.

He looked at the floor. When he spoke, his voice was so low Adelheid strained to hear him over the whine of the tram.

"They stopped talking," he said. "For a long time, they just moved forward in silence. They wouldn't take land speeders—even one that needed its oxygen supplies replenished. No matter what we said, they wouldn't respond." He paused.

Adelheid frowned. She waited for Cristavao to continue.

"We sent a team to try and find out what was happening," he finally went on. "They couldn't get too close because by then, somebody was shooting at whoever approached. We set up a listening station instead. We couldn't make head nor tail of what we heard from inside. There were screams. There were gunshots. Complete chaos. And then, the city stopped. It just sat there, waiting for the dawn to come." He took a shuddering breath. "And then it got worse."

"Worse?" Adelheid breathed.

Cristavao said nothing. He breathed slow and steady. Finally, he said, "They sent one message, broadcast on all channels. It said, 'Run. They've taken over. Everybody, just run.' Then it cut out, and the jamming signal went up. The *Apollo* started moving again, and the raids started."

Adelheid gasped. "They attacked you?"

Cristavao nodded. Then he mumbled something. Adelheid frowned. "What did you say?"

"I missed you," he whispered.

Adelheid felt suddenly warmer in her heart—a comforting feeling she'd almost forgotten the past few months. She reached out and pulled him in. He turned to her, his arms coming around her. "Lord in Sunlight, I've missed you too," she breathed.

They pressed close and held each other for a long moment until something, some tightness in Cristavao's grip, made Adelheid pull away and look up.

There were tears in his eyes.

He looked away, trying to avoid her gaze, but there was no going back. "It's falling apart," he gasped.

At first, Adelheid didn't know where to look. She pulled him closer. "It's—" She stopped herself before she said, "okay." Instead, she said, "I know."

"It's falling apart," he said again. "After the *Apollo* turned feral, everybody gave up. Everybody started grabbing what they could. They're fighting each other for every last scrap back there. At least three latitude towns are destroyed."

"Cristavao—" she began. She formed her mouth around the words, "Which three?" but couldn't bring herself to say it.

He pulled away. "And the worst thing is . . ." He drew a shuddering breath. "I understand it. I do. The culls, the food riots, the raids. There's only so much to go around, and that's not going to change. The Earth is gone. Mars and Venus can't help us. We're on our own, and there are too many of us. What in Sunlight are we going to do?"

"I don't know," Adelheid heard herself saying and hated herself for saying it. But then, to her surprise, she added, "But I have a plan."

Silence descended. Cristavao stared at her. She blinked but said it again. "I have a plan. To feed us." She drew herself up. "It's not a detailed plan. It's not really a plan at all. But I'm exploring something and, if it works, could help us."

Cristavao's brow furrowed. "What is it?"

Adelheid wrung her hands. *I haven't told anybody about my experiments except for my father. I don't know if it will work. I don't want to give people false hope.*

Then she looked at Cristavao. *But any hope, false or not, is better than no hope at all.*

"It's in my quarters," she said. "Let me show you."

☿

CRISTAVAO HAD COMPOSED himself by the time the tram doors opened. He followed her to her quarters.

As they walked, he asked, "You're a colonel, now?"

She looked back at him. "You're a commander."

"A colonel is a lot higher than a commander," he said.

She sucked in her breath. "I know. It's just—" She frowned. *Why do I feel the need to explain? As if I'd done something wrong? I haven't. But it doesn't feel right.*

She sighed. "It's been a hard few months. We lost a lot of good people." She grimaced, her mind flashing on Lizabet.

Cristavao winced. "I'm sorry, I shouldn't have—"

"It's okay. I suppose you could say we're the lucky ones left behind," she said. "Strange, but I don't feel lucky."

His voice softened. "I know."

She nodded. "I know you know . . ." She tapped the insignia on his sleeve. ". . . Commander."

They reached her quarters and stepped inside. She flipped on the lights and gestured to her laboratory table with its forge and its Petri dishes. Cristavao stared, and Adelheid tucked her hands behind her, suddenly shy. "This is . . . such as it is . . . my plan."

Cristavao reached out and, after glancing at her for permission, picked up one of the Petri dishes. It showed small amounts of growth. There were more on some dishes than others, but all had spots where you could peer through the growth medium. He looked at her. "Bacteria?"

"Extremophiles," she replied. "I've been taking samples from the bacteria we've been growing for fuel. I think, with some changes, we can use it not as fuel but as food. I've altered its genetic structure to make it something we can ingest, and now I'm trying to figure out how to grow enough to make a reasonable food source."

Cristavao stared. "Edible extremophiles?"

She reached to the back of her laboratory table and picked

up a small cracker off a plate. She broke it in half and held out a piece. "Care to try it?"

He took it, turned it over in his hands, and sniffed it. He glanced at her, then took a bite. He chewed carefully, then swallowed.

Adelheid tilted her head. "How is it?"

He ran his tongue over his teeth and nodded slowly. "Not bad."

She grinned. "Good to know. I thought it needed a little salt."

Cristavao picked up another Petri dish. "You think we can grow these on Mercury? On our latitude towns?"

"Outside the latitude towns," said Adelheid. She nodded as Cristavao gaped at her. "That's where the space is. We still need our soybeans, but extremophiles can grow in a vacuum. They can survive the heat of the Sun. I just need to find the right medium."

"This could solve the calorie gap," Cristavao breathed.

She winced. *Too much hope, too soon.* "Maybe. Assuming we can grow enough of them. A lot of things must go right for this to work. So far, I'm not having much luck. It's a long-term solution, and we need something now."

"Still," said Cristavao.

"Yeah," she replied.

They lapsed into silence. Adelheid fidgeted as Cristavao looked at the Petri dishes again. Then he frowned and picked up Adelheid's key. He turned it over in his hand, then looked at her with a raised eyebrow.

"It's from Earth," she said quickly. "A gift from my father."

"Ah." He set it down, then turned. Suddenly, he was cupping her face and kissing her. For a moment, Adelheid forgot about the present. She let out a happy sigh and focused on the immediate future.

She kissed Cristavao back and eased him toward her bed.

# CHAPTER 23
# HORROR

THE FIRST THING THEY HAD TO DO WAS FIGURE OUT HOW TO break the *Apollo*'s jamming signal.

In Command and Control, Liao pointed out on the map of Mercury the likeliest locations of the latitude towns. "We already have connections and boosters on the Robinson Rails through most of the southern hemisphere as we head to the *Baxter-Nordley*," he said to Cristavao, Adelheid, and the watching bridge crew. "If we could connect to your rail, Commander, and synchronize the signals between the *Hermes* and the *Messenger*, we could boost them through whatever is blocking us and contact the other latitude towns."

"That's brilliant." Cristavao traced his fingers along the map.

Adelheid leaned in beside him, also tracing the Robinson Rails. "Better yet, we're far enough away from the *Apollo* that there's nothing they can do to stop us."

Liao leaned back, and as Adelheid looked up, she caught him frowning at her and Cristavao, but the expression was fleeting. He turned to the map, looking as professional as a lecturer. "We'll need a second expedition to head north, and

we'd better start now. With your permission, Colonel, I'll organize the crews."

Adelheid nodded, and he hurried away, faster than he had
to. But others scurried to action as well. Adelheid and Cristavao
got to work.

By the end of the day, they'd connected the *Hermes*'s
Robinson Rail. By the end of the second day, the northern
expedition had passed the latitudes of the *Reeve-Pilkey*, the
*Anson-Bova*, and the *Nourse-Vonnegut* and were approaching the
latitude of the *Viritrilbia*. Through it all, the people of the
*Messenger* worked with a new purpose, as did Adelheid. It
didn't matter that they were rushing toward an uncertain
confrontation—after over a hundred days alone in the Far
Dark, it meant everything to be rushing back toward something. And after her duties were over and Adelheid had time to
herself, she worked on her experiments, but this time with
Cristavao watching.

On the third day, they were ready to test the booster
network and contact the latitude towns.

Copley, the junior communications officer, leaned into the
microphone. "*Messenger* to *Mókiwii*? *Messenger* to *Mókiwii*? Are
you receiving? Please respond."

Adelheid stood beside him. Cristavao and Liao stood on
either side of her. The rest of the command crew sat at their
stations, watching. Only static replied.

Copley leaned forward again. "This is a priority message
from the *Messenger* to the town of *Mókiwii*. Are you receiving?
Please respond."

Adelheid held a breath, then let it go. "Fourth one so far.
Why aren't any of them responding?"

Liao shook his head. "They could be damaged. They could
be paranoid. Maybe our connections just aren't working."

Adelheid grunted in frustration.

"Let me try." Cristavao nudged Copley aside and leaned

into the microphone. "This is Commander Cristavao D'Cunha of the *Hermes* to the *Mókiwii*. *Mókiwii*, please respond."

Static crackled. The moment stretched.

Cristavao leaned in again. "This is Commander D'Cunha of the *Hermes* to the *Mókiwii*. Are you receiving?"

Static crackled again. Cristavao stood back, disappointed. Then, the speaker clicked. "Cris? Is that really you?"

Everyone jerked up. Cristavao let out a laugh of surprise and delight. He grabbed the microphone. "Yes! Who's this?"

"It's Sam!" said the voice. "Are you really on the *Messenger*? They're alive?"

Adelheid stepped forward, giving Cristavao a bemused look. He beamed at her. "It's Lieutenant Sam Mercurio, the *Mókiwii*'s communications officer. We're friends."

She matched Cristavao's grin, then leaned into the microphone. "Lieutenant Mercurio, this is Colonel Adelheid Koning of the *Messenger*. We are indeed alive and coming back to help."

"It's good to hear your voice, Colonel," said Mercurio. "And it's good to know that Commander D'Cunha is with you."

"Are you in touch with the other latitude towns, Sam?" Cristavao added. "We really need to contact them."

The speaker crackled. "I'm happy to help, Cris!"

Adelheid smiled.

☿

ONE BY ONE, they reached out to the other latitude towns, all except the *Apollo*. Adelheid smiled as she updated the positions on the map with each new contact. She didn't let the fact that they responded more quickly to Cristavao's voice than hers bother her ... much. *At least they have somebody they can trust.*

But then the news got grim. Adelheid rubbed her temple as she stared at the report.

Out of the fifteen latitude towns they were trying to reach, eleven reported back. For those that didn't, neighbouring towns provided explanations.

In addition to the *Brook Johnson* and the *Rücker Eddison*, the *Clement-Clarke* and the *Anson-Bova* had been destroyed by the *Apollo*, their fore and aft bridges breached to vacuum, with no word on what had happened to their survivors, if any. The towns lay derelict, stripped of equipment and supplies. Whatever the *Apollo* didn't take, the neighbouring towns grabbed instead.

The *Lares* polar static was alive but turning itself into a fortress and limiting water exports. *I don't blame them one bit,* thought Adelheid, *but with the* Baxter-Nordley *not responsive, this is going to become a big problem, assuming we or anyone else is able to deal with the* Apollo.

Worst of all was the *Nourse-Vonnegut*, which now stood derelict and was being picked apart by its neighbours. They hadn't been attacked by the *Apollo*. They hadn't been attacked by anybody. Their surviving neighbours, the *Viritrilbia* and the *Reeve-Pilkey*, swore they hadn't touched them or seen anybody who had. And yet, their representatives had forced their way on board to find plenty of oxygen, even supplies, but no survivors. Everybody was dead in their quarters, many in pairs, embracing.

Adelheid shuddered, as had the representatives of the *Viritrilbia* and the *Reeve-Pilkey*—until they started fighting about how to divvy up the salvage.

*Is this what we're going to find when we get to the* Baxter-Nordley? "Any change to the ETA for the expedition team?" she asked Liao.

He gave her a sympathetic smile as he shook his head. "Still the end of the day."

The eleven towns that did reply confirmed what Cristavao had told her: the *Apollo* was attacking everyone and needed to be stopped.

She stared at the map of the dark side of Mercury, at the green lights of the remaining latitude towns struggling to keep ahead of the red light of the *Apollo*. One of Cristavao's officers entered. "Commander? Colonel? We have video links up for the leaders of the remaining towns."

Adelheid turned to Cristavao. "You ready?"

He nodded.

"Right." She turned back to the command deck. "Put them on screen, Liao."

The main screen flickered, divided, and subdivided as the faces of the representatives of the remaining latitude towns of Mercury came up. Everyone looked grim or worried. *They should be. But at least we're talking to each other.*

She stepped into the frame and motioned for Cristavao to stand beside her. She cleared her throat. "By now, we've all had a chance to compare notes. We can see the threat the *Apollo* poses to the rest of us. I know we have all faced terrible hardships these past few months, and I know we have all done things we regretted. However, the *Apollo* has crossed the line. They've destroyed the *Anson-Bova* and the *Brook Johnson*. They're now the biggest threat to all decent people of Mercury. We have to work together to deal with them."

She tried to get some sense of the other representatives' reactions, but their fractions of the screen were too small to give her enough detail. She thought she saw most of them nodding, but all were silent.

Except for one. "How?"

Adelheid frowned at the matrix of faces. "Who said that?"

A face shifted in its box. "I did. Governor Tomas of the *Reeve-Pilkey*."

Adelheid glanced at Cristavao. The *Reeve-Pilkey* was the *Hermes*'s nearest neighbour to the north. Cristavao shrugged.

"You don't have to tell us about the threat the *Apollo* poses,"

Tomas went on. "We all have war wounds. Even you—though not from the *Apollo* or any of us, it seems."

Adelheid's frown deepened.

"You're telling us to band together and fight as if fighting is easy," said Tomas. "We're starving, and the *Apollo* outnumbers all of us put together."

"We know that," Cristavao cut in. "But they outnumber us even more if we *don't* work together."

"The *Hermes* wasn't much help when an *Apollo* raiding party attacked us," Tomas snapped. "We lost fifty people fighting them off before you arrived. Not only do they outnumber us, but they attack like ants, swarming us in their land speeders. We have almost no warning. At the same time, we have our own mouths to feed."

"We've come back to help you," said Adelheid. "When—"

"Even if the *Messenger* gets back in time to join the fight," said Tomas, "at best, you'd even up the numbers. If you expect us all to fight the *Apollo*, it's possible you may be joining a battle after it's ended, with the *Apollo* having you all to itself."

"Maybe that's the plan," said another voice. It took a moment for Adelheid to locate Governor Whikham of the *Lares* Polar Static. He leaned forward, grim. "We fight and sacrifice ourselves, weakening the *Apollo*, and the *Messenger* arrives to pick up the pieces."

Adelheid clenched her jaw against her rising anger. She was going to thunder, and though she knew it would be a mistake, she also knew she couldn't stop it.

Cristavao thumped the table, startling her to silence. "How dare you!" he shouted. "You wouldn't say that if you knew what they faced in the Far Dark! They didn't have to come back for us, but they did because we asked. *I* asked, and they came. I trust this woman! She will fight, not just for herself or for her city, but for everybody who needs help. You will not insult her while I'm standing here!"

Adelheid stared at Cristavao, then closed her mouth on her gape. *He doesn't know all that happened in the Far Dark. But he still trusts me. Lord in Sunlight, I hope I deserve that trust.*

Liao came forward and cleared his throat. "Colonel? Commander? It's the expedition. They've sighted the *Baxter-Nordley.*"

☿

ADELHEID SAT at Liao's station, Cristavao standing behind her, Liao behind him. The other summit leaders had been patched into the signal to listen. "Captain Schroeder," she said into the microphone. "This is Colonel Koning." *A bit of formality is needed with the world watching.* "Report on your position."

"We've reached the lip of the Chao Meng-Fu crater," said Wilhelm. "We have the *Baxter-Nordley* one kilometre away, in our sight. The crew is in pressure suits as a precaution."

"Excellent, Captain," said Adelheid. "Captain, I have to tell you that you have an audience. We have representatives of most of the latitude towns of Mercury hooked onto your video feed."

"Good day, everyone," said Wilhelm smoothly. "I'm looking at the polar static now. Activating my helmet camera." A new screen lit, showing the front window of the land speeder and, in the distance beyond it, a large circle of metal cones rising almost to the lip of the polar static's sheltering crater, like a modern parody of an ancient Bavarian castle. "I see no signs of damage to the structure. No signs of fighting, at least from here." The camera tilted down. "I do see fresh tire tracks. We've been following a set the last little while, but there are lots more of them, now, crossing back and forth. I think there have been convoys, Colonel, to and from the *Baxter-Nordley.*"

"Has anybody been sending convoys to the *Baxter-Nordley*?" Adelheid asked the air. There were mutters and replies from the other representatives, all negative. "Have you had any communication with the *Baxter-Nordley* since we last talked?" she asked Wilhelm.

"No, Colonel," he replied. "They're not responding to our hails, and we've kept the channel open for the past hundred kilometres. Dead silence."

*No pun intended*, thought Adelheid. "All right. Continue your advance, carefully."

"Acknowledged, Colonel," said Wilhelm. "We're beginning our approach."

The camera tilted with Wilhelm's head, left and right and forward again, as the land speeder moved over the lip of the crater and followed a path that had been blasted into a reasonable slope. The *Baxter-Nordley* jounced on the screen, growing larger and closer.

*Crack!* The noise made everyone flinch, including Wilhelm, which made the image suddenly jerk. On the screen, a divot appeared in the land speeder's front window. People shouted around Adelheid and in her earpieces.

"They're shooting at us!" Wilhelm yelled. Two more sharp cracks cut through the din, accompanied by fresh divots. "Expedition force to the *Baxter-Nordley*. We are not raiders! Repeat, we are not—"

Two more divots were smashed into the window. Cracks fissured out.

Adelheid snatched up the microphone. "Wilhelm! They're not listening! Return fire!"

She saw Cristavao straighten up in shock and shook her head. "That's Mercury's water in there. Nobody gets to hoard that!"

"Expedition force to the *Baxter-Nordley*," Wilhelm shouted. "This is your last warning: let us in, or we'll open fire!"

Cristavao's brow furrowed. "What did you give them to fire with?"

Two more shots hit the front of the land speeder. Wilhelm swore. "All right, prepare to fire on my mark!"

Everyone tensed. More shots hit the land speeder.

"Aim," said Wilhelm.

"We gave them what they needed," Adelheid replied.

"Fire!"

A blast swamped the speakers and shook the video feed. When it cleared, there was a hole where one of the airlocks to the Baxter-Nordley used to be. Vapour spewed from the opening, turning to ice crystals that rained down.

Cristavao gasped. "You gave them a rocket launcher?"

"They're losing all their air," said Wilhelm, shocked. "Colonel, they're losing all their air! Emergency seals aren't falling into place."

Adelheid drew back in horror. "They must have been damaged."

"By what?" asked Liao. "The rocket launcher?"

"No." Adelheid leaned forward. "By whatever happened before. Wilhelm, go in."

"All right," said Wilhelm. "Everyone, check your firearms and your pressure suits. Is everyone ready?" He glanced around the interior of the land speeder, revealing the rest of the crew, all suited and helmeted. Thumbs-ups and calls of "Ready!" answered him.

The land speeder drew up to the airlock door as the venting gas ebbed to wafts of falling ice crystals that settled quickly. The crew stepped out and, turning on the lamps of their helmets, peered cautiously through the opening before stepping in.

Inside, Wilhelm's camera showed bodies splayed across the floor, the visors of their helmets shattered. Guns lay scattered beside them.

"These are the people who shot at us," said Wilhelm. He approached. "That's strange." He lifted an arm. "That doesn't look like . . ." He brushed frozen blood away from the upper sleeve. Where the insignia of the *Baxter-Nordley* should have been was the rising sun of the *Apollo*.

In the control room, those who didn't gasp groaned.

"Colonel, are you seeing this?" asked Wilhelm.

"Yes, we are," said Adelheid. "Keep going, Captain. Show us what happened there."

Wilhelm and the camera looked up past the bulkhead they'd destroyed. The expedition force moved forward.

The service tunnel was empty. The lights were on power-save mode. They brightened as they detected movement. Walls that were in shadow lit up—at least, where the lights still worked. Wilhelm's camera scanned the sconces, the walls.

"I'm seeing . . . scorch marks." He reached up and ran a finger along a blackened dent in the metal wall, then at smaller divots. "Blast marks." He scanned the floor and picked up some small grey things, rolling them in the palm of his hand. "Rifle shells. There's been fighting here." He looked around. "But there are no bodies other than the ones we caused. If there was a battle, they'd started cleaning up, at least." The view bobbed as he moved forward again. "We're heading toward Command and Control."

"Sir?" A woman's voice. Wilhelm turned to an officer who stood by a control panel. "I think I know why they lost all their air. Their emergency systems are offline and have been for a while. There are faults throughout the system. When we breached the airlock, there was no response. None of the vacuum shields dropped into place."

The view turned back to the scorch marks. "Damaged in the firefight, do you think?"

"I don't think so," the officer replied. "It looks too deliberate. I think the attackers cut the system to stop the residents from sealing off sections of the city. Those shields wouldn't just hold the air in; they'd keep attackers out."

This was met with grim silence.

"There's more, sir," said the officer. Wilhelm turned to look at her again. "Before this settlement lost their air, somebody—I think it was the *Apollo* attackers—tampered with the climate controls."

"Tampered?" Wilhelm echoed. "How?"

"I'm not sure if tampered is the right word," she replied. "But . . . this place was twenty degrees below freezing before we entered, sir."

Adelheid, Cristavao, and Liao shared bewildered glances.

"Maybe we'll find answers at Command and Control," said Wilhelm. "Let's go."

The expedition force hurried on into the corridors of flickering shadows, past more damage and more dead *Apollo* officers who hadn't got their helmets on in time. Watching through Wilhelm's helmet camera, Adelheid twisted her hands. She straightened up when she felt Cristavao's hand touch her shoulder. She shifted awkwardly a moment, then took it anyway and clasped it, regardless of the audience. The rest of the bridge crew stared at the displays, hardly daring to breathe. Adelheid suspected the same was true in the other latitude towns.

The expedition crew turned a corner and came into the *Baxter-Nordley*'s agora. Wilhelm froze. "What in Sunlight—"

The floor of the agora was empty, but the ceiling was not. When he looked up, they saw . . . shapes, dangling on ropes. They looked wrong and out of place but disturbingly familiar. Adelheid couldn't think what they reminded her of but was scared she'd soon know.

The slabs looked heavy. They were red, with streaks of cream, and everything was frosted in white.

Liao leaned closer. "What . . . are those things? They look like . . . meat."

The colour drained from Adelheid's cheeks.

Wilhelm gasped. "It's meat. Hunks of meat, hanging . . . this is an abattoir. They turned the agora of the *Baxter-Nordley* into an abattoir. Where could they have gotten the livestock? They don't have—wait—"

Wilhelm's camera dipped, then shifted down as he crouched on the floor. "I'm seeing scraps of . . ." He picked it up and rolled it in his fingers. "It's fabric . . . torn . . ."

"Sir!" someone else called. "We've found storage lockers."

Wilhelm hurried over to where a woman was pointing. She lifted the lid.

"Wilhelm!" Adelheid leaned into the microphone. "What is it?"

The camera wobbled as Wilhelm shook his head. "Garments. Uniforms. Clothes. Civilian and military. I'm seeing the *Baxter-Nordley* insignia—"

Suddenly, he thrust the fabric down and whirled to face the dangling hunks of meat. Adelheid covered her mouth with both hands. Behind her, Cristavao whispered, "No! Oh, no!"

There was the sound of someone retching on the radio. Wilhelm turned and saw the female officer on her knees, throwing up inside her pressure suit.

"They didn't," Liao whispered.

But in her gut, Adelheid knew. They'd only found *Apollo* officers in the corridors by the airlock. They hadn't found anybody from the *Baxter-Nordley*.

Suddenly, they heard shouts through the radio. Wilhelm looked up.

"Sir!" Shadows danced as two people ran forward, hauling a third. Two members of the expedition force dropped a man wearing a pressure suit at Wilhelm's feet. "We've found somebody alive."

The man cowered, bowing his head.

"Who are you?" Wilhelm shouted. "Identify yourself!"

The cowering man looked up.

Wilhelm gasped. "Roderick? But—"

"Roderick?" Adelheid whispered. *I know him. Roderick Jones. Apollo bureaucrat. Kept records of calorie and water rations. I sent him a report for last year's census. We talked at Terminal Day. Stiff but modest. Humble.*

Roderick touched his helmet. His voice came onto the radio. "Please!" He whimpered. "Please, don't—"

"Roderick." William shook his head. "Roderick, we're friends. Were friends."

Roderick straightened up, holding his hands where everybody could see them. He nodded. He sobbed.

Wilhelm went on. "I've known you for . . ." He glanced at the dangling bodies. "You . . . you did this. You and the *Apollo* crew all did this." He waved at the room around them. "How could you sign off on this?" His voice rose. "How could you *accept* this?"

A small voice in Adelheid's mind whispered, *He kept the record of the planet's calories.* Her gorge rose.

Roderick drew breath. His mouth opened and moved, but no words came out. The moment lengthened.

"I'm sorry," he whispered at last.

Wilhelm shot Roderick through the visor. His body fell out of sight.

Silence descended.

On the *Messenger*, Cristavao turned and left the room. Other officers followed. Adelheid sat there, watching the camera view drop as Wilhelm sat heavily on the floor.

Adelheid reached to turn off the connection, then hesitated. The only sound was the rasp of Wilhelm's breathing. Finally, Adelheid leaned forward and spoke into the microphone. "Wilhelm? We're sending reinforcements. They'll help you secure the settlement. But there's something you must do."

No response.

Adelheid spoke louder. "Wilhelm?"

"What?" he snapped.

"You need to give them a burial," she said.

Silence on the other end of the line.

"All of them," she added.

Wilhelm took a deep breath, held it, then let it go. "You're right. We'll get on that. We'll clean things up here. We still need the water." His hand reached up toward the camera. "Wilhelm out."

The screen went blank.

# CHAPTER 24
## FURY

COMMAND AND CONTROL WAS NEARLY SILENT. ADELHEID LEANED back in her chair and looked around. Some people stood or sat at their stations, staring at blank screens. Others had moved to a corner, an alcove, or a piece of blank wall and were staring ahead or at their feet. Some were crying.

Half of the people who'd been there ten minutes ago weren't there now. Liao sat at his station, his hands over his mouth. Cristavao was nowhere to be seen. On the connection to the other latitude towns, all of the squares were either blank or showed empty seats.

She slipped out of her chair and walked out of Command and Control, careful not to make much noise. She found Cristavao outside, looking like he felt. He turned toward her, but before he opened his mouth, the words that were burning inside her burst out. She clutched her hair. "By the gods!"

"I know," he said.

"They *killed* the Baxter-Nordley!" She threw up her hands. "They killed them, and then they—"

Hands clamped on their shoulders. Shocked, Adelheid turned to see that Liao had grabbed both of them and was pushing them along. "Stop it, you two. Not here. Not in front of people. Do *not* let them hear you do this out here!"

They fell into step in front of him as he hurried them down the corridor and off to one side. By the time he stopped and let them go, the gut-wrenching horror had settled, but the disgust seethed. Adelheid slumped against the wall and stared at her shoes. "Is this what we've become? We turn on each other? We see each other as threats? We see each other as *food*?"

"I know," whispered Liao.

"It hasn't even been five months," breathed Cristavao. Tears were on his cheeks. "Is that all it takes? What are we going to do?" He slumped against the wall, hitting it with a thump.

Liao leaned back on the wall between them. They stood in silence for a long moment.

"Why don't we just run?" said Liao at last, quietly. "Get the other latitude towns ahead of us and do a rear-guard action to fight off the raiders, keeping ahead of the *Apollo*."

Adelheid shook her head. "We can't do that forever. They're bigger than us. They have more resources. In a war of attrition, we lose first."

"What's our other choice?" asked Cristavao. "If we stand and fight, we just lose faster. The *Apollo* is ruthless. They've just shown that. How do we stand against that?"

Adelheid stared at the ceiling. She pictured Mercury, its latitude towns racing ahead of the Sun, now racing ahead of the *Apollo*. The city could follow them into the Far Dark, and there they would be trapped, between the Dusk Line and the *Apollo*'s raiders as the equator city ground closer on its Robinson Rail.

*The Robinson Rails, seventeen of them, and two polar statics. Eleven desperate towns against one ruthless city. What* could *we do?*

"We could be more ruthless," she whispered, then blinked when she realized what she'd said.

Cristavao and Liao frowned at her. "What are you talking about?"

Adelheid pushed away from the wall. An idea was forming, and she pulled breath into her chest, slow and hard, until she felt like she would burst. It could work. She hated it, but it could work.

She let out her breath. "Cristavao . . . how many construction bots does the *Hermes* still have?"

He frowned at her. "A few pallets," he said. "Enough for a couple of repair projects, if that. With no spare parts coming, we're really rationing their use."

She looked at Liao. "Get the remaining leaders up on screen. It's decision time."

☿

IT DIDN'T TAKE LONG before Adelheid and Cristavao stood before the leaders of the remaining latitude towns. All the leaders looked shaken. Even Governor Tomas of the *Reeve-Pilkey* looked chastened.

They watched quietly as Adelheid began to speak.

"I have a plan to deal with the *Apollo*," she said. "But I can't do it alone. We have to do what we should have done at the beginning: work together. I had no choice but to take the *Messenger* into the Far Dark, but I'm sorry we left you all behind. Now that we're back, we can marshal our forces and deal with the *Apollo* threat for good. That's why I need you all to send us the remaining construction bots in your stores."

The leaders on the screen looked uncertain.

Finally, Governor Tomas spoke. "I . . . appreciate your apology, Colonel, but I don't see how sending you our construction materials helps you or us in any way. Further, you talk about us working together, but according to our information, you're still parked. You're not that far from Terminal."

Adelheid nodded. "The plan requires that the *Messenger* be where we are."

Tomas' eyes narrowed. "Away from us. Away from the fighting."

Other voices interrupted. The chatter started to overwhelm the room, but Adelheid stayed calm. She shook her head. "Just send us every last construction bot you have," she said. "Then prepare for a counterattack."

"We can't fight the *Apollo*!" shouted the governor of the Shuixing. "We don't have the people or the resources—"

"I'm not asking you to fight," said Adelheid. "I'm asking you to run forward and meet us. We will send crews to help. We'll evacuate the polar statics to the nearest latitude towns and head for the Dusk Line."

"But what about the *Apollo*?" asked Tomas.

"They can't attack all of us at once," said Adelheid. "But give us your construction bots, come toward us, and move past us. When the *Hermes* arrives, we'll both provide a counterattack."

Beside her, Cristavao nodded.

"But what *is* your counterattack?" Tomas asked. "What can you possibly do against the *Apollo*?"

Adelheid told them.

They went silent.

Adelheid glanced at Cristavao. He stared back with mounting horror.

# PART SEVEN
# FRIEDA: A LONG-AWAITED CONFRONTATION

# CHAPTER 25
# DETERIORATING RELATIONS

*The* Messenger,
*The Mercury Colonies, May 17, 2201 CE*

FRIEDA STARED AT THE EARTH EQUIPMENT THAT NOW LINED ONE wall of her bedroom. It was both bigger and smaller than she'd expected. The hollow cube of the printer, a half-metre to a side, sat atop the table. Beside it, a touch screen was taller and wider. A tablet sat next to it. On the other side, spools of different colours of plastic fed into nozzles.

*It's like the gears and wheels around the Robinson Rail*, thought Frieda. *It's amazing it can fit in my bedroom.*

Kneeling beside it, Toshiko looked up with a sardonic smile. "Frieda, you're drooling."

Frieda jerked up. "I am not!" She touched her wrist to her mouth.

Finishing her work, Toshiko chuckled. "Don't worry. I kind of am, too."

Cara pushed back from the equipment with a grunt. "It's ready." She rubbed an eye and her forehead. She still looked a little pale.

"Are you sure you're okay?" Frieda asked.

"I'm fine!" Cara snapped. She hauled herself up from the table, knocking a screwdriver off the side. She flinched when it clattered to the floor. Josef came forward and handed over the mug of tea Frieda had ordered. Cara sipped it. "Thank you again for last night," she said. She kept her gaze away from everyone. "I still can't believe I let my mother get to me so."

*And I can't believe Grandmother tried to take advantage of that,* Frieda thought. *Thankfully, Cara's not on the news—at least, not for being drunk.*

She glanced at the media screen. The volume had been turned down, but the screen briefly showed a photograph of Cara standing over the prone attacker and then flashed to the President of the *Leigh Brackett*, looking nervous and speaking quickly, repairing the damage as best she could. Then the images switched to the Earth envoy touring the *Hermes*, President Garza beside him, showing off that city's trackworks.

Cara looked for a place to set her tea down, then handed it over when Sara reached for it.

"How much time do we have?" Sara asked. "Are we going to have to slip this between diplomatic meetings?"

"I have the day," Frieda replied. "Grandmother is handling the diplomatic duties with Earth representatives." *And I suspect I'm being quietly punished for last night.*

Dr. Daskivic knelt before the machines and peered at the gears and the assemblies. Unlike the others, he actually *was* drooling. "It's amazing the Earth has managed to keep this much of its technology in good working order over so long. They put us to shame."

Josef straightened up. "Well, you try keeping fifty-year-old technology shiny without Earth's resources. Actually, we did."

Daskivic looked up at him. "They had a nuclear apocalypse. They were sent back almost to the stone age. That they could claw their way back, re-learn, and re-use the technology they had . . ." He looked at the 3D printer and wiped his chin. "That is truly remarkable."

*If you say so,* Frieda thought. "Are we ready to test this out?"

Josef caught her eye. He frowned, looking impatient. She nodded at him. *I know what I promised, and I'll keep it. We just need time.*

Daskivic stood. "We're ready, Your Highness. Let's see what this can do. And then see what we can do with it."

They did test prints of plastic parts. Frieda turned them over in her fingers and then passed them to Cara, who tried to bend them to the point of breaking. They were durable but could be recycled as they did more tests. They called up Frieda's new prosthetic design. Daskivic, Sara, and Josef made changes to suit the new process. Cara worked to one side, adjusting the nerve interface to the new technology. Then, they called up Cara's new interface design next to Frieda's adjusted prosthetic design. They stared at it.

"I think this will work," said Cara at last.

"I daresay this is a masterwork in engineering and medical design.," said Daskivic. "It'll be one-fifth the weight and . . . functional."

A smile spread across Sara's face. "We're good."

"With training, we can teach you how to work the fingers," said Josef. "It won't be full functionality, but it will be a lot more than before."

"We're good," Sara repeated.

"All we needed was the right technology," said Daskivic.

"And the willingness to use it," muttered Cara.

Frieda stared at the revised design. She glanced at her current prosthetic, in its case, then back at the screen. "I want to print it out. I want to put it on right now. Can we?"

She frowned as the silence lengthened. She looked at her medical team and saw them looking back at her. "Well, can we?"

The team looked at each other. Cara stood. "Frieda, you do realize that this is going to require surgery, don't you?"

Frieda swallowed. "How much surgery?"

"Fairly minor," Cara said quickly. "Probably local anesthetic. But you'll need to go easy on that arm for a while afterward. It'll hurt."

Frieda looked at her old prosthetic again, and her arm twinged. *I know I'm rushing this, but* . . . "I have the day," she said. "And I don't know how long we'll have this equipment before Grandmother vetoes me. Could we . . ." She drew herself up. "I'm not ordering you to do this, but I want it done. If you're willing, would you?"

The medical team looked at each other. Cara glanced at Josef. They looked back at Frieda. Finally, Cara stepped forward. "Don't do that to us. Don't make it our choice. If you want this done, tell us to do it. If anybody has any objection, they'll resign. But if you want this done, commit to doing it."

Frieda looked away. She stared at the wall a long time, at the media screen showing images of the strikers of the *Baxter-Nordley*. She looked at her old prosthetic again, then turned back to Cara and looked her in the eye. "I want this done."

Cara turned to Dr. Daskivic. He nodded. She turned back, smiling. "Then let's get to work."

☿

CARA HELPED Frieda undo her blouse, and the team started unwrapping the bandages from her residual arm. Frieda looked away, saw the needle, and looked at the floor. She grimaced as she felt the pinch and kept her eyes away as she felt her residual arm go numb.

"Scalpel, please," said Cara.

*Still looking away*, thought Frieda. She grimaced as she felt pressure against her skin.

On the table, the 3D printer zipped along, shaping each component.

Finally, Cara wrapped bandages over Frieda's residual arm. Dr. Daskivic stood behind her, nodding. Sara swiped at a tablet. "The receptors have a good seat."

"Excellent work, Mufrau Flores," said Daskivic.

Meanwhile, Josef assembled the parts of the new prosthetic as they came off the printer assembly. Gradually, it took shape, looking as much like an arm as her previous prosthetic did, but the way everyone handled it without hefting it made it look much lighter. They brought it over, and Frieda craned her neck to see.

"Should we try it on?" Josef asked.

"We've just re-bandaged her," said Cara.

"I want to try it," Frieda cut in.

The medical staff looked at each other.

"Please?" said Frieda.

Cara sucked her teeth. "Okay," she said uncertainly. But she and Josef brought the new prosthetic in. Frieda felt it click into place. To her shock, there was no jolt of pain. She looked down and saw the new prosthetic, the artificial palm on her lap. She swallowed. It felt uncannily familiar.

And as she watched, the fingers twitched.

"You should be careful," said Cara. "You probably should rest."

"But it's so much lighter!" Frieda hefted her prosthetic. "I can hardly feel it."

"You'll feel it when the anesthetic wears off," said Daskivic. "I'm getting you some painkillers now."

"Thank you," said Frieda. "But . . ." She gasped as her prosthetic fingers twitched, like it belonged to somebody else, trying to turn away. Then she stared, focusing. The twitching hand stilled, then lifted up.

"Frieda . . ." Cara warned.

But, thinking hard, staring hard, Frieda watched as one finger flexed and extended. Then another, and another. She let out a gasp of joy. "I think it's working!"

Cara grabbed it before it smashed into Frieda's face.

Frieda stared at the knuckles of Cara's hand. "Maybe we need to turn the sensitivity down on those receptors," she said.

"Yeah." Cara tapped a part of Frieda's new prosthetic, and the appendage relaxed.

Before they could do anything else, there was a sharp knock at the door, which then burst open as Anna staggered in, looking frantic. "Your Highness," she gasped. "You're needed at Terminal. The leaders of the latitude towns have called a summit. Your grandmother needs you there!"

Around Frieda, everyone looked either guilty or confused. Frieda's eyes widened at Anna's frantic state. "Why? What's going on?"

Anna's brow furrowed. "You haven't heard? Something's happened at the *Baxter-Nordley.*" She looked over at the media screen, which mutely showed confusion, jostling crowds somewhere. Anna stepped forward and turned up the volume.

A reporter faced the camera as security officers shoved shouting people away in the background. "We've no confirmation of who threw the Molotov cocktail," said the reporter. "While the protests had been loud, they'd been peaceful up to this point. In any event, the security forces responded quickly and arrested the protesters in the *Baxter-Nordley's* agora. The polar static is now under martial law."

Cara stiffened. Sara put her hands to her mouth. Josef and Dr. Daskivic stood. "Oh, gods," Josef muttered.

On the screen, the reporter faced a security officer, glaring down. "Clear the square, please!" said the officer. "There's a curfew."

"You can't do this," the reporter snapped. "We're journalists; we have a right to report!"

"You need to go *now*, Your Highness," said Anna. "Your grandmother has—" Then her eyes fell on Frieda's new prosthetic, on the tools and equipment that lay about, and on Frieda's old prosthetic, still lying in its case. Her eyes fell on the guilty expressions throughout the room. "What's happened here?" she asked.

"Um," said Frieda.

There was a knock at the door, and they heard one of the security officers call, "Your Highness? Are you ready?"

Anna turned sharply, opened the door partway, then planted herself in front of it. "Be patient and wait outside. Her Highness needs time to prepare. No one else is to disturb her." She slammed the door, then faced the room, looking uncertain.

"Anna," Frieda breathed. *I don't want Grandmother to know about this yet because I commandeered the Earth's gifts without her knowledge. Because I'm having this done, and she might have said "no." And because it could get complicated if she found out about this now.* "Anna," she said again. "Who do you serve?"

Anna looked from Frieda to the prosthetics to the rest of the people in the room. She focused on Frieda again and her new arm. Then she straightened up. "The Crown, Your Highness."

"Okay," said Frieda slowly.

Anna came forward. "And you're needed. Grandmother needs you at the summit so the *Messenger* can speak together. You need to get ready." There was another knock at the door. She glared at it. "*I* may need to forestall the attendants." She looked around at the others in the room. "Do *any* of you know how to dress a person?" she snapped.

People looked at each other. Cara raised a hand. Anna nodded. "Good. Get her uniform on her now. I'll keep the advisers out of the way while you do that, but *hurry*! The Regent needs her at her side for this!"

☿

FRIEDA EMERGED from her bedroom in her uniform, feeling only moderately dizzy. Her prosthetic twitched, but she put her hand on it as she walked down the halls of the Royal Apartment, carefully but smoothly placing her feet. Security officers slipped in before and behind her. Cara stayed close beside her. Anna led the way.

"Are you sure about this?" asked Cara. "You could claim illness."

"That'll cause more trouble than it will solve," said Frieda. "Besides, what's going to happen? She wants me as a prop to show unity. All I need to do is stand there." She winced. "Or, hopefully, sit there."

They reached the reception room to find Adelheid waiting, tapping her cane. She nodded as Frieda stepped forward. "Finally." She winced, then softened her gaze and her tone. "Thank you, Frieda, for coming on such short notice."

Frieda tried not to sway. "I serve Mercury," she said quietly.

Adelheid nodded. "Good." She turned to Cara. "Thank you, Mufrau Flores. We'll take it from here."

"But—" Cara shifted closer to Frieda.

"It's okay," Frieda muttered. "I'll just sit there."

Cara frowned, but she nodded and stepped back.

Adelheid turned away. "Let's go and see if we can't put back what those strikers ripped out."

Objections formed in Frieda's head, but she saved them.

Her cane clicking, Adelheid led the way out of the Royal Apartment and onto an empty tram. Frieda took her seat with Anna standing close by her, facing forward. Frieda's arm was still numb, thanks to the painkillers, but there was an ache around it that felt threatening. *Also, I'm sweating. Even though the trams are kept cool. That cannot be good.*

The tram sped along for a few minutes before easing to a stop. Frieda looked up in surprise. *Didn't Grandmother order an express?* Her grandmother, she noticed, was standing straighter, holding her cane against her side.

The door opened, and the *Hermes* ambassador entered with an entourage of her own. The doors shut. The tram accelerated. Adelheid shifted back as Ambassador Flores gripped a handle beside her. The two faced forward.

"Ambassador," said Adelheid.

"Your Majesty," said Flores. "I assume that this is more than a social call."

Adelheid took a deep breath. "I need to know what President Garza will say at this summit."

Flores cocked an eyebrow at Adelheid. "He doesn't give me a script. Like you, I will find out in a few minutes. We are almost at the Terminal stop."

Adelheid glared. "You know, and I'm sure Garza knows, that we had nothing to do with the incident on the *Baxter-Nordley*. I'm horrified by what happened, but we have restored order. I don't see the reason for this summit."

"I appreciate your regret," Flores replied. "But you can pass that on to President Garza directly, and he can tell you the reason for this summit. It will only be a few more minutes."

Adelheid's jaw tightened. She took a deep breath and said, "We shouldn't be having this argument now while the Earth delegation is here."

"I don't see why we should suspend Mercury's business just because of visiting dignitaries," said Flores.

"This is just the sort of discord the Earth could take advantage of if we're not careful," said Adelheid. "For the good of the planet, let us speak with one voice."

Flores lowered her voice. "You hate them."

Adelheid didn't reply.

"All of Mercury is eager to re-establish trade and relations with Earth, but you resist," Flores prodded. "It's more than a lack of trust. Because of what happened fifty years ago, you hate them."

Adelheid looked away.

Flores' expression softened. "Earth's collapse was uncontrollable. Everything they faced with the onset of the Silence, everything they did, we did too."

Adelheid's voice was so soft Frieda could hardly hear it. "That's why I hate them."

The ambassador straightened up. "My father talked a lot about you. He said that you gave your soul to the people of Mercury. And he's right: you are rightly a hero to this whole planet. But you gave everything regardless of whether the people wanted it or not."

Adelheid's brow furrowed. "What was your father's name?"

"Cristavao D'Cunha," the ambassador replied.

Silence stretched.

"Well. He would know, wouldn't he?" Adelheid said at last.

The tram eased to a stop. The doors opened. Frieda struggled to stand without using her prosthetic, but then Anna reached out a hand. Frieda glanced up at her impassive face a moment before she took it and hauled herself to her feet.

They followed the crowd into Terminal. Adelheid's cane didn't click. She held it under her arm as she strode into the reception hall, which had been converted into a meeting space with a long table and chairs around it. Monitors on one wall faced the table. Frieda spotted the leaders of the other towns, either in person or on screen. The president of the *Leigh Brackett* stood to one side, silent but looking relieved. The mayor of the *Baxter-Nordley* was nowhere to be seen.

In one corner, Envoy Stevens stood, hands clasped in front of him, watching the room. Food and drink had been set on a nearby table, but he was the only one eating, having grabbed a handful of bac-crackers and munching on one.

Adelheid strode toward Stevens. "Envoy Stevens." Her voice was crisp. "In what capacity are you serving at this meeting?"

He raised his hands. "No capacity at all. I'm here only to observe, at the invitation of a few of the latitude town leaders."

Frieda looked around the room. The other leaders were giving Adelheid a wide berth, casting glances when they thought Adelheid wasn't looking.

But Adelheid turned away from Stevens and strode to the table, calm even though all eyes were on her. She took her chair and looked around at the room. "I have been called to this meeting, so let us have it." She sat. Frieda followed, sitting beside her, stifling her breath of relief. Her residual arm was starting to ache.

The other leaders sat around the table. Frieda couldn't help but notice that President Garza of the *Hermes* sat across from Adelheid, and most of the leaders sat on his side of the table.

"Thank you for coming, Your Majesty." Garza nodded at Frieda. "Your Highness." He refocused on Adelheid. "I think you can understand the concern all the latitude towns of Mercury feel regarding the recent . . . incident . . . in the *Baxter-Nordley* polar static."

"As I told your ambassador," said Adelheid levelly, "we had nothing to do with the 'incident,' as you call it, and the situation has been brought under control. There have been injuries, but they are being tended to and no lives were lost. The *Baxter-Nordley* is now under a curfew, which Mayor Huang is even now heading back to administer."

Garza took a deep breath. He looked almost apologetic. "I'm afraid that's not good enough, Your Majesty. The fact remains that the water shipments from the Baxter-Nordley have been suspended."

"Temporarily," Adelheid cut in.

"Until the situation is resolved and the curfew lifted," Garza replied. "And when will that be? The strikers have made it clear they still intend to strike. Will you force them back to work? I believe this situation calls for a neutral observer so that the strikers feel confident enough to return to work."

Adelheid sucked in her breath. "You have no right to interfere in the operations of our client town!"

"They are the producers of half the water of Mercury," said Garza levelly. "All the towns of Mercury have a vested interest in this situation."

Frieda watched the back-and-forth between Adelheid and Garza through a growing haze of pain and alarm.

Adelheid crossed her arms in front of her chest. "What can I say to assure you that the water shipments from the *Baxter-Nordley* will resume and that the situation will be resolved?"

Garza leaned back. "I think all of Mercury would feel better if representatives from other cities could come and help keep the peace."

Adelheid's gaze narrowed. "Representatives? Keep the peace? Are you suggesting soldiers?"

"Of course not, Your Majesty," Garza replied. "Consider them peace officers."

"And what do you propose to do if the citizens of the *Baxter-Nordley* don't allow your 'peace officers' aboard their town?" Adelheid snapped.

Garza tilted his head. "Are you suggesting that representatives of the *Baxter-Nordley* would impede the activities of peace officers representing the legitimate interests of the overwhelming majority of Mercury? Should we put this to a vote?"

Frieda winced and leaned away from her prosthetic. Light though it was, it still pulled her down, and her residual arm's ache was intensifying. Sweat beaded on her temple and slipped down the back of her neck.

The Earth envoy cleared his throat. "I realize that this is an internal matter, but in the spirit of friendship, perhaps I can offer some assistance to ensure this situation is resolved to the satisfaction of all involved."

Adelheid shifted her glare to Envoy Stevens, but Frieda caught an edge to that look. *She's losing the room, and she knows it,* thought Frieda. *And the Earth envoy isn't helping.*

"You're presuming too much, Mr. Stevens," Adelheid began.

"There's no harm in hearing him out," said Garza. "What are you offering, Mr. Stevens?"

"Only our ongoing friendship with all of the settlements of Mercury," Stevens replied. "It's my hope and expectation that this will be the first of many visits, and we can build a new relationship based on mutual friendship and trade."

Even with the rising ache in her residual arm, Frieda could see Stevens leaning into the words "and trade" and some of the other leaders leaning toward him in response.

Adelheid narrowed her eyes. "What do we have that you could want, Mr. Stevens?"

Stevens shrugged. "Your modesty is to your credit, Your Majesty. But even on Earth, we've heard of your work with edible extremophiles."

Adelheid straightened up.

Stevens nodded. "That discovery would have earned you a Nobel Prize, Your Majesty, if there was still a Swedish monarch to award it." He held up a bac-cracker. "You take it for granted now, but it's your miracle. If we'd had access to that technology, our Troubles would have been shortened by at least a decade. We could have clawed our way out of our collapse that much faster."

"The technology is not a state secret," said Adelheid. "Why don't you just use it?"

Stevens shrugged. "We would if we could, but we haven't had much success. It may be that these extremophiles can only be grown under Mercury's conditions. If we wish to use these, we'll have to import them, at least to start."

"The bac-crackers are a critical part of our food supply, Mr. Stevens," said Adelheid. "What we have isn't for sale. We could ramp up production, but last time I checked, there were two billion people still on Earth and one million Mercurians. I doubt we could contribute much to the Earth's food supply."

"Well, as they say, every little bit helps," said Stevens. "And we would be happy to pay you handsomely in return."

Even through the rising pain, Frieda could see the suspicion in Adelheid's stare. But she could also see how others were looking at the Earth Envoy, the hungriness of their gaze. *He's isolated her even more. They're ganging up on her. I should do something, but what? Lord in Sunlight, my arm hurts!*

Adelheid turned to Garza. "If I didn't know better, I'd ask if you planned this. It's a hell of a coincidence that we're having this meeting the day after the Earth envoy arrives."

Garza laughed. "Well, I'm glad you're not stooping to that level of paranoia."

The Earth envoy cleared his throat. "Really, I'm sure we can work together and resolve any issues we have in a peaceful manner. I'm sure, after our rotation—as you call it—together, we will have a better understanding and a solid foundation for our friendship."

Adelheid glared. "So, you're staying for a full rotation?"

Stevens nodded. "President Garza was kind enough to extend the invitation. And, truly, the few days we've had are not enough to properly reconnect with an old—planet."

Adelheid seethed, but Frieda frowned at Envoy Stevens. It had been the barest of catches, but she was sure she'd heard it. *He was going to say, "old colony," wasn't he?*

*How much further are they going to prod Grandmother? And how is she going to respond? With all that's been happening, this feels like it's tipping toward a war, but that's silly. With all that we've been through, we shouldn't fall on each other, but if nobody backs down . . .*

*I really need more painkillers* now. *I wish Cara were here!*

She didn't hear President Garza call for an adjournment, but he said something, and he stood up, as did Stevens and the other representatives in the room. As did Adelheid. Automatically, Frieda stood, too and regretted it.

Her arm blazed with pain. The floor shifted beneath her, and her vision tunnelled. *Are we moving again? Wait, no. We're on Terminal. So why is Terminal moving?*

The tunnel got longer and deeper and was accompanied by a ringing in her ears that became a roar. Suddenly, Frieda saw the floor rising up to meet her, and she closed her eyes against the impact.

When she came to, cries of "Your Highness!" ran together with a general throng that made Frieda's head ache. Through the clamour, she heard a softer, though no less worried voice. "Frieda?" Her grandmother's face filled her vision, furrowed with concern.

Frieda reached up and clasped her grandmother's outstretched arm with her prosthetic hand.

Adelheid stared as the gloved fingers dug into her arm. She gaped at Frieda.

That's when Frieda realized her mistake.

Adelheid reared up. "Clear the room! Now! Give her air!"

Footsteps approached, but Adelheid waved them back. "I said clear the room!"

Frieda closed her eyes against the dizziness and blacked out again.

# CHAPTER 26
## A PLAN TO ABDICATE

WHEN FRIEDA RECOVERED CONSCIOUSNESS A SECOND TIME, Adelheid and Anna were heaving her into a chair. Once seated, Frieda almost tipped off it again, but Anna caught her and shoved her upright. "Your Highness," she breathed. She looked terrified.

Frieda pulled herself together and straightened in her seat, putting her arms on the table for support. She nodded to Anna, too tired to tell her she was all right.

"Thank you, Mufrau Petrov," said Adelheid to Anna. "Please leave us and guard the door."

Anna bowed quickly and left. Adelheid poured out a glass of water and pressed it to Frieda's lips. The icy cold jerked her alert. She took a sip.

"Feeling better?" Adelheid asked.

Frieda winced. Her head and her residual arm throbbed. "No."

There was a knock at the door, soft and tentative. Adelheid looked up. "Ah. And if I'm not mistaken, that will be your chief medical adviser." She got up and left Frieda's vision. Frieda heard the door open, and Adelheid say, "Thank you, Mufrau Flores. That will be all."

"But—" Cara's voice was cut off by the closing of the door. Adelheid returned and pressed a pill into Frieda's hand, then pressed the cup of water to her lips when she took it.

"There," she said. "The painkiller should help, eventually."

"Thank you," Frieda muttered.

"You have the grip of an Earthman," said Adelheid quietly.

"What?"

Adelheid nodded to her arm. "That's going to bruise."

Frieda blinked, then looked closer. Where her prosthetic fingers had gripped, five welts reddened on Adelheid's arm. Frieda's gaze fell back to her prosthetic, and Adelheid's followed it.

"When did you have that done?" she asked, her voice low.

"Earlier today," Frieda replied.

Adelheid nodded slowly. "You used the Earth's 3D printers."

Frieda felt bravery rising. *In for a gasket, in for a cog.* "And my engineering design skills. And Cara's surgical skill."

Adelheid exhaled, but she tilted her head. "Could you show me?"

Frieda hesitated, then focused on her left arm. For a moment, nothing happened. She tried to remember what Cara had told her. *Think of flexing my arm, like I'm lifting a barbell, making a muscle—*

The gloved fingers splayed, then curled. Frieda bent the prosthetic's elbow and raised her hand. Adelheid reached out carefully, tentatively, and touched the tips of Frieda's gloved fingers. For a second, Frieda thought she'd feel her grandmother's touch, but to her disappointment, nothing registered. *Still, to be able to do this . . . it's liberating.*

Adelheid paused, her arm outstretched, and said, "May I?" At Frieda's nod, she grasped Frieda's new hand and turned it. She traced her finger along the palm and flexed the wrist. She nodded as the clockwork clicked. Finally, she moved the arm back toward Frieda's lap. "How does it feel?" she asked.

Frieda shrugged, then winced as her shoulders protested. "Hurts."

"Other than the surgical incisions, I mean," said Adelheid. "I'm sure those will heal. It's good work. Indeed, I would say it's a masterwork, both of your engineering design and Cara's surgical abilities. It looks better than anything we'd be able to build here on Mercury. And, of course, it's way more functional."

"Lighter, too," Frieda added quietly.

Adelheid looked up. "Why didn't you talk to me before doing it?"

Frieda looked at her grandmother. Her gaze hardened. "Because *you* would have told me to wait."

It was an accusation without evidence, but Adelheid didn't contradict her. She looked away. For a flash, she looked guilty, but then she growled, "You're a naïve child. You let the Earth buy us off with gifts—"

Frieda gasped. "What? I was not bought off!"

Adelheid's voice rose. "You would risk the *Messenger*'s position on a masterpiece of Earth technology and the discretion of a young *Hermes* woman you hardly know, whose mother I have to fight with—"

"How dare you!" Frieda yelled, shoving herself to her feet so vehemently that Adelheid scrambled up and backed away a step before she caught herself. "What do I owe Earth? What do I owe Cara except gratitude?"

Adelheid laughed mirthlessly. "Clearly, the painkillers are working."

That just made Frieda angrier. "What do I owe them that I don't already owe to other people? What makes you think I would sell out the *Messenger* because of what I owe?"

Adelheid folded her arms and kept her voice low. "If people

find out that Mercury's young queen was given new arms by generous Earth benefactors, how could we possibly refuse them any request they make? You have given them a hold over us!"

"Why are you so paranoid?" Frieda shot back. "You question Cara's character; you assume the worst of her mother and Envoy Stevens. You turn your back on the interests of the people, cheering for contact with Earth, and you get angry at me when I speak out for peace! You swoop in, Mother's crown barely cold, give me a useless prosthetic, and start battling with the *Hermes* president and threatening the strikers on the *Baxter-Nordley*. Do you want war?"

"No, of course not," Adelheid yelled. "But the *Hermes* is looking after its own interests, and I don't think the Earth is acting in Mercury's. You don't know what they're capable of because you weren't around when they went silent and saw what we had to do to survive! All the other leaders are blinded by the promises of new technology and trade, and they don't take a second to look at who they are trading with. I don't want war. I don't want to go against what the other latitude towns think they want, but I have to move in Mercury's interest, especially if Mercurians can't see when their interests are being threatened. As Stadtholder, I have to make the hard decisions!"

"Well, the Stadtholder won't be around to make those decisions when I come of age," Frieda jabbed.

Adelheid's brow furrowed. "What are you talking about?"

"I'm talking about what Mom planned to do, what *I'm* going to do once I no longer need a regent," Frieda yelled. "When that happens, and I wear the crown, my first decision will be to formally abdicate as Stadtholder." She smiled as she saw Adelheid's flash of horror and pressed on. "And unlike when Mom was alive, you will have no one else to shove the position onto. I will see to it that the line of succession ends with me. I have no cousins, and I won't have children!"

Adelheid let out a short laugh. "You don't know that—"

"I'm very sure!" Frieda shot back. "I have no interest in this . . ." She waved her hand and prosthetic at herself. Her nose wrinkled. ". . . this relations stuff, beyond friendship. And I will not be married off as some political prize to encourage peace. I'll take my place as a private citizen and cede all power to Parliament. The people will just have to figure out how to govern themselves the old-fashioned way."

Adelheid and Frieda fell silent, staring at each other.

Adelheid sat in her chair and slumped back, staring at her lap. For a second, Frieda felt a surge of guilt. *She looks so old suddenly.* She breathed in to bolster her resolve.

"I daresay you'll do well as an engineer," Adelheid said slowly. "You've always had the mind, and possibly your new arm will serve."

In the new silence, seeing how exhausted Adelheid looked, Frieda felt her anger ebbing despite herself. "Um . . . thank you."

Adelheid looked up. "You say you don't want to be Stadtholder, but you mention my 'swooping in' before Beatrix's body was even cold."

Frieda winced. "I'm sorry—"

"I *did* swoop in," said Adelheid. "Because you weren't ready. Not because of your arm and not because you were too young, but because you were grieving and traumatized. You were in no fit condition to lead. I had no choice but to intervene."

Frieda swallowed. She nodded at the wrought-iron crown atop Adelheid's head. "So, you didn't actually want to wear that again?"

Adelheid rolled her eyes. "I want it as much as you do."

Frieda frowned in disbelief.

Adelheid sighed. "I'm an old woman, Frieda. I gave the crown to Beatrix for a reason. She was ready. She was good. And though she was scared as hell, and though she said she didn't want the position, she was willing to accept the responsibility. She thrived on it." She chuckled. "And now you, while my back was turned and with hardly any push, figured out how to work with the budget the office gives you. You gathered a team and made things happen. I underestimated you, granddaughter. There's hope for you yet."

"What do you mean?"

"Always make your enemy underestimate you if you can," Adelheid replied. "That will always trip them up. Even me."

Silence descended, but one that wasn't as cold as it had been. Frieda thought this over. "What happens now?"

Adelheid looked up. "I don't know. You have your new arm. That's good. If the press notices it and asks the right questions, your masterwork will surely come out, and that will give the Earth leverage in any future negotiations. Nothing we can do to change that. In fact, covering it up will only make it worse." She looked away again and sighed. "I'm probably going to have to let the peacekeepers into the *Baxter-Nordley*. I'll probably have to accept the strikers' demands for independence. That makes my leverage less and less. Nothing we can do about that. I'll just have to do the best I can to make them see reason."

Frieda shook her head. "What do you think the Earth wants so badly that they'd have to force you to do something you disagree with?"

Adelheid shrugged. "Again, I don't know. I'm sure they will reveal it eventually."

Frieda nodded slowly. "And what about us?"

Adelheid looked up again. After a moment, she looked away. "I don't know. In the end . . . I think it's up to you."

There was a knock on the door. "Your Majesty?" Toshiko's voice. "You called me?"

"Ah." Adelheid nodded to Frieda. "I took the liberty of summoning your new chief of staff."

Frieda's cheeks flushed. "So you know about that, too?"

"I know my way around a ledger, Frieda."

Toshiko entered. "Your Majesty," she said. She nodded at Frieda. "Your Highness."

"Thank you for coming, Mufrau Nakajima," said Adelheid. "I think the Crown Princess would appreciate a chance to rest after her strenuous time here. If so, would you escort her home?"

Toshiko looked at Frieda, who nodded and stood. "Thank you, Grandmother."

"I'll make sure the way back to the tram is clear," said Adelheid. "But, Frieda?"

Frieda turned.

"Nobody wants the responsibility of being Stadtholder or anything like it," said Adelheid softly but earnestly. "It gets thrust on them, or they fall into it before they know it. You'll probably fall into it too. When that happens, be prepared. Find out what Earth wants. There are things they aren't telling us, and people only do that if they're afraid of you or want to take advantage of you. Both of those things are bad for us. Look closer at what the Earth is and prepare yourself."

She turned away and said no more. Frieda stared a moment, then she and Toshiko left.

☿

FRIEDA AND TOSHIKO boarded a private tram back to the Royal Apartment. Once the doors closed and the tram accelerated, Toshiko asked, "What was all that about?"

"Family drama," Frieda muttered. She ran her grandmother's words over in her head. "But, strangely enough, I think we understand each other better now."

"That's good, isn't it?"

Frieda gave a little shrug. "It is, I guess. Why is Grandmother so paranoid?"

"Didn't she tell you why?"

"Sort of." Frieda sighed. "She's being isolated. I mean, part of that is her own doing, but that's what I saw: the other leaders isolated her, and that seemed to suit Envoy Stevens just fine. So, what *does* he want?" She looked up at Toshiko. "She told me to look closer at what the Earth is. How do I do that?"

Toshiko leaned back in thought. "I know somebody you need to see. Your grandmother might be leery of you seeing her, however."

Frieda raised an eyebrow. "Who?"

☿

FRIEDA WONDERED, as she and Toshiko approached the local offices of the Journalists' Guild, whether she should have donned some disguise or arranged for security to clear a path. But if they were worried about Grandmother's feelings about this visit, that sort of production would have gotten back to her. As it was, quietly and quickly striding along the corridor, just the two of them, was enough of a disguise. Any bystanders looking for the Stadtholder would be expecting an entourage.

The receptionist inside the entrance to the Journalist's Guild *did* recognize Frieda, however. His eyes widened, and he stood up.

"Please don't," said Frieda, quickly, quietly.

"We'd like to speak to Malika Beidl, please," said Toshiko. "As discreetly as possible?"

The receptionist nodded and led the way through hallways to a small but crowded room full of desks and chairs, with a messy sofa in the corner. There were reporters here, and Frieda and Toshiko entered among the chatter almost unnoticed.

Malika sat at her desk at the edge of the room, tapping away at her tablet. The receptionist came over and whispered in her ear. She looked up, saw Frieda, and stood, her chair scraping back. "Your Highness!" she exclaimed.

The room went silent. Everyone looked up, then stood up.

Frieda's cheeks flushed. *Well, so much for discretion.* But she stood straight. "Thank you," she said. "I'd like to speak to Mufrau Biedl alone, please?"

The other reporters filed out, and Toshiko went with them. Frieda suspected she was going to make sure their royal visit didn't make the news. This left Frieda alone with Malika, who stood staring, looking nervous.

Frieda looked around the room. The floor hadn't been swept. The sofa was old. "Nice place," she said.

Malika shrugged. "It serves, Your Highness."

"Please don't call me that. It's just us."

"Okay . . . Frieda."

Silence stretched. Both women looked at each other awkwardly. Finally, Frieda said, "Listen, I wanted to thank you for your question at the start of the Grand Tour. It was hard, but it was . . ." *Human?* "It didn't badger the way the other reporters did when they asked questions of my grandmother."

Malika tilted her head. "You're welcome. Though to be fair, your grandmother knew what she was getting into. You do realize it was your grandmother who helped set up the Journalists' Guild to be independent of the settlements of Mercury?" She nodded at Frieda's expression. "She doesn't talk about it, and neither do we, lest it impact on our objectivity, but soon after she took the Stadtholder mantle, she encouraged the other leaders and got them to agree to make us like a longitude town, stretching from the *Lares* to the *Baxter-Nordley* and covering everything in between. She did that as a power check so that those who ran the latitude towns, even her, would have someone looking over their shoulders."

"Somebody to watch over us," said Frieda. She frowned as

she remembered some of the pundits talking about her injuries and her mental fitness. "But who watches the watchers?"

Malika shrugged. "That question has been asked for centuries. Nobody's come up with a suitable answer. I suspect that's because the question is a distraction. So . . . if I may ask, why are you here? Shouldn't you be resting after collapsing at the summit?"

Frieda winced. "You heard about—no, no. Of *course,* you heard about it."

"*Are* you okay?"

Frieda gave her a wary glance, even as her residual arm twanged. "Yes." She sighed. "The thing is . . . well, you probably know about what was said at the summit. You probably know about Grandmother's . . . suspicions about the Earth?"

Malika nodded. "It's starting to get play among the pundits."

"What are they saying?"

Malika frowned. "Normally, I'd suggest that you watch them, but given that we're classmates . . . Most pundits outside the *Messenger* seem to think that the Dowager Regent is increasingly out of touch with the aspirations of the people of Mercury. That she's on the wrong side of history, as seen with the strike on the *Baxter-Nordley.* At best, she's irrelevant; at worst, she's standing in the way of progress."

"What do you think?" asked Frieda.

Malika shook her head. "I'm a journalist, not a pundit."

"There's a difference?"

"Yes."

"But, still, what do *you* think?" Frieda leaned in. "Grandmother told me I needed to look closer at Earth, and Toshiko suggested I come to you. Why would Toshiko do that if you didn't know anything?"

Malika thought a moment before she answered. "However you feel about the pundits, Frieda, or how I would feel about how the Dowager Regent handles the media, there's a . . . relationship between us and the leaders of Mercury, a relationship of equals. That's good. So . . . some of what we're seeing from Earth . . . disturbs us."

"What do you mean?"

Malika picked up a tablet and swiped through some files. She passed it over. "Have a look at this Earth media report."

Frieda took the tablet with her remaining fingers as the video played. It showed an Earth newscaster at a desk, wearing a grey jacket over a white blouse, an image of a grey city stretching out behind her. Except for the woman being stockier, broader-shouldered, and fuller of face than any Mercurian newscasters she'd seen, and except for the Earth background, the setup could have been any broadcast she'd seen on the *Messenger*.

The Earth newscaster didn't smile. Her delivery was businesslike. She clasped her hands on the desk in front of her.

"The Director-General of the Federation of Earth Nations officially announced the pacification of the McMurdo Republic and its formal acceptance into the FEN Charter," the newscaster intoned. Beside her, a screen-in-screen image showed soldiers working with civilians in a town bounded by white-grey mountains. "The move brings an end to the rogue state's acts of piracy on the Southern Ocean. The new administration has kindly channelled their nation's mineral reserves into the planetary reconstruction effort; officials say the move will ease fuel rationing for years to come."

Frieda frowned. There was something . . . wrong about this report. It sounded like what she'd seen in the *Messenger*'s media, but . . .

"McMurdo Republic?" she asked Malika.

"Antarctica," Malika replied. "One of the few areas that made a big population gain as a result of the Earth's climate shift. As far as we can tell, they managed to avoid the nuclear strikes at the start of the Silence, so they maintained a pretty good quality of life in isolation."

"But . . . piracy?"

"Well, yeah," said Malika. "That's what the Federation newscaster says. We can't confirm the claims of either the Federation of Earth Nations or the old McMurdo government. It appears there were incidents. So, we can't say for sure who's right or who's wrong, but . . ." She gestured at the tablet. "The reporting feels wrong. The reporter is taking the Earth government's side. It condemns the old leadership of the McMurdo Republic without question and praises the newly installed leadership, also without question. And this goes with other reports. No reporters question FEN policies. What we have here doesn't feel like reporting. It feels like propaganda."

"What are you going to do with this?" asked Frieda.

"I'm not sure," said Malika. "We're not sure how to report this, and the pundits haven't yet formed their opinions. We've passed these reports on to the leaders of Mercury, but they haven't responded yet. Some may think this is an internal Earth matter that has nothing to do with them. I wonder if some are just unwilling to rock the boat now that the Earth has re-emerged."

"What *should* we do about this?" asked Frieda.

"That's your call, not mine, Your Highness," said Malika. "It's your grandmother's call. I'm only here to report on what I see. But if you're wondering why your grandmother might be worried about the Federation of Earth Nations, this may be the reason. Take care."

☿

FRIEDA RETURNED to the Royal Apartment with Toshiko in tow.

She found Cara, Dr. Daskivic, Sarah, and Josef waiting for them in her bedroom.

"Are we out of our jobs?" asked Daskivic.

"Are we under arrest?" asked Sara.

"What? No! It's fine. I'll make sure it stays fine."

"Told you." Cara glared at them. Then she turned to Frieda. "Are *you* okay?"

Frieda's residual arm twinged again. "I think your painkillers are working anyway." She rubbed her face with her good hand. "I shouldn't have rushed this. I'm sorry. Please take this off me."

As the medical team worked, Frieda noticed Josef looking frustrated, and it took a moment for her to realize why. *I did promise I'd help him get his evidence.* "I haven't forgotten you," she said. "It's just that . . . I have had a lot to deal with."

"I can tell," said Cara. "What's happening between your grandmother and the *Hermes* president?" She bit her lip, then continued. "Mother talked to me again—urged me to come back to the *Hermes*. Seemed worried." She shivered. "Scared, frankly. Frieda, what's going on, and what can we do about it?"

"Scared?" Frieda frowned. *Why should she be scared?*

*But if she and the* Hermes *leadership are scared, that's bad because they actually have the power to act on being scared. If nobody backs down . . .*

*This is going too far. But what* can *I do?*

*So much is happening. Grandmother fears the Earth. Tensions are rising over the* Baxter-Nordley, *and the leaders of Mercury are getting stupid about it. And the mountains are in the wrong places and something stalled both the* Messenger *and the* Hermes. *Is there anything that I can do that can cover all three of these at once?*

An idea came to her. She straightened up. "I need to talk to Grandmother."

☿

THE ATTENDANTS OPENED the doors for Frieda as she walked to her grandmother's bedroom. She winced as her residual arm twinged. *I'm going to need more painkillers before this day is through. Should I be doing this?*

She looked up at a media monitor as she passed. Among the headlines: "Earth envoy moves to the *Hermes*." "*Baxter-Nordley* security prepares for arriving force."

*Force*, thought Frieda. *Not peacekeeping force. Just force.*

Adelheid looked up as Frieda entered. Before she could say anything, Frieda said, "I want to lead an expedition. Myself, representatives from the *Messenger*, the *Hermes*, and the Earth." *Can't exactly leave them out.* "I'll take the envoy's representatives ahead and tour the iron cornrows. We can start tomorrow morning."

Adelheid raised an eyebrow. "An interesting idea. What brings this on?"

Frieda shrugged. "I thought it would help."

Adelheid tilted her head. "You want to help?"

"You said you took over because I was grieving and traumatized," said Frieda. "Thank you. But I can help you now, and to do that, I am going to speak out for peace. I'm going to show that the *Hermes* and the *Messenger* can work together. It will change the story, especially after the summit."

"Why the iron cornrows?"

"Envoy Stevens wants to know more about how we make the edible extremophiles of our bac-crackers," said Frieda. "I'm sure he'll jump at the chance for his representatives to see the cornrows. My team will organize this. We'll set out tomorrow morning. With your blessing, of course."

Adelheid looked Frieda up and down a moment. Then she nodded. "Granted. Very good. That's leadership. I always knew you had it in you, Frieda."

Frieda's jaw tightened, but she didn't comment. "Thank you, Grandmother."

She strode out the door.

# CHAPTER 27
# A NEW UNDERSTANDING

FRIEDA WISHED SHE COULD IGNORE THE BABBLE OF VOICES THAT played over the tram's newsfeed, but it gnawed at her.

"For the Earth delegation to move to the *Hermes* during this fraught period sends a signal," shouted one pundit. "They're picking sides. It's an insult to the *Messenger*."

The other pundit tried to sound calm. "The Earth envoy speaks for himself, and the delegation came to visit all of Mercury. They acknowledged the *Messenger*'s importance when they first arrived."

Frieda glanced up at the screen. *Pundits are not the same as journalists*, she reminded herself. *Still, who watches the watchers?*

Standing above her, Cara cleared her throat. "We're almost there."

"Thanks. Help me up?" She'd hoped to stand on the tram for once, but the vacuum suit was an extra bit of weight she hadn't been ready for. She grunted as Cara helped her lever herself to her feet. She remembered not to use her prosthetic and grabbed a stanchion with her thumb and forefinger instead.

Cara, wearing her own suit, picked up Frieda's visor. "Are you sure you're going to be okay inside that vacuum suit?"

"Well, that's why you're here, isn't it?" Frieda replied. "And it's why you gave me that dose of painkillers before we put it on."

"I hope this doesn't take too long, though." Cara handed over the visor. Frieda carried it in the crook of her uninjured arm. "Dosing you again out there would be . . ."

"Tricky, I know," said Frieda. "I'll manage."

The tram eased to a stop, and the doors opened. Frieda and Cara walked from the tram to the land speeders' docking area, followed by the security detail. The *Hermes* and the Earth delegations stood waiting, along with, to Frieda's surprise, an honour guard. Then she spotted Adelheid standing in front, smiling. Frieda's father, looking proud, stood behind her.

*One of my first official duties as Stadtholder,* thought Frieda. *Their little girl has grown up.*

Keeping her prosthetic limb by her side, she came forward, took Adelheid's outstretched hand, and gave a quick bow. "Your Majesty."

Adelheid bowed her head. "Your Highness. Thank you for doing this."

Frieda lowered her voice. "You mean this bit of show-manship?"

Adelheid chuckled. "Never waste an opportunity."

Frieda turned to her father. "Dad."

She opened her good arm. He stepped in and hugged her. "Frieda," he breathed.

*He sounds relieved. Has he been worried? What did he want for me as his daughter? I'm sorry I didn't get a chance to ask him.*

"Dad," she said again, stepping back. "I'm ready."

Adelheid's brow furrowed. "Where's your delegation?"

"Here, and coming . . ." She nodded over her shoulder. Cara came forward, showing her papers to one of the security officers. "Cara Flores," she said. "Medical adviser to the Stadtholder."

Adelheid frowned at this but said nothing. Frieda smiled at this until she noticed Cara getting strange looks from the *Hermes* delegation as well.

Another young woman stepped out of the crowd to show her papers: Isolde from school, apprenticing for the Security Guild, and having just passed her pilot's test. Frieda nodded at her as the young woman bowed.

Finally, Josef came forward, showed his papers (co-pilot), and stepped into the circle, passing Frieda's father as he went. Her father blinked as the young man passed. He opened his mouth, but Frieda touched his arm.

"Forgive him," she whispered. "*I* did."

Her father closed his mouth. For a moment, he couldn't look Frieda in the eye. His jaw clenched. Finally, he said, "I'll do my best."

Frieda squeezed his arm, then turned to her grandmother. "It looks like everybody is here, so we should head off."

Adelheid looked at her again. Her gaze narrowed. But Frieda waited patiently. Finally, Adelheid said, "Right then, Your Highness. Off you go."

Frieda took a step back and saluted with her human hand. Taking a moment to wave to the audience, particularly to the journalists with Malika among them, she walked to the land speeder bay.

☿

THE LAND SPEEDER they'd picked was the largest on the *Messenger*. It had to hold twelve people. Isolde took the front seat, and Josef sat in the row behind her with Cara. The other dignitaries took their seats in little groups: *Hermes* representatives and Earth people. People put on their helmets even though the cabin was pressurized.

Frieda took the seat on the other side of Cara, who was again getting frowns from the *Hermes* delegation.

Josef leaned forward and helped Isolde with the pre-launch checks. "Your Highness," said Isolde. "We are clear to launch."

Frieda nodded and touched her radio. "Take us out, pilot."

Isolde touched a button on the console. Warning bells rang. The door to the land speeder locked with a *shunk!* Fans started, loud at first, the sound fading as the air was sucked from the loading bay. Ahead of them, giant doors opened, and lights illuminated the first few metres of Mercury dust ahead of them. Isolde pushed the power lever forward, and the land speeder left the docking bay and picked up speed.

The kilometres ticked away. They kept the Robinson Rail on their starboard side as the *Messenger* disappeared behind them. Frieda made small talk with the *Hermes* and Earth delegates. Everyone was polite, but everyone stayed in their groups and kept their radios on semi-private. Mostly, people sat in their seats, watching the landscape pass by.

Frieda returned to her seat beside Cara, tapped her radio, and selected a private channel. She cleared her throat. "Cara? Did your grandfather know my grandmother?"

Cara looked at her for a long moment. "Why do you ask?"

"It was something your mother said to Grandmother when we were coming to the summit," Frieda replied. "She implied that your grandfather . . . disapproved of what Grandmother did at the start of the Silence."

Cara faced forward. "Maybe. Mother never talked to me about it. I never asked."

Frieda lowered her voice, even though they were on a private channel and the roar of the land speeder was loud within the cabin. "How do you feel about . . . what she did?"

Cara gave a tight shrug. "She did what was necessary, even

if it was cold. I don't see there was any alternative. Still . . ." She looked at Frieda. "Am I right in guessing that this is the first time you've mentioned what happened fifty years ago to anybody?"

Frieda didn't bother to nod. "Does Garza and your mother . . . do they resent Grandmother? Is that why there's so much tension between our two towns?"

Cara's gaze narrowed. "I'm not an ambassador, no matter what you say. I can't speak for the whole city."

"But you lived there and here," said Frieda. "What do *you* think?"

Cara shrugged again. "There's always been a bit of a rivalry. That comes from being the two biggest towns after the *Apollo*. But I think that if the *Hermes* resents anything, it's that when the *Messenger* asks that Mercury should speak with one voice—I think that's your grandmother's term—it assumes that the *Messenger* should be that voice."

"Do we do that a lot?" asked Frieda.

"Yesterday, your grandmother did," Cara replied. "She seemed offended by the thought that the other latitude towns could come to a decision without her, as though we're variants of the client cities that the *Messenger* took over at the start of the Silence."

Frieda frowned. "You make us sound like conquerors."

"No," said Cara. "Just imperialists."

"Those client cities were depopulated," said Frieda. "We had to supply the people to get them moving again. The people living there today are those people's children and grandchildren. And we gave the *Leigh Brackett* independence when they asked for it."

"Yes, and I know the *Hermes* took on client cities of its own, too," Cara cut in. "I didn't say the resentment was wholly rational. But you asked what fuelled it, and I told you."

Frieda grimaced. "Sorry."

"That's okay," said Cara. "There's one more thing, though. You said the *Messenger* gave the *Leigh Brackett* its independence. Good for you. But things aren't going as smoothly for the *Baxter-Nordley*, and I suspect that's because that polar static has half the planet's water supply, and the other towns don't like the idea of the *Messenger* controlling it."

Frieda's jaw tightened. "We haven't restricted water exports. We've given all the latitude towns their fair share."

"Again, with the word 'give,'" said Cara. "Which implies that it belonged to you at the start. We gave our client towns, including the *Lares* polar static, their independence. Yes, I know I also said 'give,' but whatever. They have control over their own affairs now. That's a source of the resentment and distrust we're dealing with."

Frieda looked away. "Huh." She turned back. "All that and being a republican, and you still want to immigrate here?"

Cara shrugged. "The job that I want is here, not at home. Doctoring is worth putting up with a crowned leader. Besides, you've made it pretty easy for immigrants to the *Messenger* to become citizens. Good for you. And your citizens have the right to ask their governments to do better. Your grandmother put that in the *Messenger*'s constitution."

Frieda raised her eyebrows. "Oh."

"So, that's what I'm doing," said Cara. "What are *you* going to do? The citizens of the *Baxter-Nordley* have asked their government to do better. Whether you like it or not, that includes you. What happens next?"

Frieda looked ahead, thoughtful.

Isolde's voice crackled in Frieda's ear. "Your Highness? Something's wrong."

Frieda tapped her radio. "Isolde? What do you mean, something's wrong?" She looked up at the front seat to see Isolde craning her neck to look at the Robinson Rail.

"I mean, this isn't where we're supposed to be," said Isolde.

"We're not lost. I'm looking at our location on the Robinson Rail, but the topology around it doesn't make sense anymore. All the landmarks are out of place."

Josef's voice crackled in Frieda's ear. "This is even worse than I thought. Everything has shifted."

Frieda tapped her radio, bringing all the members of the *Messenger* expedition into the loop. "How bad has the landscape changed?"

Cara looked around at the three of them. "This is what Josef was working on?"

"What are you three talking about?" snapped Isolde. "I can't make head nor tail of these readings. What's going on?"

"I thought something was happening to the landscape," said Josef. "Something that could throw up enough rocks to stop the *Messenger*."

Isolde's brow furrowed. "Meteor strike?"

Josef shook his head. "We'd have noticed that."

"Well, what could we not notice that could change the landscape this much in 176 days?" Isolde sounded scared. Frieda heard murmurs behind her and looked. The Earth representatives were frowning, looking from the *Messenger* crew to the *Hermes* representatives. The *Hermes* people had their hands to their ears, listening.

Isolde cut in. "Your Highness, I'm getting reports from the *Messenger*, including a Priority One. It's a bit garbled."

Frieda tapped her radio but caught snatches of reports. ". . . *Baxter-Nordley* polar static under martial law . . . violent confrontation between *Baxter-Nordley* security officers and peacekeeper delegation . . . representatives of the *Hermes* diplomatic delegation arrested . . ."

Frieda swore.

The land speeder growled louder as it topped a rise. Isolde leaned closer to read a panel. "Your Highness, I have orders from the Dowager Regent. They're calling us back."

Josef straightened up in his seat. "Wait."

Isolde kept reading. "The *Hermes* president is requiring all citizens of the *Hermes* to leave the *Messenger* and return to their home city. They're pulling out of Terminal in the next fifteen minutes. The Earth delegation is going with them—"

Frieda's stomach sank as if pulled by Earth gravity. *Severing of diplomatic relations. In some cases, that's a prelude to war.*

Josef raised his voice. "Wait!"

Voices rose among the *Hermes* expedition. Cara lowered her hand from her radio. "Frieda? I think I have to go."

Josef smacked his radio. "Wait! Stop this speeder and look ahead, dammit!"

Isolde jammed on the brakes as they topped the rise. Frieda looked around, confused, until she focused ahead. In the lights shining atop the land speeder, there were black gaps in the ground. The way forward was strewn with holes. At the edges of some, the iron cornrows could be seen, toppling into them.

Frieda looked around, but outside their spotlights, the land was in darkness. "Isolde," she said. "Call up the radar. Show us the local topology."

Isolde tapped at the console. The front display changed to a black-and-white image of the area a hundred metres around the land speeder, seen from above. Sinkholes covered the land.

The *Hermes* delegation leaned closer, peering at the screen in horror. "What?" breathed one.

"Lord in Sunlight," Cara gasped. "Frieda, they're all around your Robinson Rail."

"They've undermined the Robinson Rail," said Josef in horror.

Frieda punched up the topographic map and focused on the Robinson Rail. There was a clear bend in it.

She swallowed. "We need to warn the *Messenger*, now!"

Suddenly, the land speeder shook. People cried out. Frieda

gasped as she saw the bend in the *Messenger*'s Robinson Rail increase. She saw it split.

The ground kept shaking. Isolde's voice cut across the radio chatter. "I don't understand these readings!"

"The ground's collapsing under us!" Josef shouted. "Reverse!"

Before them, the grey landscape dropped from their headlights, revealing blackness. It was all around them. It was under them. Frieda had just enough time to grab something with her prosthetic hand before the land speeder fell.

# CHAPTER 28
# THE SINKHOLES

THERE WAS A TWISTING AND A FLAILING AND A CRASHING. Everything not nailed down or boxed in bashed around them. The radio was filled with screams and cries. Frieda yelled as her helmet smacked hard against the side of the land speeder. When things stopped spinning, Frieda looked around, dizzy and disoriented. She felt for her seatbelt and released it, then grunted as she fell out of the seat and landed hard on what used to be the land speeder's ceiling.

She looked around. The world was at an odd angle, but she was alive. *I am, aren't I? Do I have all my parts? Legs, chest, arms— oh, right. Never mind.* That thought shook her out of her panic, and she took a moment to assess herself properly. She flexed her prosthetic arm, then her uninjured one. *Everything still works.* She tapped her radio. "Is everybody all right?"

She tuned in to a babble. She saw shadows flailing, struggling to get upright. "Hey," she yelled into the tumult. She pressed a button and caught everyone's attention with an electronic screech. "Hey, is everybody all right? There are twelve people her,e and I don't have time for a roll call, so if you are all right, turn your helmet light on. I want to see twelve of them."

Her beam cut into the semi-darkness. She counted off the lights as they flicked on. "I have eleven. Who's missing?"

"Isolde!" Josef knelt unsteadily on the land speeder's upended ceiling and gingerly touched Isolde, hanging upside down in the pilot seat. He peered into her visor. "She's unconscious, but she's still breathing. She's pretty banged up, though."

"Okay." Frieda let out the breath she was holding. *Eleven out of twelve, and no one dead. That's a good start.*

"Your Highness?" The voice of one of the *Hermes* representatives cut into her radio, and she heard the fear in it. She looked up and saw him—a lieutenant named Almeida—point forward. "The window!"

Frieda looked at the front window and saw the crack and the thin jet of air turning to ice crystals in the land speeder's headlights. As she watched, the crack fissured out. "We're about to breach! Check your suits!"

"Um . . ." Cara's voice quavered on the radio. "Hi. About that?"

Frieda turned, and saw Cara dangling from her seat, fingering a crack that cut across her visor. She scrambled forward. "Do we have replacement helmets?"

"The storage cabinet's damaged." Almeida yanked at the door. "I can't get it open!"

Cracks broadened on the front window. Josef tucked Isolde's arms under her safety belt. He nodded over his shoulder. "That thing is going to explosively give way unless we depressurize the cabin."

"No!" Frieda shouted as Cara's eyes went wide. "We need to seal Cara's visor!"

"Are you nuts?" shouted an Earth delegate from the back. "We could lose our reserve oxygen if that window goes!"

The cracks on the front window branched out again with an audible *creak!*

"Frieda." Cara's voice whispered in Frieda's ear. "They're right."

Frieda glared at Cara. "You are not a sacrifice. We still have time." She tapped her radio. "Hold depressurization! What's the status of the storage locker?"

"I can't—" Almeida groaned as he and another *Hermes* representative strained against the locker's lid.

*We need something else!* "Sealing tape! Have we got any?"

Josef leaped for a smaller storage locker by the exit door. "We do! Here!"

He yanked open the box, and its contents cascaded out. He fumbled around and brought out a roll of silver tape, passing this to a *Hermes* delegate, who passed it to Frieda. Without thinking, Frieda snatched it up with her prosthetic. With the thumb and forefinger of her good hand, she tore off a strip and planted it over the crack in Cara's visor before she even realized what she'd done. She didn't pause. She scrabbled for another piece of tape and laid it over the first. A third left Cara's face half obscured. Josef came over and smoothed the tape down. He gave Frieda a nod.

Frieda looked hard at Cara. "Are you ready?"

Cara drew a shaky breath. "As I'll ever be."

Frieda took Cara's hand. Cara stared at it, then at her.

"Josef," said Frieda. "Depressurize us."

Josef pressed a button. Everyone put a hand to their helmet as the air rushed out of the enclosure. The hissing ebbed in volume until the only sound everybody heard was their own breathing inside their small spaces.

The cracks on the front windshield stopped branching.

Frieda and Josef stared hard at Cara while the woman took slow, steady breaths. After a long moment, Cara let out a soft laugh. "I think it's—"

"Don't jinx it," said Frieda. "Just be careful."

Cara gripped Frieda's arm. "Got it. And . . . thanks." She

released her safety belt and Frieda helped her to the floor—the floor that used to be the ceiling.

Frieda smiled at her. Then she looked at the others in the land speeder. All looked confused or frightened. Nobody had said anything about what to do next. *Maybe that's my job?*

*There are eleven of us here. Time to delegate.*

"I need damage reports," she said into her radio. "Check whatever's nearby you. What's working? What's not?"

"Communications with the *Messenger* is down," said Josef. "Internal communications only."

"Dawnfire," Frieda muttered. "How are the engines?"

"Um . . . Crown Princess?" Almeida raised his hand. "Are you assuming you're in charge here?"

Frieda tilted her head. "Do you have another suggestion?"

She realized that the people inside the upended land speeder had clumped into three groups: the *Messenger*, the *Hermes*, and the Earth reps. Everyone in each group stayed close together and whispered to each other over private channels. Two of the Earth reps stood to one side and were leaning close while they spoke. She frowned at this.

But Almeida moved out of his group and crawled over. He tapped his radio, and she acknowledged his request for a private channel.

"We got a message from the *Hermes* telling us to return," said Almeida in her ear. "Something seems to have happened at the *Baxter-Nordley*. I suspect that relations are . . . more strained than ever between our cities. It's possible we're not supposed to be cooperating."

Frieda raised an eyebrow. "Really? Are you proposing we suspend diplomatic relations right here, right now?"

Almeida let out a laugh. "We have no choice, do we? We have to work together if we want to get back to not working together."

Frieda chuckled at that. More seriously, she said, "I don't

know what's happened on the *Baxter-Nordley*, but I can tell you, I didn't want violence. I want us to work together in peace."

He nodded. "What does your grandmother say?"

"She doesn't speak for me, and I don't speak for her," Frieda snapped.

"You might have to," said Almeida. "We heard the peace-keeper force was arrested as they arrived. We can't stand for that. Can you?"

Frieda swallowed. After a moment, she touched her radio so everyone could hear her. "If Mayor Huang arrested the peace-keeping force, it wasn't by my order, and I would never have ordered that. I don't think my grandmother ordered that, either, but if she had, I would tell everyone that she's wrong."

The *Hermes* representatives straightened up. One of them, a sub-lieutenant—"Ramos" had been the name listed in Frieda's briefing notes—leaned forward. "You're saying that Mayor Huang has gone rogue. If you rein him in, what happens next? If the people of the *Baxter-Nordley* hold their referendum on independence, will you allow it? If they vote for independence, will you let them go?"

Frieda looked at Cara. The woman looked back at her, expectant, nervous, hopeful.

"Yes," she said, looking Cara in the eye. "If the people of the *Baxter-Nordley* indicate they want independence, I will support them. My mother was not a dictator, and neither am I. We let the *Leigh Brackett* go, so the *Baxter-Nordley* should be given the same respect."

Silence descended. Josef looked shocked but looked at Cara. Cara smiled at Frieda, and Josef nodded slowly. Almeida, Ramos, and the two other *Hermes* representatives also nodded, eyeing Frieda with respect. The four Earth representatives looked confused.

"So," said Frieda. "Shall we get to work?"

Everyone struggled up and went to different stations.

"Engines aren't responding," said Almeida. "I think it can be fixed, but it may take time. And we're going to have to dig ourselves out."

"Oxygen tanks are holding," said Ramos. "We could repressurize just as soon as we fix the front window."

"Okay," said Frieda. "We're forming teams. Cara, you're the medical officer; see if you can help Isolde. Lieutenant Almeida, please form two teams, one to fix the window and one to fix the engines."

Almeida straightened up. "Yes, Your Highness."

Frieda faced the door. "Let's get this open and see what's out there."

Josef crawled to the door controls. After a moment, the panel switched from red to green, and the door unlatched silently, but with a vibration they felt in their feet. It swung open before smacking against a rock wall. The motors shuddered, then stopped. The door to the land speeder sat partly open, the gap just a few centimetres wide.

Frieda sighed. "Oh, well. It will have to do. Josef—"

She didn't realize her mistake until a second passed, and Josef stayed silent. She turned and saw him staring at the small gap that they'd have to crawl through—and seeing another gap from when this all started. Her residual arm twinged as she thought about it.

Before she could say anything, much less cancel her order and apologize, Josef leaned into his crawl and shoved himself into the opening.

On the radio, she heard Josef's heavy breathing. "This opens up. Just a few feet of tight quarters here."

"Keep going." Frieda nodded to one of the Earth delegates to follow her, then leaned forward to squirm out behind Josef.

On her radio, she heard a *clunk!* Followed by an "Oof!" Then Josef said, "Huh."

Something about Josef's tone made Frieda look up. "Josef?"

He grunted again. "Well. I see. That's instructive."

She saw his legs in the light from her helmet, his body wedged between the roof of the land speeder and the rock wall. "Josef, what is it?"

"I'm stuck." He scrabbled at the dust, grunting with effort. "I can't go forward." He gathered himself and shifted back, straining, before collapsing again with a nervous laugh. "And I can't go back. I know I haven't gotten any fatter. I wondered what would have happened if I hadn't frozen back then. This is very instructive."

"Josef, don't panic," said Frieda, frantic. Then, an Earth delegate tapped her arm. She nodded at Frieda, then crawled toward the gap, looking determined. "We're getting help," Frieda continued. "Sit tight."

"Don't say 'tight'!"

The Earth delegate, a slim young woman, slid easily into the gap and then braced herself against Josef's boots. Pushing against the wall and the land speeder, she shoved forward. Frieda felt the land speeder shift, and Josef slid forward, saying, "Whoa!" Motioning for the other Earth delegates to follow her, Frieda slipped out the door.

They were on top of a mound of rubble. Josef stood at the base of it, brushing himself off. The Earth woman looked up and around, the light from her helmet bouncing off smooth, rounded grey walls. The other Earth delegates slipped out behind Frieda and turned their attention to the upended underside of the land speeder. "I don't think the axles are damaged," said one.

"That's good." Frieda looked back at the land speeder, upside down under a circle of stars. "How are we going to get this upright?"

The Earth woman who'd shoved Josef out clasped a corner of the land speeder. She pulled, grunted, and strained, and the land speeder rose a few centimetres before she had to set it down. "We can do this if everybody gets out and helps," she said. One of her colleagues called into the land speeder, asking everybody else to come out. Cara grabbed Almeida, and they went to unhook and carry out Isolde.

Frieda looked around. Grey sloping sides angled up about four metres around them. "A sinkhole," she muttered. "How is that possible? You can't get a sinkhole without flowing water."

"Or flowing something," said Josef. "You're right: nothing natural on Mercury could make this."

Frieda tapped her helmet and set her link to Josef to private. Taking him by the elbow, she turned him away from the rest of the group. "What in Sunlight is this place, Josef? If this isn't natural, then who made this?"

Josef looked up and around. "I don't know. We didn't mine when we dug for coltan before the Silence; we quarried. We certainly wouldn't mine beneath our Robinson Rails." He looked ahead. The light from his helmet vanished into the darkness. "This goes deeper."

She walked past him. "Let's go."

They entered a tunnel, round as a drainpipe, sloping down. The stars vanished as the ceiling closed overhead. Frieda brushed the smooth walls and flicked away dust that shone silver as it fell from her hands. Her breath caught as she thought about her next question. "Do you think somebody's trying to undermine us?" *The* Hermes *wouldn't do that! They wouldn't dare!*

Josef ran his hand against the wall. "We don't have the technology to do this, not since we scrapped the last construction bot. Even then . . ." He gestured at the wall, the dust falling from his hand. "These walls are airtight. Construction bots couldn't do that on their own." He frowned as he focused on the dust on his fingers. "And this isn't rock dust."

Frieda leaned forward. "What?"

Josef rubbed his fingers. "This is something different. I . . . I think it's metallic."

Frieda marvelled at the way the falling dust shimmered in her visor light. It looked like silver sand, except it didn't move like sand. "Get a sample."

She looked back the way they'd come while Josef patted the pockets of his pressure suit. She saw the Earthwoman and the Earthman pushing and rolling the land speeder away from the wall while the Mercurians either pulled at the other side or stayed well out of the way. The two remaining Earthmen stood by the wall of the sinkhole, looking up at it, touching it, rubbing dust from their fingers.

*Huh*, she thought. *They're curious, too.*

She looked back at Josef. "So, if Mercurians didn't build this, was it Earth people?"

"They've only been here a few days. This couldn't have been built even within one rotation." Josef scraped dust into a cloth wipe, which he pocketed. "At the same time, this doesn't predate the Silence. Remember the debris? The changing heights of the mountains?" His breath caught. "This is a network of tunnels . . . a *big* network of tunnels. And it's been growing."

"Digging," Frieda breathed. "Undermining us. Maybe even undermining the *Hermes*." Her chest tightened. "And the *Messenger* is running right into this." She looked up at Josef. "We have to warn them!"

They hurried back to the land speeder, passing the two Earth reps still examining the sinkhole walls. Cara was tending to Isolde inside the now upright land speeder. Almeida and Ramos had a panel open in the front and were peering in at the speeder's engines. The Earthman and Earthwoman who'd rolled the vehicle had pulled apart the jammed storage locker and were applying sealant over the crack in the front window.

Frieda tapped Almeida onto a private channel. "Can we move?"

"Eventually," Almeida replied. "Some of the wires were ripped loose by the crash. We'll have to repair them." He reached into the panel. There was a spark, and he yanked his arm back, shaking his hand. "Tricky."

Frieda stepped closer. "We need to hurry. Show me what's wrong." She peered in, then flinched as some of the dangling wires sparked. "Can we remove the link to the battery?"

"Yes," said Almeida ruefully. "Unfortunately, by sticking my hand in there. I can handle this, Your Highness."

She glanced back at the panel. "If those wires touch you, you're fried."

"I know."

"You'll need something non-conductive to hold the wires aside."

"Again, I know, Your Highness," said Almeida with exaggerated patience. "I was about to look for something—"

She held up her prosthetic arm and flexed her fingers.

He looked at the hand. It took him a moment to put it together. "Your fingers . . . ?"

"Vulcanized rubber."

He nodded. "Let's get to work."

She and Almeida turned back to the engine. The others continued to work. The Earth reps who'd been standing by the wall stepped to a toolkit. Cara continued to tend to the unconscious Isolde.

Frieda focused on the panel. She reached with her prosthetic. The dangling wires sparked. She flinched at the lightning flash but pried the wire aside, pulling it from its connection. The arcing stopped. Almeida nodded.

A change in light told her someone had stepped up behind her. She glanced back to see one of the two Earth reps looking over Almeida's shoulder, curious. "Just a few minutes," she said. "Almeida, have you got space?"

"Yes, Your Highness." Almeida leaned in.

Suddenly, the Earth rep stumbled forward. Frieda grunted as he knocked her against the land speeder. Her prosthetic arm slammed into the engine block, and the wire arced like a Tesla coil. Almeida shouted and leaped back. Frieda yelled as her pressure suit started to smoulder. Her mind screamed at her to jerk her arm back, and it did. Her prosthetic elbow shot back and jabbed the Earth rep in the side. He staggered and fell.

She whirled around and saw him on the ground, clutching his side. "What the—you—" She gasped in disbelief as realization hit her. "You did that deliberately!"

Then she saw Almeida on his back, wheezing, clutching his ribs, and the rock that rolled out of the Earth rep's hand. On her radio, she heard pandemonium, people shouting and struggling. The other Earth rep, who'd been examining the wall so closely with his colleague, swung a crowbar in the middle of a melee of officers. Ramos and another *Hermes* representative were on the ground. The Earthwoman and her partner were staring in horrified confusion. Josef launched himself at them, only to be knocked away.

And suddenly, she saw the scene. If searchers found them, herself electrocuted, Cara's visor broken, the land speeder crashed, everybody else dead, the Earth reps could make it look like they were the only survivors of a tragic accident.

But they hadn't counted on the non-conductive prosthetic.

Almeida rolled up and shoved the struggling Earth rep back down. He tapped his radio. "*Messenger* officers! Protect your Crown Princess!" Her attacker sat up despite Almeida's best efforts to keep him down.

Frieda swallowed. *Earth strength in Mercury's gravity. We don't outnumber them as much as we think.*

Ramos went flying. Almeida grunted as his Earth assailant rose to his feet.

Suddenly, the wall fountained out in a silent cloud of dust. The impact shook the ground beneath their feet. The fighting stopped. Everyone turned and saw Isolde, standing in front of Cara, leaning against the land speeder, holding a gun.

"Don't try it," she snapped. "This will go through pressure suits, no problem. And I have plenty of shots left."

Almeida stared as he got a grip on the Earthman's arms. "What is she doing with a gun?"

"She's a security officer," Frieda replied.

Isolde nodded. "The piloting experience was a bonus." She swung her aim at the other Earth reps. "Raise your hands. Don't move."

The members of the Mercurian teams helped each other to their feet and glared at the Earth reps. The two who'd helped right the land speeder raised their hands; their voices gabbled through the radio. "I swear, this has nothing to do with us," said the man.

"What the hell, Largo!" the woman shouted at the rep in Almeida's custody.

Frieda raised her prosthetic hand. "Let's just get back to the *Messenger*. We'll sort things out there."

"Until then . . ." Isolde gestured at the Earth reps with her gun. "You're staying where I can see you."

☿

THE LAND SPEEDER REPAIRED, they raced back the way they'd come. Josef drove, and Frieda sat behind him. Cara sat behind her, along with Almeida, Ramos, and the other two *Hermes* representatives. Isolde sat facing the back seat, eyes on the Earth representatives, gun ready.

Cara nudged Frieda. Frieda looked over, then set her radio to private. "What?"

"Are you okay?" Cara asked.

Frieda looked ahead. "That's the second time somebody's tried to kill me."

Cara nodded. "Well . . . I suppose it's not something you'll get used to."

Frieda let out a short, sharp laugh. "I hope not."

She looked left. She saw more breaks in the Robinson Rail, flickering in the spotlights. Her stomach twisted. *We need to hurry!*

They topped a ridge, and Cara gasped. Josef stiffened. Frieda looked ahead. Her hand went to her mouth, even though her visor was in the way.

"No," Cara breathed. "Oh, no!" Others swore.

Ahead of them, the *Messenger* was stopped, its front section tipped forward into a massive sinkhole.

For a heart-stopping moment, Frieda thought her whole city was dead, but as they pulled closer, she could see lights on in the windows behind the front section. *Maybe it's not as bad as it looks.*

"Can we radio the *Messenger*, now?" she asked.

Josef tapped at the controls. "Land speeder to *Messenger*, are you receiving?"

No response.

He tried again. "Land speeder to *Messenger*, we have the Crown Princess. We're ready to dock."

More silence. He grimaced. "I don't understand. They should hear us at this range."

"It must be chaos in there," Cara muttered.

The drop of the sinkhole lay before them, blocking their way to the *Messenger*. They pulled to a stop, and Frieda opened the door and stepped out onto the surface. She stepped to the edge of the sinkhole and looked up at the towering bulk of the *Messenger*'s front section, tipped toward her.

Near the top, she saw the window into the forebridge and a figure in silhouette staring back at her.

# PART EIGHT
## ADELHEID: THE ABYSS

# CHAPTER 29
# FACING THE APOLLO

*The* Messenger
*Mercury Colonies, January 17, 2152 CE*

OVER THE NEXT FEW DAYS, THE REMAINING CITIES OF MERCURY rushed land speeders to the *Messenger*, bringing their supplies of construction bots. The *Messenger's* crew gathered them in storage rooms. The *Mókiwii*—the nearest latitude town to the north pole—evacuated the *Lares* polar static, and the *Messenger* crews brought supplies to feed the refugees.

The *Messenger* moved forward again—Adelheid surprised herself by how much she thought of it as reverse—to get to the Near Curve west of Terminal that put the *Messenger* and the *Hermes* within a few kilometres of the *Apollo's* Robinson Rail. Assuming they had the *Apollo's* location right, and assuming it was travelling at top speed, this gave them another day to do what they needed to do.

Liao came in and handed Adelheid a slip of paper. It was the latest count of the planet's construction bots in the *Messenger's* holds. The last city—the *Reeve-Pilkey*—had given all it could. *Let's hope it's enough.*

On the map, the lights of the remaining latitude towns flashed green as they passed the *Messenger*'s longitude. One by one, the pieces fell into place. She sat alone and silent on the forebridge, where people bustled on their duties. *Cristavao*...

Cristavao was with his crew. He was suddenly busy. They had always been busy, but suddenly, it seemed that they couldn't be busy together.

*What is his problem? What have I done wrong? I should talk to him, but*... She looked at the map, the approaching *Apollo*. *Now is maybe not the time.*

But she'd reached the point where all she could do was wait.

She straightened up. "Captain, how long before we're at the location?"

Liao glanced at his screen. "Two hours, Colonel."

She stood. "I'll be in my quarters. You have the comm."

In her quarters, Adelheid sat at her lab desk and did up another set of samples, placing each Petri dish in the portable forge. The minutes ticked away.

When there was only one Petri dish left, she leaned back with a groan. She glanced at her logbook, with its record of failure after failure, and flipped it closed. This last batch had done nothing but eat up time. Whatever comfort this work had once offered, this batch just left her numb.

She shoved herself away from her desk. *I'm done being disappointed.*

She went to her porthole and stared out at the horizon. In the distance, she saw the lights of the *Apollo*'s Robinson Rail draw closer as the *Messenger*'s Robinson Rail tracked nearer to Mercury's equator.

She glared at the last Petri dish. *I've been wasting my time for months. I've tried every possible fertilizer we could make. Some things work better than others, but nothing produces the growth we need to eat. Not unless we want to plant something to harvest ten years from now when we're all dead from starvation.*

*I told Cristavao about this because false hope is better than no hope at all. But it doesn't change the fact that the hope is false. I know it's false. There's no hope for me.*

*Is there?*

She stepped back to the desk and turned the last Petri dish over in her hand.

*What's the alternative to false hope, even if I know it's false?*

*Maybe pretend to hope one last time.*

*What should I use for this last sample?*

She sat and looked around her desk for inspiration. Her eyes fell on the antique key, her father's gift.

*Why not? I've tried everything else.*

She scraped off the old rust with a knife. The flakes floated down onto the Petri dish. Finally, she set it in the forge, closed the door, and turned on the timer.

Her intercom chirped. "Colonel." Liao's voice. "We've reached the planned location."

She pressed the button. "Thank you, Captain. I'll be right there."

She shrugged on her jacket, took a last look around her quarters, and left for the command centre.

☿

THE *MESSENGER* SAT at the end of the Near Curve, with the lights of Terminal on the horizon. Airlocks opened. Land speeders emerged, heading north and south. People in pressure suits cast out squat metal spheres on tank treads at regular intervals. The land speeders returned to the *Messenger* when their supplies ran out to be refilled and sent out again.

They worked for a whole Earth day. Near the end of it, more land speeders came, bearing people. At the *Apollo* Robinson

Rail, one stopped and opened its doors. Adelheid emerged, flanked by Cristavao and Liao and other members of the bridge crew.

Here, the lights of the *Hermes* Robinson Rail could be seen in the distance as it came out of its own Near Curve. Lights moved along it: the *Hermes*. Adelheid and Cristavao tracked the lights as the latitude town breezed across the landscape until the city passed, heading toward Terminal.

Adelheid touched the radio controls. "Captain Fang. Status?"

"The last latitude towns are past, Colonel," Liao replied.

"Good," she said. "Commander D'Cunha?"

"The *Hermes* stands ready," said Cristavao.

"Good," said Adelheid again. "Now."

Liao touched his helmet. "Control? Now."

They stood, waiting, staring. At first, there was nothing to see. Adelheid held her breath.

Then, the shadows along the ground started shifting. The people who were watching took steps back.

Slowly at first, then in a widening and lengthening line, the ground collapsed, making a sinkhole that spread out from *Apollo*'s Robinson Rail.

Adelheid peered over the edge. The light of her helmet caught a glimpse of the descending ground until it vanished from sight, leaving only a dark and gaping hole.

The sinkhole spread further, north and south, widening as it went, uncovering the concrete trench of the *Apollo*'s Robinson Rail. It sagged without the ground to support it.

On the dawn's horizon, new stars flickered to life and grew brighter.

Cristavao lowered his telescope. "It's the *Apollo*," he said through a private channel. "And dozens of land speeders."

Adelheid nodded slowly. "Staying close to the city?"

"Yes, Colonel," he replied. "They must be anticipating our attack."

"Their mistake."

One of the first land speeders came close enough for them to see the separate headlights. Then, suddenly, the lights swung upward, illuminating a surge of dust as the land speeder disappeared.

Other land speeder headlights started to vanish as the traps did their work. Other lights slowed to a stop. But the *Apollo* pressed forward.

"Captain Fang?" Adelheid's voice was calm as the lights of the *Apollo* drew even closer. "Now."

Liao stepped forward, wrapping wires around the contacts of a box with a large red button. He flipped a switch, looked up, nodded, and pressed it.

Red and orange flashes lit up across the *Apollo*'s Robinson Rail. The silent shock travelled through the ground and hit everyone's pressure suits with a bass thrum. Concrete shrapnel arched. The Robinson Rail crumbled, its pieces separating and smashing together as they descended from sight. Where the *Apollo*'s path had been was now a hundred metres of open space.

Through the radio, Adelheid heard a collective gasp. Even though everyone knew the plan, people stared in horror now that they'd done it.

Then the chatter rose as the *Apollo* approached, taking shape as more than just lights. They could see its bulk and then the portholes within that bulk. It came forward toward the new gap at speed. People gasped when they realized it wouldn't stop.

Adelheid stepped to the edge of the chasm and faced those lights down.

On her radio, she heard people around her yelling in fear.

"Stay calm," she said, and the chatter quieted, but only a bit.

The *Apollo* didn't slow. It kept its steady pace as it reached the lip of the wide trench and moved out into open space. The first section was ten metres out over the gap, then twenty, then almost halfway. It didn't even tilt.

Then, when the *Apollo* was eighty metres out, the ground beneath it on its side of the trench collapsed.

The front of the *Apollo*, all five storeys of it, with its windows into the front of the trackworks, the offices, and the viewing galleries, swung down in front of Adelheid, missing the edge of the trench, and her, by less than ten metres. If not for the vacuum, the rush of wind it would have produced would have knocked her back. Instead, she stood as the front of the *Apollo* hit the base of the trench so hard the ground shook. Flames erupted skyward.

Adelheid waited until the flames vanished in the vacuum. Then she stepped forward, gun at the ready.

*Hermes* and *Messenger* officers, holding guns, crowbars, and makeshift spears, stepped to the edge of the trench. It should have been too steep and too deep to climb up, but they weren't taking chances. However, nothing happened. Below, the nose of the *Apollo* sat like a crumpled tin can, windows and portholes smashed, their insides dark or flickering, exposed to the vacuum.

Adelheid looked up along the top of the *Apollo*'s front section until she spotted the windows of the forebridge, around fifty metres back. In the flickering lights of the bridge, she spotted a figure staring out. A flash of light illuminated a pressure suit and helmet.

Adelheid touched her radio. She spoke quietly for all the world to hear. "We have used all our remaining construction bots. The trench is fifty metres deep, a hundred metres wide, and nearly twenty kilometres long on either side of you. You could climb through it, but that would take time. You could drive around it, but that would also take time. By the time you get to the other side, all the latitude towns will be far ahead of you. We have taken all available supplies out of Terminal. You will not be able to catch us before your land speeders run out of fuel. You cannot repair your city or your rail before the Sun comes up, and you are too far away to run to the polar statics. Your choice is to either suffocate in the dark or burn in the light.

"We buried the bodies you desecrated," Adelheid went on. "We know what you did. But we expect that not everybody agreed with it. So, we will accept and give refuge to all children and to anyone who has not engaged in cannibalism. We can do tests. If you try to hide from us, we will find you, and like the rest of you who crossed the line, you will face the dawn. Those are our terms. What is your answer?"

There was silence on the other end of the line. On her right, Cristavao shifted his feet in the dust. On her left, Liao flexed his fingers. The radio remained silent. The dark face staring out from the window to the forebridge didn't move. The world held its breath.

There were no pleas, no shots, no arguments. Instead, the figure behind the forebridge window raised a hand and then brought it down.

Along the flanks of the *Apollo*, the airlocks opened, and the air burst out of them. Adelheid saw a body fly out of one, hit the ground, and lie limp.

They could hear no sound beyond their own exclamations picked up by their radios. The air continued to spew out of the airlocks, second after second, as the *Apollo* depressurized. Adelheid gaped. *They've exposed their entire city to the vacuum.*

On the other side of the trench, the crews of the remaining land speeders stared at the venting airlocks. Then, one by one, they got back into their land speeders, turned their vehicles toward the Sun, and drove off.

The radio filled with chatter.

"What in Sunlight?"

"What have they done?"

There wasn't a single word from the *Apollo*.

Finally, the air spewing out from the open airlocks ebbed. Adelheid looked back up into the forebridge window, but it was dark.

"Why . . . why did they do that?" Cristavao's voice was a drawn-out breath. "*Why would they do that?*"

Adelheid stared at the distant land speeders as they vanished toward the horizon. She heard herself say, "They decided they couldn't live with what they'd done. They decided *no one* on the *Apollo* could live with it. Ever."

"What have we done?" breathed Liao.

*What we needed to*, thought Adelheid, and closed her eyes.

☿

THEY RETURNED to their ships in silence, Cristavao walking away with the rest of the *Hermes* officers back to the *Hermes*. Adelheid watched him go. He didn't look back.

Once inside the *Messenger*, Adelheid removed her helmet and found Liao staring at her. She frowned. "Go to command and order the trackworkers to move us forward again," she said. "Let's put some distance between ourselves and the sunrise."

He nodded. "Yes, Colonel." He hurried off.

Adelheid went back to her quarters. *I'm not ready to face the command deck yet. I just need a little time to clear my head. Then, back to work.*

Back in her quarters, she stripped off her pressure suit and pulled on her uniform. She sat at her desk and rested her head in her hands. The memory of the airlocks opening and the air escaping from the *Apollo* played and replayed across her vision. She took a deep breath, held it until her chest ached, then let it out slowly. She stared at her ceiling.

*Do I believe in gods enough to pray for forgiveness?*

*Maybe it's not for me to decide, whether I believe or not.*

Another deep breath and slow release. She turned to her desk and opened her incubator.

She stared.

There was a fuzzy blue-green pile inside, about the size of her hand. It looked disturbingly alive, though it didn't move. It was so out of scale it took her a moment to realize what it was.

*Extremophiles! They've covered the dish! Which dish?*

She grabbed a set of tongs and picked it up, peering under it, looking for her writing.

*Father's key! Iron! Rust! How could I have missed this?*

She set the Petri dish on a ceramic tile, scooped a sample with a glass slide, pressed it together, and fed it into her microscope. Her breathing quickened as she saw everything she needed to see.

*It's perfect! That level of growth? If we nurtured it through a rotation—*

*We could have enough to feed the* Messenger! *Two rotations, and we could have enough to feed Mercury! The growth here is enough that we could—*

She froze. She looked up from her microscope into the middle distance.

*We could have fed everyone.*

In her mind's eye, she saw the figure in the *Apollo*'s forebridge staring out at her.

☿

LIAO WAS RETURNING from the command deck when he heard Adelheid scream. He ran, overrode the lock, and shoved his way into Adelheid's apartment. He found her prostrate on the floor, wailing. He grabbed her by the shoulders. "Adelheid? What's wrong? What is it?"

It was a long time before Adelheid could make him understand.

☿

FIFTY YEARS LATER, Adelheid rushed from the tram toward the forebridge, outpacing her attendants as they struggled to keep up. The doors parted ahead of her, and she ran in. "I'm here," she yelled. "What happened? What's stopped us?"

Frieda's father turned from the window, his face pale. "You're majesty. We're facing a sinkhole."

"What?" Adelheid shoved forward and staggered to a stop before the forebridge window. In the lights ahead, it was clear that there was a gap in the Robinson Rail. Around it, the circle of ground dipped into darkness.

Then she felt a rumble beneath her feet. It took her a second to realize it couldn't be the *Messenger*. They were parked. She looked out at the sinkhole and saw shadows growing.

"Reverse," she breathed, then shouted, "Reverse!"

Frieda's father shouted orders. Communications officers called down to the trackworks, but it was too late. The shuddering increased. The sinkhole opened out, and the *Messenger* pitched. People on the forebridge shouted. Adelheid grunted as she fell forward and smacked hard against a console. She clung on, desperate, as the floor tilted and rocked. Lights flickered, then went out. Finally, the ground stopped pitching, and a relative silence fell, broken by people groaning and calling out.

"Get the lights on," Adelheid shouted. She hauled herself to her feet, clutching her left shoulder. A pain jabbed down her arm. *Damn! Must have really whacked it!* "Get the lights back on!"

"Yes, Your Majesty!"

She strained to stare out the front window, but Mercury was

dark. A complete power failure. She thought she saw lights approaching. A land speeder, perhaps. She gripped her left forearm. *Damn, this really hurts!*

Somebody stepped close to her. "Your Majesty, are you okay?"

"I'm fine," she said through gritted teeth. "There are other people here; tend to them first." She raised her voice. "Where are we on those lights!"

The lights flickered on, blinding her momentarily. But she could look out the forebridge window as the headlights clicked on. She looked. "Lord in Sunlight," she gasped.

The *Messenger*'s Robinson Rail stood broken. The *Messenger* tipped forward; its nose bent into the sinkhole. She could see the lip on the other side and the land speeder near the edge.

Behind her, reports were coming in. "We're stuck!" "Dawn is just in a few days!" "We're not going to be able to repair this in time!"

Adelheid looked out the front window as a figure exited the land speeder, stepped to the edge, and stared up, arms limp in horror. Adelheid couldn't see the woman's face, but she recognized her. "Frieda," she breathed. They stared at each other across the gap, across fifty years, and Adelheid remembered staring back into another forebridge where someone stood waiting.

The pain in her arm intensified and spread into her chest. She let out a cry as she fell to her knees, her vision tunnelling.

People surrounded her, caught her as she fell back. She stared up at the ceiling as faces drew close. She tried to draw breath, but it was too painful. She tried harder. "Get . . . get the Stadtholder," she gasped.

"Your Majesty!" Frieda's father held her, his face pale. "Your Majesty, we've got you."

Adelheid struggled to take a deep breath. "Get . . . Frieda! Bring her here! *Bring the new Stadtholder here!*"

# PART NINE
## FRIEDA: THE STADTHOLDER IS DEAD

# CHAPTER 30
## STALLED

STARING UP AT THE TILTED BULK OF THE *MESSENGER*, FRIEDA tapped her radio. "Frieda Koning to the *Messenger*, please respond." Only static replied. "Frieda Koning to the *Messenger*, can anybody hear me?"

Cara nudged her. "Look!"

Lights appeared from the side of the *Messenger*. As they watched, the lights jounced across the landscape, skirting the edge of the sinkhole. Frieda straightened up as the land speeder approached, stopping a few metres away. Security officers in pressure suits piled out. Their voices shouted over her radio. "Your Highness! Can you hear us? You need to come with us now!"

Frieda tapped her radio. "Is everybody okay? What happened?"

One of the officers stepped forward. "Please, Your Highness. Come with us now. Your grandmother needs you."

Frieda looked from the security officers to the expedition crew.

"Go," shouted Isolde. She held up her gun, then nodded to Josef beside her. Almeida, Ramos, and the *Hermes* representatives were next to her, keeping a wary eye on the Earth delegates. "We've got things under control. You need to go."

"I'll come with you," said Cara. As the officer from the *Messenger* frowned, she added, "I'm medical. I need to be with the Crown Princess."

The officer nodded and beckoned them to follow. Cara and Frieda strode to the land speeder with the other security officers falling in behind, forming an honour guard.

They entered the *Messenger* through an airlock and came out into a corridor of chaos. The air was full of shouts and screams. People ran. People stood by the walls, looking confused or crying. The security officers closed ranks around Frieda and Cara.

Frieda pulled off her helmet. "What's happening?" She struggled to hear what people were shouting. She caught the news only in snatches. "It's just a few days until Dawn! We can't repair the damage in time!" "Who's in charge?" "Why isn't the forebridge responding?"

The other officers had pulled off their helmets. They had to shout to be heard. "Your Highness, please, we have to hurry!"

"Why is there so much chaos? We should talk to these people—" As Frieda watched, doors parted, and other security officers emerged, reaching out to people, shouting at them to return to their quarters. People weren't listening.

Then, someone familiar shoved through the crowd. Toshiko struggled forward and stopped in front of Frieda, looking pale and breathing heavily. "Frieda," she shouted. "I'm glad you're here. Come with us to the forebridge."

"Why is it like this?" Frieda shouted back.

"Communications are down," Toshiko yelled. "We're on emergency power. We need people in charge on the forebridge. Come on!"

The security officers formed a wedge to push past the knots of people blocking their way. Cara and Frieda followed Toshiko in the middle of that wedge as they rushed toward the fore-bridge. They didn't stop until they reached the front section, and Frieda saw the floor tilting down beyond the articulation joint. Her breath caught. For a moment, she could only stare.

The officers, Cara, and Toshiko looked at her.

Frieda swallowed and drew herself up. "Come on," she said, and they pushed forward again.

They half-ran and half-skidded down the corridors until they reached the forebridge. The door had been left half open, with guards and medical teams standing ready. It was quieter here, and as Frieda looked around, she saw people standing near the walls, staring down. Many were crying.

The security team fell back. Toshiko gently took Cara's arm and stepped to one side, leaving just Frieda. As she approached, one of the guards touched his ear and whispered into his radio. "She's here."

Frieda swallowed, but she didn't hesitate. She entered the forebridge.

It was crowded here but nearly silent. She had trouble picking out individual officers, and she couldn't see her grand-mother. She stepped farther into the room, and some in the crowd saw her and nudged others until all stepped aside. Frieda advanced, hardly aware that she was walking. The clarity of the light and silence made her feel light-headed. She blinked and realized she was crying before she even knew why.

The final row of people parted, and Frieda saw her father kneeling by the command chair, holding her grandmother's hand. Adelheid lay on her back.

"It's her heart," her father gabbled to no one in particular. "It's why she abdicated to Beatrix after the death of her husband. Gods."

Adelheid's eyes were closed, her skin pale. For a moment, Frieda thought she was staring at a corpse, but as she looked, Adelheid's chest rose, and she shifted. Frieda came forward and took her grandmother's other hand as the woman's eyes fluttered open.

"Frieda?" Adelheid breathed.

"Yes, Grandmother?"

Without thinking, Frieda had grabbed Adelheid's hand with both of hers. The woman squeezed Frieda's artificial knuckles gently. "Closer."

Frieda sniffed. She leaned closer. "Grandmother?" she whispered.

Adelheid struggled for breath. She whispered into Frieda's ear. "I'm sorry, Frieda. I tried to serve for you, but the *Messenger* needs you now."

Frieda's jaw ached from the strain of staying composed. "I understand, Grandmother."

"I didn't," Adelheid wheezed. "Until it was too late. You have to look them in the eyes, Granddaughter, and be what they need you to be. Show them who you are. I looked into the eyes of the people of the *Apollo*, and they knew I was going to let the Sun come up. They knew I was going to leave them to die."

Her voice faded. Frieda strained to hear.

"I see their eyes, even now," Adelheid breathed. "I hope to Sunlight you never have to make such a decision. No one ever should, but . . ."

Frieda said nothing. She kept her hand on Adelheid's wrist, feeling her grandmother's faltering pulse.

"You shouldn't have to do it, but I know you can," said Adelheid at last. "It's your turn now, Frieda. I'm sorry."

She let out her last breath.

Frieda stared as Adelheid's arm went limp in her grasp. Then she laid it gently across her grandmother's chest. Not knowing what to do, she stood up and looked at her father.

Her father stared at Frieda, then at Adelheid, then back at Frieda. Then he went down on one knee.

"Dad!" Frieda gasped. "Dad, what are you doing?"

"Your Majesty." Her father cast his eyes down. "We commit the Stadtholder's body to the Sun, to the stars, and to the dust of Mercury. May she watch over us through our rotation. The Stadtholder is dead. Long live the Stadtholder."

A security officer beside Frieda's father went down on one knee as well. "Long live the Stadtholder," she whispered. As did the man beside her and the woman beside him.

Frieda stared as a wave of everybody kneeling, eyes down, went through the forebridge, sweeping back through the door into the corridor beyond. All her problem now.

There was one island left in that sea. At the back of the room, Cara stood, her arms at her sides, staring. Frieda stared back, imploring.

Then Cara, her eyes not leaving Frieda's, put her hand to her heart and went down on one knee. She bowed her head.

Frieda looked around at the assembled, not one looking back at her. *Get up! Please get up!* she pleaded inside her head. *It can't be up to me! Everybody has more experience. Everybody has more knowledge.*

*But nobody knows who else can be in charge. They'll talk over each other. They'll stumble into each other. Somebody has to give them direction.*

*And it's me.*

*Lord in Sunlight, that somebody is me.*

# CHAPTER 31
## TAKING CHARGE

FRIEDA LOOKED DOWN AT HER GRANDMOTHER, FEELING EVERY EYE in the room on her, waiting on her. *Well, they can wait a moment longer.* She knelt by her grandmother again, reached out, and closed Adelheid's dead eyes. She closed her own eyes and made a silent prayer. Then she stood up.

She had tears on her cheeks. She sniffed, drew a long, shuddering breath, then let it go slowly. Finally, she faced the people in the room.

*My people.*

*Whether I like it or not.*

*I don't like it. But I love my people.*

She cleared her throat. "Everybody, get up." *Please!* "Who's in charge of security? I need the highest-ranking security officer here now."

People started to stand up. Some turned to their consoles. Others stared disconsolately ahead. A young captain stepped forward, looking terrified and bewildered. Frieda thought she recognized him from school, but if so, he'd graduated a few years ahead of her. "Um . . ." he said. "We're still figuring that out, Your High—Your Majesty. Communications are down throughout the *Messenger*. We lost people in the crash. We're trying to re-establish contact with the other departments."

"I need to talk to the person in charge here," said Frieda firmly. "Is that you?"

The colour drained from the captain's cheeks. "Uh . . ."

She looked him in the eye. "What's your name, Captain?"

"Lambert, Your Majesty," said the captain. "Royce Lambert."

*As Grandmother would say, don't be afraid to delegate.* "Well, Captain Lambert, you're now my second in command. How are we trying to restore communications?"

"Diagnosing the systems, mostly," he said. "Our personal radios only have about a hundred-metre radius, and it's chaos out there."

Frieda's father stepped forward. "Fr—" He caught himself and bowed. "Your Majesty. If we can't fix the systems quickly enough, we can set up personal relays. Officers stationed along the length of the *Messenger*, sending messages back and forth."

"That sounds good," said Frieda. "Take whoever you need and get on it."

Her father nodded. He tapped a couple of bridge crew officers and hurried off.

"We're also trying to reach the trackworkers to send teams out ahead to assess the damage to the Robinson Rail," Lambert continued. "We hope we can have a full report in an hour."

Frieda straightened up. She looked at the clock above the bridge, counting down to the dawn. *I've been out ahead. There's no way we can repair the Robinson Rail in time. That means—*

She turned back to Captain Lambert, then raised her voice to the forebridge. "Everybody, listen to me. The rail ahead of us is ruined for the next few kilometres, at least. We can't repair the damage quickly enough."

A groan went up among the forebridge crew. Frieda saw people putting their faces in their hands. She knew how they felt. *But I mustn't freeze. We need to do this now.*

"So, I'm ordering that we evacuate the *Messenger*." She looked at Lambert. "Prepare everyone. Tell everybody to gather supplies and get ready to head to the nearest latitude town." She looked up. "Toshiko! Work with Lambert!" Toshiko nodded and came forward as Lambert bowed. The two hurried off, tapping two other officers to follow.

"Your Majesty," said a new voice from the entrance door. Frieda looked up as Prime Minister Solberg entered the fore-bridge. Frieda let out a breath of relief seeing her, but Solberg was frowning. "We can't evacuate the *Messenger*, Your Majesty. It's an impossible task. We have no control over the town."

"Then we have to get it under control," said Frieda.

"The people are in a panic," said Solberg. "They're not going to accept an order to evacuate. We've tried everything to stop the riots short of firing shots."

"Thank you for not firing shots," said Frieda icily.

Solberg winced at that but nodded. "Nobody wants to get violent, but we don't have many options until we restore full communications. And we don't even know if the other latitude towns can take us. Evacuating the *Messenger* is too risky."

*I've seen the rail ahead; you haven't*, Frieda thought. *We can't not evacuate.*

Her father came back. He cleared his throat and lowered his voice. "Frieda—Your Highness—" He winced. "Your Majesty. Sorry."

Despite herself, Frieda gave him a soft smile.

He nodded. "The nearest latitude town right now is the *Hermes*. And after what just happened, they might not be willing to listen to us."

Behind her father, Frieda heard another officer mutter to his colleague, "The *Hermes* would be the best choice. We could both backtrack to Terminal. It would make the transfer of supplies and people *much* easier."

Frieda turned to Solberg. "What *did* happen with the

*Hermes*? I heard a garbled message about arresting peace-keepers on the *Baxter-Nordley*. Did we start a war?"

Solberg grimaced. "We're not sure; it happened very fast. Mayor Huang came back just before the peacekeeping force and did something. Apparently, shots were fired, and the peace-keeping force is in custody. Envoy Stevens boarded the *Hermes* with his entourage, and they left Terminal, moving on ahead. We moved out, too. We tried calling them, but then we ran into . . ." She waved her hand. "This."

Frieda winced. *Every second we waste makes the evacuation harder.* "We need to get through to them."

"They weren't responding even before we lost communications," said her father.

"Well, first things first, we need to get the *Messenger* back under control," said Frieda. "Communications are down, and people are rioting. It's happening because we're stuck, and they don't know who's in charge." *We have to show them that someone is in charge.* "Where's Grandmother's crown?"

☿

WHILE LAMBERT and a team went to find the wrought-iron crown, Frieda spent the next ten minutes working with Toshiko and the bridge crew, assessing what supplies they had and how best to move them. The time slipped past, and the crown did not arrive. However, now that the personal communications relay network was working, injury reports did. Tensions were rising. All the agoras were full.

At fifteen minutes, Frieda looked up at the clock. "We can't wait any longer." Willing legs that didn't want to move to move, she left the forebridge, keeping her pace measured. Officers fell into step beside her, but she raised her hand. "No. I go first. Do *not* surround me. I need the people to see me."

The corridor stretched ahead. Officers running along it

stopped to see her, then stepped to the side. Behind them, she heard the people roar. There were no words to it, just fear and confusion rushing toward a tipping point. Frieda kept walking.

Finally, she stepped out into the foremost agora, behind the line of security officers that stood against a plain of shouting, shoving people. Frieda tried to hear what they were shouting about, but all words were lost. *Maybe it doesn't matter at this point what they're saying.*

She had no crown on her head. *I hope this is enough. We're finished if it isn't.* She stepped to the line of officers. She cleared her throat, but they couldn't hear her. "Step aside, please," she yelled, but her voice was lost to the throng. "Hey!"

*How am I going to do this?*

Suddenly, she sensed someone running toward her. She turned in time to see an out-of-breath Captain Lambert rushing up with the wrought-iron crown. Frieda took it with the hand of her uninjured arm and braced it with her prosthetic. Concentrating, she made her artificial fingers wrap around the crown. She turned it over and back, then looked out at the yelling masses and the grim-faced officers staring back at them.

She swatted the nearest officer on the arm with the crown.

He swung around, then stared as Frieda placed the crown on her head. She smiled at him and mouthed, "Step aside, please."

The officer nudged the officer beside him. Soon, everyone on the line was looking at her. They hesitated, even though it was an order. It *was* an order, though, so they complied. A gap opened. Frieda stepped through, wearing the crown. She clasped her hands in front of her and faced the people.

Before her, the shouting and shoving reached a tumult.

Then somebody saw her. They pointed. Others saw her, and they pointed or nudged people beside them. Frieda kept silent, and the volume throughout the agora lowered. It was still too loud for anybody to hear her, so she waited. The volume kept lowering.

*How much of leadership is just staying calm?*

Finally, the volume dropped to near silence. People could hear themselves breathe.

*Now.*

"I know you are afraid." Frieda spoke softly, but it carried in that silence. People strained to listen, and that helped them hear. And, as she paused, Frieda heard people speak up and pass her words to the people behind them. Slowly but surely, her words got to the end of the agora. *Good.*

"I know you're afraid," she repeated. "I'm afraid, too. But we have faced five decades of the worst things fear could throw at us, and we never gave in. We fought back against fear, and we will do that again."

She swallowed. "Queen Adelheid has passed on ahead of us. The *Messenger* is grounded, and we don't have time to get it running before dawn. Therefore, I am ordering an evacuation. We will gather our supplies and will prepare to leave the *Messenger* and seek refuge with our neighbours. We will have to move fast and move with care. We will not stampede like animals. We will organize, prepare, and, above all else, we will survive. That's what we do."

She started to say, "Are you with me?" but halted. *A queen does not ask. A queen leads.*

The people in the audience were straightening their backs. Many were nodding. But an edge of uncertainty remained. *They just need one more push.*

Her voice rose. "Pass this on. Pass this on to anybody who isn't here. Pass this on to all who need to hear it: we *will* survive. We are Mercurians, and we don't give up!"

Now, it felt like the air was leaving the room. People were drawing breath, gathering strength.

"Gather your families," Frieda ordered. "Tell them to

prepare themselves and to listen to the evacuation officers. Report to your duty supervisors. Do the jobs that need to be done. Prepare to evacuate!"

People started to cheer, but Frieda raised her prosthetic hand, and silence fell. "No time. Just do it, please."

The crowd, no longer a mob, broke up, filing out of the agora individually and in small groups. The security officers on the line sagged in relief.

Frieda turned and walked back to the forebridge with her father, Prime Minister Solberg, Cara, Toshiko, and Captain Lambert among the forebridge crew falling in behind her.

"What happens next, Toshiko?" she said.

"We're going to need to direct traffic when the evacuation starts," Toshiko replied. "We'll need officers and officials at the airlocks to manage the crowds."

"I can arrange that, Your Majesty," said Captain Lambert.

"Very good," said Frieda. As Lambert hurried off, Frieda faced the forebridge crew. "How are we going to get the *Hermes* to stop and reverse back to Terminal? Are there any *Hermes* officials still on board?"

Prime Minister Solberg shrugged. "There's still the *Hermes* ambassador."

Frieda blinked at her. "Where is she?"

"In custody."

"*What?*" shouted Cara.

"Protective custody," said Solberg hurriedly at Frieda's expression.

Frieda grimaced. "Because of the mob?"

"Yes," Solberg replied. "But she wasn't happy about it."

"Great," Frieda muttered. "We need to talk to her."

☿

CARA FUMED as she and Frieda strode down the corridor to the cells. "You locked my mother in *prison?*"

"Not me—Grandmother," Frieda replied. "And it was for her protection. The mob could have used her as a scapegoat."

"And that's supposed to make me feel better?"

"I'm getting her out," said Frieda. "And I need your help to talk to her."

Cara glared at the floor ahead of her.

"Why would she still be here, though?" Frieda asked. "If all the *Hermes* representatives left after . . ."

Cara looked up, her eyes widening in horror. "It's because of me. She wanted to bring me home. Of all the stubborn—"

"This helps us, though," said Frieda. "If there's anybody who can talk the *Hermes* into reversing, it's her. Will you help me?"

Cara looked away. "I'll try my best. Knowing her, it might not be easy."

They swept into the cells. The security officers on duty snapped to attention as Frieda approached. "Take me to the ambassador, please."

Ambassador Flores stood up from her cot as Frieda entered her cell. She looked at Cara, then back at Frieda, her expression carefully neutral. "Your . . . Majesty," she said. "My condolences on the death of your grandmother."

Frieda nodded quickly. "Thank you." She took a deep breath. "Ambassador, we need your help."

Flores raised an eyebrow. She folded her arms, just like Cara. "So, we're not at war, then, Your Highness?"

Frieda drew back. "Not with me, Ambassador. And hopefully, not at all. We don't know all of what Mayor Huang did on the *Baxter-Nordley*, but rest assured, I oppose it. But there are more important things to deal with. The *Messenger* is grounded. The Robinson Rail is ruined for kilometres ahead of us. We need to evacuate. We need shelter for our refugees."

Flores blinked at Frieda. Then she stepped back and sat heavily on her cot. After a moment, she looked up at Frieda. "You're asking for a lot. We don't have the resources. And in the current political climate—"

"We'll bring resources," Frieda cut in. "And we can call on the other latitude towns to help, but we need you to bring us aboard. You're the one with access to Terminal. And the current political climate shouldn't matter, given that a lot of people will die if we don't act."

Flores opened her mouth to object, but Cara cut in. "Mamae, before you say 'no,' you need to know that Frieda saved my life out there. I trust her. And she's right: people are going to die if we don't act." She stepped forward and placed something on the table beside her mother's cot.

Flores's brow furrowed as she looked her daughter up and down. She took in Cara's pressure suit. Then she looked over at what Cara had set down. It was her cracked visor, with the patch Frieda had hastily put on. She stared at the patch for a long moment.

"Ambassador," said Frieda. "Will you help us contact the *Hermes*?"

Flores turned to Frieda. "All right, Your Majesty. I'll see what we can do."

# CHAPTER 32
# THE LONG MARCH

DOWN THE LENGTH OF THE *MESSENGER*, THE DOORS OF THE LAND speeder terminals opened, and vehicles eased forward, speeding up as they headed south. On the horizon, lights flashed as the first of an earlier set of vehicles returned. Frieda watched on the display in Command and Control. Cara and Toshiko sat close by while other officers worked at their stations. The lights were now on three-quarter power. The place buzzed with people pouring over inventories and checklists for the evacuation.

Toshiko stepped forward. "Your Majesty, we've established a communications relay to the *Shuixing*. Their prime minister is on the line."

Frieda nodded. The Shuixing was the closest latitude town to their south. "Thank you. Any word on when full communications will come back online?"

"They're still working on it."

"Flare." Frieda straightened up. "Well, put the prime minister of the *Shuixing* on." She sat in the command chair and pulled the communications panel toward her. The picture flickered, then displayed the image of a dark-haired young man. "Mr. Prime Minister," said Frieda.

"Your Majesty," he replied smoothly. "My condolences on the passing of your grandmother. She was—"

"I appreciate your thoughts," she said quickly. "But we don't have time for mourning right now. I trust our first teams have told you what happened?"

He nodded. "We stand ready to take refugees. We'll reach out to the *Takeuchi* as well for assistance." He sucked in his breath. "Understand, though, Your Majesty, that we're less than half your size. Our space is limited."

"I understand," said Frieda.

"How are you doing restoring your full communications?" asked the prime minister. "This is the first we've heard from you. We can tell the other towns what happened if that helps."

"It will," said Frieda. "And we're still working on restoring communications and getting in touch directly with the *Hermes*." She looked past the monitor and saw Ambassador Flores striding into the bridge. "I'm getting other help. If you'll excuse me, Prime Minister?"

The prime minister nodded and waved an official over as Frieda passed the monitor to a bridge officer of her own. She stood up to meet the ambassador, and her face fell as she saw the woman's expression. "Were you not able to get through to the *Hermes*?"

"I'm sorry, Your Majesty," Flores replied. "The *Hermes* is not responding. They've gone into complete blackout, likely because of the political situation."

"Where is the *Hermes* now?" Frieda asked the bridge.

An officer consulted a screen. "Our last records suggest they were about twenty or so kilometres ahead of us."

Ambassador Flores looked grim. "They'll soon be hitting the Far Curve. When they do that, they'll be heading back to our regular position at ten degrees north."

Frieda grimaced. "If we don't get them to turn back to Terminal soon, we won't have time to evacuate everything. We'll save the people but not the supplies to support them."

Cara, listening, winced. "How do we make them listen?"

"What if we actually went out there?" Toshiko asked. "Intercepted them?"

"A group of land speeders rushing to catch the *Hermes* could be seen as a raiding party," said Flores.

"What if we had them broadcast our peaceful intentions," said Frieda. "What if we had them bring letters of marque—"

"If they're feeling especially suspicious, they might think it's some kind of a trap," said Cara. She paused, then added, "Unless we sent *you*."

Frieda looked at Cara, not sure if she'd heard correctly. "*I* should go?"

"It would be quite a gesture," said Ambassador Flores. "They couldn't ignore it."

"But—" Frieda looked around Command and Control, at all the people working on the evacuation plans and on getting her city back on its feet enough to return to Terminal. "You expect me to leave the *Messenger*? Now?" *It feels like running. It feels like cowardice. The captain goes down with the ship, the Stadtholder Queen with her latitude town.* She turned to Flores, "What if you lead the team—"

"They might think she was a prisoner," said Cara. "They wouldn't think that if you were with her."

Her father, who'd been standing in the background, leaned in. "The ambassador is right. We're looking at a long march to the *Shuixing*, and they don't have the space to house all of us. We need to get the *Hermes*'s attention now. This is the best way to do it."

"We can keep the *Messenger* running, Frieda," said Toshiko earnestly. "We all know what to do."

"And I'll help you reach the *Hermes*," said Cara.

Frieda wrung her hands, but as she thought about it, she began to nod. *I've done everything I can here, delegated what needed to be delegated. Sure, I can stay and be a symbol for people to rally around, but they'll still have that if I go to the* Hermes, *and I can do even more good there.*

"All right." She shoved herself to her feet. "I want a small convoy of land speeders ready to move out to meet the *Hermes* in fifteen minutes."

☿

FRIEDA SWALLOWED hard and didn't look back as the land speeder jounced across the landscape of Mercury. Two other speeders followed as they headed north to where the *Hermes* hopefully still was. Isolde drove. A security team sat in the seats around Frieda. Cara and her mother sat in the back seat.

The inside of the land speeder was pressurized, so Frieda could hear, though she didn't mean to, Ambassador Flores talking to her daughter. "You're still sure you want to immigrate?"

Cara sighed, exasperated. "Yes, *Mamae.* I haven't changed my mind. I want to be a doctor, and the space for that is here."

"Well, I daresay, *Filha*, you won't have as much trouble immigrating as I'd thought."

Frieda could feel Flores's eyes on her back, but she didn't respond.

Finally, Flores sighed. "I'll miss you, is all."

"You know you can visit, right?"

"Hopefully," said Flores. "I'll do my best to make sure."

Frieda smiled.

Isolde's voice cut through the radio. "We're approaching the *Hermes*'s position."

"Get ready, everyone," said Frieda.

The land speeder whined as they topped a rise. For a

moment, the front window showed only stars; then, the ground swung into view. They saw the line and groove of the Robinson Rail stretching toward the peaks.

Frieda leaned forward. *Where is it?*

Isolde pointed. "There! They're topping the next rise!"

Frieda peered ahead, as did everybody else. Movement caught her eye. In the distance, lights played off the ground. She could barely see the red dots of the rear lights of the *Hermes* pulling away. "We've got to pick up speed!"

"Doing it!" Isolde shouted. Inertia pulled Frieda back into her seat.

"Contact the *Hermes*," Frieda called. "Let them know we need to come aboard."

The officer beside Isolde picked up a communications relay. "*Messenger* land speeder to the *Hermes*, please respond. We need assistance. Land speeder to the *Hermes*, please respond."

The land speeder whined and jounced. The back end of the *Hermes* gradually came nearer. The communications officer looked back. "No response, Your Highness."

"Let me try." Ambassador Flores grabbed the communicator. "*Hermes* command, this is Ambassador Alanza Flores. I have representatives from the *Messenger*, and we need to talk. Please respond!"

The radio returned static.

"Your Majesty," Isolde called. "I'm getting weapons-lock reports. They're taking aim at us!"

Flores slapped her communicator. "*Hermes*, this is Alanza Flores. We are on a diplomatic mission with the queen of the *Messenger*. We are not raiding you!"

"Stop the other land speeders," said Frieda.

Isolde looked back. "Your Highness?" Her voice squeaked. "That will make us easier to hit."

"We look like a raiding party to them," Frieda replied. "Order the other two land speeders to stop. We press on alone."

Isolde nodded to the communications officer, who relayed the order. The escorts fell back. The main land speeder pushed on in the dwindling light of their headlamps.

The communications officer flipped another switch. "Land speeder to the *Hermes*, we are not raiding you, repeat, we are *not* raiding you. We need assistance! Let us in!"

The back end of the *Hermes* drew closer, and then they were beside it. They slowly passed exterior panels and darkened portholes. Isolde leaned hard on the accelerator. "They're not shooting at us, but they're not stopping."

Frieda looked up at the ten-storey bulk of the *Hermes* rumbling beside them. *They don't have to stop. We're not a threat to them. How can we make them listen to us?*

Cara tapped Frieda on the shoulder. "Frieda, we're going to have to climb."

The others in the land speeder exploded with exclamations of disbelief. Frieda just stared. Cara pointed out the front window. Frieda followed the gesture and saw ahead, five storeys above them, approaching slowly, one of the airlock gaskets for Terminal protruding from the side of the *Hermes*. "They won't stop unless they see you," Cara added. "So, we've got to get up there."

Frieda swallowed. "You want me to climb aboard while it's still moving?"

Cara nodded. "You wanted to be an engineer. You know how our cities are built. You've climbed up the *Messenger* before, haven't you? The *Hermes* isn't very different."

*I have.* But her heart pounded. She held up her hands. "Not with these!"

"I'm coming with you," said Cara. "I'll get you up there."

Frieda swallowed. "Prepare to depressurize the cabin."

There was a pause, but Isolde faced forward. "Yes, Your Majesty." The other officers got to work.

They pulled closer to the moving mountain of the *Hermes*.

Everyone checked their visors and gave the all-clear. Finally, Frieda nodded, and Isolde punched the button. Alarms sounded, then faded as the air was sucked out of the cabin. Then the doors parted. The line between the edge and the ground wobbled as the land speeder jounced.

Frieda and Cara stepped toward the door. Frieda looked up at the ten-storey hulk.

Cara's voice came on Frieda's radio. "You need to grab in the direction the *Hermes* is going: left hand on the rung, then left foot on the rung, then right hand, right foot. That way, if you lose your balance, you fall toward the ship and its handholds."

Frieda concentrated. The fingers on her prosthetic flexed. She nodded at it. "Are you sure this will take my weight?"

"Probably," came Cara's reply in her ear.

"*What do you mean, probably?*"

"They'll work better than your original prosthetics, at any rate." Cara took Frieda's hand in her own. "Look, you trust me, right?"

"Yes," Frieda cried. The *Hermes* rumbled beside them, a permanent quake.

"Then walk with me." Cara grabbed Frieda's left wrist—her prosthetic one—and raised it up as a handrail approached. She pressed her body behind Frieda's. "Count of three, okay?"

Frieda nodded. "One," she rasped.

Cara patted her shoulder. "Two."

"Three!" Frieda pressed ahead, and Cara stepped forward. Frieda's hand closed on the rung. Her right foot found a foothold, and the *Hermes* mountain picked her up. Frieda swung forward and grabbed the rung with her human hand.

"Now, go!" Cara's voice crackled. "Up to the airlocks!"

Frieda slipped out of Cara's embrace and climbed while the land speeder peeled away.

The path up the *Hermes* meandered, shifting to where they could get a grip or find a foothold. They ascended one level, then two. Finally, when Frieda was level with the gasket locks, she looked at the gap and blanched. "That's awfully far!"

Cara scrambled up behind her. "Lean out. Keep a hold of your handhold and stretch out. I've got you."

Frieda gripped the handlebar. She could just reach the next foothold with her toe. She stretched . . .

She cried out as her fingers slipped from her grip, then jerked as Cara caught her wrist. Her residual arm twanged as her harness took her full weight, but Frieda didn't struggle. She flailed her hand until she grabbed a handhold that helped her steady herself. Then she looked up into Cara's eyes.

Cara nodded. Frieda nodded back. She looked ahead and stretched out her leg again. Keeping her grip firm around Frieda's wrist, Cara leaned out. Frieda scrabbled, got a foothold, and then thrust herself forward onto the small ledge in front of one of the airlock doors. She turned, reached back, and caught Cara as she leaped. They landed hard but steady.

They turned and pounded on a porthole beside the airlock door. Frieda saw a worker inside, staring at them in wide-eyed astonishment. Cara shouted, even though there was no way for the worker to hear her. Frieda caught her hand and held it for a moment until Cara calmed down. Then Frieda stared pointedly at the worker within. She raised her prosthetic hand. *You know who I am.*

A few minutes later, they were inside.

☿

Frieda and Cara removed their helmets as they stepped out of the airlock into one of the *Hermes'* Terminal agoras. They were met by security officers wearing sidearms.

Frieda tucked her helmet under one arm. "I need to speak to President Garza."

The captain of the security team looked Frieda up and

down. He blinked at her and took note that she was not armed. "Crown Princess—" he began.

"Queen," said Frieda. "The correct form of address is 'Your Majesty.'"

He coughed, looking bewildered and uncomfortable. "Your . . . Majesty. Where is Queen Adelheid?"

Frieda kept her gaze firm and neutral. "She's passed ahead of us. I speak for the *Messenger* now, and I need to speak to your president."

"As you wish . . . Your Majesty," said the captain slowly. "If you would accompany us?"

Frieda glanced at the guns, then up at the agora around them, where crowds of curious onlookers were gathering. She heard the buzz of shutters. She turned back. "I need to speak to President Garza now, out here."

The captain frowned. "You can wait in proper quarters, Your Majesty, and meet with the president in private—"

"This meeting is too important to wait or be conducted in secret," said Frieda evenly. "Or do you intend to arrest me—a visiting head of state who stands alone and unarmed—in front of your citizens?"

The captain's frown deepened, but he raised a hand, and one of his officers hurried off.

Then, all they could do was wait in awkward silence as crowds continued to gather around them, curious and confused. Fortunately, minutes later, a new crowd approached from one of the corridors: more guards, officials, and President Garza of the *Hermes*. Envoy Stevens walked behind him. Frieda stifled a flinch when she saw him. The two Earth representatives who hadn't attacked her kept swearing they had no idea why the other two had attacked her. *He looks surprised to see me. Is it just because I climbed my way in here? Or does he know what happened at the sinkholes because he ordered it?*

"Mr. President," said Frieda. Keeping her expression neutral, she nodded to the Earth envoy. "Envoy Stevens."

"Your . . . Majesty." Garza shook his head. "Why are you here? Given the diplomatic situation—"

"You say that like we're at war," Frieda snapped. "Are we?"

"Well, no, not technically," Garza stumbled.

Frieda raised an eyebrow. "Technically, eh?"

Garza rallied. "But, Your Majesty, given the arrest of our peacekeepers at the *Baxter-Nordley* and Mayor Huang's refusal—"

"I did not authorize that, I oppose that, and I will reverse that just as soon as I can," Frieda cut in. "But we can't let that delay us. I need your help *now*." She took a deep breath. "By now, you should be getting reports about what happened to us. The *Messenger* is grounded, and we can't repair things before sunrise. The *Shuixing* and the *Takeuchi* are taking refugees, but it won't be enough. We need to back up to Terminal and bring our supplies and our people over here."

Garza came forward. Stevens followed but frowned when Garza waved him back. Garza lowered his voice to Frieda. "You're asking for a lot. What will you do if we say 'no'?"

Frieda clenched her jaw. "A fair question, Mr. President. What will *you* do?"

Garza frowned. "Your Majesty?"

"What would desperate people do?" asked Frieda. "I don't know what my people would do if you said 'no,' but I can promise you that I will not order my people to try and take the *Hermes* by force. That's my gift to you. We both know that out in the vacuum, you have all the advantages. We're grounded. You could fend off any attack—in fact, you're ready for one. You could outpace us and leave us to die. But your people would have to live with that. It's the worst thing you can ever ask the strong to do. It's the worst burden you could make them carry."

"I don't believe this!" Cara's voice made both Frieda and

Garza jump. She strode forward and prodded Garza in the chest. "I can't believe I voted for you! People need saving now, and you're talking politics?" Her voice echoed through the agora. "This woman saved my life because it was the right thing to do. Saving thousands of people from the sunrise is the least we can do!"

Garza coughed. Frieda turned away self-consciously. She couldn't help but smile at Cara's outburst, but she wondered, *Could it do more harm than good?*

Just then, an officer ran up to President Garza. "Mr. President, we've sent officers to intercept the convoy that pursued us . . . it's just three land speeders, sir. We've looked back for a few kilometres as well. That's all they sent."

Garza stared at Frieda. To his officer, he said, "The land speeders you found: what are they doing?"

"Um . . ." The officer took some notes from his subordinate. He frowned at them, then shook his head, bewildered. "Nothing, sir. They're standing in plain view." He looked up. "That's all."

Frieda let out the breath she was holding. "They will not approach unless they're invited, Mr. President," she said softly. "But, please. We are running out of time."

Stevens stepped closer to whisper carefully to President Garza. He reddened a little to see Frieda staring hard at him, but he said, "Mr. President, we have some experience with this back on Earth, with McMurdo. This could be a trick—"

Garza rounded on him. "No, it's not. If this were a trick, they would not have sent their queen here, alone and unarmed."

Frieda cleared her throat. "Mr. President, if there is any lingering doubt about my intentions, if there is any possibility that we're even 'technically' at war, then here and now, on behalf of the *Messenger*, I surrender." And as the reporters' shutters clicked like crickets, she solemnly got down on one knee.

Garza blinked at her. Then he took her prosthetic hand and helped her to her feet. "No, you don't." He turned to his aides. "Gather the heads of all the departments. Contact the infirmary and gather people at the airlocks. Tell the trackworks to stop and prepare to reverse. Tell everyone to prepare to take aboard refugees." He turned back to Frieda and offered his hand. "Your Majesty. Please join me in our offices as we return to Terminal."

Frieda smiled. She shook his hand.

# CHAPTER 33
# THE RECKONING

THE MOOD OF THE PEOPLE OF THE *HERMES* SHIFTED IN THE HOURS ahead. Frieda saw it change by watching the news media in between helping to organize the *Hermes*'s refugee relief effort.

When President Garza ordered the *Hermes* to stop and open its doors to the first convoys from the *Messenger*, commentators fretted over how the population of the *Hermes* would double. How could they handle all the extra mouths to feed?

But the first convoy to arrive had Malika, and she had cameras on the first refugees as they arrived. She showed them delivering supplies—lots and lots of supplies. The *Shuixing* and the *Takeuchi* showed images of themselves taking in refugees from the *Messenger* as well. Finally, the *Messenger* repaired its communications array, and all of Mercury saw the grounded ship and the people working to repair it enough to return to Terminal. That's when the hand-wringing stopped.

The *Utarid* and the *Reeve-Pilkey* stepped up with offers to take in refugees as well. Every latitude town offered support.

Meanwhile, Frieda contacted Mayor Huang of the *Baxter-Nordley* in private. An hour later, the curfew lifted and the strikers went back to work, the multi-town peacekeeping force providing security.

Through all the work, with cameras on her, Frieda smiled, offering sympathy and help wherever she could. Wearing the wrought-iron crown, she greeted every refugee as they arrived on the *Hermes*.

Then, the *Messenger* freed itself from the sinkhole and began reversing to Terminal. The *Hermes* moved back to meet it, and the transfer of people and supplies began in earnest.

Finally, the last resident came aboard, along with the last crate of supplies. Frieda stood in the *Hermes* Command and Control, Malika's cameras on her, as the *Hermes* disengaged and pulled away from Terminal. She watched the spaceport and the *Messenger* shrink in the distance before they glowed brightly in the rising Sun.

It was only when her father came up behind her to report that she broke protocol and embraced him in front of everyone.

☿

THE HARD WORK continued for another couple of days before there was space enough to call a meeting of Frieda, President Garza, and the leaders of every latitude town and polar static on Mercury. Envoy Stevens arrived with one officer from his entourage and entered the meeting room. Frieda nodded at him as he looked around at the table where Frieda and President Garza sat and the video screens showing the other leaders of Mercury. Frieda caught a brief flicker of a frown before he smiled and bowed. "Good morning, Your Majesty and Mr. President. It's been a busy few days, to say the least. I regret we weren't able to have a face-to-face discussion earlier."

He took a deep breath and continued, "Your Majesty, I want to convey my government's sincerest condolences on the passing of your grandmother. It is a loss to the whole solar system, and it is a shame that she will not live to see the full restoration of interplanetary contact."

"Thank you, Mr. Stevens." Frieda gestured wither her prosthetic at the third place at the table. "Have a seat." Although off to one side, the chair still faced Frieda and Garza. The Earth envoy sat, his aide standing behind him. Frieda went on, "I regret it's taken this long to hold this summit. We've needed to clear the air for some time." Garza nodded, and Frieda added, "Speaking of which: Mayor Huang?"

The image of the mayor of the *Baxter-Nordley* expanded on the video screen. He blinked as the attention of everyone in the room focused on him. "Your . . . Majesty?"

Frieda clasped her hands in front of her. "I would like to thank the security officers of your town for working with the peacekeeping taskforce—after the initial . . . confusion, anyway. I've heard from *Baxter-Nordley* citizens, as well as people in President Garza's office, and the situation now appears to be peaceful. The water workers seem happy to be back to work under this supervision."

Still looking flustered, Mayor Huang nodded. "It has been peaceful, Your High—" He coughed. "Your Majesty. I hope that the current stability removes the need for the peacekeeping taskforce, and we can return full control of this town to this office."

Frieda tilted her head. "Well, 'stable' may not be the right word. The situation for now is more calm than stable. I've seen no indication that the calls for independence have gone away. And then there's the matter of the violence during the strike that brought the peacekeeping taskforce to the *Baxter-Nordley* in the first place."

Huang coughed. "Well, Your Majesty, that just illustrates the need for us to be back in control of the operation of our town, to find the perpetrators—"

"The peacekeeping taskforce has done its own investigation

into the violence around the strike, Mr. Huang," Frieda cut in. "We at the *Messenger* have audited it, and we've found no reason to dispute its findings. The task force found no evidence that the strikers had the weapons necessary to create that disturbance. We've started questioning the *Baxter-Nordley* security officers who were on the scene."

Mayor Huang fell silent. Frieda raised an eyebrow. "So," she said. "Given the exemplary performance of the task force in maintaining a just calm in the *Baxter-Nordley*, I have confidence in them to extend their tour of duty for the next two months— time enough to organize a proper referendum on the independence question and new elections for the municipal government."

Mayor Huang's lips tightened. Then he stood up and walked out of the frame. His screen flickered and went black.

Frieda glanced at President Garza. "Well," she said. "That's the first thing off our list."

Garza nodded.

Then Frieda turned to the Earth envoy. "Mr. Stevens, I owe you a debt of gratitude."

He raised an eyebrow but said nothing.

Frieda raised her prosthetic hand in a half-wave, half-salute. "By now, people have noticed how well this prosthetic operates. This is thanks to Earth's gift of 3D printing technology, which allowed my people to rebuild my prosthetic to be more flexible and light." She smiled brightly at Stevens. "It also saved my life when one of the representatives of your delegation shoved it into exposed wiring, hoping to electrocute me."

Stevens nodded and smiled, but it was brittle. "A most fortunate mistake on his part, Your Majesty. And, given that I'm here and not being questioned by your security, I assume you've come to accept that we had nothing to do with Lieutenant Ferrier and Sub-Lieutenant Manx's actions during your expedition. I apologize for it, nonetheless. We're horrified by what they did and are really glad you weren't harmed as a result."

Frieda rubbed where her prosthetic met her residual arm. She remembered how the electricity had vibrated under her non-conductive fingers. "Yes, Ferrier confirms he and Manx were operating on their own. We found nothing to contradict his statement."

Stevens leaned back in his seat. *He looks relieved,* Frieda thought.

He said, "We've been in communication with the Federation government. We've determined that Ferrier and Manx had ties to an independence movement in the old nation of France. They were working against all our interests, and, again, I deeply apologize for our lapse in our security."

Frieda looked down at her notes. "Noted."

Stevens went on. "If you want him deported, it will be our pleasure to take him into custody and get him out of your hands as soon as is convenient for you."

Frieda looked at Stevens with a raised eyebrow. "Noted. But we still have questions, Mr. Stevens. Ferrier hasn't been cooperative in explaining his reasons for attacking me, but I think he was trying to hide something. He was examining the wall of the sinkhole, just as Josef and I were doing. And then there's the question of the sinkholes themselves. How did they form? Why did they appear so near the *Messenger*?"

She tapped at her tablet, and the video display changed to a 3D display of the surface of Mercury. Lines appeared and stretched down, connecting blobs of space like an ant farm. "Now that the work on the evacuation has finished, Garza and I have had engineers investigate the sinkholes. They're part of a larger complex of tunnels stretching deep beneath the surface of Mercury and, except for the ones that are right at the surface, they're well-constructed. The sections can be made airtight. How did we miss this?"

Stevens nodded slowly.

Frieda focused on him. "Mr. Stevens, I appreciated the kind words you said about my grandmother, though I think many would be forgiven for believing that they were . . . a polite exaggeration. The Earth still has two billion people, and we number barely a million. The Earth is unlikely to pay much attention to one Mercurian woman who ran a few latitude towns, even if she did save them from starvation." She tilted her head. "But the Earth does know her name, doesn't it? Or, at least, her father's name: my great-grandfather, Colonel Abraham Koning?"

Envoy Stevens frowned, but he stayed silent.

Frieda reached down beside her and, using both hands, picked up a metal and glass canister and hefted it onto the conference table. Inside the container, silver mist shimmered.

Stevens stiffened.

"They're inert," said Frieda. "The container blocks electromagnetic radiation and other signals, so they'll stay inert. These were collected in the caverns that ruined the *Messenger*'s Robinson Rail."

"Ah." Stevens nodded, but he didn't relax.

President Garza leaned forward, peering at the silver mist. "So, these are nanobots?"

"Microscopic robots capable of transforming molecules into, well, anything." Frieda kept her eyes on Stevens. "Even copies of themselves. The *Hermes* file clerks found Cristavao D'Cunha's papers in their archives. Fifty years ago, my great-grandfather broke the Earth's embargo and smuggled three crates of nanobots to Mercury. But we couldn't unload them before the shuttle exploded when the Earth went silent." She gestured to the container. "This is the real reason the Earth rushed here as soon as it was able to, isn't it, Mr. Stevens?"

Stevens stared at the canister of nanobots, looking almost hungry. Finally, he leaned back. "Yes, Your Majesty. You have here before you some of the last pieces of nanotechnology in the known solar system."

Frieda stared at him. He nodded and added, "You know what happened to us at the start of our silence: there was nuclear war. None of the nanobots we had survived the electromagnetic pulses, and the technology to make these machines vanished in the chaotic decades that followed. These machines, more than your edible extremophiles, could help us regain the old technology and finally free us from the hole we've spent the last fifty years clawing our way out of."

"Why did we have to find out the way we did?" asked Garza. "Why didn't you just ask for your technology back?"

Stevens shrugged. "You might have said 'no.'"

Garza let out a short, sharp laugh. "You could have taken it from us easily."

"No, they couldn't," Frieda cut in. She looked at Stevens, who sat stone-faced. "I saw the report about how the Federation of Earth Nations handled the McMurdo Republic—the last independent nation on Earth. I know enough to read between the lines. The Earth does not handle 'no' very well—when nobody is watching. But that's not the case now."

She leaned back. "The Earth announced to the solar system that it had made contact with Mercury and was re-establishing diplomatic relations. Venus and Mars heard you. To turn around and crush us days later—what message would that send? Mercury is no threat to the Earth. We are tens of millions of kilometres away with no spaceships and no useful weapons and the Earth outnumbers us two thousand to one. Crush us, and the Earth tells Venus and Mars everything they need to know about the Federation of Earth Nations. They'll treat you like the plague."

Her glare softened. "And possibly you won't do it because you don't want Earth to be that planet. We are all afraid that what we do in the dark defines us, Mr. Stevens. My grandmother taught me that. But in that fear, there's hope for us yet."

Stevens ran his teeth across his upper lip. Finally, he said, "So, what happens next?"

"You can have your nanobots back," said Frieda.

Garza frowned at her.

"They may be inert now, but they're still a hazard," she added.

Stevens nodded, satisfied.

"But that's our act of goodwill," said Frieda. "*Your* act of goodwill is to help us remove the remaining nanobots from this planet, help map the caverns they've built, and bring us soil."

Stevens raised his eyebrows. "Soil?"

Frieda nodded. "Soil, and lots of oxygen and nitrogen— Earth air, basically. Please make sure it's clean. We haven't been able to map all of the caverns, but there are plenty that are deep enough and stable enough to hold an atmosphere. With artificial light, soil and air, there are hectares we could farm."

Stevens nodded slowly. "And Mercury can be self-sufficient."

"We've been self-sufficient for fifty years," said Frieda. "But with this, we won't just survive, we'll thrive. These are the terms, Mr. Stevens. Will the Earth accept them?"

Stevens looked at her. He folded his hands in his lap. "I think I can persuade them, Your Majesty."

"Then this is the deal you will take to Grandmother Earth," said Frieda.

Stevens chuckled. "Don't you mean Mother Earth?"

Frieda shook her head. "I am a daughter of Mercury."

☿

THE MEETING BROKE up soon after, with the leaders of the other latitude towns signing off their video links. Envoy Stevens nodded at Frieda before he left. Finally, Garza gathered his tablets and stood up. "Well, I think that went well."

Frieda nodded. "We pulled together as Mercurians."

"It's not the first time we've done that," said Garza.

Frieda smiled softly. "No. And it won't be the last."

Garza nodded and turned away.

"Mr. President," said Frieda. He turned back. "I've checked. My grandmother didn't authorize any action against the strikers on the *Baxter-Nordley*." She shook her head. "Mayor Huang acted alone. If Grandmother had heard about it, there would have been hell to pay."

Garza smiled sympathetically. "I find that, however much you're thought to be in charge, you're not in control as much as people think. People can and do act without your knowledge. I suppose it's better than the alternative."

"Maybe," said Frieda. "Grandmother did not like the idea of letting the *Baxter-Nordley* go. I fear Mayor Huang acted thinking he was doing what she wanted."

Garza chuckled. "Well, the ironic thing is, now that you're allowing that referendum on independence, the townspeople may decide not to do it."

She looked up at him. "What do you mean?"

Garza tilted his head. "Have you been following the media, Your Majesty?"

Frieda winced. "Only as much as I have to."

"I noticed that the strikers—or, rather, former strikers—at the *Baxter-Nordley* held a rally after the end of their shift. They were chanting your name and best wishes for your health."

*Long live Queen Frieda*, she thought. *Well, thanks.*

"You've become a popular figure throughout Mercury," said Garza. "And, of course, you're seen by your own people as their saviour. And honestly? Not without reason."

Frieda nodded. "I've been thinking about putting my own position up for a referendum. I told Grandmother I wanted to abdicate, but I see now that something like that requires the people's permission. If I put the question of replacing me with an elected president to a people's referendum, I'll lose, won't I? They'll reject my proposal."

President Garza nodded, though he looked apologetic. "Sometimes, the people choose their leaders whether the leaders want to lead or not."

Frieda sighed.

Garza paused at the door. "However . . . it's still up to the leader how they want to lead."

He left, then. Frieda looked ahead thoughtfully.

☿

As FRIEDA LEFT the conference room, she spotted Toshiko, Josef, and Cara waiting in the corridor outside. They approached. "How did it go?" Cara asked.

Frieda shrugged. "I think we're going to get some good help from Earth. They may need watching, however. How are things on the medical front?"

"No accidents or injuries since we transferred everybody to here, the *Shuixing*, and the *Takeuchi*," Cara replied. "Most of our most serious cases have recovered. The medical teams are moving to stand by."

Frieda tilted her head. "How does it feel to be working as a medical officer in your hometown?"

Cara smiled, not quite certain. "Strange. I didn't think it was going to be possible, so it's a bit like a dream come true. At the same time, I'd planned to do this on the *Messenger*, so . . ."

"Daskivic tells me that, if you wanted to, you could ask to be promoted to a junior doctor," said Frieda. "Your surgery on my arm was a masterwork, he said."

"Maybe," said Cara. "I think I need more in-field practice

first. We'll see. There are a bunch of things where we'll just have to see." She glanced quickly at Josef.

"So, what happens next?" asked Josef.

"Well," said Frieda, "everybody will be in close quarters with each other for the next rotation. We'll figure out ways to keep from getting under each other's skin. The *Hermes* is moving at twice Mercury's rotation, and we'll meet Terminal as it emerges from daylight. Then we'll have the whole night, and the *Hermes*'s help, to repair our Robinson Rail, shore up our rights of way, and see Envoy Stevens on his way. We'll probably take aboard more Earth shuttles as they help us remove the nanobots."

Josef chuckled, "I mean, what about now? I don't think we have anything else on our schedules this evening."

"Oh," said Frieda. She glanced at Toshiko, who nodded. *It's been such a busy time. I haven't had a chance to think about what happens once we get a moment to breathe.*

Then she looked closer at Josef and Cara. They were standing together, and as she watched, their hands brushed. She smiled at the two of them. "Things going well?"

Cara blinked, then looked at her hand brushing Josef's, looked up at Josef, and blushed. Josef looked confused, then, seeing Cara's blush, blushed as well.

Frieda stepped back. "If there is nothing left on our schedule for today, I think you three deserve the rest of the day off." She raised her hand before Toshiko could object. "I'll head back to my quarters. I may meet Anna on the way there. I can manage by myself for the rest of the evening. Me, and the other help I still have assigned to me."

They smiled and parted. Frieda walked—by herself for once—to the *Hermes*'s trams. People passed her without noticing, and Frieda relished this strange feeling of anonymity.

Still, at the tram stop, she waited until the crowds had boarded and requested a private car from a monitor. One arrived, and she got on board. When the doors shut, she released the breath she hadn't realized she was holding.

The people and the places of the *Hermes* streamed past, reminding her of the *Messenger* and the views through the windows of its trams. Stars willing, they'd be back soon. And then . . .

*The* Messenger. *It was all my responsibility. I didn't ask for it, but it fell to me, and somehow, we survived.*

Frieda closed her eyes and began to cry. She planted her face in her hands, breathed deep, and let the tears flow.

She didn't realize the tram was slowing down until it came to a stop. She looked for the express button, but it was too far away to push. She hurriedly wiped her cheeks on her sleeve and cleared her nose with a sniff. She straightened to attention as the tram stopped, and the doors slid back.

Anna stood on the other side. Frieda blinked to see her.

Anna bowed quickly. "I was just heading back to the guest apartments, Your Majesty. If I may?"

Frieda nodded and stepped to one side. Anna stepped in. The two faced forward as the tram accelerated. Frieda swallowed against her tears and sniffed once more.

Suddenly, Anna turned and put her arms around Frieda, holding her so tight she grunted. Frieda blinked as she stared, then slowly patted the arms around her. It felt . . . good.

The tram began to slow again. Anna let go and stepped back. She flashed Frieda a nervous smile. Frieda sniffed but also smiled. "Thank you, Anna," she said.

Anna nodded. "You're welcome, Frieda."

The doors opened, and Anna straightened up. "Is there anything else you need, Your Majesty?"

Frieda gave her a regal nod. "No, thank you. That will be all. I think I actually want to spend some time to myself, watching the people of this town. I'll be back in presently."

Anna bowed and hurried on her way.

# EPILOGUES: LONG LIVE THE STATDHOLDER

# EPILOGUE 1

*The* Messenger
*Mercury Colonies, January-June 2152 CE*

THE *MESSENGER*, THE *HERMES*, AND THE OTHER LATITUDE TOWNS rolled across the surface of Mercury, keeping ahead of the Dawn Line.

As they did so, crews got out of the front airlock of each town, dozens of them, each man and woman carrying a hammer. Another group followed, pulling carts laden with long, rusty iron rods. They spread out, ten paces between them, and started walking, the carts leading the way. Every ten steps, the men and women with the hammers picked up an iron rod and pounded it into the ground. The latitude towns rolled slowly past them. When they were done, they waited for the rear airlock, which opened as it approached. At the front of the towns, a new shift took over, moving onto the surface. Slowly, the iron corn rows stretched across Mercury and entered the daylight.

Through these days, Adelheid kept busy. She didn't talk to

Cristavao, and Cristavao didn't talk to her. They had their own cities to look after.

Then, one rotation around Mercury, they drew level with the *Apollo* again, and the *Hermes* and the *Messenger* crews moved out to it, working together to salvage it. Nobody wanted to stay long in the dead city, so the salvage was moved over to Terminal to be sorted and distributed.

When Adelheid went to supervise the crews, she saw Cristavao standing on a balcony overlooking the loading bay. She stared at him, but he didn't see her. So, she squared her shoulders, left the loading bay, and made her way up to the balcony.

She came out and leaned on the railing beside him. He glanced over at her, then resumed his stare across the loading dock. They stood in silence for a long moment.

Finally, Adelheid said, "We haven't talked."

Cristavao took a deep breath. "No, we haven't."

Another long moment of silence, and then Adelheid said, "You think I went too far."

Cristavao thought a moment, then shook his head. "No. You did everything that had to be done. You did everything I would have had to do if you hadn't been around. And I would have done it, or else we would not have survived." He swallowed. "And I hate that."

Adelheid looked at him. "Then can't we move on?"

Cristavao looked away.

Adelheid looked down. "We finally have enough food, and hope for food, that we can increase our rations to nearly a full diet. Another rotation, and we'll be back to a healthy day's requirement and able to store food for the long term."

"And I suppose the reduced population helps reduce our caloric needs," Cristavao muttered. "That's the dusk on the dawn line."

Adelheid clenched her jaw. She took a deep breath. "What

would you have done? What could we have done? Please tell me?"

He shook his head. "I already told you, I don't know."

She looked away. "I really wish you did." Then she frowned at him. "So, what's your problem now? The raids have stopped. We're distributing food. Have the supplies been divided unfairly?"

"No," he said quietly.

"Then what?" she snapped.

He looked up. His expression was grim and dark. Adelheid took a step back.

"I hear you're taking over the other latitude towns—"

"The *Baxter-Nordley* was completely wiped out by the *Apollo*," Adelheid cut in. "If we want them to continue supplying the planet with water, we need to recolonize it and rebuild. The same goes for the *Brook Johnson* and the *Rücker Eddison*—"

"And the *Leigh Brackett*?" Cristavao asked.

"They asked us in," said Adelheid. "They lost a lot of people, including their leadership. They need help with maintenance and growing the extremophiles."

"You're taking them over as colonies of the *Messenger*!"

"You're doing the same thing with the *Anson-Bova* and the *Nourse-Vonnegut*," Adelheid shot back.

"Only until things stabilize!"

"Same here!"

"Really?" He gave her a look that was halfway between wariness and fear. "You're not reforming your civilian council."

Adelheid spluttered. "We will when they're ready. The civilian advisers agree we aren't ready yet—"

"But what about this . . ." He waved his hand. ". . . this title you've given yourself. 'Stadtholder'? That doesn't sound like a temporary position. It sounds like a monarchy."

"On the contrary," Adelheid replied. "The term comes from

my Dutch heritage. It literally means placeholder, a steward. I'm not a monarch or some head of state; I'm just holding the position until others are ready to take it on. It's better than being a colonel, anyway."

His frown deepened. "For how long?"

"As long as necessary."

"How's a stadtholder better than being a colonel?"

She glared at him. "My people deserve better than to be ruled by a military government."

He tilted his head. "*Your* people?"

Silence stretched. They stared at each other.

Cristavao looked away first. "Well," he said. "I shall leave you to your affairs of state, then." He turned and left.

Adelheid watched him go, swallowing against the rising ache in her heart. He did not look back.

Finally, Adelheid left Terminal and returned to the *Messenger*, walking through the corridors. She saw the people passing: fellow officers, who nodded at her, workers at the new extremophile farms. Everyone looked tired, but they looked . . . happy. Hopeful. Determined. *That's something we didn't have not so long ago. I should relish this.*

Adelheid faced forward and kept walking. Her chest still ached.

Finally, she entered the crew quarters, stood outside a door, and rang the door chime. Liao opened it. He was in off-duty clothes. He stared at her.

"I wanted to talk to you," she said.

He smiled as he waved her inside. "I've always been here for that."

She smiled, then sighed.

He frowned at her. "What's wrong?"

"Nothing," she said quickly. Too quickly. "I know what we need to do. I know there's a future ahead of us at last, and I know how to get to it. It's just . . ."

*It's too much. There's too much to manage. Too many opportunities to fail. Not enough...*

Liao reached out and touched her shoulder. He looked into her eyes. "What do you need, Adelheid?"

Adelheid took a deep breath, then let it go. "I need a friend, Liao. More than that, I need a partner. What do you say?"

For a long moment, neither said anything. Then he reached out and took her hands in his. "I can be both."

She smiled sadly, then came forward and hugged him.

# EPILOGUE 2

*January 1, 2153 CE*

THE BLACKSMITH'S GUILD HAD BEEN SET UP AND OPERATING FOR a few months, but Adelheid called for a ceremony on New Year's Day to mark the occasion.

And at the ceremony, when the guild leaders and the Civilian Advisory Council met with her, Adelheid handed over the Blacksmith Guild's charter and said to them, "Make me a crown."

Later that day, she watched as the top blacksmith twisted glowing iron, bending it around a guide to make a graceful curve. Using tongs, he held the iron in the torch flame again before bringing it out and hammering it, each clang spraying sparks.

Adelheid watched him work, her hands clasped behind her, an orange sash over her blue uniform.

Finally, the blacksmith took the glowing lacework and dipped it into water, which gushed with steam.

Bringing it out, wet and still steaming, he placed it on a towel to cool.

Finally, Adelheid picked up the wrought-iron crown. She turned it over in her hands, inspecting every detail. The dark bar curved and wound around itself in a tiara shape, beautiful without jewels and strong.

She nodded and gripped it tight. "Thank you. Let's go."

She placed the crown on her head and turned to face her future.

# EPILOGUE 3

*The* Hermes
*Mercury Colonies, August 14, 2201 CE*

NEARLY NINETY DAYS AFTER THE EVACUATION OF THE *MESSENGER*, with the *Hermes* travelling at twice the planet's rotation, they finally approached the Dusk Line. Terminal was just a few hours away. With that would come farewells to the people of the *Hermes* and to Envoy Stevens and his team, and a lot of work. But first...

Frieda stepped into the meeting room, full of department heads and community leaders from the *Messenger*, not to mention reporters with cameras. She crossed to the podium as everyone in their chairs stood to attention. She kept her face composed.

*I'm still not used to all this pomp and protocol. I really hope I never get to be.* She took the podium and faced the crowd. "Thank you. Please be seated."

She looked out at the rows and rows of faces, everyone looking expectantly at her, wanting something. *What? Hope? We've had that, thank the gods. No, something more.*

She stood silent a moment. Then it came to her, and she smiled. She gripped the podium. "We're going home." She stepped back.

The room erupted in cheers.

She didn't go with them right away. As she stepped out of the meeting room, Toshiko came over, carrying an urn.

"You have her, then?" Frieda asked.

Toshiko nodded.

"Good. Let's go."

Toshiko fell into step beside her. "It seems odd doing this by ourselves."

"We've had the funeral," Frieda replied. "This . . . she told me through her will that this is what she wanted done with her ashes. One last moment to herself."

Toshiko nodded. They reached the doors to the land speeder docks. Toshiko set down the urn and helped Frieda put on her pressure suit. Soon, they sped along the dust of Mercury, perpendicular to the *Hermes*'s Robinson Rail, toward the *Messenger*'s latitude. An hour passed before Toshiko brought the land speeder to a stop. "We're here," she said through the radio. "And..." She twisted the roof lights until they illuminated the cairn. "There it is."

Frieda clasped the urn on her lap, prosthetic and uninjured fingers interlaced. "Depressurize the cabin, and let's go."

The land speeder door opened, and Frieda and Toshiko stepped onto the dusty surface. They walked toward the cairn. Toshiko stopped and stood in respectful silence as Frieda approached. Around them, casting stark shadows in the lights of the land speeder, stood other cairns. She paused at the one that held her mother's body and bowed her head a moment in prayer.

Finally, she moved to the next cairn and gently placed the urn inside it. "We commit our Stadtholder's body to the Sun," she whispered. "To the stars and to the dust of Mercury. May she watch over us through our rotations."

Then she opened the pouch she was wearing over one shoulder and brought out the wrought-iron crown. She turned it in her hands a moment in the beam of the land speeder's headlights, watching the lights and shadows that played through it. Finally, she laid it atop Adelheid's cairn and stepped back.

"Goodbye, Grandmother," she said. Then she nodded at the space beside her. "And Grandfather."

She brushed dust away from the plaque that was obscuring the name: *Liao Fang*.

She stepped out of the lights of the land speeder and looked at the cairn and the sweep of the Milky Way rising above it.

Toshiko's voice came through the radio. "Frieda? I just heard: Terminal and the *Messenger* have cleared the Dusk Line. The repair crews are ready."

Frieda took a deep breath and let it out slowly. "Thank you, Toshiko. Let's go."

THE END

# LIST OF LATITUDE TOWNS ON MERCURY

## FROM SOUTH TO NORTH

1. *Baxter-Nordley* (polar static; killed by *Apollo*, recolonized by *Messenger*). Named for authors Stephen Baxter and Gerald D. Nordley, both of whom have stories set in the Chao Meng-Fu crater near the Mercury's South Pole. (*Cilia-of-Gold* by Baxter, *Crossing Chao Meng-Fu* by Nordley).
2. *BepiColumbo.* Joint mission by the European Space Agency and the Japan Aerospace Exploration Agency to Mercury, launched October 20, 2018, expected to arrive on December 5, 2025.
3. *Brook Johnson* (killed by *Apollo*, recolonized by *Messenger*). Named for author Jessica Brook Johnson, who wrote the short story "Blind Mystic," set on Mercury, published in *Vanishing Point Magazine*, Issue 2, Winter 2022.
4. *Rücker Eddison* (killed by *Apollo*, recolonized by *Messenger*. Named for author Eric Rücker Eddison, whose novel *The Worm Ouroboros* (1922) is set on Mercury.

5. *Leigh Brackett* (cull, attacked by *Apollo*). Named for the science fiction author (1915-1978) called "the Queen of Space Opera." First woman shortlisted for the Hugo Award. Some of her stories, including "Queen of the Martian Catacombs" (1949) feature Mercury.

6. *Utarid.* Malaysian word for the planet Mercury.

7. *Takeuchi.* Named for Naoko Takeuchi, the author of the Sailor Moon series, whose characters include Sailor Mercury.

8. *Shuixing.* Chinese word for the planet Mercury.

9. *Messenger.* Taken from Mercury, the Roman God, who took messages to other gods. Mercury had wings on his shoes to make him go faster. Also the name of a NASA robotic space probe that orbited Mercury between 2011 and 2015. The name is an acronym of MErcury Surface Space ENvironment, GEochemistry and Ranging.

10. *Apollo* (dead). A Greek and Roman sun god. Half-brother to Mercury.

11. *Hermes.* A Greek god who was an emissary and messenger. His Roman equivalent was Mercury.

12. *Reeve-Pilkey.* Named for authors Phillip Reeve, whose Larklight trilogy includes a stop on Mercury, and Dav Pilkey, whose Mighty Robot series includes *Mighty Robot vs. The Mutant Mosquitoes from Mercury.*

13. *Anson-Bova* (killed by *Apollo*, recolonized by *Hermes).* Named for author Mark Anson, whose titles include the novel *Below Mercury*, and author Ben Bova, whose Grand Tour novel series includes *Mercury*, published in 2005.

14. *Nourse-Vonnegut* (ended itself, recolonized by *Hermes).* Named for authors Alan E. Nourse

(*Brightside Crossing*) and Kurt Vonnegut (*The Sirens of Titan*).

15. *Viritrilbia*. The name for planet Mercury in C.S. Lewis's Out of the Silent Planet trilogy.

16. *Mókiwii*. The Navajo word for Mercury.

17. *Clement-Clarke* (**killed by** *Apollo*, **recolonized by** *Hermes*). Named for authors Hal Clement, whose 1953 novel *Iceworld* features aliens that set up a base on the day side of Mercury, and Arthur C. Clarke, whose 1973 novel *Rendezvous with Rama* features the descendants of human colonists on Mercury.

18. *Susan Forest*. Named for the author of "For a Rich Man to Enter," published in *InterGalactic Medicine Show*, Issue 62, April 2018.

19. *Lares* (**polar static**). Guardian deities of Ancient Rome who, in a story written by Ovid entitled "Fasti," are children of Mercury.

NOTES: Each colony was set up by a different Earth space agency over a century before. The *Messenger* was set up by the European Space Agency and the *Hermes* by the Brazilian Space Agency. Transfers between the colonies happened, but not extensively, and got rarer when the Silence started and population controls were imposed.

# ACKNOWLEDGMENTS

There are many people I need to thank here, and I'm sure I'm going to forget some, and for that, I apologize. This book has been more than ten years in the making, and that's a lot of drafts, a lot of readthroughs, and a lot of conversations. Looking through my e-mails has been a trip down memory lane.

Let me start with my fellow writers, whose kind words and constructive criticism made *The Sun Runners* a much better novel. Starting with J.M. Frey, one of the book's first readers and supporters, I must also thank John Baglow, Kate Blair, Leah Bobet, Cameron Dixon, Susan Fish, Mark Richard Francis, Ishta Mercurio, Terry Rudden, Arthur Slade, and more. Thanks to Marsha Skrypuch and the good folks at Kidcrit, who helped with the early drafts of this story. I'm also thankful for the literary influences that helped me build up this story, from the rail city of Terminator in Kim Stanley Robinson's *2312* to the steampunk derring-do of Phillip Reeve's Larklight series, to the pressurized societies of *Snowpiercer*, to the "anything can happen" confidence of *Doctor Who*. Don't let anybody tell you that watching and reading science fiction is a waste of time.

I could not be here without the support of my family: my partner-in-crime, Erin; my kids, Wayfinder and Eleanor; my father, Eric; my father-in-law, Wendell; his wife, Judy; and my step-father-in-law, Michael. You all supported and encouraged me to continue, and not one of you ever suggested that I should get a real job since writing was clearly my job, and I am glad to work at it. Thanks especially to my mother-in-law, Rosemarie. May she rest in peace.

This story also received direct support from the Ontario Arts Council Works in Progress grant, an invaluable program that offers hope and encouragement to artists throughout Ontario and should be maintained and expanded.

If you've wondered how valuable the work of writers and artists is, consider how much work AI coders are putting in to try to steal it. Our society is much better off if our artists can live while making their art, so support our artists. And speaking of support, thanks to my editor and publisher, Edward Willett, for bringing this story across the finish line, and Bibliofic Designs for their stunning covers.

They say that reading opens up whole worlds to readers. For the past ten years, it has been my privilege to explore a whole solar system through *The Sun Runners* and its companion stories. My first thoughts on *The Sun Runners* came around Christmas 2013 while I was visiting my in-laws in Nebraska, as I imagined a young queen on Mercury who would rather be an engineer. It took me a while to find the story around Frieda, and it was in exploring Mercury to find that story that the universe opened up. At first, the conflict was between Frieda and her mother, and the Earth had been silent for centuries and was only now coming out of that silence. Then, as I asked why Frieda's mother was so distrustful of Earth, I realized I needed somebody who had experienced what had happened at the start of the Earth's silence, and Frieda's grandmother Adelheid was born.

As the story expanded, so did the universe. How did the Earth fall silent? What did it want now that it was back? What other colonies did they abandon with their collapse? What were their stories? I have had a great time playing in the vast sandbox that the Silent Earth universe represents, and I'm privileged to share that sandbox with the contributing authors of the companion anthology, *Tales from the Silence.*

Before I go, there is one final person I must thank, and it's my mother, Patricia Bow. Throughout my life, she was not just my biggest cheerleader, but my best editor, who could spot a typo at fifty paces and could take apart and rearrange a plot, identifying key links between characters, alternative solutions, and just better ways of doing things. My wife, Erin, can do many of these things as well, but she admits that my mother was in a class by herself. *The Sun Runners* was the last story of mine that she looked at. As she passed away in 2017, she only got to see the early drafts. I've already dedicated a book to her, but here, I'll dedicate my whole career. I rue the fact that she won't see this finished product, but I'm glad she saw part of it, at least.

Thanks to everyone for their time and attention, and I hope you've enjoyed the book!

—James Bow

# ABOUT THE AUTHOR

James Bow writes science fiction and fantasy for both kids and adults. He's been a fan of science fiction since his family introduced him to *Doctor Who* on TV Ontario in 1978, and his mother read him classic sci-fi and fantasy from such authors as Clifford Simak and J.R.R. Tolkien. James won the 2017 Prix Aurora Award for best YA Novel in Canada for *Icarus Down*.

By day, James is a communications officer for a charitable land trust protecting lands from development in Waterloo Region and Wellington County. He also loves trains and streetcars.

He lives in Kitchener, Ontario, with his two kids, and his spouse/fellow writer/partner-in-crime, Erin Bow. You can find him online at jamesbow.ca.

# ABOUT SHADOWPAW PRESS

Shadowpaw Press is a traditional publishing company, located in Regina, Saskatchewan, Canada and founded in 2018 by Edward Willett, an award-winning author of science fiction, fantasy, and non-fiction for readers of all ages. A member of Literary Press Group (Canada) and the Association of Canadian Publishers, Shadowpaw Press publishes an eclectic selection of books by both new and established authors, including adult fiction, young adult fiction, children's books, non-fiction, and anthologies, plus new editions of notable, previously published books in any genre under the Shadowpaw Press Reprise imprint.

Email: publisher@shadowpawpress.com.

facebook.com/shadowpawpress
x.com/shadowpawpress
instagram.com/shadowpawpress

# MORE SCIENCE FICTION AND FANTASY AVAILABLE OR COMING SOON FROM SHADOWPAW PRESS

### For Young Adult Readers

*The Headmasters* by Mark Morton

*I, Brax: A Battle Divine* by Arthur Slade

*Blue Fire* by E. C. Blake

The Shards of Excalibur series by Edward Willett

*Song of the Sword, Twist of the Blade, Lake in the Clouds, Cave Beneath the Sea, Door into Faerie*

*Spirit Singer* by Edward Willett

*Soulworm* by Edward Willett

*From the Street to the Star*s by Edward Willett

### For Middle-Grade Readers

The Canadian Chills Series by Arthur Slade:

*Return of the Grudstone Ghosts, Ghost Hotel,*

*Invasion of the IQ Snatchers*

### For Adult Readers

*The Downloaded* by Robert J. Sawyer

*The Traitor's Son* by Dave Duncan

*Corridor to Nightmare* by Dave Duncan

*The Good Soldier* by Nir Yaniv

*Shapers of Worlds* Volumes I-IV

*Duatero* by Brad C. Anderson

*Ashme's Song* by Brad C. Anderson

*Paths to the Stars* by Edward Willett

*The Legend of Sarah* by Leslie Gadallah

The Empire of Kaz trilogy by Leslie Gadallah

*Cat's Pawn, Cat's Gambit, Cat's Game*

The Peregrine Rising Duology by Edward Willett

*Right to Know, Falcon's Egg*